The Evolution of Kami's Soul

M.B. Heard

authorHOUSE®

AuthorHouse™
1663 Liberty Drive, Suite 200
Bloomington, IN 47403
www.authorhouse.com
Phone: 1-800-839-8640

First published by AuthorHouse   5/4/2009

ISBN: 978-1-4389-4001-4 (sc)
ISBN: 978-1-4389-4002-1 (hc)

Printed in the United States of America
Bloomington, Indiana

This book is printed on acid-free paper.

A good traveller has no fixed plans, and is not intent on arriving.

Lao Tzu

Table of Contents

Table of Lives

	Life 1	Life 2	Life 3	Life 4	Life 5	Life 6	Life 7
S E N T I E N T B E I N G S	Karlos	Mei Hua	Khalid	Keizo	Marta	Molly	Krishna
	Karlos' Father	Shu Chi	Amir	Aoi	x	x	x
	Merlo	Bau Yu	Fida	Tatsuo	Jon (husband)	baby in traffic	Morani Botsu
	Victor	Ying	Misha'il	Midori	Jon (son)	Henry	x
	Emilio	Madame Wang	Bahroum	Aiko	Little Marta	x	x
	x	Yen Chang	Nuri	Hiromi	x	x	x
	X	girl given voice	Shaymaa	Hirochan	x	Mr. Prizzani	x
	x	X	x	x	x	rapist	Sammy

KARLOS

Evil begets evil

Karlos first heard the low cries of the Lisbon dungeon when he was twelve, and they drew him in. It was more than hunger that enticed Karlos to lurk about in the shadows of the entrance. Something sinister permeated the superheated air that careened off the brick and bounced between this world and hell, carrying with it the scent of blood and faint moans. The dungeon promised Karlos a place that was comforting by virtue of its familiarity, something he could not put his finger on, having blotted out his past long ago.

He had been living by his wits for several years and, lacking the good sense bestowed upon some, was near death with privation. One day, as he was skulking about the entryway trying to get a glimpse of a torture victim, he was asked to carry out two buckets of excrement and given some bread for his troubles. After several days, he was offered a place to sleep for carting out the refuse. He accepted. Soon he was a regular fixture in the dungeon, working his way from charboy to guard in three years. Evincing the kind of proclivity for cruelty required by the position, and in possession of a physique able to carry out his threats, he was promoted to senior guard after five years. He has been in that position for the past twenty-two years.

The dungeon is ancient. Constructed twenty years after the Palace out of the same hand-hewn stone, its deadly caverns are a testament to the dark side of power. The prisoners themselves dragged each stone overland from the quarry and fit them expertly in place. Dying of thirst, starvation and infections from their lashings, as many men perished from labor as there are rocks in those buildings.

An addition sits atop the underground structure, built several decades ago, housing a temporary jail and some of Lisbon's Guard. The city has since enveloped the dungeon; its cries are barely audible now amidst the din of the metropolis.

Sentences to this little piece of hell are rarely lived out. If men are lucky, they find a way to die before they enter its diseased walls. It is not money but poison that is most often smuggled into the holding cell once an unfortunate is sentenced for stealing a crust of bread or slighting an official. If they are unlucky, they take that shackled walk into the bowels of the earth and are never seen again. Gradually, the same look takes over every prisoner's face, and if that look were put into words they would be, "God, please let me die."

Karlos is the prototype of a prison guard. He has an imposing build and a foul character. His chest is as broad as an ox's, and his legs are as big around as tree trunks. He stands a good head higher than most of the men he meets. Clenching and unclenching regularly, his fists are like hammers warning onlookers of impending violence. The scent of his body is overwhelmingly acrid, the kind of smell that signals death and won't be deterred by soap and water. Not that he bathes, other than the rare inadvertent drenching he might receive in a downpour.

The sight and scent of this big man hit simultaneously, and the immediate reaction is to retreat. When he manages to talk, his voice is guttural and harsh, his words few and threatening. His brow is forever furrowed above his large nose, and his eyes squint in perpetual misunderstanding. Thick lips, a square jaw, and huge ears that jut out from the ragged brown hair framing his face is what one sees if they dare glance at his face. The overall effect is one of ugliness, though in the softness of death one might see that he is not unattractive: it is only his internal deformity confusing the surface of his being that makes him reprehensible.

He is a man who goes out of his way to harm those he perceives to be guilty of wrong-doing, as is often the case with people who have been wronged. If a man has been sent to the dungeon, Karlos surmises he must be a wrongdoer. This is simple enough. Once within his sights as a wrongdoer, other men are subject to his merciless attacks. He has experimented with cutting off or cutting out nearly every part of the human body. He has explored the length of time it takes a man to die from various sorts of wounds and their subsequent infections. He has tortured men beyond the point their bodies and minds can bear, causing death from pain itself. He has pulled human bodies apart.

It is his job, but it is also his nature.

Karlos has no wife or children. He has been celibate all his life, though it has not been a conscious choice. He feels no sexual urges except at night sometimes, in his sleep. There are no women in the dungeon anyway. The ones in the taverns are repulsive to him, and repulsed by Karlos as well. In fact, Karlos shares this relationship of mutual repulsion with all beings, though he doesn't dwell on it. There is nothing he wants from anyone except for them to stay out of his way. He may have been average in his ability to reason when he was young, but the horrors of life have encouraged him not to think much. He has no desires, save to survive, and to this end he heads out from the guard's cottage to the prison at the break of day and heads back when the sun sets. He survives rather well in the underground system and life has moved on without a hitch, until recently.

For some time now, strange things have been happening in Karlos' mind. Bits of memory have unexpectedly appeared, causing him to think. Thinking, an activity he is not accustomed to, has created turmoil. Conclusions are hard to come by, and when they are finally reached they imply an awareness so foreign to him that the only reaction he can muster is that which is most familiar to him: anger.

Worse than these memories, Karlos is experiencing vivid dreams that engender immediate and powerful feelings in him. Feeling anything beyond his bodily drives is not his norm. In the past, his dreams were like insects, swatted at and forgotten before they hit the ground. Now they are inescapable in the cold, dank mornings. They make him cower. They make him shake. They make him think.

He has been thinking about what might be happening to him. He has been pondering. Maybe these odd thoughts have come from his gathering years, or maybe he has been cursed. Perhaps he is being haunted. He cannot understand what is happening. All he knows is that this strangeness has taken more and more of his time and energy and is starting to frighten him, a man who fears nothing. His brain is being driven to a level of activity it has never known. At times he fears it will explode. He has been experiencing this for the last three days, maybe longer.

Karlos lays on his wooden cot, staring up at the ceiling in the dark, the sound of his three roommates snoring and tossing in their sleep barely gaining his attention. It must be an hour before dawn, and something has awakened him. He does not know why he is awake, but he suddenly recalls that yesterday he remembered one of the times his father raped him. He was dragging a prisoner along the floor toward his execution, the thin man yelping now and then, when Karlos remembered being raped in his bottom when he was six years old. As soon as the scene came into his mind, he dismissed it again to go about his business. He remembers the thin man dying rather quietly, quicker than expected. Karlos had cut off his legs and held him down while the blood drained into a bucket. He just fainted away and died. But now, here, this morning, the rape memory is back. Against his will, Karlos feels the memory as though he were experiencing the rape again.

His nostrils are filled with the smell of pigs because his face is pressed down in filthy hay. He and his father have taken refuge in a manger whose owner must not mind the loss of pigs from disease for the smell is sickly and putrid. It is dark and cold, and his father has simply rolled him to one side, tiny Karlos still half asleep, and pulled down his trousers. With no small effort, holding Karlos by his shoulders and pushing with both hands, his father forces his penis into Karlos' anus. Karlos hears his own voice yelp as though it were coming from somewhere else. He remembers the fist against his head as though it were someone else's head and he simultaneously remembers the burning tear of his behind.

He tries to push the thought of remembering out of his mind. He thinks about drinking wine. He is panting. He feels like vomiting and is nearly frozen with fear. "What the hell is happening to me," he thinks. He tries to remember how long this has been going on. He realizes it has been the same day after day. These thoughts are waking him up; they must be coming into his dreams. He realizes they are about his childhood. He has a powerful foreboding and would like to crawl right out of his skin to escape feeling vulnerable, but he cannot get away. For days he has been running from these memories, but they keep catching him. There is no escape. This memory of his childhood vulnerability, something he drove from his life on the eve of adulthood, has returned with a vengeance. It is the one thing on earth he cannot withstand.

Karlos notices the others have gotten up and are heading out the door without him. He jumps from his cot, pulls his trousers on, slips into his shoes, and runs down the dirt lane after them. He throws open the door leading down into the dungeon and takes the stairs three at a time. He has been a guard in the Lisbon prison for over twenty years, and this is the first time he has been late.

No one seems to take notice.

He goes through his day in a daze, now and then slopping gruel into bowls and barking orders at the char boys, but otherwise ambling about aimlessly. Devoted solely to not feeling or thinking anything, he forgets to torture anyone. In fact, he has lost track of who is due to be tortured. He had a method of deciding who lives and who dies based on some convoluted logic that no one ever dared question, but now it is gone.

He finally notices that he is not behaving properly. It is late afternoon, and he has tortured no one. He sits dejectedly on a three-legged stool by one of the mainstay columns, leaning his back against the cool stone and staring up at the ceiling.

"Am I not the master of this underworld? Why shouldn't I do what I want?"

He wonders what it is he wants to do, if he is holding himself back from torturing or if he is sick of torturing. He cannot seem to follow these thoughts to their end. He looks down, and his eyes meet a man's, some man's, they all look the same. He is chained to the other side of the column, and he has somehow managed to crane his neck around and up at Karlos. The touch of their eyes is a shock to them both. The chained man instantly drives his eyes downward while his face snakes back around the column and disappears. Karlos bolts up from the stool, sending it rolling. He heads away from the man with panic in his stride.

He finds himself climbing the stairs out of the dungeon, and another memory flashes forth between the tenth and eleventh steps. He is lying on a dirt floor, curled up in a ball, his stomach aching. He is hungry and exhausted. He seems to hear his father moving about somewhere, but he does not have the strength to lift his head to look for him. Suddenly, his right hand is shocked with pain, and he sees his father's boot pressing down against it. He dare not cry out. He bites his tongue as the boot slowly twists a little to the left, then a little to the right, until he hears a soft yet audible crack. Then the boot goes away. Blood from his tongue trickles down his throat, and his hand feels like it is dead. Karlos remembers the throbbing and how his hand was unusable for weeks. He looks down at his right hand: the middle knuckle protrudes.

He leans against the wall of the stairway, shaken. He fights a wave of nausea and fear. After he catches his breath and calms down some, he is struck by the idea that it may be this very spot on the stairs that caused the memory to come, and he rushes back down into the dungeon.

He is afraid to do anything that might trigger a vision, and so he stands in a corner holding a broom, pretending to sweep. He waits for night to fall knowing it will bring no solace.

Several days of dark skies and cold rain pass before the other guards begin to notice how Karlos now stands in some dark corner, muttering to himself. Each remarked the change in Karlos separately, but now their collective awareness reinforces their individual perceptions: something in their leader has changed.

"Did you see that?"

"What is wrong with him?"

"Karlos has been acting very strange."

The truth is, for fear of triggering a memory, Karlos has begun to hesitate before taking any action. His foot now pauses before it takes that first step, for fear of inadvertently cueing a memory. When he is eating, it is the same: as the first spoonful rises to his mouth, he fears he will find himself trapped in the past. Or when he pulls on his trousers in the morning, or when he pulls the cork from a jug of wine.

He has tortured no one for days.

He has tried to identify every situation that makes him have a memory, but he can't be certain. It occurs to him that he is losing weight. Should he stop eating, stop climbing the steps? Maybe it is everything he does. Maybe every action is cursed. He cannot even lie in bed.

He was on his way to another part of the dungeon for reasons he can't remember, but now he has stopped and is leaning against the wall of a narrow passage, staring into space and talking out loud.

"I am getting old."

"I might die soon from this madness or be tossed out into the streets."

These are distinct possibilities. He has seen old guards be pushed out to scrounge as beggars when their usefulness was gone. He has seen them crumple in this underground cavern and just stop breathing. He looks from left to right but, finding no one to blame or attack, he stares ahead again.

"I will be next," he thinks.

"I want to stop thinking, especially about the past! It is not what went before that I want to know but how to stop things from changing. And what's worse, I don't know when it will happen, when a memory will attack me. I hate remembering. To have things come into my mind like this without warning is not good. Everything is going to the dogs."

He has never thought about the future and what it means in terms of his power in the dungeon. Now he thinks if his power wanes, his life will be over. Of course there has to be an end to his life, but so soon? He closes his eyes and feels something in his throat.

"Hey Karlos! Old man! Go or stay, but move out of my way!"

That is Emilio. He is young, strong, and vicious. His father worked here before him, and his mother was a whore who died shortly after he was born. His father was killed by a prisoner, who consequently had his eyes gouged out and was left to die some three months later from infection. It is not unusual to blind a prisoner, but they are usually put out of their misery several days later, being pathetic beyond endurance. It was a special punishment to keep this prisoner alive until the infection took him. Karlos remembers punching him and force feeding him and telling him how horrible his death would be. It was.

That was many years ago.

"Go find your mother whore and beg for favors," Karlos growls at him. Emilio does not answer, being unsure of his strength when compared to Karlos' viciousness. There was a time when Karlos would never have been questioned. Has that time passed? Emilio is uncertain. Instead of taking the bait, he jacks his shoulders to the right to avoid hitting Karlos and continues down the passageway, thinking, "Your day will come, old man, and I shall be none the sorrier for it."

Emilio's passing is dimly noted by Karlos, who suddenly becomes aware of his surroundings. The ancient brick walls are filthy with grime. Decades of foul human mucus and condensation from the rainy season have coagulated with all manner of granulated detritus to form a glossy layer over the brick. The filth nearly writhes in the dark shadows on the walls, and the stench hits Karlos' nose sharply. He realizes this smell has lived unnoticed in his nostrils all these years. Why does he smell it now? The movement of a bug catches the corner of his eye, a large cockroach, and Karlos can remember the feeling of such creatures touring his prostrate form. Was it just last night?

He finds himself bolting down the passageway and up the narrow earthen stairs, looking for the way out and into the light. He takes the corridor to the left, still loping at top speed. Another jog to the left, another smaller flight of stairs, and he is at the door guarded by Victor the Cripple.

"Open the door!" Karlos shouts, ready to force the door himself. Judging by the unaccustomed panic in his fellow's voice, Victor thinks there must have been an escape, so he heaves back on the door handle, using all the weight of his tiny frame, then jumps to the side. He watches in amazement as Karlos hurls his body outside and stands retching in the sunlight.

"What, Karlos, are you unwell?" Victor calls.

Karlos takes some time to finish heaving and then growls without straightening or making eye contact, "Have you ever known me to be sick? I am not sick! There is some curse, some bad spell, and when I find the man who cast it, he will not live another day!"

"Cursed? By one of the prisoners, perhaps?"

"No, you idiot, no prisoner could do all this to me! It is a special curse. One has to buy this kind, for it goes deep, to the very heart of its victim, and plagues him like bees setting upon a small child. I have only heard of curses like this, I have never experienced one before! Foul it is. Unbearable!"

"What is it like?"

Karlos straightens up and takes a step closer to Victor. He peers down at his small deformed face. Some childhood disease no one is meant to survive twisted Victor's left leg and the left side of his face so that joy and anguish are not easily differentiated. Karlos wonders how Victor has managed to live so long. As though seeing another human being so clearly has sapped him of his strength, Karlos pauses and leans against the outer wall. There is vomit on his face and sweat matting his graying hair, though it is still very cold, just early spring. Slowly he turns his head to eye Victor again, this time calculating whether he was the one who bought the curse or knows who did and is keeping the secret.

Victor's expression seems concerned, not the face of a conspirator. Either way, thinks Karlos, I will see what his reaction is.

"Every night I feel the torture of twisted memories. Every bad thing that ever happened to me comes back, only not as it was but ten times worse. It is worse than being chased by demons. Night and day I am plagued. Pictures flood my head until I cannot think, walk, or speak. I am possessed. If I were a religious man, I would buy a redemption to end this curse, but as it is I dare not even speak the names of the holy ones for fear that my tongue would burn in my head. I do not exist in the eyes of heaven. My only hope is to find the one who placed this curse on me and kill him!"

With these last words, Karlos clearly reconsiders Victor as a possible suspect, his gaze on the former so piercing that Victor stammers immediately that he has never met anyone selling such curses, nor does he know anything about them.

"No, Karlos, believe me, you are the first man I have ever seen afflicted by a curse, and it has frightened me. I cannot help but wonder if one of my enemies might buy a curse and place it on me. What will you do, Karlos? Are you sure it is a curse?"

"What else could it be, you fool? And how should I know the buyer? Have I not tortured and killed hundreds of men? Surely they have relatives or friends, but who would dare? How could anyone dare do this to me? Don't they know I will hunt them down and kill them in the most horrible way?"

"No man would dare it, Karlos, no man. Could it be a ghost, then, Karlos? Come to get his revenge?"

"And how would a ghost find his way into my very soul? Turn my senses against me? Rob me of my strength? It's no ghost, nor bad food, neither, but a curse for sure. I must see who sells these curses in Lisbon and you must help me. Next Sunday, when we get our day off, you must come with me. We will find all those selling curses, and they will tell us who bought this one!"

Karlos is surprised that he has asked for this man's help, and is still more surprised when Victor genuinely consents. A chill catches him, yet the sun seems abhorrent. He feels too visible standing outside the door. He darts within, and Victor tries to pull the heavy door closed, still shaken by the strong man's sickness. Karlos lopes back the way he came. Victor, not knowing what to do but feeling very strange, calls out after him.

"Sunday next, Karlos. We shall find the dog that dared to curse you!"

Victor thinks he hears Karlos mutter agreement, but he cannot be sure. A shudder runs through him and he hunkers down next to the door, thinking of all who may wish him harm.

The guards' quarters are above ground, two small cottages down a dirt lane a few minutes from the dungeon. They sleep four to a room and in shifts. Since news spread that Karlos is cursed, no one has wanted to be his roommate. There is nothing any of them can do besides bring it to the attention of the Captain of the Guard, and this none would dare. The Captain of the Guard is not a superstitious man nor does he take kindly to having his dungeon disrupted. He has more important things taking up his time. He would surely cast out anyone appearing to start trouble.

No one dare provoke Karlos' anger, either. Throughout the long years that Karlos has labored as a prison guard, no man has ever bested him in strength or ability to kill. He has been the unspoken ruler. And yet, as the rumor of this curse has spread, the idea of being able to overpower Karlos has been planted in his fellows' minds. Each in turn has considered the possibilities that might present themselves in the underworld of the dungeon were Karlos somehow overthrown.

At the end of his shift, Karlos usually goes to the tavern down the street where the guards gather to drink and have a go at one of the skinny whores, should they come upon some money. But this evening, following the episode with Victor, Karlos drinks some wine he has put aside in his trunk in the guards' quarters, eats some dried meat and stale bread, and goes to his bed alone. He fears the questions he may face at the tavern, and he fears the walk home, intoxicated, in the deep of night. In case it is a ghost haunting him, he does not want to be alone on the road at night.

He is not sleepy but an overwhelming tiredness moves through his body. Visions of the past assail him, replete with scents, sounds, colors, and temperatures. Cold, lonely, hungry and abandoned, the scenes rotate in his head, but the basic deprivations remain constant. He changes his mind about going out and wishes to get up, to go to another place, any place, but he cannot rise. He commands his body to get up from the hard wooden cot, but nothing happens. He lays in the dark, alone.

For a long time he lies there, then finally manages to conjure up images of the others, Lazaro, Juan, and Merlo. They are senior men like him and share his sleep shift. None asked him to go with them tonight, though they never make any formal invitation. For the most part, they head off to town at the same time and therefore end up accompanying one another. He thinks about one or the other of them playing drinking games. He begins to grow calm, swimming in familiar thoughts.

Caught off-guard, a new image appears to him. His father is standing before him. There is no mother; there never was a mother. It is as though Karlos had simply crawled out from under his father's boot and lived just there, at his feet. Karlos is a small boy, maybe five years old. He has stolen a man's purse and has presented it to his father. His father's lips are pinched together, his face is narrow and angular, his eyes are like glass - transparent, unfathomable. Instead of being happy, his father takes hold of Karlos' arm and slowly, very slowly, he begins to twist the tiny flesh of his half-starved upper arm. He twists harder and harder until Karlos cries out in pain, but not a shadow of sympathy crosses his father's face. He continues to twist and pinch the flesh until his fingers slip off, having knotted the skin to nothing. His father takes the purse and disappears.

Karlos is alone. He is so tired. It is dark, and his arm feels like it will fall off. His eyes close. He hears a howl and realizes he is in a black forest. There are wolves all around him, circling unseen in darkness so black he cannot see his hand in front of his face. He hears a snarl to the left; a branch snaps to the right. He realizes they are creeping closer. Karlos is perfectly blind.

He falls to the ground, scrambling in the darkness, frantically feeling about on his hands and knees until he finds the trunk of a tree. He jumps to his feet and throws himself at the trunk, tearing into the bark with his fingernails, trying to hoist his slender body to safety. He feels so small. He hears the wolves snarling beneath him and frantically tries to climb higher, though he cannot gain but an inch up the trunk with even the most Herculean effort. His breathing is jagged, and primal fear pumps his blood, pounding in his throat, hurting his ears. He hears a low growl and suddenly feels the sharp penetration of teeth clamping down on his ankle. He finds himself falling back to the ground.

Instantly the wolves are upon him, attacking from all directions. Karlos screams and flails at them with his thin arms, but he fails to deter them even slightly. With the breath of wolves all around him, he feels his flesh being torn from his limbs. Pain rips through his brain and howls with the sound that the first wolf made, howls deep inside him. It is the sound of death.

He tries rolling from side to side, struggling to keep this limb or that from the powerful jaws, but he is bitten over and over again. He hears his skin tear, he feels his muscle rip from his bones. He hears his own screams turn into moans, and he can no longer move.

He knows the wolves are dining on his flesh; there cannot be much left of his body. The sound of their snarling over his meat lessens and abates, and he is suddenly alone again.

So this is it. It is over, and there is some peace. He is horrified, but there is no more pain.

Suddenly, he feels the slightest breeze on his bones, and the jolting caw of a crow hammers against his eardrums. A ripping starts up again, less severe than before, as more crows join the first and clean up after the wolves. His heart is barely beating. He hears the crows flap noisily away.

He lays in the darkness, alive, wishing he were dead. Then he feels the air being stirred by wings once more and hears the soft sound of feathers tucked up against a body. The crow hops closer until Karlos can see the black monster leaning over to pluck his eyes out. The crow takes the right and swallows it whole. Then he takes the left.

Karlos awakes screaming, running with sweat, and jumps from his putrid bed. He tries to flee but crashes into Lazaro's low wooden bed and falls to the floor. Lazaro cries out lustily, and in one swift movement he leaps from his cot and yanks Karlos to his feet by the neck. Merlo and Juan have struggled up from their cots and are ready to attack the man in Lazaro's clutches when Karlos manages to call out, "It's the curse! Get your hands off me before I break your arms!"

"Hey, Karlos, is it you?" Lazaro calls out, though he has the man not ten inches from his face.

"Yes it's me, of course it is me! Are you going to let go? This is your last chance!"

Quickly turning Karlos loose, still in darkness, Lazaro stammers, "You fell upon me! You are the one who is wrong! Are you threatening me?"

In frustration, Karlos bellows, "Yes, I fell on you, it was an accident, it is the curse, goddamn you, as I have said! But I would break your arm, both your arms, if I chose to! Keep away from me!"

"Who would go near you? You stink, you are mad! You have grown mad, Karlos, and we don't want you in our room anymore!"

"Then throw me out, you diseased dog, I dare you! Throw me out, throw me out!" Karlos thunders these words with such fury that the other three fall back, Lazaro first among them.

"Hey, Karlos, what's the matter? Take it easy, you must have had a bad dream. Don't draw attention, we will be set upon and cast out. Karlos. Remember that time the prisoners rioted? They got ol' Pedro and twisted his neck, then went for Merlo here and knocked him senseless. They nearly got us that time. But you charged their ranks, killing two at a time with your staff, and they fell back. That was a good one, eh Karlos?" It is Juan speaking, nicknamed The Phraser because he knows how to use words to get out of tough situations.

Karlos stands dumbly in the half-light of the cold room, breathing easier now, adrenaline-stoked sweat drying on his body. The others slowly backed away while Juan was praising the big madman.

Karlos remembers the story and grunts.

"I have saved the day more than once down there, not that I got anything for it. Listen, Juan, you Merlo, Lazaro. I am not mad. I have been cursed. Victor the Cripple knows this. Someone with power and influence…they have bought a curse and placed it upon me, a curse of the past. Do you, any of you, know of such a curse being sold?"

The men peer into the darkness to get a fix first on Karlos and then on each other. No. None of them has heard of a curse of the past. Then Merlo speaks up, slowly and steadily.

"I know of curses where the victim's head rots and rolls straight off his body, and I've seen it, too. I know of curses because my third master, when I was young, sold them. But not many hit their mark. Not many made a man die or even suffer. My master sold them to eat, that is all."

Merlo's voice is soothing. "He is a strange one," Karlos thinks. "He is not vicious. He is often the one with good information, like now. Merlo is right. Most indulgences and curses affect men in no way. If they did, I would be dead."

But the story about the curse of the rolling head has captured Karlos' attention.

"Who is this man whose head rolled off his body? Did you see it? Are you certain it was from a curse?" Karlos strides over to Merlo and, grabbing him by the nightshirt, pulls him closer as he interrogates him, though not with his usual roughness.

"Yes, I saw him suffering. I saw the yellow curds roll from his ears, though I was only told the head itself finally fell off. And I know this was due to one of my master's curses because the old man's wife herself bought it and applied it and came every day to check its strength, to see that it hit its mark. Her hatred was very powerful and must have helped the curse, which would otherwise have been far less deadly."

Karlos turns Merlo loose and takes a step back, pondering these words. He begins to shiver, thinking of what might come dripping from his ears.

"Then I will die for sure. I cannot remember all those who bear that kind of hatred for me! But what if the old man killed the old woman first? Wouldn't that have ended the curse? Can't I find the one who bought the curse and kill them? Can't I be free of it that way?"

"I don't know," Merlo says, pausing to consider. "How can you know who cast the curse? If you did know who cast it, I do not know if killing them would lift it. It might make it worse, as the hand of God is said to guide such curses because they are bent on righteous revenge."

Karlos, as if under Merlo's spell and taking on his qualities, stops to consider this for a while. The other two have taken to their beds, Juan snoring loudly already. Then he speaks again.

"Have you ever heard of a curse that brings the past, never before remembered, to haunt the victim until he loses his senses?"

"No, I have never heard of such a curse. Karlos, it may not be a curse. It may be the spirits of the dead bent on destroying you."

"How could it be spirits? I never see any spirits. I only remember things, things I have never remembered before. The memories are so real, exactly as they happened. I fight very hard to send them away, but as soon as one goes, the next one comes. And just now, I dreamed I was eaten by wolves and picked clean by crows, and every night it is the same, one bad dream after another. All day and all night. I am going mad."

Karlos is broken, on the point of tears. He stands limply in the ghostly light. Merlo has never known Karlos to be anything but emotionless until tonight. In his present pathetic state, Merlo's heart goes out to him. He remembers when Karlos saved him during the prisoners' uprising.

He puts his hand on the big man's shoulder and ventures. "You may want to go to church and buy an indulgence to expiate your sins. If the memories are of your wrongdoing, this can do no harm. They say The Lord accepts repentance from anyone."

"I wish they were only scenes of my misdeeds, but they are of my father and the unspeakable things he did to me. I am accustomed to the things I do. And you are wrong. I will never be forgiven for the things I have done. There is no sense to ask."

"Perhaps it is the ghost of your father, then. Do you hate him very much?"

"I do not even know if he is dead. He left me in this town when I was ten, and I never saw him again. I have never thought about it, but now I am beginning to hate him. It is more than hate. I am afraid. I do not know what the feeling is. These memories are dragging me under, like being in the ocean and not knowing how to swim. It is true, what Lazaro said is true: I am mad."

"Do you not believe in God, then?"

"I do not even speak His name. I have always been bad."

"But if you asked forgiveness..."

"Look at me, remember who you talk to! Do you think I can be forgiven? If that is the only way, I am as good as dead. I will not step foot in a church. As sure as I am standing here, I would be struck down."

"I am full of sin myself. I do not go to church, and I don't like the hypocrites who do. I am sorry, though, that I cannot help you. Your father must have done some terrible things if the very memory of him can drive you mad. I do not know what to say. There is nothing for it, Karlos, and I must go to bed or suffer the more for it tomorrow."

Karlos stands looking long at Merlo, wanting to thank him. He finally says nothing. Merlo turns to his cot. Karlos senses that this weakling knows something he does not, and Karlos respects him for it. Karlos also feels something else, something he does not know how to name: it is gratitude.

★ ★ ★

On Sunday, Karlos finds Victor waiting at the tavern. He is perched like a wounded bird on the edge of a tall stool, leaning his elbows against the bar with his head in his hands. He flinches and nearly falls when Karlos' heavy hand on his shoulder jolts him from his reverie. Karlos' eyes are bloodshot, and his breath is worse than ever. His eyes narrow at Victor, who jumps off the stool to show his faithfulness to their mission. Without a word, the two men head off in the direction of the great cathedral. They believe they will find men of portents and other mystical remedies loitering about the vicinity.

Victor glances sidelong at Karlos as they move down the lane, the one lumbering, the other limping at double-time to keep up. In just two weeks, Karlos has grown much thinner, and the reek of his person is more pronounced and sour. He looks like a sick man.

Victor wonders whether it is necessary for him to go along with Karlos. Perhaps he has nothing more to fear from the now emaciated brute. But he reconsiders.

"Karlos is like an animal, he is hard to predict. Also, this could happen to me and if it does, I will know what to do." Victor feels settled by these thoughts and thinks no more.

Karlos is not thinking, either. He is overwhelmed with gloom and foreboding. He strides alongside Victor with what for him is an unnatural sense of purpose. Something in him remarks how much cleaner the stones on the outside of buildings are and how much nicer the air smells, but it is not so much a conscious thought as an instinctual perception. The passerby's faces register instinctually in his mind and float off again, monitored only for their capacity to harm and nothing else.

Victor takes in the scent of foods he has never eaten, meat-filled buns and jellied breads, delicacies not meant for the likes of him. Passing the time in silent sensation, it is not long before they find themselves at the foot of the Cathedral.

For a while they stand dumbly staring out at the square, their backs to the Cathedral. There are stalls selling food, drink, and religious trinkets. The commotion of human activity comes to them like sound waves underwater. Time has slowed to the tempo of their breathing. Neither wants to be aroused from this inert state. They have no idea who the sellers of portents might be. They watch men and women come and go as they pass before the square and sometimes enter the cathedral.

Remembering why he is there, noting that his very life depends on his achieving his mission, Karlos begins to feel frustrated. They are here, but the next step is not clear. He glances about in earnest this time, trying to apprehend the situation. He looks over to Victor.

"Who sells curses here?"

"I do not know!"

Karlos' agitation is growing by the minute. He finally stomps over to the nearest seller of trinkets and, leaning forward in a menacing way, snarls into the man's face.

"Where is the one who sells curses?"

This seller of trinkets is a short man with a patchy complexion and jolly countenance. He immediately makes Karlos out to be the half-mad, dangerous brute that he is. He will have to humor him.

"Good sir. Esteemed sir. What kind of curses are you talking about?"

Karlos eyes the man and thinks to himself, "Could this be the one who sells them? And if he is, can't he see that I am suffering from one? Perhaps he will protect the buyer and refuse to give the man's name. This seller is a tiny man with a funny face. This is not a man who means anything. I'll kill him if he does not tell me the name of the man who bought the curse."

Karlos leans closer with murder in his eyes and demands again, "Who sells curses? That is a simple question. Who sells them?"

Sensing his deadly intent, the tiny stall keeper gulps in air and looks about for some possible escape, but there is none. He turns back to Karlos and gives him a sweet smile.

"Sir. Not so loud. I will tell you everything I know. There are men who travel through; they never stay for long. They sell indulgences and sometimes curses, and there is such a man in this area now, I don't know exactly where! He could be in the tavern or staying at an inn, there are several near here. That is all I know!"

"What does he look like?" Karlos bellows in exasperation, leaning even closer.

"He is easy to recognize, sir! He has only one eye and no patch. It is a leering eye he has and a hole where the other one should be. You will recognize him, surely! Try the tavern. He has some money, I saw him talking with several people yesterday. He must have sold something. At least ask at the tavern!"

The man is pleading for his life now, knowing that Karlos has made up his mind to kill someone today and it could just as well be him. He looks as sincerely as possible into the crazed man's eyes, given that he is scared out of his wits. He nods his head approvingly and points in the direction of the tavern. These gestures, having no effect on the madman, will have to be replaced with a better strategy. The seller gestures more widely, putting his whole body into it, and says, "Yes, the tavern is over there, it's the place you want to go to. You will find the one-eyed man right over there, over there..."

Karlos seems at last to be satisfied with this information. The seller sighs with relief as the mad stranger and his crippled companion turn in the direction he has gesticulated so emphatically towards: the tavern.

The gathering warmth of the day alone does not account for the rivulets of sweat running down Karlos' face. It is the wildness in his eyes that makes him sweat. After passing five shops on the north side of the street, just east of the Cathedral, he spies a tavern. He pushes open the creaky door and begins sifting through the faces of the men clustered at the tables closest to the door, assessing them for eyeballs. He does not see a one-eyed man. He searches from table to table all the way to the back, upsetting beer mugs and stepping on feet. Nothing. Then he starts going through the men sitting at the bar, pulling on their shoulders to spin them around in their seats so he can see their faces. He ignores their initial objections, which are cut short by the spittle flying from Karlos' mouth and the crazed look in his eyes. He is unaware of Victor, who is still timidly at his side, nodding greetings and smiling weakly as each man in turn is disturbed.

Finally Karlos finds the man he is looking for and bellows out, "Aaaa-Ha! A one-eyed man! It is you! You have done this to me!"

It is as if his face itself speaks what he is thinking: "And so you die!" Veins bulge from his skull, and his lips stretch into a snarl. Karlos lunges forward. He has his hands around the man's throat, but the one-eyed man abruptly stands, easily breaking Karlos' hold on him.

This one-eyed man is even bigger than Karlos. He is certainly half a head taller.

The man thunders, "Are you mad? Or are you just intent on dying today?"

With this, Karlos falls back. Has this man read his mind? "He speaks just like me and he is even bigger! He will be difficult to kill!"

Karlos' hesitation lasts only a moment, survival being his life-blood. He reaches into himself for the nastiest feeling he has ever had and comes toward the man again, snarling:

"Are you the one who sells curses? Just answer me that!"

"I have sold curses. Has one made you mad?"

Now Karlos does look as though he is stark raving mad. He is pouring forth sweat, his skin is an odd yellow color, and there is foam on his lips. Rage causes his body to tremble. He shouts at the man, "Yes! One has made me mad! How do I stop it?"

Ignoring Karlos' imminent violence, the huge one-eyed man coolly turns to the others in the tavern, saying, "I only sell the curse. It is the buyer's hatred that works these kinds of evil deeds. See the power of my curses! Is it not as I have said?"

Karlos suddenly swings his hairy arm and connects with the man's temple. Taken unawares, attacked from the side, the big man goes down as quickly as he stood up, banging his head on a table as he falls to the floor. In an instant Karlos is on top of him, pinning his shoulders down, his hot breath nearly gagging the man.

Words tear forth from his mouth, spraying saliva everywhere, "GIVE ME THE CURE NOW!"

The one-eyed man looks concerned for the first time. He struggles to throw the crazy man off, but Karlos' strength has somehow doubled in his fury. There is nothing he can do but deal with him verbally. He musters his own strength and straining against Karlos' bulk, manages to raise his head and say, "You can buy an indulgence and perform obeisance, and the curse should get weaker."

"WHO BOUGHT THIS CURSE AND PLACED IT AGAINST ME?"

Karlos' knee has edged up and is now pressing down on the one-eyed man's throat, forcing his head back against the dirt floor of the tavern.

The thought crosses the one-eyed man's mind that this mad fellow could kill him, and he grows scared.

"I have not sold a curse, in truth, all the time I have been in this city! I have tried to sell them, but folks have only bought indulgences!"

"LIAR!" Karlos screams, pressing his knee down on the man's Adam's apple. His one eye visibly bulges from its socket. This time he responds in a shrill voice.

"I swear! I SWEAR! I don't even make money this way! Only a little, only indulgences! I trade in trinkets, love potions sometimes, rarely curses. I have a farm! This is only a side business! I sold a curse in Lisbon last year. I don't know the name of the man! They buy them, a few minutes of dealing, and they are gone! I can't breathe, I can't breathe!"

Karlos takes this information in. He rolls the words around in his brain.

"You don't ever get the buyer's name?"

"You -- must move -- knee!"

Karlos eases some of his weight to the other knee but remains hovering menacingly over the man who sputters with precious air.

"No names! Would men buy from me if I insisted on getting their names? What do I care what their names are?"

Karlos eases some weight back onto the knee pressing down on the man's throat. The man cries out with his final breath, "They don't work! Curses are nonsense, for the ignorant! For the love of God! I have not done this to you! There are no such curses!"

The room is dead silent, save for the gasping of the one-eyed man. Karlos eases his knee up again, and the man's one good eye fills with tears of relief. A look of resignation floats over Karlos' face, bringing in its wake a feeling of hatred for this one-eyed man who has failed to solve his problem.

In a deeply antagonistic voice he asks, "Do you know anyone else who sells curses?"

"There are many! It is like selling air to idiots! We never work the same area at the same time. Frederick of Four must have come through here a fortnight or more ago. But I swear, I have never seen a curse work!"

Karlos considers killing the man. He could crush his windpipe, he could gouge out his one good eye and eat it. Then he has another thought.

"Do indulgences work?"

"They may. Here, I will give you one for free." The one-eyed man has given himself over to fear now. He understands clearly that he has met a man more vicious and evil than any man alive.

Karlos considers killing him just to vent his frustration but worries that the indulgence might not work then. He eases off the man enough to allow him to fumble with a cloth bag hanging from his belt. The one-eyed man pulls out a small medal wrapped in paper. He fumbles at stripping the paper off and holds it up to Karlos. There are words written on the back of the medal.

"Say this prayer on the back every hour. Wear the medal. This is all I can do."

Karlos takes the object and gets to his feet. It is as though he sees nothing. He does not see Victor, trembling at his side, grateful that he never dared cross the madman. He does not see the shocked faces turned to him in repugnance. Karlos glances absently about the tavern as if assessing his environs for danger then heads out the door into the blinding light of day. Victor follows quickly behind.

The following weeks bring continued suffering for Karlos. He had Merlo read the words out on the coin, and he committed them to memory.

"Oh Holiness, have mercy on me. Protect me from every evil, and grant that I be delivered safely from my enemies."

He recites these words every hour, but the indulgence does nothing to abate the constant parade of nightmares and memories. He has lost all ability to distinguish waking visions from dreams. He manages the walk to the dungeon every day and that is all.

The prisoners whisper to one another with delight. An absent-minded fool has replaced the ogre of the dungeon. Preoccupied with his visions, Karlos forgets to terrorize them. He fails to notice the look of thanks in a clumsy prisoner's eyes when Karlos quietly passes the spilled gruel without a lashing or even a kick. The prisoners see him wasting away before their eyes, losing his mind. Several of them hypothesize that Karlos' madness is the work of God.

Lacking the heart for it, the other guards have failed to keep up with the pace of torture and death that Karlos previously set. They avoid Karlos the way the prisoners used to avoid him, stepping aside and muttering about the curse as though it were the plague. Ironically, the prisoners have become heartened while the guards have become demoralized, all because of Karlos' memories.

One night, while the others are off at the tavern, Karlos prays while lying on his bed. His prayer goes like this:

"Oh Sir," (for he still dare not speak the Lord's name), "if you can do things on this earth, make me the way I was. When I wake up, I don't want to have any memories, no remembrances of any kind, no visions in my head. When I go to sleep, I don't want any dreams at all. Otherwise put into my head the name of the person who placed this curse against me, and I shall kill him."

"Sir, I should have killed my father. None of this would be happening now if I had. Is it my father who has cursed me? But surely he is dead by now, and good riddance. Just take away these odd things that have been happening to me, and I will give you anything you want. I will do whatever you tell me to do."

He knows he does not mean it. He cannot see himself doing anything else. He cannot imagine what God might ask him to do. There is a sharp pain stabbing his skull behind his eyes. He knows that if he were God, he would kill a man like himself. He sighs and gives up praying and begins examining the cottage ceiling, the contours of which he already knows so well from many sleepless nights. He feels himself drifting off to sleep and he can't bear the thought of another nightmare, but he is gone before he can fight it.

Suddenly, Karlos is lying in a lane covered in filth. His father approaches and picks him up. He hurts all over and has sores running with puss. His father, as always, is silent and angry, his face set hard. Behind his eyes the menace of the Devil glows red like burning coal. Karlos quakes in his arms, averting his face from the specter of his father's eyes. In his mind he calls out to his mother, certain she is dead and in heaven, for she would never abandon him like this, would never let her boy suffer this way.

The stars shudder in the heavens overhead with each step his father takes. His little heart begs to be somewhere else or to be so small that he might fall through the hairy arms and be free to hide in some obscure corner forever. But Karlos has no such luck. His father trudges along with Karlos in his arms, through the empty lanes and down the scary streets, winding this way and that. The chill of the night invades his bones because his clothes are too thin even for rags. Only the warmth of his father's body comforts him, an irony lost on one so small and broken.

The man marches with his son in his arms for what seems like an eternity. Karlos does nothing for fear that his father will kill him. At last he smells the ocean and knows his father cannot walk much further.

But his father keeps walking. He carries Karlos out over a pile of rocks jutting into the ocean. Karlos can see faraway lights jittering over the water with every pounding step his father takes. He slips and almost drops the child more than once, grabbing him back up in his wicked arms at the last moment. Karlos thinks, "Free or dead, it wouldn't matter, if only I could get away from him!"

When his father has journeyed to the very edge of the very last rock, he looks down into the child's face and says with disdain, "You are a very bad boy. You should never have been born. It is a mistake I will fix."

And so saying, he throws Karlos into the sea.

Karlos barely feels the cold hard impact of the water. He knows instantly that he is no longer dreaming and that he has jumped into the sea. It feels much better than the dream had, better than anything he has felt in his life. Floating softly down through the water he experiences this new feeling, and it is good.

This is his first time in the ocean; he cannot swim. He does not struggle. He feels warm. He is unconcerned as he drifts down, down, down beneath the waves, and he feels grateful for this new feeling. For the first time in his life, he is free of worry.

His body begins to get lighter. His eyes are open, his mind is at ease. Suddenly, just for a moment, he struggles to breathe and is flush with panic, but it passes. He lets the world of fishes and kelp float gently past as everything grows darker. He thinks he might be hearing the quiet music of sea angels playing on wispy underwater harps. It is the best and last moment of his life.

Karlos after Death

Kami (the Sentient Being Who Was Karlos) stays close to his body, which slowly rises up through the dark water, buoyed intermittently by the current, until it breaks the surface. It bobs there for awhile then moves imperceptibly toward the shore.

It is some time before Kami realizes he is not inside his body. Once perceiving this, he tries desperately to reenter it. Nothing seems to happen. He hovers over it frantically as it drifts. Finally, it nudges the sandy beach.

As the hours of the night draw on, Kami becomes reconciled to the fact that there below him is his body and he cannot get back inside it. It is face down, its arms slightly spread to either side. He wishes he could flip his body over and look at his own dead face, but he does not know how to make this happen; his will is ineffective.

So he sways gently in the space just above his corpse, falling in rhythm with its motion as the surf rocks it back and forth. Sharing the motion of his body makes him feel a little less agitated, although he can't help notice it is beginning to bloat and discolor. From time to time, when he is not gazing at his previous form, he looks up and down the beach or up at the stars.

Early morning, just before the glow of dawn, two fishermen approach. Kami feels great apprehension and moves back several feet. It seems that the men are going to pass right by when the shorter of the two shouts, "Aiee! Omar! Look at that!"

"God in heaven!"

They stare at the body without moving, engrossed by the macabre specter of the bloated dead man peacefully bumping against the shore. Then the short one says, "See if he is dead."

"You see if he is dead! I'm not going near him! His spirit is probably still nearby. Hey! Juan! Listen now, don't go near it!"

But the short one called Juan edges closer and closer to the partially submerged form and pushes it with his foot. The body rolls free for a moment then settles back onto the sand.

"Now see!" the taller one barks. "You'll anger his spirit and he'll plague you! I'm going!"

The taller one starts backing up in the direction they came. Gurgling sounds issue forth from the corpse, and both men turn and sprint away down the beach.

Kami feels dejected and then angry, angry that they came, angry that they touched his body as though it were a dead fish. He tries to settle back into the space over his body where he was before, but for some reason he can't get that close. He hovers in the air several feet above his body and begins to sway rhythmically again. Just when he is beginning to feel settled, a group of men approach from the same direction the fishermen had fled. A dim lantern glows in the early dawn, and gradually Kami can make out six men, two of them dragging something through the sand. It is a handcart.

The men timidly approach the body. They talk about what is to be done and who this man could be. Kami notices the shorter man is among them, but not the taller man. The shorter man hurriedly describes how they found the body then they all fall silent for a spell.

Finally, one of them says in a loud voice, "Come on then. Everyone grab a piece and let's get him on the cart."

The men move in unison and manage to wrestle the water-soaked body onto the cart, flipping it over on its back. Kami can see his face for the first time: his mouth is caught up in a ghastly snarl and his eyes leer up at the heavens. Although death has made him more gruesome, he realizes for the first time how hideous he looks and he is shocked. Surely, this is not his body, not his face.

The men move in silent trepidation as they wheel his body down the beach. Every now and then there is more whispered speculation about the identity of the corpse, but Karlos' name never comes up. They finally reach the outskirts of town and wheel the body into an old shed. Then they all leave.

Kami stays with his dead body in the dark shed. Finally, at midday, a man comes and wheels his body out. There in the sunlight are Merlo and Victor, looking down at his body, wincing from the smell and the horrible sight of his decaying form.

Kami cries out, "Hey, Merlo, Victor, it's me, Karlos!"

But no one hears him. He tries to touch them, but he moves right through their bodies. He feels panicked, as he did when he tried to get back into his body, only now it is because he cannot get anyone's attention. Not even Merlo can tell he is there.

Meanwhile, the men have been talking.

"Oh, that is Karlos for sure!" Victor starts.

"Poor Karlos. It is he. He drove himself mad or had a curse upon him. Did he drown?" Merlo asks.

"He was found floating in the bay," the man who wheeled the body out says.

"In the bay?" Victor is puzzled. "Must be forty minutes from the dungeon to the bay. He must have walked there while we were sleeping and thrown himself into the sea."

"He was tortured by memories," Merlo explains. "He must have killed himself."

"Looks that way. There's no mark of a fight on him, and no one could drown a big man like that without a struggle," the unknown man says.

The three are silent for a moment. Merlo and Victor furtively glance at the corpse, but feel immediately sickened and quickly avert their eyes.

"Hey! I did not drown myself! My father threw me in! My father threw me in!" Kami screams shrilly, but they can't hear him.

"You sons of whores are deaf! You idiots! Listen to me! I'm telling you I'm right here, and I did not kill myself!" But the men have taken up talking again, and Kami has to be quiet to follow their conversation.

"I know where that is. When?"

"It'll have to be in a few hours. This body stinks worse than most. Got to get it into the ground."

"We were only excused to name the body. We have to go back now," Merlo tells him.

"And I thank you for your trouble," says the man.

The two former acquaintances move softly away, and Kami is torn between following them and staying with his body. He wants to follow them, but he can't seem to control himself; he stays with his body.

Some hours later, the same man wheels his body down a dirt lane to a grave site where a second man begins to dig the grave. The first man exchanges a few words with the new one, then leaves. Kami watches as the new man digs a shallow grave. Using all his strength, he shoves Karlos' body off the handcart and it hits the ground with a thud. The man gets on his hands and knees and rolls the body over a couple of times until it tumbles into the grave. He starts shoveling dirt over the form, which did not land straight in the grave; he leaves it the way it fell, half twisted at the hip. Kami feels horror as he watches his body disappear beneath the earth.

When his body is covered and the dirt begins to mound, the man stops shoveling and starts to stomp around on top of the grave. He shovels on some more dirt then stomps around some more. At last the job is finished. He gathers up his things, takes up the handcart, and moves on.

Kami stays by the grave day after day. It is not unpleasant. He does nothing but mark the passage of time. Once, another body, the body of a young girl, was buried not far from his own grave.

Gradually, without giving it much thought, he drifts away. He finds himself on the streets of Lisbon, and this is not a nice feeling. For close to a week he floats here and there, observing fights, watching deaths, seeing discord and anger. He has given up trying to talk to or touch anyone living, and he sees no other dead people. He would like to see a dead person so that he might find out what happens next.

Eventually he finds the cottage he shared with Merlo and the others. He feels something like happiness at seeing the old place again. For many months he stays inside the cottage watching the men change shifts or stumble in from the tavern. At first he listens to everything they say. Juan complains of chills and Merlo talks about Karlos from time to time. He suggests to the others that Karlos is now a ghost, but they do not heed him.

Kami tries several times to talk to Merlo. He tells him about being dead and about how he died. Merlo pauses at his work sometimes when Kami is talking and looks around with a concerned countenance, but he never answers.

A new man replaced Karlos several days after his death. He had grown accustomed to the position before Kami found the cottage. He is about twenty years his junior, and Kami feels some resentment. He realizes they divvied up the few belongings in his chest long ago, and now the chest belongs to the new man. This new man keeps to himself, just as Karlos had.

Gradually, even Merlo stops mentioning Karlos, though it is clear that he can sense his presence. Kami seems content to watch these four men move through the same routine he had kept most of his life.

He stays in the cottage for a year. One day, Merlo does not return with the others and he, too, is quickly replaced.

Kami finds himself floating down the stretch of lane leading to the dungeon. He is looking for Merlo. He searches throughout the structure but does not find him.

He stays in the dungeon now, morning and night. He gravitates to the torture and execution of prisoners. He watches raptly as each man is killed, but he never sees the person leave their body. He witnesses death after death. At first he feels the excitement he knew when he was alive, the reason he liked to kill. However, he begins feeling revulsion, thinking how death came to him just like it came to these others. There doesn't seem to be any difference. They have the same pained and horrified looks on their faces as Kami had seen on his own. Death in general, and killing specifically, stops making any sense to him at all. He reasons that death is not some kind of consequence. It is just repetitive.

After awhile, Kami stops going down the stone steps into the dungeon, preferring to stay close to the door leading out to the light where he had vomited that fateful day when his dreadful memories first came to him. Victor still stands there. Kami listens to him hum to himself. He listens to the occasional conversations Victor has with the other guards as they come and go. After awhile, everything starts to blend together; all the men start to look the same. Kami cannot distinguish Victor from any other man.

Three and a half years after his death, Kami suddenly finds himself drifting away from the dungeon, without thought, without purpose. He drifts through the city. He drifts out over the countryside. He never stops moving. Sometimes he notes his surroundings, and sometimes he is in a daze.

After another year or so he finds himself hovering above a pond. It is the first time he has stopped moving in years. The pond is bordered on three sides with forest, and on the forth there is a rock outcropping. He moves beyond the rocks and perceives a cave. As soon as he enters the cave, he finds himself in "heaven."

There are a myriad of sentient beings all around Kami. Some appear only for a second and then quickly disappear again. Others hover hesitantly, looking around as though they were waiting for something. Many others just float like Kami, without pain, without thought, in a state of suspension.

Kami, The Sentient Being Who Now Vaguely Recalls Being Karlos, exists in heaven for nearly four years. He stops seeing beings appear and disappear. He does think from time to time but not about anything he can follow, as though he were trying to remember a complicated dream.

When he no longer knows quite who he is or where he is, he finds himself drifting into position for rebirth. He does not know he is in position for rebirth, but he can tell something is about to happen.

He hovers there. Then he has a thought. "I am a bad person. This is true. But there is one thing. Yes, one thing. I was raped many times when I was very young, but I never raped anyone. That is the one good thing I have done." With this thought comes the desire to be happy with himself, and with this desire he is immediately born again.

Transmigrations

Karlos to Mei Hua

Karlos	becomes	Mei Hua
Karlos' father	becomes	Shu Chi
Merlo	becomes	Bau Yu
Victor	becomes	Ying
Emilio	becomes	Madame Wang

MEI HUA

Love is lost and found

At the top of the wooden stairs is a red lacquer door that opens and closes for many. It is the entrance to the boudoir of a fifteen year old prostitute named Mei Hua. The small town of Wutai is known for such girls, but none compare to Mei Hua, whose beauty and talent is fated to become legend.

Several years after buying her, Madame Wang let her two older girls go to fend for themselves, like scavenger chickens gleaning the back alleyways. Madame let them go even though they were only in their twenties, not quite past their prime in the World of Fallen Flowers. She did not need them anymore. One Mei Hua is all a Madame needs.

Madame Wang lives quite comfortably on the feminine charms of the little orphan. She, too, had supported her mistress' household when she was young with the draw and gyration of her body, but unlike the others who beg or hawk edibles until their death, Madame Wang was an excellent thief and so had prospered enough to avoid the streets after her prime. And now, her mercilessness toward her little 'adopted daughter' ensures her a comfortable life.

Madame Wang is determined to shield Mei Hua from her future decline so as to guarantee her present compliance. When Mei Hua goes out, it is in a covered rickshaw or an enclosed palanquin, if the occasion is especially auspicious. Their rented living quarters provide everything they need: a place to eat and a place to do business. It is one of many narrow brick buildings lining the road situated right off the major thoroughfare. The downstairs has a small kitchen and a bedroom for Madame while the upstairs consists of Mei Hua's richly appointed boudoir, with a small living area for entertaining guests. The rooms on the first floor are dark and sparsely furnished because Madame puts away every penny she makes so that she will be able to eat when her luck runs out. Their young maid sleeps in the kitchen on a grass mat she rolls up every morning before day break.

The bed Mei Hua lies in is luxuriant. It has several coats of rich black varnish that mirror her movements when she least wants to see them. The bedding is turquoise, green, and red quilted silk. Next to the bed is a black lacquer dressing screen with deftly painted snow-white cranes for customers who prefer privacy disrobing. On the walls hang classical paintings of famous courtesans for inspiration. The ornately carved lantern overhead is rarely snuffed out at night. Business is good.

The little prostitute feels the morning sun creep into her room like a messenger from another world. At first she remembers some pain and wonders if she was dreaming of something wicked again. It is hard to tell. She easily dismisses it. She lies on her bed, focusing on the lantern, then beyond it to the ceiling, then back again. Before her eyes swim a plane of translucent worms, all dipping and turning at the same slow pace, shooting out of sight when she focuses on the lantern, floating gently into view when she focuses beyond it. She feels light and happy for a time, watching the bobbing waves of squiggles.

Then she hears a harsh female voice and recalls the instant she was orphaned. Her mother had coughed blood into a rag for many months until she died. Her merchant father was gone, never to return. As if these memories formed a single thought, she remembers the property owner selling her to Madame Wang to pay the tenant debt her mother left behind. She remembers the slave housework until she was twelve, then the smell of men.

Only a second passes, but the sun ceases to amuse. The room curls in upon her like the thin twig bars of a cricket cage. If she does not get up now she will have her hair pulled. Madame Wang, the sculptor of her life, knows how to hurt her without marring her beauty. The Madame's voice rips through the floorboards.

"Everything you touch rots!"

Bau Yu, the homely serving girl, must have angered her, and Mei Hua is most likely next.

Yet she does not move. She has no will to continue this life. Tears form but do not fall. The June swelter of the northlands, with their infestations of vermin and wet heat, has been oppressive for so many days she does not believe the fall will ever come. She feels the marrow in her bones fermenting like cabbage.

Now a vision in her mind brings reprieve. There is a lush garden, vividly overgrown, with a stone settee carved at a forty-five degree angle. She sees herself lying on it, heavy as lead, looking up through the branches of a loquat tree whose shadows dapple her body. The leaves tilt back and forth in the breeze. An iridescent blue bird flies at her face, cutting upwards at the last moment to land on her high cloud coiffure. Mirth bubbles up in her throat. The bird flies down her body and lands on one of the turquoise silk embroidered slippers covering her lotus bud feet, cocking its head and eyeing her. Swift as a fairy it flies toward her face again, then stops and hovers there. It slips its thin beak between her lips.

The creak of wood comes too late, and Madame Wang bursts into the room.

"You little slut! Still in bed, are you? Hung over, too, no doubt. The wine is not for you, you know! I'll go broke trying to slake your thirst, you lazy whore! Why I waste my money training you, who could know! Get Up! The Ying's party is today. You really are one, you!"

Mei Hua starts up for the dressing screen as Madame, looming taller than her five odd feet, lunges forward and grabs her hair, conquered as usual by rage.

"You idiot! Wash first! From head to foot you smell of semen! How revolting!"

Mei Hua remembers being with someone last night, was it just a few hours ago? She struggles to recall whom. It seems an overwhelming task, and soon she gives up.

Her scalp smarting, she keeps her eyes down, not from fear or hatred but from habit. The hand has left her head, but she remains bowed and motionless. The stair boards creak loudly as Madame storms away. Then a gentle creaking takes its place. Mei Hua looks up to see Bau Yu.

Her cheeks color to have her hideous shame observed, but when her eyes drift up they meet nothing but warm sympathy in Bau Yu's, who is holding a basin of water.

"The precious mistress would like to wash," Bau Yu says softly. She breaks eye contact to set the basin down and gaze around the ill-gotten room.

"Bau Yu," Mei Hua whispers. These two words sound like the first words of a holy chant. Her eyes fill with tears that cannot escape; she does not know what good deeds she must have performed in an earlier life to have Bau Yu as her maid and only friend.

Bau Yu smiles at the sound of her name and takes a cloth from the warm water scented with sandalwood. She begins by wiping away last night's makeup. Then she pulls Mei Hua's undergarment over her head and offers her a second cloth to bathe her private areas. Mei Hua shivers, perhaps from a chill or from Bau Yu's free, gentle touch.

The little maid washes Mei Hua's back while Mei Hua cleans herself in the front. Bau Yu is fourteen. She hums the tune from the Chao Clan Orphan. Her simple voice is the only guide Mei Hua knows to what is decent, what is fine. Her body relaxes.

"A moment ago I thought I was in a garden. It was luxuriant, everything was resplendent. I had a little friend there, a bird, it was so blue. What does that mean?"

"Ah, it is surely a lucky sign for you."

Bau Yu sits next to her and they hold hands. Looking into each other's eyes, they find hope and admiration. The sun dances again.

"Maybe it is about happiness. It could be the Ying boy. They say he is handsome, a great scholar. He is going to take the National Examination in the Capitol soon. Maybe he will fall in love with me and take me for his concubine. I will bring you with me!"

Mei Hua notices the softest look of consternation on Bau Yu's face.

"Am I not pretty? Clients say I sing like the nightingale. But I am not very clever, like you. My calligraphy is poor."

"No, no. You are beautiful. Any man who does not fall in love with you is blind. Maybe it will be the Ying boy, Mistress. Who knows?"

Mei Hua hugs her and asks what gown she should wear. Bau Yu counsels her to wear the red gown of Double Happiness and the spring-green sash. Quietly, as the morning extends into afternoon, Bau Yu sweeps her mistress's hair up into the cloud coiffure she favors and paints her face as she has for years. Mei Hua lets her mind play with the hope that she will escape this life of servitude, riding on the back of her beauty, but in her heart she knows only Bau Yu's love, like a spider's thread from heaven let down into hell to save one forsaken.

She is looking at herself in her handheld mirror. Her thick black hair is caught up in puffs and swirls, her mouth is painted cherry red, her face is white as dou fu. Her heart is racing; she feels an abnormal level of upset. The house seems to be breathing. Reflecting back strangely from the mirror, her face changes from light to dark, fading in and out, becoming at times grotesque: it is not her face at all. She watches in rapture as various configurations of faces she has known slip over her real face. She hears a sharp order to hurry and leaves with the image of someone else's eyes staring dumbly back at her.

She rides with Madame Wang in a covered rickshaw, plowing through the crowded streets, weaving in and out of the shadows thrown by rickety two story buildings. People dart about in the street like bats at dusk. Mei Hua thinks of the lucky bat-shaped broach of blue-green jade fastened to her sash. She knows tonight will be special. Madame Wang stares straight ahead in deep calculation.

Mei Hua suddenly notices the veins bulging in the impervious legs of the rickshaw runner. She can see them under the edge of the curtain. They seem acutely susceptible to gouging by a rock or shard. The movement of the coolie's legs mesmerizes Mei Hua. Each leg lifts up and slams right back down, and the soft slap of rope-soled shoes against the rammed-earth street creates a beat that somehow syncopates with her heart. She watches the legs, entranced.

When the legs finally stop moving, Mei Hua's relief is tremendous. There has been no accident with a shard. Madame Wang steps down and tosses the coolie the copper she has been gripping in her hand as if to say, "Take it or leave it, it's all you're going to get." Beads of sweat shake on the man's upper lip. He looks down at the copper and is crestfallen. He turns to leave without a word, and Madame walks over to the gatekeeper.

Mei Hua lingers, extracting a small coin from her girdle and pressing it urgently into the runner's grimy palm. "Perhaps a Taoist Priest could help with matters of breath and circulation," she whispers. His head bowed, he shoves the coin into an inner pocket. She sees the faintest smile play about his lips as though he were holding back laughter. She feels flustered: he knows she is only a little girl pretending to be a famous courtesan. At the same time, she realizes he will die without ever seeing a doctor; the coin will go to some other purpose. Just like that, the coolie has made her aware of her position.

"Mei Hua! Don't stand there like an idiot!" Madame Wang hisses loudly from the inner courtyard. She scampers on tiny feet to her jailer's side.

An old man comes striding out of the main doors, conceited and self-contained. He is like a varnished tortoise shell hanging in the Ancestral Palace, only the semblance of what was once great. She instantly drops her head and hears Madame Wang purr in an amber voice she saves for clients like a precious drug not to be squandered.

"Master Ying! You are so robust! I have brought my worthless daughter as you requested. She is not much to look at, but she can sing a note..."

The insidious drug of Madame's voice is working on Mei Hua. She feels a familiar coyness spread through her body, producing a sweet pout, a limp wrist. The old man looks at the girl, slightly unnerved by her attractiveness. She glances up and feels his lecherous eyes on her face. Her chin cradles back to its demure resting place, pointing to her breasts, her head bowed. Her limbs become heavy with the knowledge that if Madame says so, he might be the one to have her tonight. Her knowing of old skin—all the passionless scenarios, all the haggard faces and wrinkled "golden rods" too many to count—tortures her mind.

As she hears him speak of his son's twentieth birthday, she develops a profound hatred for the old man. She envisions him in the various throes of death. Now he is turning his wretched body, heading stiffly back into the main hall. Impulsively she affects a stumble towards him. He swings his arm out to catch her around the waist. Her knees, bent beneath her gown, support her weight, but he thinks he has saved her from a fall. Blushing, she looks askance at his face and airily thanks him.

He is at a loss. His night will now be haunted with the memory of her touch, purchased for his son.

She keeps her eyes cast down as she enters the banquet hall. The tiled floor laughs at her with richness. She feels many eyes upon her. She stops walking. There are introductions, first through the old man, then Madame, but they are unable to create any movement in her. She understands at once that she is creating mystery around herself through her silence, through her immobility. This ploy will serve her ends. But as always, somewhere inside, she wishes she could disappear.

"Mei Hua! Do you have some sickness? Greet the Young Master!"

"She is still shaken from her near fall," the old man coos, captivated.

"What? Are you all right, Miss? Is it your ankle? Hurry a little, call the doctor to come." This voice sounds too certain for twenty.

All eyes are drawn to her pretty little feet, the famous lotus buds of erotica that help her fetch more than a meal's price. Madame Wang could not have done better, though she had coached Mei Hua on that particular fall. At the perfect moment, the point where the Young Master cannot bear her inaction anymore, Mei Hua looks up to the face addressing her, and in doing so, it becomes hers. Young Master Ying's breath catches at the sight of her beauty; the sound he makes is audible in the now silent hall. With his eyes fixed on her face, he takes her arm and leads her to her seat.

Madame chatters away, indicating that a doctor is not necessary, Mei Hua is a bit clumsy, that is all. She is beginning to irritate the men, a nice counterpoint, for she makes Mei Hua seem all the more demure.

Ying's upper body edges close to Mei Hua's as he guides her through the hall. The sound of conversation starts up again. Mei Hua hears a voice in her head saying, "Give him no peace."

She drops her head, addressing the floor. "It is a rare honor to meet your acquaintance. Please excuse my having troubled you." She hardly recognizes her own voice, it is so high and light.

"It must be that you are exhausted from your journey. Please sit and rest a moment." He leads her to the seat next to his at the head of the table.

"Oh no, I could not presume upon you. If I could just have a little water..." With silent mincing steps, she moves to the offered seat but does not sit down.

"Please, go ahead," says the old man, a bit perturbed. "It is my son's twentieth birthday. His wishes must be observed." He motions toward the high-backed chair of cherry wood inlaid with mother of pearl and cushioned with red silk. She whispers a thank you and floats downward, her gown brushing the Young Master's knee; she observes his body tense out of the corner of her eye.

They are the only women in the hall. Madame Wang sits next to the old man, pouring words over him like sugarcane syrup, each drop agitating him more than the last. These men are Ying's male relatives and friends; they have the feel of pigeons in a coop.

As the others talk, occasionally stealing glances at the famous Mei Hua, there is one man on Master Ying's right who stares at her boldly. He is beyond her wiles. Shortly he turns to Ying.

"Now that you have scaled the rise of manhood to twenty, the next peak will bring you to the Examinations, surely."

"Ah, yes. What you have said is true, surely," Ying perfunctorily replies as if brushing away a beetle. The other man looks over Ying's head at Mei Hua. His eyes say: "You little whore." Ying never stops attending to her, and his eyes say: "You sweet mourning dove!" Mei Hua has a great desire to laugh, to throw off her humility like wiping steam from a window and just laugh at both these men. However, if she did this, she would find herself with a ruined reputation and many customers each day to make up for her drop in value, so she does not even color. She recedes into herself so as not to anger the man on the right.

During speeches, wine, and delicacies she indulges in a fantasy. Ying cannot bear to be separated from her. He has fought his father and won, taking her as a concubine. She avoids the old man and produces several heirs. She praises Ying and his venerable father, sends presents to her mother-in-law. It could be done. She sees her future spin out against the backdrop of this hall, sees the banquets to come that will celebrate her children's births, her place thereby secured amidst the feasting and drinking. Her son will be tutored in matters of state and become the rising star of the Ying clan.

She turns her face to Ying, his eyes standing ready for the chance to look into hers. She blushes and drops her head, tries to meet his eyes again, then blushes and drops her head. She does this several times, as his love for her shyness seems inexhaustible. In the end, she says nothing, so he begins speaking.

"Please eat a little something. There is 'Phoenix Chasing Dragon,' 'Double Shrimp Dumplings,' or 'Spring Vegetable with Dou Fu.' I can have them make anything you like. You have not touched your wine. Please, Miss, eat a little something. You must not become weakened."

"Master Ying. I do not wish to trouble you. Everything is too fine. I am exhilarated to be in your presence. I am unable to eat."

"That is unacceptable. Perhaps the dishes are too heavy. Shall I call the cook to make you Sea Scallops in the Grass?"

"No, please, do not trouble yourself. To honor you I will attempt a morsel."

When all present know Mei Hua should feed the Young Master, he breaks etiquette and fills her dish with savory delicacies. It is a great triumph indeed. She dare not look to Madame Wang, who has no doubt witnessed this transaction with satisfaction. Ying offers her a cup and watches with fascination as she deftly brings the white porcelain to her tiny mouth. She only pretends to drink.

It is not long before the men's heads begin to sway on uncertain necks. Stories have been told, and many flasks have been heated. Madame Wang seizes the moment and stands with flamboyance to announce, "The distinguished gentlemen allowing, I will now request that your humble servant's daughter perform. She will sing 'Lovers Parted' and perform The Rainbow Skirt Dance." She cuddles back into the seat next to the old man, flushed with exertion as if *she* had just danced.

Mei Hua thinks she will have Ying make Madame a scullery maid when she becomes his concubine. She quickly notes the musicians in the corner: a lute, a flute, a bowed instrument. She will need to carry the beat. She takes in the drunken state of the men, knowing it is good. As a few stray notes from the players urge her to her feet, she looks to Ying. Frozen in the pressure of the moment, she wishes she had actually drunk a cup.

Sensing her hesitation, Ying murmurs softly, "Please dance."

Gripped with the sense that this moment is her only chance to get away, she smiles warmly at Ying and bows her head in acquiescence. Rising like morning fog on a lake, she floats to the center of the floor. She stands radiant. The players begin.

Like a flower bursting into bloom, she whirls around, dipping and twirling on her toes, the unfurled sleeves of her gown wrapping lightly about her body. Her weightlessness is so unnatural that her viewers become convinced that she is not of this earth. She is ecstatic and silent, undulating with the music. Waves of tender movement ripple out and engulf the room. When all feel light as air, the music stops like a leaf wafting to the ground.

There is a spontaneous cry for Mei Hua to keep dancing. Settling back into herself, she revels in the pleasure and awe of these men.

She stands looking from face to face until she finds Ying. His face radiates pure rapture. Looking straight into his eyes she begins to sing unaccompanied, a song she has never heard before. The melody is simple and plaintive. She hears a voice rising full and high, beautiful beyond imagination. It is her voice. She sings as though she was alone, beseeching the gods. The melody weaves a cord that pulls her listeners into an aesthetic heaven:

The butterfly floats without worry,
Leaves flutter down without strain.
But an orphan's lot is struggle,
Each breeze attacks the flame.

The sun woke the birds this morning
The cricket escaped its cage.
With certainty I know
The blossom will not die in vain.

No one can tell if she still sings or if it is an echo reverberating around the hall. A tear rolls down Mei Hua's cheek, and Ying gasps, staring at her.

"Too fine!" he finally whispers. The masculine murmurings weave together, forming a chorus of praise.

Mei Hua has become faint. She begins to teeter towards her seat when a rough hand grabs her arm. The harsh voice attached to it whispers, "What song is that? I've never heard that one before. I told you to sing 'Lovers Parted!'"

Madame Wang's insensitivity is just enough to rouse Mei Hua from her fairy tale. Strength returns to her limbs.

"Unpolished, but likable in a rustic way!" Madame Wang gives commentary to the men, now edging out of their stupor.

"Rustic?" Ying says incredulously. "It was stunning! Please, Miss, who taught you that song?"

She drops her head in embarrassment.

"Now what? Answer the Young Master!" Madame Wang snaps.

Her eyes again become intimate with the floor. "It is nothing. I made it up as I sang, moved to wish you long life on this your twentieth birthday. That is all. Please forgive its coarseness. I am silly and sometimes act on a whim. I can sing another if you like."

"There isn't any other. That was the most beautiful song I have ever heard," Ying answers in admiration. Others murmur agreement.

The women return to their seats. Some talk starts up at the other end of the table. Happy and exhausted, Mei Hua feels Ying's knee pressing gently against hers beneath the table. She dare not return the gesture.

She hears the men's voices as though they were all far away. The only thing anchoring her to this world is the mischievous pressure from Ying's leg.

After awhile, Madame announces they must go. Young Master Ying protests, but Madame insists that they trouble him and his venerable father no longer. The old man goes as far as the gate to see them off, a great honor. He hands a red envelope to Madame Wang and a small package to Mei Hua. She will find the two silver hair combs once she is in the waiting rickshaw. Before she can climb in, the old man squeezes her arm and says, "I hope we will be graced often by your presence."

"Always your humble servant," Mei Hua mumbles in reply. She suddenly feels queasy.

It has been a week since she rode home in the rickshaw. No word from Ying. Is he suffering, too? But he is free, he could send a message. Maybe there have been other parties, other singing girls.

These thoughts torture Mei Hua. Could he be that fickle?

But his eyes were so sad! His eyes said he loved her.

His eyes float before her in the darkness of her room, eyes of love and compassion. She has not left her room since that night. She has refused to entertain customers. Her feigned illness has sent Madame past the bounds of hidden injury into bruising and slapping, but to no avail. Mei Hua will not eat. She moans his name. She vows she will have no lover but Ying. Let Madame kill her, let Madame send her away. Mei Hua cries and pleads.

Madame curses her. There will be more men, even if she must bind her.

Memories of her past customers come to haunt her in the glow of her new love. Four years of nameless men torture her like ants crawling over her skin. Leering faces with exaggerated lips spin around her in the darkness on free-floating heads whose mouths move soundlessly, forming silent words, chanting spells powered by the silvery moonlight. She is getting thinner.

What had she done in a past life to atone in such a way? How could anyone have been that wicked? "Heaven is blind; it treats men like straw dogs." It is so true! Ying is merely an extra torture. She hears the gods laughing at her, drunk on ill-gotten libations of wine. Her spirit-soul beats against her skull, seeking escape, while her heavy body-soul presses her spine so far into the bedclothes she can barely rock from side to side. She feels trapped inside her bed, the instrument of her destruction. There is no Ying, and her beauty is fading.

She hears a sound like a bird being impaled and remarks it as Madame Wang's voice. Her limp body finds enough agony left to respond to the violence in the air, instinctively tensing for a blow from the woman downstairs. Her mind routinely reviews various hiding places; all were exhausted long ago when she still had the hope of a child. Dully, she ponders killing Madame Wang.

Creaking wood, a slamming door, and frenzied breathing tell of Madame Wang's approach. Mei Hua nearly jumps out of her body at these sounds.

Madame Wang sneers, "Bathe, and fix your hair. Young Master Ying will be here in the hour."

It takes a moment to sink in.

He is coming! They will be together at last! She flies from her bed and starts to fix herself up. She stands at the window, fighting the braided ropes of her long black hair with pins, trying to secure them at the back of her head. Bau Yu is busy cooking in the kitchen below, so Mei Hua dresses herself. It occurs to her that she has missed her neck, it is not clean. She moves over to the basin to wash it then drifts back to the window like a moored boat nudging a dock. Somehow between standing at the window and leaving briefly to complete a task, the bed is made, the gown is donned properly, and the make-up is applied. Mei Hua stands ready, forever looking down from her window.

The fried dou fu seller comes and goes. Rickshaws file aimlessly past like beetles. There is no knock at the door. Surely more than an hour has passed. Mei Hua grows desperate.

She tries to see herself in Ying's home, a picture so easily painted just days before. No scenes come to mind. She imagines seeing Madame Wang for the last time, but it does not feel real. She will tell Ying that she must bring Bau Yu to live with her. No mode of travel presents itself. No color appears for the bridal chamber. There is no knock at the door.

Finally, she hears a male voice, but it is not his. Madame Wang's approach sounds again, but Ying is not the one treading heavily on the stairs behind her. She can tell. It has all been a lie, a ruse to force her to see customers again.

When the door opens, she sees a strange man behind Madame Wang. He is in his forties, short and fat, and has the look of Ying's father about his face. When she sees the lechery there, she falls to the floor and cries.

It is as if the tears of a lifetime pour from her eyes.

Mei Hua stands at the window, mechanically scanning the faces below for Ying. The throbbing in her wrist interacts with the aching from the lump on the back of her head. As she eyes a coolie for familiar traces of the face now dominating all her decisions, she remembers after the kick to her kidneys how she agreed to see customers again. But she won't.

The beating was actually good, because Madame Wang has given her one more day before she arranges the next customer.

Mei Hua has sent a message through Bau Yu to Ying. She wrote it in her best hand and sent along a strand of her hair. It says, "If you love me, come quickly, before my spirit passes from this realm of sorrows. If you do not, please tell my trusted maid and end my suffering. Mei Hua."

A richly painted palanquin hurries past, and her breath catches as it bobs on down the lane. Still, it could have been his.

What could be keeping him? What will she do tomorrow? She considers the trick of "monkey leaving the tree." It is a technique used to get the customer drunk and later wake him to coo about his deftness at "rain and clouds." She has used it successfully before. She also knows she is Madame's only source of income. Surely she will not be beaten to death.

Bau Yu has come to look in on her several times, bringing salves that Mei Hua accepts only because Bau Yu looks like she might cry. Mei Hua does not want to heal until she knows that Ying will be hers. Standing at the window so long her muscles are numb, Mei Hua thinks about Bau Yu and how they have always taken care of each other and felt each other's pain.

She remembers when Bau Yu first came into her life. There were two prostitutes in the house, and Mei Hua was the only servant. She remembers being very skinny and constantly tired. Madame Wang realized the household tasks were too difficult for a ten year old, if she expected the girl to last long enough to provide for her retirement. Because Mei Hua's beauty and singing ability were already showing themselves, Madame Wang bought another girl to help.

Bau Yu must have been almost eight when she entered their household. She was an orphan, too, a war refugee from a southern province. Mei Hua and Bau Yu developed a simple, unspoken pact: they would be kind to each other. As young girls, they shared everything from hiding places to trinkets. The two figured out rather quickly that Mei Hua would become a prostitute while Bau Yu would remain a servant due to her homeliness. Neither life seemed desirable. Lying on their mats by the door after it was dark and everyone was in bed, they would talk about their dreams and fantasies. Mei Hua always pretended that her mother got stronger and never died and that she lived with her still, selling sweet cakes. Bau Yu talked about the lovely life she had before the war. Her parents and relatives worked a large piece of land together and no one ever wanted for food or clothing. She was happy then. Now they are all dead.

They could see no way out of their situation, so they let their minds go to the places where children's minds go, to happy times, past and future. On days when they were treated to some particular cruelty, they would talk about their actual lives.

"Heaven has assigned us these lives to balance our past misdeeds. There is no escape," Bau Yu once said.

"But there must be a way out, Bau Yu! I will practice my singing every day, every day, and then someday I will be a famous singer, and we will not have to work so hard!"

The two would snuggle down close to each other and dream of that day.

Even now, late at night, if a customer leaves before dawn, the girls share Mei Hua's comfortable bed, feeling warm and safe for a few hours together in the fleeting world of dust.

A young man walks by as Mei Hua shifts her weight from one hip to the other. She has been standing at the window for so many days there is a mark on the wall where she rests her hand. She drinks in every face she sees. She wonders at Bau Yu, how she is always so quiet and calm though she has no future outside these walls. Bau Yu just listens when Mei Hua describes their future in the Ying mansion and smiles a sad, empathetic smile that reaches far beyond her fourteen years. Mei Hua truly loves her.

She thinks of going downstairs to find her and realizes she hasn't left the room in eight days. She determines to find Bau Yu, but she cannot leave the window.

"I am growing weary, or perhaps I am just mad. What am I waiting for? Ying would have come by now if he cared for me," Mei Hua thinks to herself.

Suddenly she feels a hand on her shoulder and jumps before she realizes it is Bau Yu. She whirls around to see her smiling friend and grabs her up in a hug. They stand embracing for a long time, long enough for Mei Hua to hear the birds chirping in the dusk. Slowly she pulls her body back and looks into Bau Yu's eyes. It is in her face.

"The message?"

"He is coming tonight. Madame knows he is coming, but she knows nothing about the letter."

"Ahhhh! Is it true? Ying is coming? Is it true? Did you see him?"

"He came to me after I sent the letter to him through the gatekeeper. He has grown thin, too. He grabbed my arm and made me tell of your plight. He swore to kill Madame," Bau Yu answers wryly. She, too, has had this thought. But in an instant the look fades to one of sad concern.

"What? What is it, Bau Yu?"

"Nothing. Nothing of importance. I am happy for you, Mistress Mei. You must hurry now."

In what seem like minutes, Mei Hua is dressed and back at the window with her mirror in her hand. It is amazing what a job Bau Yu did to hide the bruise under her eye. Mei Hua shares her time equally between the street and the mirror, measuring her beauty against the approach of the man she loves. A flicker from the candle blots out her image for a moment; she wonders who lit it and when. She is beyond picturing Ying's face, so much time has passed since she last saw him. It feels unreal to be standing and waiting for him, and suddenly she imagines that she does not know who he is or how to recognize him. She shakes off the feeling and returns to waiting without another thought.

Now the voice she has longed for comes up through the floorboards. Like liquid she turns softly from the window, hearing all the sounds around her: a bell, the thin hum of human voices, a baby crying far away, a wheel turning, the crickets' songs. She imagines hearing footsteps on the stairs even before they fall; perhaps she has confused them with the beating of her heart. Then redemption for her entire meaningless life stands knocking faintly at her door. Still she cannot move altogether away from the window nor can she utter a sound. Her chest is hurting, and she fears he will go away, but the handle turns and he is standing there.

A single note - "Ying!" - lifts the lines of worry from his young face. "Mei Hua." His deep voice cracks with emotion, startling them both. She leans forward but does not move, as if a vortex were swirling between them, pulling her forward and repulsing her at the same time. Ying begins to walk toward her, quickening his steps when he sees her tears. She sweeps her head away to the window, speaking out into the darkness.

"This is where I stand waiting for you. I live to look out this window. I have stood here day and night. I fear now you are a specter, the last of my tortures. How could you be real? Surely it is the strain upon my eyes."

"Mei Hua!" he whispers, his breath on her cheek betraying how he slid closer without her noticing. "I wanted to come so badly it was unbearable. My father forbade me to see you as soon as you left that night. He has watched me like a stone temple guard. I have not left my house alone. I climbed the wall tonight, telling only my servant. Do not cry! I am here!"

They fall into each other's arms. Mei Hua's tiny frame shudders with relief. He pulls her to his breast and kisses her head. He tips her mouth up and kisses it, then moves his hand to her breast. The feeling is so familiar she is stunned and pulls back. Taking his handkerchief, he wipes her tear stained cheeks, uncovering the bruise. He gasps. Her stomach tightens. He caresses her shoulders and face. This caress is like a thousand other caresses she has known; one cannot erase the past. She feels separated from her body. It is a feeling she knows well, and she struggles against it. "You are a prostitute," a voice in her head mocks.

"I have heated wine," is all she can say. He looks at her, puzzled, but moves to take a seat on the bed. She scurries to get the wine. Only in the ritual of pouring does her hand slow, measuring out the acrid liquid with her head bowed. With some confidence now she begins saying the words she knows so well:

"Please drink. May you live ten thousand years, Young Master Ying."

"Please. You must drink a cup, too."

"I could not presume. Would you like to eat a morsel? I cannot offer much..."

"No, no, not hungry. Thank you. Mei Hua. You do not need to be formal."

"It is no formality. The humble creature that I am, excuse me, I am not well-studied."

"Mei Hua. Do you still like me?"

"I...I...you must forgive me!" She turns her head aside and cries, wiping the tears quickly and trying to regain control.

"Mei! What is wrong?"

The candle sputters with a sense of urgency. She does not know if she should let her heart roam to him. She thinks of the coolie's grin, but feels compelled to speak her mind.

"You call me 'Mei' with apparent fondness. There is nothing I can say to that. But should I not please you, it would be worse than angering a God. The irony is, 'Before the sticks are thrown, the number's known.' How can I be anything more than a Fallen Flower to you? How can you be anything less than my very existence? A newborn could not be more dependent. This is unfair to you. Even though it means my death, how can I not, with the profound love I feel for you, urge you to leave now and be free from the stain of my temporal world of sorrows?"

"Do not 'cut the tree before the seed is planted.' Who is to say what past deeds have brought us together? Chuang Tzu said: 'Wherein am I happy? Standing on this bridge!' You are like that bridge. The seasons revolve, and life passes away. Do not call out for winter while it is still spring!"

Suddenly, Mei Hua hears the crickets and feels the moonlight flooding the room. The wine is aromatic.

"You understand, then, and I am not afraid," she whispers contentedly.

He smiles, offering her a cup. Together, they begin to laugh.

It is late morning and he is gone. He did not leave while she was sleeping; she would not sleep. She watched his back disappear through the door. She watched him wake the driver, glance up at her window, and climb in. Before he left, he said, "You should know, I will find some way to return."

She has the time now, before the smell of the morning's dou fu milk evaporates into the muggy afternoon and is replaced with the steam of boiling rice, to repeat once more in her mind scenes from their love making. There were kisses and the gentle touching of secret places through the finest cloth. He loosened her sash and exposed her small, firm breasts. He knelt by her where she sat on the edge of the bed, intending to roll her gown up, but lingering long in his play with her tiny feet. He squeezed and tickled them, placing them against his cheek. He rubbed her marble smooth thighs. He stood and uncovered his flaring manhood. It bobbed anxiously in the dim candlelight. With mock roughness, he pushed her thighs open with his knees and pressed the quilt into the small of her back to maintain an arch without discomfort. How many times he thrust into her, mouthed her nipples, squeezed her waist, she could not say, but at some point their voices merged into a long, low moan, and the moon erupted over the bed as if the clouds obscuring it had spread apart and released a most gentle and titillating rain.

There is no place in her mind that is not dominated by the thought of Ying. She can only think about when she will see him again and how she can put off other customers.

"You have left your body," Bau Yu nearly whispers, an astute commentary delivered between mouthfuls of rice.

"I have never felt so happy. I have never seen with these eyes," Mei Hua says, eating with relish. "Being with Ying is like the silk worm freed from its cocoon. He is so gentle! He loves me in a way I have never been loved before. He would do anything for me!"

The girls sit in the kitchen on new straw mats, the old ones having been little more than breeding ground for vermin. The house of Madame Wang has reached new levels of prosperity. Not only is Mei Hua entertaining her old customers again, there are also new customers, drawn by the mystery surrounding her long absence.

Bau Yu finishes eating and says, "Please be careful, Mei Hua."

"You don't need to worry. Ying loves me. I know he does."

"Love is one thing. What is real is another."

"Don't worry! Everything is perfect!" Mei Hua laughs to her friend.

At first, Mei Hua refused to see any other customers, especially after her first night with Ying. So Madame Wang threatened her with a well-known and dreaded customer, the first Mei Hua ever had. He was meant to break her in, and he did. Master Chang only likes it when the girl is unwilling. The more they struggle, the more he hits. He performs quite a service for the ladies managing boudoirs. He quickly taught Mei Hua how to lay still and succumb. Madame Wang only cancelled his appointment with Mei Hua after she agreed to entertain a high paying old timer who had grown remarkably fond of her. She realized that without Madame Wang, she would be out on the streets and her chances of seeing Ying would diminish greatly. Not that she would have gotten away; the law protects Madame's property. The constable would have dragged her back, and Madame would have beaten her and forced her to see twice the usual number of customers.

As it is, she need only play a game in her head: each man's thrust is a wave sweeping her closer to Tuesday, Ying's day. Their moist odor is like that of the coolie's, who first brought her to Ying. Like the days of hiding from Madame Wang, she need only close her eyes to leave the room, journeying to the banquet hall where Ying first became hers. Several of her customers have asked her what song she hums, assuming she was pleased with their performance of rain and clouds. She smiles and says she made it up. When she hums, it means one less man between herself and the One. She is one step closer to heaven than she was a moment ago.

Without warning the door flies open, and Madame is back from her errands.

"Oh, 'Sit and Eat Until the Mountain of Wealth is Gone,' is that it? I do not keep you to sit on your butt, Bau Yu. And look at this gown! As if it isn't enough to have to deal with a fickle Caged Bird like Mei Hua, Liu has to send the laundry back dirty. Bau Yu! Run this back to him, and tell him if it is dirty again, it will be the last gown he launders! And if you, Caged Bird, think because your precious Ying is a Regular that you won't do parties, you thought wrong! You are doing the Chiu party tomorrow night."

Mei Hua bounds to her feet, but Bau Yu sits placidly finishing her rice. When she rises, she rises slowly, taking up both bowls and walking to the water bucket to clean them. Mei Hua shifts her weight, thinking of something to say.

"Oh, is there something you want to say? What do you want to say? You'll do anything to hang onto your precious Ying. You think you are in love with him! You think he is in love with you! What a fool you are, really! I taught you better than that. When he has had his fill, like any man, he will wander off to fresher flowers. Love! Where do you get these ideas? You are just weak and lonely, and that's the truth of it. You'll go crazy with such thinking, believing in such lies. Those songs you sing are for tricking men, not yourself, you idiot!"

Bau Yu is standing next to Madame, staring into her face. She is not threatening; she is not afraid. In a voice collected, like a mother addressing an angry child, she says, "I will take that gown now, Madame. Mei, go rest. Have you forgotten it is Tuesday?" With these simple words, she takes up the gown and goes, undoing Madame's heartless tirade.

Mei Hua wants to scream that if it wasn't for her Madame could not purchase the new mats or the gowns or the porcelain that have found their way into the Wang house over the last several weeks. She wants to tell her that she should be in charge because she makes the money. But she knows that without Madame, she could wind up a beggar in the street, or a scullery maid. All the mistresses of fallen flowers are like Madame, some even worse. She might never see Ying again. She remembers the look in the coolie's eyes and puts herself in her place. She turns quietly and goes up the stairs to her prison.

Mei Hua lies on her bed. She thinks about the only two people who call her Mei. One she knows well for the gentle girl wise beyond her years. The other is Ying. She recalls a poem she learned, maybe from a book Madame made her read to become cultured: "My heart is not a stone. It cannot be rolled." They say water only flows uphill if you beat it with a stick. Even Madame cannot force her to feel other than what she feels. Perhaps she learned the bit of poetry from her tutor, Madame Chou, who came to teach her when she first started entertaining. She was light and friendly and encouraged Mei Hua. "You are very bright. You learn quickly! Not every girl in your trade can be taught to read. Madame did well when she purchased you!" Mei Hua remembers her with gratitude.

She sees a tree, huge and black, scraping at her face. She opens her eyes, and Bau Yu is sitting on her bed. She must have fallen asleep.

"Mei. Ying is not coming tonight. Madame has arranged another customer."

"Bau Yu! I have had a terrible dream. Still it clings to me, I am not fully awake. Ying not coming? Do you know why?"

"I don't know. A messenger was sent. He said Master Ying is indisposed. At any rate, you must get up. Mei Hua, I must tell you. I cannot bear to stay here any longer. My heart is sour. I must find another place. I have a friend, she is also a servant, who says her Mistress is kind and needs a kitchen girl. I have not been adopted. I must leave."

Mei Hua is pushing the branches out of her face, half asleep, half alive. "But Bau Yu! How can I live without you? You know I cannot leave! Ying may not come today, but I know he loves me! We can both find a way out!"

She sees sorrow in Bau Yu's eyes. Bau Yu knows something Mei Hua does not. Mei Hua feels the earth sinking beneath her feet, but she struggles to hang on.

"Bau Yu. Go now, you must. Remember. When I am in Ying's house, I will call for you. You will never be beaten or ridiculed. Wait and see. Heaven has eyes!"

"Mei! If you choose, I can help you. You are like a sister to me. Come now, come with me. This place will surely kill you. You were not meant to be a Fallen Flower, you have no ability to endure it."

Even as Bau Yu speaks, Mei Hua shakes her head. "How can you know? You have never been in love. This love is beyond heaven and earth. But go now. Soon we will be together again. Bau Yu. There is no way I can repay your kindness. I will think of you every day."

Then she remembers their stash of coins underneath the floorboard in the corner. She runs to the spot, pries up the board with her fingers, and pulls the bag out.

"Take it, Bau. We saved it together. I want you to have it."

"No, Mei. You will need it. I will have a new job. I will work and save more coppers. You will need this, Mei! Save it for a time of need, or give me my share later!" Her voice sounds so desperate, so out-of-character, Mei Hua becomes frightened. She returns the coins to their hiding place and stands thinking for a moment.

Then she walks over to her dressing table. She takes the precious mirror and places it in Bau Yu's hand, looking deep within her eyes.

"Good-bye for now, my little sister."

"I will contact you when I am settled. You are like the flesh of my bones. I will not forsake you."

Mei Hua feels Bau Yu's arms around her, feels the amazing strength in her little body, the warmth coming through her worn blouse. It strikes her: she is only fourteen! She has great daring.

A week has gone by. There is another serving girl named Yi Ya. She is twelve and appears to be mentally deficient. She moves like a small animal, and her eyes are dull. People keep passing below the window. There have been men, one or two a day. None have been Ying. This is his night. Mei Hua is beyond worry. She stands at the window, observing the sun as it briefly rests on top of the low buildings. She is dressed in her finest. Yi Ya did her hair, pulling at the roots as Bau Yu never did.

Madame Wang bursts in, looking to see that she is dressed as though checking on an infant.

"Your precious Ying will be here soon. He sent a message." Madame says this just to spite Mei Hua because it is clear she does not believe their love affair will amount to anything. Anger lines on either side of her mouth indicate this might have happened to her. Certainly, if she ever had a heart, it died some horrible death long ago. Her only desire now is to ensure the productivity of her golden mountain, this little prostitute.

"Well, have you prepared the wine?" is all she can say as she sweeps out of the door and pulls it closed behind her.

Hours have gone by. Rickshaws and hawkers take over the night that followed so hard upon the heels of dusk. Suddenly there are voices, and Ying fills the doorway. Mei Hua turns from the window and runs to his arms.

"How could you leave me for so long? Do you not love me? Oh, Ying, it is unbearable here. Please! You must take me away. I cannot stay another hour. Bau Yu is gone, and I am all alone. Madame is so cruel! Oh Ying, you love me, don't you? You can do something!" The words come pouring from her like a rainstorm. She looks into his eyes with desperation. She feels his body tense, draw away. Something is wrong.

"It is not easy for me to get away to see you, never mind the expense. And this is how I am greeted? I have told you, my father won't allow it. You are lucky I come to see you at all. That, too, will be coming to an end. I will need to leave soon to sit for the Imperial Examination."

Mei Hua takes a step back. She looks away from his eyes as if this will help her focus on what he just said. She wants him to come through the door again, to say different words, or to just hold her as he did that first night. What was that he said? It was important. She cannot remember. She looks back and sees his eyes have gotten cloudy. A look of disgust floats over his features.

"I'm sorry. What did you say?" She sees his lips move, but the sound is slow to reach her ears. He says he must leave to take the Imperial Examination. "He must leave to take the Imperial Examination," she repeats in her mind. She has fallen back against the window. His lips are moving again as he turns away to pour himself a cup of wine, but a low-pitched buzzing obstructs their meaning. Gradually the words take shape in her mind.

"Don't I give your stepmother enough? Every copper I get goes to Madame Wang! How can you be so ungrateful? Why do you ask the impossible? My father would disown me if he knew I came to see you, spent his money this way. I am not proud of it myself. And who is this Bau Yu?"

He has raised his voice, striding closer to Mei Hua. He looks defiantly into her face, but cannot hold the stare and turns in anger to gaze out the window. Mei Hua finds her hands have been twisting her sash. A tiny voice inside her whispers, "There. So. It has happened, as you always knew it would. It is over." A counter voice takes up the cry, "No! It cannot be true. You have suffered enough. This is not your fate!"

In between these extremes she finds her outer voice and says, "Please do not be angry with me. I am grateful to a degree you could never know. I had no life before I met you. I would do anything for you, even for the memory of you. I see I ask the impossible. The ancient books say love ends this way. Only look into my eyes and tell me you must leave. Hold back your tears, and I will let you go. If I knew I weren't alone in my suffering, that you, too, feel haunted by the lonely nights strung together on the whisper of my scent, I could help you on your way. My heart! Ying!"

She is weeping now, uncontrollably. Through her tears she sees the lines around his eyes harden and narrow. A balmy wind blows in through the window, threatening the candle flames. She hears his voice come back at her as though it had traversed a dark wood before reaching her.

"Huh. So you are going to be like this. My friends scolded me, spending my money this way. If you want to cry, then cry! I don't want to spend my last days in town with a bird whose song is so discordant!"

"You will carry this betrayal until the day you die," she sobs with vehemence now.

With one swift motion, Ying glides over and strikes her with the back of his hand.

Mei Hua is sinking down on her knees. She feels the ceiling creeping down, forcing her against the old wooden floorboards. She imagines a delicate spine, suspended from a thread hanging in midair. With a swift kick, it breaks to pieces and falls to the floor. She cowers. There is a pain shooting up her back. She hears her voice weeping. "Ying! Do not do this! Ying!" In her mouth is the salty taste of tears. She cranes her neck up to see Ying pausing, considering some action. He looks down at her for a moment, then turns and sweeps out of the door.

She wonders if she could run after him and beg his forgiveness. At the same time, she wonders if she could find a knife and drive it through his heart. She feels the floorboards beneath her vibrating with his footfalls on the stairs. Madame's voice, pleading coyly for him not to go, carries through the house. There is a brusque reply, more vibration through the boards, and Madame is standing over her, cursing.

"Ai ya! Isn't it what I have said? Didn't I tell you? He was your best paying customer! We could have gotten one if not two more visits from him! And your reputation! Professing love is a curse for a girl like you! Just look at your face! Haven't you learned at least to shield your face? Who will want you now? We will lose two or three days of business! Just forget it! If you do not heal in three days, you are out on the street! How impossible you are! So stupid! How like a child!"

Madame's voice swirls above her. All the days of her life join in the harangue. She feels her body for the first time, feels the throbbing create such havoc that all her other senses are shutting down in the face of this pain. She moves her hand up to explore the pain and finds her left eye swollen shut. Her fingers slide off in the blood. She feels the floorboards vibrate again and searches in the sputtering candle light for her mirror, but it is gone. Yes. She gave it to Bau Yu, and Bau Yu is gone. She finds her make-up cloth and daubs at her face. There is surely more blood than can come from an eye. A bubble rises in her throat and erupts with the words, "Bau Yu! Come back! Take me with you!" The pathetic cracked whisper that reaches her ears cuts the knot in her throat, and her tears come pouring forth. She lies back on the floor, crying without sound, wishing it were her coffin.

She is in an expansive hall, its high ceilings magnificently carved with intricate designs. She hears steps approaching from the far side of the hall, knowing right away it is the Empress. There are odd designs floating in the air all around her. They are symbols that form a language only the Empress can decipher. They are somehow the key to her being. As the Empress draws near, great monstrous heads thrust forth from the massive columns lining the hall, rolling their eyes, exposing their long, writhing tongues. The Empress, robed in a garish orange gown, is nearly upon her, she can almost see her face. Whose face is it?

She senses she must get beyond the Empress to the back chamber. She must kill her. The walls are bare, she has no weapon, and the Empress is growing. She is only twenty feet away. There is no escape. She looks into the Empress' eyes, and her heart swells with a loathing so great she can barely breathe. She hurls herself across those twenty feet with superhuman speed, grabs the Empress by the throat, and squeezes with every ounce of her strength. A wonderful power flows up from her lower abdomen into her hands. The Empress goes slack. Her head bobs with the throttling, and her eyes bulge out. The Empress' dying eyes strike her with horror, and she lets go, sensing immediately that this was a mistake. She leaps over the body and rushes down the hall to the gigantic wooden doors leading out. She heaves her body against them, and they tiredly creak open.

She is face to face with a sea monster. Long feelers trail from the sides of his hideous, lipless mouth. He has a sword and strikes at her. She ducks and sees behind him a couple bound with ropes heavy and mildewed. They have been captive for so long! She urgently wants to free them, but sees in her mind's eye both the monsters' intention to strike again and the Empress gaining the doors, having rallied the gruesome columns to trudge behind her in her defense. The building begins to crumble. She springs up and flees down a dark side corridor.

The dull ache of abandonment has turned to irritation. She says nothing to the endless stream of customers and refuses to sing. Those that bother to look see that she is no longer even trying to pretend. This does not seem to affect business though, as the emotions of a prostitute rarely do. Her irritation grows, and she directs it at Madame Wang.

Mei Hua insists on the finest dishes now and clamors for new gowns. She weeps impetuously when certain customers arrive. The customers actually seem to enjoy the drama as Madame tries to soothe the Caged Bird, cajoling her to eat a bite or sing a song. It is worth the hair-pulling Mei Hua receives after they have gone.

Then one day she awakes with the conviction that Ying actually does love her, has always loved her and only forced himself to say those cruel things in order to save her from the pain of separation. Without giving it much thought, she waits for Madame to leave on her daily errands and packs a few of her favorite gowns and most valuable jewelry into a cloth bag. As she packs, her heart begins to beat faster, and an inner voice starts up with warnings and discouragement. Her hands tremble as she urges them to pack faster than the inner voice can dissuade.

Going out the door, she remembers the coins and runs back to pry them out from under the floorboard. She stuffs them into her sash.

On the stairs she runs into Yi Ya, who stares dumbly at her in disbelief. The little servant opens her mouth to say something, but no words come out. Mei Hua whisks past her. She marches straight to the door, throws it open, and walks outside, alone for the first time in her life.

She feels exhilaration, imagining Madame's fury when she finds the bird that sat in her cage with the door wide open for so many years suddenly up and flew away.

Ten thousand sounds, sights, and smells assail her simultaneously. The noodle man's cart smells of boiled chicken as he methodically chants his noodle call. A mother and child turn the corner and stare at Mei Hua, but it is of no consequence to her. She only notices the little girl's hair is caught up in the pigtail fashion that she used to wear. A bell strikes, echoing hollowly down the side street. Dogs bark and crickets cree in the smoldering heat of late afternoon. She hurries along, letting her feet retrace the way to Ying's mansion, memorized through the pounding of a coolie's feet so long ago.

She bumps into a gentleman who eyes her shrewdly. She blushes and hurries past, thinking, "Can they all tell what I am?"

She is not certain where she is going. She stumbles several times from looking about. She has traveled these lanes in rickshaws and palanquins, but now as she walks they are littered with sights and sounds she has never known up close. She keeps moving.

She fears she is lost. Hours have gone past. When her tired feet refuse to move any further, she sits down by the roadside. Her legs are throbbing. She has never walked so far in her life. When she looks up to get her bearings, she sees the inscription on the archway over the entry gate connecting the high wall encircling the house: Long Live Ying Mansion. She has found it! Suddenly, she hears the voice of an elderly man.

"You there! What are you doing?"

She turns to face the gatekeeper. He immediately recognizes her and shrinks back. Seeing a ghost resting on the curb would have been less surprising than seeing this Fallen Flower. She drops her head, not to escape his stare in shame as she has done so often in her life but to examine her blistering feet. They swell so badly that her dainty slippers pinch them. For a while, she can only sit and feel her body pump blood, her breath heaving in and out. The sun is warm though there are gray clouds gathering. She detects the scent of rain in the air.

"It is the beginning of the rainy season," she offers to the old man, craning her head up to meet his eyes and smile. He nods in astonishment. "The rains sweep the cooking oil from the air. It makes me so happy. The other smell nauseates me all summer."

"It is true. It is oppressive... Young Miss...may I ask why have you come here?"

This question startles her, like a creature finding itself in a trap. Her brow furrows. She hesitates.

"I have come to see Young Master Ying," she finally manages, her unusual situation becoming clearer by the second, creating agitation and misgiving.

"Young Master Ying? That is not possible. He is preparing for his journey in the morning. Your being here is not permissible, anyway. You really should go now," he adds in an almost fatherly tone.

"Go? Where do I have to go? Where is it you think I should go?"

"But...you must go home. Your Madame will not like your being here."

"She does not like anything about me. I will die before I return to the Seventh Level of Hell. If I have committed some grievous crime, as I must have in a past existence, it is surely paid off by now. Believe me. I have no more suffering left. I have nothing left but Ying. Please tell him I am here. He will certainly want to see me."

"Not allowable. You should go."

"Just try for me, please. Do not tell the old man. Go straight to Ying and tell him I am in great danger and need his help. Please. I am begging for your mercy."

"Ai ya! I certainly shouldn't do as you ask. I will be cursed."

"But you may be rewarded. I am Ying's favorite. If this is not so, it is the end of my short life."

"All right, all right. I will tell the Young Master. But I should not. It is not proper," he mumbles as he limps halfheartedly away.

Mei Hua feels the clouds blocking out the sun. If only they were there a few hours ago, she would not have spoiled her gown so badly with perspiration. She smoothes her coiffure, replaces a hairpin, and stands to stretch. She is very anxious now and has nothing to do as she waits. Her heart starts pounding again, harder than before. She strips a mulberry leaf from its branch and begins peeling the green tissue from the healthy vein. After stripping five leaves, the old man returns.

"You must leave now," he says with a gruffness he orchestrates for the role.

"Did you tell him? What did he say? Oh, please, just give me his answer!"

"He knows no Mei Hua. There. Now, you must go," he says in a quivering voice, betraying his sympathy for the girl.

"Knows no Mei Hua? But I am Mei Hua! He does know me! I am his favorite! Surely you know that. He does not speak the truth! Why does he lie? Is it the old man? Did he stop you? But you must get to Ying!"

"No!" he nearly yells. "It was Ying himself who said it. He is tired of you. He won't see you. Don't you understand? You shouldn't have come here. You don't belong here. Master Ying has been promised since an early age, it is unseemly that you should be here at all. Now go!" With the resolve of his station, the gatekeeper turns and pulls the gate shut.

Again, there is a chorus of contradiction in Mei Hua. She is not surprised, yet she is aghast. "Ying denies my existence," she whispers aloud. She has a strong urge to push past the gate and find him, or to dance in the street and rend her hair like a mad woman, but she does neither. She stands sentenced. She ambles away from the gate and sits down to think. A new voice begins to speak, clearer than any other in her head.

"My life is through. My heart is dead. If I go back to Madame, she will beat me, and then the men will begin again. I will have to work hard and learn fast to save enough money to be in Madame's position when the years show on my body. If I succeed at survival as well as Madame Wang, will I end up buying 'daughters' of my own?

"Yes. After my beauty and talent are spent, I would turn to those of other girls. In the same way a peasant lives off the land, I would squeeze out an existence from the men I loathe through some young girl's body. I would be like Madame. She has no doubt I will return. She knows I am weak.

"She is wrong. I am not that weak. I could hire myself out as a servant. But where would that get me? I would merely be raped without pay by the gentlemen of the house, become used up and die young. I could search for a new Madame, one who might be kinder. Should I hope for that, as I have hoped for Ying? I wish hope could kill my body as it has so easily destroyed my heart. Surely, death is better.

"Enough! It is enough. I can no longer live. I disdain this life. I shall die now and end this predictable cycle of pain. Bau Yu was right. I cannot endure it."

She feels comforted by this decision. All is quiet and peaceful. She feels a great inner sense of exhilaration now that she will be free, free from anxiety and pain, from hoping and dreaming, from suffering and crying. She feels lucky, like the bats flying about the lights ringing the exterior of Ying's mansion not far off. It is only a few steps away, yet it feels as though she has traveled many li! It was only moments ago that her dreams died, yet it feels as though they never lived.

As the bats herald the coming of night, she feels remarkably hungry and winds her way to the main thoroughfare, looking for a noodle cart. She follows a rich savory smell and finds an old man hawking soup. She buys a bowl with one of her coppers and stands with her head over the rich steam. Has there ever been such a bowl of noodles? Without hesitation, she gives herself over to the nourishment.

Having finished the bowl, she is suddenly at a loss. How will she kill herself? After a quick mental review of stories she has heard, she decides on poison. Only poison would work. She returns the bowl to the old hawker and politely asks, "May I make an inquiry? Is there an apothecary nearby, one that is open?"

"Heh. Let's see. Old Chu has one, right around the corner. Yes. However, it may be closed. I don't know. You can try Chu's." He points the way.

"Thank you," Mei Hua breathes. She sees him looking at her, wondering who she is and what she wants with an apothecary. He ventures, "Is your head hurting?"

"No. It is my heart."

"Ah. That's too bad."

It has grown quite dark. Mei Hua hurries in the direction of Chu's Apothecary.

★ ★ ★

The storefront is closed up, but there is a light on inside. She considers sleeping in an alley until the store opens the next morning, and her previous joy fades to familiar anxiety. Someone may find her, may even be looking for her now. They will drag her back to Madame. Her death must be now, tonight! Oh, why didn't she think to get Bau Yu's address! She was too busy numbering her offspring with Ying. Bau Yu would have harbored her. "It is too late!" she whispers out loud. Without further thought, she bangs on the apothecary door. When there is no answer, she cries out, "Sir! Honorable Sir! Please! Open the door!" She continues pounding until a man's face appears and the door opens. He is a young man.

"What? What do you want? Oh, it's you..." He gapes at her in shock. He seems to know her, but she cannot place his face though she has seen it before. It is of no consequence.

"Honorable Sir. You have done me a great favor opening your door so late. I am sorry to have troubled you, but there is an urgent situation. Please, I need some...I need to get some medicine, like a poison."

"I know you. You are the one who sings like a nightingale. It is true, I have heard you myself, though you don't remember it seems. Poison? For what use?"

"I...I...I need some, very much. I cannot tell you why. Please, Sir. Your face is kind, you have done many kind deeds in the past, no doubt. Do one more and heaven will reward you, double fold."

"But...buying poison is not a usual thing, unless it is for rats or the like."

"Will poison for rats be enough to kill...someone my size? Oh, but it's not for killing anyone. I cannot say what it is for. Oh, please! And if you were kind and did not want the rat to suffer much...is there a poison like that?"

"You are speaking craziness! Mistress Mei Hua! What is your business? Is something wrong?"

"Oh, never mind. I am sorry to have bothered you," she breathes out, as though they were her last words. Tears tremble on her lashes, her head drops down. She turns to go.

"Please, wait a minute!"

She whirls around.

"Yes?!"

"I will give you what you ask. But the kind that does not cause pain, only sleepiness, is very expensive..."

"I have money! If you can wait a moment, I will find it for you! Oh, thank you! Please, get some for me right away!"

The younger Chu disappears back into the store. Mei Hua begins fumbling through the gatherings of her gown and finds the coins she and Bau Yu saved. She finds three silver pieces among the copper. Young Chu returns with a tiny paper package.

"How much money should I give you?"

"It is the equivalent of a silver piece. Here, just give me fifteen coppers."

"I will give you the silver. You have been so kind!"

She gives him the money, and he describes how to use the poison. "Mix it with heated wine. The effect will take place almost immediately, beginning with befuddlement, followed by warmth..." She interrupts him with a gesture from her hand, and their eyes meet. Her gratitude is uncontrollable in her eyes. Several teardrops have already managed to escape. Quietly, she reaches out and takes the packet, whispers 'Thank you,' and runs off into the night. He wants to call out, but she disappears so quickly he cannot even discern the direction she has taken. "Do not use it wrongfully," he calls out into the darkness, his last good deed of the night.

She runs blindly but soon finds with surprise that she is at Ying's once more. She walks stealthily past his gate and follows the wall as it wraps around the mansion. She discovers a wooded area behind the house, to the south. It appears to be an extension of the property's gardens. "It will be good to die in your garden," she laughs, unnerved by the queerness of her own half-hearted laughter. She enters the woods and walks until the darkness obliterates the light from the mansion.

She cautiously moves through the trees then feels numbly for a trunk and sits shakily at its base. For a second, she thinks about what she is going to do, about taking her own life, but she drives the thoughts away. She feels a chill and senses the eerie loneliness of the deepening night. "Take the poison now," a voice in her head suggests, "before you change your mind!"

As she fumbles with the packet, thoughts of her mother's death consume her. Truly, at that moment, her life ended, too. Looking back at her life following her mother's death, she finds few redeemable moments. Worse yet, she cannot conjure any vision of happy moments to come. She will take the poison. This much she can do.

She has the packet open but can barely see the white powder. She curses herself for not bringing wine with her, but it can't be helped. Quickly, she rolls the edges of the thin paper into a small cone, tips her head back, and lets the powder sprinkle down on her tongue and throat.

The acidic bite is more than she expected. Her tongue leaps from her gaping mouth afire with nothing but her own saliva to kill the flame. She closes her mouth and swallows hard. The burning rushes through her mouth and halfway down her throat. The bitter, chalky taste, like heated sandstone dust, creeps up her nasal passages. She suddenly realizes the poison will destroy the tissues of her mouth before it ever reaches her stomach, with no water to wash it down. Tears come streaming over her cheeks as she rips through her bag and shoves a piece of silk into her mouth. It is the sash she wore the night Ying left her. She is rocking back and forth, the sash muffling the cries of pain trying to escape her throat. She begins to gag but forces herself not to vomit, gulping again and again, rocking harder and harder, snorting air through her nose, focusing on the curious ringing in her ears, hanging on, doing the very best she can to die.

At last, she has stopped rocking. The ringing seems to be funneling different sounds, amplifying the calls of the night birds and crickets. Like a jade ball rolling in a tin basin, the metallic-tinged chirping seems to sweep past her head in a circle. Shadows suddenly form where before there was only darkness; the light of the moon punctuates the movement of the trees bending in the gathering wind. Moonbeams reveal a small field mouse scurrying for his burrow. Grasses and ferns wave back and forth, then stop, then wave back and forth again. The deep blue images entering her poisoned eyes, painting the pre-storm dance of the tiny forest, are the most beautiful she has ever seen.

She feels warm though the wind is blowing harder now. She senses the tiny hairs on her body as though the wind were emanating from beneath her clothes. She pulls open the front of her gown, as much to encourage breathing through her constricted throat as to alleviate the heat generated by her dying body. The blue wind feels so good she laughs, and the laughter somehow reminds her that she is dying.

This singular thought breaks through the sensory onslaught of the blue trees and metal chirping; it is powerful enough to pull her to her feet. "It is not good to die!" she whispers, falling back against the tree, dizzy and nauseous. A strange and distinctive panic rumbles up from the pit of her stomach, bringing with it the terror of death. Her mind casts about wildly for a means to survive, assessing the capabilities of her body already weak with poison. "Run!" is the only command she can give it. "Run, run!" reverberates throughout her being. She observes herself like a ghost floating above the trees. She sees roots fly beneath her feet and feels tree limbs tear at her clothing. She is running.

New images tumble forward in her mind. Scenes of beatings and abandonment mix with the games she played with Bau Yu and the times steaming rice sweetly met her starving lips. The Rainbow Dance, her first kiss with Ying, the mellow light of a candle, Bau Yu's sincere smile... The vivid pictures fall through her mind like heavy rain, one huge drop after another.

Rain is falling now, falling on the top of her head where her lighter soul waits to escape, falling on the ground and turning it to mud. In a single, sweeping movement, Mei Hua slips in the mud and scrambles back to her feet. She keeps running. She tries to concentrate, to remember what she is doing, why she is running through the rain, but the situation won't quite come together. There is this movement of her body from the woods back into the street. There are these memories crowding her mind like circling birds looking for a place to land. There is this desire to live.

Now the rammed earth street slams up against her face and she cannot move. She breathes softly, feeling her body pant as tiny rivulets of rain course through her hair and trickle over her face. She smells the mud in her left nostril and feels it against her cheek. She sees the base of a brick building and realizes she is on the ground, able to hear and see but not move. She tries to get up, but her body only twitches. She has killed it. She relaxes into the mud and the rain, into her death on the street in the night, feeling very much alive.

Then she hears voices, many of them, all around her. She sees a tiny foot right in front of her face. She has the sensation of being lifted and sees for a fleeting moment a face: Bau Yu's.

There is a great amount of darkness, like blindness, and a whispering voice floating softly through her head. The voice makes a low pitched sound, like humming, beautiful yet unintelligible. A hand slips beneath her head and tilts it. Fingers pry open her lips and something cool and bitter slides down her throat, soothing the throbbing tissues of her mouth. The hand removes itself as the humming stops. The darkness settles in, swirling on and on throughout time immeasurable like a black boat drifting over the chill night ocean.

Mei Hua opens her eyes. It is a silent, peaceful morning. The ceiling is made of simple boards, water stained from the recent rains. She stares at it for a long time, then closes her eyes again.

When she opens them, she finds she can move her neck and turns her head from side to side to take in her surroundings. There are two coarse platform beds jutting out from the wall, each six feet long and four feet wide. Mei Hua is on one and the other is empty, its bedding folded up neatly at the foot of the bed. Muggy air filters slowly through the open window, wooden storm shutters pinned against the earthen wall. There are no pictures on the wall, no adornments of any kind, but the room feels kind to Mei Hua. Looking down, she sees a form curled up on a mat at the side of the bed and recognizes Bau Yu. She tries to get up but only manages to lift her head for a moment. "Bau Yu," she says in a voice so cracked and weak it comes back to her ears as little more than a groan.

She falls back on the pillow for a while then tries to get up again. This time her hand moves, flopping like a fish. And she can still move her head.

It dawns on her that she is alive. A knot rises to her throat. Her eyes sting, and tears come pouring forth in a profusion of sorrow and joy: "I am sad this is my life, but I am glad to be alive," she thinks.

The sound of her weeping brings Bau Yu to her side. She is beaming, and tears begin to roll down her cheeks, too.

"You have saved me. Now my life is yours," Mei Hua whispers in a cracked voice, smiling through her tears.

"You did not want to die. You told me so. When I heard you had left Madame Wang's, it was already quite late. I figured you had gone to Ying's, being the unconventional Fallen Flower that you are. I brought my friends with me, in case you were in trouble. We carried you to Chu's, the closest apothecary to Ying's, and woke him up. He told us what you had bought and sold us an antidote, which we administered on the spot. That you are alive, that you swallowed the antidote, told me you wanted to live. I am very glad, my friend."

"You are right. After I took the poison, I changed my mind, but it was too late. Where is this place?"

"This is the servants' quarters of the Lau's. I told you I had a friend who worked for a house that was upstanding. She is Mei Ying. I know her from the laundry and the market. There is a new baby, so they needed another girl for the kitchen as Mei Ying now helps the Mistress with the baby."

"How do you know all these people?"

"Mei, I am not attractive, so I come and go as I please, doing errands for Madame Wang. Girls are not threatened by me, and men do not molest me. Anyway, we half dragged you to Chu's. You must thank him... he helped carry you here."

"It has been a long night. Excuse me for being muddle-headed. I cannot remember anything."

"You have been unconscious for two days now! I have nursed you with medicinal teas and broths. No one thought you would survive. Madame Lau has been most kind to let me stay with you. They will be happy you are alive!"

"I am undeserving of their kindness, and of yours, my sister Bau Yu. I have troubled you much and inconvenienced your house. I will try to get my strength back and leave as soon as possible."

"What are you saying? You are dearer to me than anyone. I will not let you leave alone. Madame Wang has been searching for you. She has reported your absence to the Magistrate and is clamoring for your return. You must not go back there. She will surely be your death. We will think of something. Rest now. You have already grown ashen with your exertions. There will be time to talk."

As Bau Yu holds her hand, Mei Hua drifts gently off to sleep.

★　★　★

There are four women in the room. Many days have passed with Mei Hua struggling to keep down simple foods and testing her strength one step at a time. Bau Yu has brought her special tea to hasten the healing of her mouth tissue. Her speaking voice is nearly back to normal.

The women are discussing Mei Hua's flight from Wutai. The infant is crying in another room across the courtyard. Mei Hua is not sure what their urgency is about, except that it has to do with Madame Wang's rights to her. Bau Yu is to leave with Mei Hua within the week, on foot. They will journey to Kuai Le, where reportedly a troupe of traveling players currently resides. It was decided that the girls locate this troop and join them, Mei Hua being skilled in song and dance, Bau Yu being adept at costuming, hair, and make up. Should things go awry, they are to return to Wutai and lay low with the Lau's again.

This plan appeals immensely to both girls. They have their savings still; only a little was spent for the poison and its antidote. They stay up late making plans and talking.

"Bau, I think the poison has changed my voice. It may be ruined."

"It's true, your speaking voice has changed, but not for the worse. Have you tried to sing? Perhaps the change will be an enhancement."

"I haven't tried. Will we be found out if I sing?"

"I don't think so. We are on the far side of the city. No one is likely to recognize you. Still, maybe you should sing at night. Then only our closest neighbors will hear."

So Mei Hua practices her singing after dusk. The quality and tone, the timber and vibrato, have indeed changed, but it is as Bau Yu predicted: her voice is even better than before. It is somehow richer, deeper, like the eyes of a woman who has given birth. Bau Yu says it is the touch of wisdom.

During the day she helps with the household chores. At night, her voice drifts in and out of windows like jasmine, soothing the baby to sleep and preparing gentle dreams for the household. This is her gift to her rescuers.

She is stronger now in a quiet way. She has come back to a self she had left behind when she was first orphaned.

On the day of their departure, Master Lau himself presents the girls with a small carved box filled with coins on which is written: "Longevity enduring as the mountains, Happiness as deep as the sea." In addition to admiring the beauty of Mei Hua's voice, the friendship between this Fallen Flower and her maid touches his heart. He assures them that his home will forever be open to them.

Mei Hua wakes on a wooden platform bed with Bau Yu curled up beside her. Arriving in Kaui Le well after sunset, they squandered a few coppers for a meal and a room for the night. Their food, carefully prepared by Bau Yu's friends, had given out the day before.

Their journey has been pleasurable. During the day, they walked between fields and through small villages, talking freely. In the evenings, the chill was remedied by the warmth of their bodies huddled together, wrapped in a single blanket. They slept in the woods or by the roadside. It has been three days, and they have arrived safely to their destination.

Mei Hua lets her mind drift with the timid scent of morning dew, back to a chance encounter on the second day of their journey. A Taoist priest they met on the road, rather young and healthy, sat down to lunch with them. He was on his way to Wutai, having come from Kaui Le. He confirmed that the troupe of Tsa Chu players was still in that town, lodging and performing at a temple on the city's outskirts. He did not know if they were in need of new players. When he heard Mei Hua could sing, he beseeched her to sing for him. She sang "The Girl from Hua Mountain." He was stunned by the beauty of her performance. She remembers the look on his face when he said, "Feeling and execution in perfect harmony. This is not easy." He told Mei Hua that she captured the sorrow of an autumn day and that she had no equal among the players they sought.

Lying in bed with Bau Yu beside her, knowing that their food and much of their money is gone, Mei Hua hopes that the priest was right. She dreams of repaying Bau Yu's kindness. Someday, Bau Yu will know that her loyalty has not been in vain. Mei Hua gently nudges her awake, and the two prepare to leave for the temple.

It is late morning when the girls arrive at the small wooden temple. The red lacquered gateway is carved with sweeping clouds and dragons painted blue and gold. They follow the sound of voices and find a large awning held high by carved wooden columns sheltering the players as they rehearse.

They watch for a while, drawing stares, until Bau Yu finds courage enough to ask for the manager. A thin young boy points to a man standing near the stage.

The production manager is a short man with thinning hair, wearing the somber blue gown of a scholar. His eyes sparkle as the girls introduce themselves to him and their purpose is made clear.

"Do you know any plays? 'The Chou Clan Orphan,' or 'Li K'uei Carries Thorns?'" His tone is surprisingly gentle, somehow at odds with his business-like demeanor. Mei Hua internally remarks how his eyes are always laughing.

"Your servant has seen them performed. She has studied song and dance, and is told her voice is not without merit. 'See the dance, do the dance;' your humble servant is able."

"There is no strong leading lady in our troupe. Pu Yi has performed these roles. See if you are better than him." He grins, delivering this challenge. He motions for her to sing.

Mei Hua sings unaccompanied. As her naturally sweet voice moves up and down the scales, hitting high notes she alone can reach and hold, the company slowly stops moving and talking. All eyes turn to Mei Hua as Bau Yu smiles triumphantly at her side as if to say, "See this and believe, that such a sound can issue from a human girl!" When the song is over, murmurs of approval fill the void left by her voice. The look of rapt contentment on the production manager's face tells everyone that Mei Hua has won the distinction of Female Lead. He will come to be called Yen Chang the Goodly by the girls as the passage of time brings to fruition, at his paternal hand, the dreams of a lifetime.

During the course of that cool autumn afternoon, Mei Hua sings all the songs she knows amidst the scratching of bowed instruments and the rustling of stage costumes. There are breaks for tea and the examination of scripts. Yen Chang is well pleased with Mei Hua's ability to quickly memorize the most exacting arias. Members of the troupe drift over to the pair, introducing themselves and breathing out praise for Mei Hua's talents. They note the uncanny closeness between the two girls. The subtle glances and gestures that float softly between the two create an immediate sense that these young women are closer than sisters; they are connected on an ethereal plane. By the end of the day the Tza Chu troupe has accepted Mei Hua and Bau Yu as Female Lead and Costumer.

Her first performance two weeks later as the female lead in "The Romance of the Western Chamber" causes Mei Hua's name to be carried far and wide on the four winds. With each performance, she becomes better known. The troupe travels from temple to temple and where they were lucky to call in the hands from the fields previously, they now have dignitaries traveling substantial distances to experience the famous Mei Hua. Their retinues are large, replete with soldiers to guard against roving brigands.

When her entrance comes, Mei Hua floats onto stage like an apparition, creating the effect that she is not of this earth. Her movements are not limited to her limbs but flow from her waist, emanating outward like a ripple on the stillest of waters. By accentuating the wrist or the neck, her gestures symbolically relay the anguish or joy of the character.

As if this were not enough, with a crowd already mesmerized by her movement, she opens her mouth and the purest sound known to heaven spills forth with a strength startling in one so young and petite. Her notes are like crystal raindrops falling on parched earth. She becomes the character she is portraying, transporting her viewers into another dimension. No viewer is able to control themselves; they weep tears of sorrow for the plight of her character in the play, on top of the tears they shed from the sheer beauty of her performance. The interaction between actress and audience is complete. Having experienced her once, no other performer will satisfy.

Their audiences double from performance to performance. Bau Yu waits on Mei Hua exclusively. They are always together. It is like the days of their childhood, only now they are free and happy. The other players treat them with respect and honor.

Although several men with the troupe have vied for Mei Hua's affections, their suits are never forced, nor are they ever accepted. Men from the audience have also tried, with the same outcome. Rumors arise concerning Mei Hua's affections and the sequence of events that brought her to the stage. Someone catches wind of the Fallen Flower's broken heart, and word of the lovesick star's devoted chastity increases her fame and estimation.

Yen Chang's captivation with Mei Hua grows with each performance. He has taken a personal interest in the success of his young charge. Many afternoons pass in meditative study as he schools her in the operatic meaning of various gestures and poses. None can improve upon her vocal talents, but Yen Chang offers tips on air control and breathing, being a master at Tai Chi, which he faithfully practices every day. Bau Yu and Mei Hua now rise with the sun to exercise and practice various disciplines. Mei Hua has observed that what was once level-headed in Bau Yu is now serene. They are both happy in a way that only those who have suffered deeply can know.

One evening, after a particularly moving rendition of "The Chaste Wife of Ch'iu in the State of Lu," Yen Chang approaches the girls where they sit in the temple garden sharing tea. They have just finished the time consuming task of cleaning away makeup and storing away gowns.

"We have been invited to perform in the Capitol. A magistrate was in the audience tonight and approached me to offer his home for our stay. He believes you are too talented to play to the uneducated in the outlying districts. We have kept closely to our current circuit for nearly ten years. It seems time for a change. What do you think?" It is as though his eyes are speaking, they twinkle so brightly.

"Your servant cannot presume to play before such an exalted crowd, but if you think it's a good idea, I cannot dissent," Mei Hua answers. Yen Chang detects trouble in her voice beyond the polite and humble words, and inquires further.

"Do you have some concern?"

She waves him off, but looks more troubled than before.

"Mei Hua. Please tell me. I am asking you, so please answer. What is troubling you?"

After some hesitation, she begins.

"Master Chang, you are wise and know these things, I cannot presume. However, is the journey far? What of the bandits? I am not one to fear—I have lost many lives and now live by grace—but I have heard

of a brash brigand, Shu Chi, and I worry for the safety of my friend."
With this, she lets a tear drop.

"Oh, no, Song Bird! You have nothing to fear! Did not the magistrate come through the same land to observe your performance? He is not hurt. I have not heard of any attacks. We will hire several men, if that will help you feel safe." Yen Chang seems to be laughing at her, and she grows indignant. She turns to Bau Yu and sees that she is not concerned, either.

"That would make me feel better, Master Chang, thank you. You are very kind. I will make this journey, if Bau Yu agrees."

Bau Yu nods her consent and reaches out for her friend's hand, as if to explain to Yen Chang, "She has had a hard life!"

They plan to make the trip to the capitol without any stops. Mei Hua, Bau Yu, and several other ladies ride in the only carriage. The rest are on horse or on foot. Though the weather is colder, the two girls are reminded of the journey they took from Wutai to Kuai Le the year before. In the early afternoon the two get out and walk, and at night they sleep together as always, sharing a room at various inns.

By the third day they reach a mountainous pass with sheer cliff face on either side. Mei Hua and Bau Yu walk briskly in the rear, taking in the afternoon sun. It is as though decades formed the silent closeness between them as they point out a bird high above on a ledge or the emerald blossom of a mountain flower. Time moves slowly like mountain honey dripping from a tree. Into their peaceful revere comes a foreign, frantic sound. They turn their heads in unison.

A herd of hooves thunder toward them. They are overtaken by a band of riders pounding down the cavernous passage. They think at first it must be a military brigade then they see that the band is small and chaotic, dressed in rich but varied clothing. They are brigands! Before the girls can even make out the features of their masculine faces, the highway bandits snatch them up, reel around, and head off in the direction they came.

Mei Hua screams, struggling against the strong male arms clasping her tight. She manages to turn her head in time to see the rider with Bau Yu speed past. She sees the rest of the troupe scatter before her captor butts her in the head. She ducks down to avoid another blow, a cacophony of shouts and screams ringing in her ears.

The pounding of the horse's hooves match the beating of Mei Hua's heart. She cannot think and does nothing but struggle against the unseen man holding her from behind. He squeezes harder every time she moves, making her squirm all the more. The flesh on her arm is bruising. She wrenches her neck to see his face, but he forces her head back against his chest with his chin so she can't get a good look. It occurs to her to call out to Bau Yu. She calls out once and then twice before the man head-butts her again. A small figure begins to struggle against a larger figure on the horse right ahead; is it in response to her calling? Is that Bau Yu? She finally stops struggling and begins to cry, addressing the man who holds her.

"Please! You are hurting me! Let my friend go. I will do anything you say. Are you abducting me? Why are you doing this? Whatever you have to gain, I can pay you. Please listen to me! Have you no heart, to steal girls from their homes? Listen to me, please! I am frightened. Can you hear me?"

The unknown rider, never having said a word, places his hand over her mouth to silence her. Tears roll down her cheeks, and she feels the motion of the horse beneath her for a moment. Then she takes advantage of his hand thus occupied and throws her elbow into his side, biting down on his hand at the same time. He hisses, recovering his balance in an instant. Moving his hand down to her throat, he begins to squeeze. She struggles, but he does not let go. She recognizes the desperation of not being able to breathe and feels again the rush of life throbbing in her veins, the rush she had known in the woods, reigning in her mind and heading her toward life. She chokes out words beseeching him to stop, hearing the shrill pitch of panic in her voice. She feels her legs begin to kick and her back to arch. She cannot breathe.

When she comes to, it is dark and she is still on the horse with the man. She surmises she must have passed out. Her body feels sore, and her chest hurts. She lays her head back and sees the stars in the sky, so beautiful to her now. She weeps silently because all is lost: the beautiful dream of being cherished, of being free, swept away by these men on horseback.

They ride through the night. Mei Hua calls out to Bau Yu several times, each time thinking she hears a muffled reply. She can see the horse Bau Yu is on, right up ahead in the dark. She hears more horses behind her, but her captor will not let her turn around. At one point, she begins to sing the last aria she performed, both to mollify her captor and to let Bau Yu know she is near, but she is quickly squeezed into silence. Still, the high notes hang in the air like a hawk floating over the forbidden riders.

Sometime after the morning breaks, they arrive at their destination. It is a nomadic camp of eight or nine tents, pitched in the dry mountains. The man who so single-mindedly secured her abduction brings Mei Hua to one of the Mongolian-type tents and roughly shoves her inside. His fat leering face, as it withdraws from the tent, creates in her a startling hatred.

The tent is dark and empty. It seems remarkably quiet. Mei Hua feels completely lost. Her body aches, her stomach churns with fear and hunger, and her head seems too heavy for her neck. She feels dirt in every pore.

She slowly assesses her condition. She has been abducted, possibly for ransom but more likely as a passing fancy of some renegade warlord. She will be raped repeatedly and made into a slave after she is no longer wanted. If she survives. Thinking of such tortures brings her friend Bau Yu sharply to mind. The memory of Bau Yu's kind face smiling over her where she lay dying in the street a lifetime ago pulls her to her feet. She pushes through the flap of the tent and is shoved back so roughly she falls. This smarting bleeds together with the agony of the day, yet there are no tears. There is just a longing to see Bau Yu. She begins to cry her name out methodically, over and over again, like a night creature calling. The man outside the flap sharply orders her to stop, but she does not. Like a trapped animal, she cries even louder, "Bau Yu! Bau Yu!"

Like an answered prayer, Bau Yu suddenly crawls into the tent. The girls fall into each other's arms and weep.

They must have fallen asleep from exhaustion because awareness comes with the late afternoon sound of activity. No sooner do their eyes open than the fat-faced man and two others enter the tent with what they intend to be ceremony but they only look ridiculous, aping pious ways. They know nothing of ceremony. They ring the blanketed ground upon which the girls lay petrified like stones and address them.

"You have been chosen to be the consort of Shu Chi, Warlord of the Red Banner. You have been allowed to keep as your servant this girl. You will entertain as ordered and please our Lord as he sees fit. Your garment trunk will be arriving shortly. Prepare yourself to meet your new Master." The men exit with what little pomp they can muster following this announcement.

Shu Chi! It is the name Mei Hua feared! The prop man told her a story of rape and carnage with this name attached. Mei Hua's heart is ready to burst with terror; she trembles and whispers the name, "Shu Chi." Bau Yu shudders, grimacing at the thought of being raped. Mei Hua knows Bau Yu has never known a man; her fear must be the greater.

As they look at each other, imagining the dreadful fate that awaits them, a peculiar resolve begins to bubble up in Mei Hua, and a rage that has been forming all her life bursts forth.

"This will not happen! I am not a person to be resigned, never again! Whatever happens, Bau Yu, know this. It has been my doing, and I will find a way out. I will not let them hurt you."

"'When the Big Wind comes, who can hold it back?' Surely it is some fate of ours. You are one small woman against a hoard of men. I do not expect you to save me, Mei Hua. That is crazy talk. But know this: whatever went before that has brought this day down upon us, in our lives long past, I am glad that I have known you. I love you. I do not decry having shared this fate with you. You are my truest friend. You are my sister!"

"And you are my life! Bau Yu! I will think of something! I must think of something!" The girls hold each other and cry.

Time is passing. Their trunk arrived but they refuse to touch it. The guard has come and lit the lamps, admonishing the girls to hurry and get dressed, but Mei Hua has no intention of dressing for the occasion. Instead, the young women talk until the men arrive, reminiscing about their time with the drama troupe and mulling over their situation.

Escape would be very difficult, but they will watch for a chance. They both agree they would rather die than live as slaves to these men. They make a suicide pact and this softens the beating of their hearts a little.

Whenever the guard looks in on them, urging them to hurry, they feign obsequiousness and move about until he closes the flap once again.

Then they hear a shout from right outside the tent. "His Superior Shu Chi!" The flap is raised and two men enter, momentarily hunching their backs to get through the opening. They are big men. The first is obviously a close advisor or confidant to the one standing tall behind him, who must be Shu Chi. The men eye Mei Hua with pleasure despite her disheveled appearance, as though they were judging some ill-gotten horse. A third man enters with heated wine and a plate of food. He places them to one side and exits immediately.

The two men sit, unceremoniously flapping their gowns. The girls have barely left these blankets over the past nine hours. The advisor addresses Mei Hua with pleasantries but she does not respond. She returns their adoration with a cold empty stare. Then he motions to Bau Yu to pour the wine, and she does so very slowly. The two men drink many cups rapidly, Mei Hua easily pretending to drink hers as she has on so many nights. They are getting drunk. Mei nods discreetly to Bau Yu so that she will be diligent in keeping their cups filled, but suddenly Shu Chi lunges forward and grabs at Mei Hua, attempting to touch her breast with one hand and her thigh with the other. She easily evades his drunken movements. He becomes enraged.

"Whore! Who do you think you are? I know who you are! You are the greatest whore of all, the Nightingale, Mei Hua! Don't pretend to some other station!"

Bau Yu intercedes, saying: "Lord. My Mistress, the Actress Mei Hua, is not yet acclimated to this place. It is foreign and frightening to her. I therefore apologize on her behalf."

While Bau Yu is talking, Mei Hua wonders if she could kill one or both of these men and how it might be done. She has never thought of killing before; she has been too timid. But now when the clear choice is to be passive and hope for the best, she cannot do it.

"Men like these must carry weapons of some sort, but I cannot see any," she thinks to herself. "The sash, the girdle, these are the only places they could be hidden. I must be certain to get their clothes off and keep them away from Bau Yu."

Shu Chi has gotten to his feet in frustration. Shu Chi's advisor speaks up.

"Honorable Shu Chi. Perhaps a tune from the world-renowned song bird would cheer your heart." It is clear from his gestures and diction that he has had a different upbringing than Shu Chi, who sits back down with arms folded, scowling at this advice.

Mei Hua chooses a song she disdains so as not to ruin the memory of a favorite piece, and she moves to the side of the tent. She begins to sing. The song is sad and discordant because there is hatred filling up her heart. Without warning, in the middle of the song, Shu Chi stands and strides over to Mei Hua, who stops singing and slowly backs away. He abruptly pushes her down and straddles her, one hand pulling up her skirts, the other yanking at the sash at his waist. He is exposed in an instant, attempting to enter Mei Hua. Mei Hua's scream propels Bau Yu up from the blanket to her aid, but she is caught by the advisor, who pushes her down as well. Bau Yu lands right next to Mei Hua.

"'Two horses ride abreast!'" Shu Chi shouts gaily, goading his friend on. The advisor has undone his sash, and together the drunken men search for entry into the petrified women.

Mei Hua's mind burns as she struggles with her assailant. "If I can get a hand free, there may be a knife tucked away on him somewhere." In his frenzy, he seems not to notice any of her movements. She feels around on his back and down his legs but finds nothing. Then, like a tiny gift from heaven, she sees a dagger lying on the ground within reach. It must have fallen when he undid his sash.

As soon as her hand finds the knife, she begins a careful but rapid assessment. "If I kill this man, his supporters will rape us, torture us, and eventually kill us. If I manage to kill both these men and we make our escape, we will be going through their country. On horse or on foot, they will surely catch us. If I kill myself, Bau Yu will be left alone here with them..." Suddenly, five drunken men break into the tent. When they see the rape in progress, they begin laughing and goading the rapists on. "Leave some for me," "Breach the gate, scale the wall!"

Their voices act like a drug on Mei Hua, slowing everything down. She turns her face as if in slow motion and sees her friend biting her lip to keep from screaming in pain, tears streaming down her face. She turns away, envisioning a brief life of servitude and suffering ahead for Bau Yu, the kindest human being walking the earth. She knows Bau Yu is suffering this fate because she is her friend.

Remotely now, for she is detaching from the world, Mei Hua hears Bau Yu's attempts to stifle sobs sick with fright, sobs Mei Hua has never heard from her before. She cannot bear her friend's pain another moment, so wild is the grief she feels. In the next instant, she swings the knife in an arch with her one free arm and lays the blade hard across Bau Yu's throat.

Bau Yu rolls her head toward Mei Hua. Air hisses from the opening and blood sprays from the arteries in her severed neck, but her eyes soften in gratitude and she seems to smile. Then she is gone.

Mei Hua hears shouts of disbelief and anger. She feels a pain shoot through her right shoulder and hears the sound of a bone cracking. Shu Chi's knife has been wrested from her and is lodged in her shoulder. Superimposed on these sounds is a harsh and sadistic voice saying, "I'm going to fuck you until you die!"

She feels pain shoot through her vagina and another lacerating pain in her breast but the world has gone dark. Mei Hua can't track what is happening to her. Even the pain is distant, like the first time she was raped. She feels like she is floating far away from the tent, hovering in the crisp night sky high above with the stars. Her life has been one long preparation for this kind of pain. It is not so bad. It is nearly over.

She smiles to herself in the darkness. "I have at last repaid Bau Yu's kindness..."

Mei Hua After Death

Kami (*The Sentient Being Who Was Mei Hua*) *feels herself wafting out of her body like a puff of smoke curling up from a candle. She experiences a delicate tug to keep floating upward, but she is confused. She looks down through the tent and sees the men checking her for signs of life. Then she sees Bau Yu's body lying next to hers and realizes they are both spirits now.*

"Bau Yu! Oh, my dearest friend, where are you?" she calls out. Kami starts searching telepathically for Bau Yu's spirit. She assesses the area inside the tent but does not feel her friend's presence. This thought, to find her friend, spreads out from the tent into neighboring tents: nothing. Her awareness expands throughout the surrounding area and even into the foothills, but there is no trace of Bau Yu. When Kami realizes that Bau Yu is gone, her pain is unimaginable.

She begins to cry. Her wailing mounts to a horrifying pitch, and she flies madly about the tent. She sees Shu Chi and the others standing about in shock, and she flings herself at them, screaming and crying. Although the others are unaffected, Shu Chi cries out and leaps in terror, as if burnt. He can feel Kami's powerful desire for his death, and it scares him. His men turn to him in astonishment. As she sweeps through his body again and again, weeping and wailing in her beauteous deep voice, he becomes more and more hysterical. He storms from one man to the next, shouting for the bodies to be dragged from the tent. Kami screams back at him, from deep within her soul, demanding that he be punished. Her rage is huge and nearly explodes from her as she flies at him. Shu Chi runs at one of his men, grabs the other's sword, and swings it about wildly as Kami sweeps violently through his body. He arches his back and the sword falls from his hand. He calls out again, this time in abject terror.

"She is a demon! Don't you see her? Woman, go to hell!"

In that instant, Kami realizes with certainty that she is dead and that she is, in fact, in hell. Never has she known hatred as deep as this. It is consuming her. She stops and thinks, "Bau Yu is dead, and I am dead, but somehow we have been separated. Where are you, Bau Yu? Let me go with you, do not leave me!"

She looks around. The tent is perfectly silent: every man holds his breath. Shu Chi scans the tent's dome in fear, as though he hears Kami's thoughts— as though he, too, waits for an answer.

There is no answer. There is no Bau Yu. Kami teeters on the brink between fury and sorrow. She thinks about tormenting Shu Chi, but her anger is drifting away. She feels her love for Bau Yu. She remembers setting her friend free, the look in Bau Yu's eyes. Bau Yu understood the sacrifice, she was thankful. Kami suddenly feels happy that her friend is gone.

She flies close to Shu Chi again and whispers in his ear, "I will not go to hell, because my friend is not there. You will go to hell, someday, in payment for what you have done." And with this she turns away.

Instantly, Kami begins to weep, silently, without effort. She floats aimlessly into the night.

★ ★ ★

Day comes and she is in the hills, high in the hills. She wanders for days. Weeping, she watches rabbits and foxes, birds and insects. She watches the storm clouds slowly roll in, release their waters and dissipate. She thinks about Bau Yu and wonders if she is roaming the hills like herself. She knows Bau Yu is gone, but she cannot help continuing her search.

She moves down from the hills and comes to a village. She shoots out her awareness to see if Bau Yu might be there, but she is not. She moves from village to village, looking for her friend, and with each disappointment the quiet weeping is prolonged.

Weeping, she sees babies being born. She sees men and women working in the fields and in their houses. She sees animals eating and resting. She weeps as she gazes at the faces of people laughing, talking, shouting, crying. She hears all their words and sees all their deeds. Their deeds are like her deeds when she was alive, only they are much clearer because she is free to observe them.

She finally gives up her search for a while, stopping in a little village. For almost a month she stays and watches the people who live there. She sees them fight and copulate. She sees them wipe their noses with their fingers. She sees some lavish kindness upon others, and she sees others take advantage and hurt people.

One day, a troupe of traveling players comes to town. Weeping, she remembers her days with Yen Chang's troupe and drifts over to see them rehearse at the local temple. She sees the girl who will play the roles she once played. The girl is young and vulnerable.

At dusk, the townspeople begin filing into the temple for the performance, and soon it begins. Weeping, Kami watches as the play progresses. The play is the Chou Clan Orphan, a play her troupe had performed many times. It is about a male orphan, the last of his clan, who is the rightful ruler. The infant is being hidden from the rival clan, who has managed to kill everyone in the Chou clan except for the infant, in order to gain power. The orphan's father has already died in his defense, and his poor servants are all the baby has left. Now the servant woman, nursing the infant at her breast, steps on stage to sing the piece's finest aria. It is the young girl Kami saw practicing. She looks frightened and sad, and her voice carries this sorrow out into the crowd. Although this girl has minimal talent when compared to Kami's when she was alive, she is sincere and knows the pain she sings of deep within herself. Kami is so touched by the simple performance that she stops weeping to hear the singing better.

Her ears are instantly filled with the sound of the voice that used to be hers. She begins to laugh, the sound is so fine. She laughs and watches, and when the show is over, the crowd claps loudly and calls for the female lead. The young girl comes back on stage, her face flushed, and she seems to look right over everyone's heads into Kami's eyes. Love for the girl and a profound sense of beauty permeate her being. Instantly, she feels herself floating upward, and she is in heaven.

She knows she is floating but more than this she cannot tell. She sees other beings. Some appear for a flash and disappear again, and others float as though asleep, buoyed on an invisible ocean. There are others still who go from being to being asking if a loved one has been seen. They ask without speaking. Kami is among this group.

At first she moves frantically from being to being, inquiring about Bau Yu. She begins to hear the names that the others are searching for and forms a list. Soon, she is asking about the other names as well, all listed behind Bau Yu's. She is tired, but she searches ceaselessly. Her list has grown to some twenty names; she tries very hard not to forget anyone.

Gradually, she begins to understand that no one has found anyone. She sees that she has asked the same being the same names, possibly many times. Moreover, she has never been able to tell anyone where their loved one is. No one has an answer. Once again, she feels despair rising up within herself. But she knows the feeling well, and she thinks, "Bau Yu is in a better place. Why would I want to find her here? I am glad for her."

She moves aside and sees that she has been on a track going around and around. She wants to laugh. She is done searching. She thinks, "Good-bye my friend. If our fate brings us together again, I will do better next time. I will always love you."

With these thoughts, the searching beings recede and she finds herself in a queue. There is a being there who is very kind, with a radiant face. This being mind-talks for a long time to the being in front of Kami, communicating without spoken language. Then the being turns to the Sentient Being Who Is Now Forgetting That She Was Ever Mei Hua and says, "Hello little sweetie. You are going back to earth. You have chosen. I will see you again in a few moments or decades. I have one gift for you. It is this thought: 'No more fear.'"

Kami feels released, like a bird slipping from a cage, and she is instantly born again.

Transmigrations

Mei Hua to Khalid

Karlos/Mei Hua	becomes	Khalid
Merlo/Bau Yu	becomes	Fida
Victor/Ying	becomes	Misha'il
Emilio/Madame Wang	becomes	Bahroum
Karlos' father/Shu Chi	becomes	Amir Ibn Saud
Yen Chang	becomes	Nuri
girl who is given voice	becomes	Shaymaa

KHALID

Past evils are repaid

The hottest time has passed, and the man-child Khalid, the third and youngest son of Mataa Fuaz, plays alone in the sand of the Nufud desert.

"This is the great horse of the king. It can run forever with the king on its back, over the Nufud, far, far away they never stop. But the sun is so hot. The king is all covered in a big cloak and turban, what has he to fear of the sun? And water? He catches rain in a great cloth pulled behind the horse. Well, I don't know about the water, unless he stops. He is not thirsty.

"Here is the great horse. He always holds his tail up stiff, its hairs waving in the breeze made by its speed. But Oh! Here comes the evil spitting camel of the Shammar, with long stretching legs, to bite off the tail, ahhgh, and then the horse's buttocks, ahh! The king lashes the camel with his whip, he whips its eyeballs out, the camel screams, heee! and falls to its knees..."

"What's that?"

Khalid knows that voice. It's big Mamoud. He has hit Khalid several times before. That's his big fat toe.

"It's the great black stallion! It can kill anyone it chooses!" he shouts at the toe.

"Looks like a blob of dung to me. Dried goat dung, that's what it is!"

"You are..." Khalid dares not call him dumb, for fear of being hit again, but he thinks it. He thinks, "When will my father give me a knife? Nuri and Bahroum have theirs!"

"What am I?!" Mamoud taunts.

"You are...wrong! This is the great horse!"

"You have never ridden a horse, but I have. My uncle has a horse!"

"I have too!"

"Yeah? When?"

"At the big meeting, I have too!"

"You are lying. Should I hit you again?"

"If you do, my brother will hit you!"

"Oh? Where is he?"

"He is in our tent!"

"Liar! He went away with the men!"

"If you hit me, I will throw sand in your eyes!"

"I'll throw sand in yours first!"

"Mah-moood! Mah-moood!" a scratchy thin voice wails out over the sand. Ah! Mamoud's mother is calling him. He looks at Khalid, debating whether he should hit him once before he runs to her. Then again comes the call, "Mah-moood," like an Imam calling out painfully to Allah. He sneers and runs off, each footfall splashing up the sand.

It is amazing to Khalid how the sand springs up and then falls like it is alive. He supposes Mamoud has been called to cut up some meat. The women must be preparing the evening meal. Or maybe he has to milk. He has no sisters, only a baby brother, and his mother always coughs and wheezes. They say Father of Mamoud should have taken another wife long ago, this one is so sickly, but she has made another boy, so he is honoring her. Khalid heard his father say, "Maybe this one will live, Insha Allah."

Khalid thinks, "Well, Insha Allah, maybe Mamoud will grow skinny and weak like his mother, then I can hit him. My three sisters, they do everything. My mother pretends she doesn't see or hear when they squeeze my arm for doing a bad thing to them. They are strong! I wonder why such girls, taller than me, grow weaker as they get older, while I am certain to grow stronger like the men, Insha Allah, though Father of Ali is not such a big man. Shaymaa will go through Female Rites soon, she will cry for sure. Maybe that's what makes girls grow weak, because my sisters are certainly strong now. I asked my mother what Female Rites are and she said, 'It makes a girl into a woman.' I asked her how, and she looked at me like I was being trouble again and said, 'It is a secret only for girls. You are a boy.'

"My sisters won't tell me, they like secrets. I don't think Shaymaa knows because she looks worried. I'm going to ask her. Why don't we have 'Men's Rites?' Maybe they need some help now. I could cube the lamb and ask Shaymaa. I need a better horse. This is just an old piece of dung. I need a real horse, or one made of metal, but I can't ask father again. Well, it is not a bad horse, but I will make a better one."

Khalid has prepared the meat for the fire. Two hares from the night before soaked in salt water and vinegar. They are in his older sister Duhiya's hands now. He cannot be involved with the cooking.

Duhiya is fourteen, soon to be married. She should have been married a while ago, but a match could not be found. She has no time for Khalid now. Khalid remembers the stories about how she took care of him when he was a baby. She held him in her arms like a prize and showed him around to her friends. It occurs to Khalid that Duhiya is not happy; he cannot begin to imagine why. This saddens him, and he looks again for Shaymaa, who is still young and would play with Khalid all the time if their mother let her, but boys and girls are kept separate.

He sees Shaymaa and his mother in the women's tent where the food is prepared, and he enters. His mother frowns to discourage him from loitering about with the women, and walks past him out to the fire. He is alone with Shaymaa, for the moment. He strides up to where she squats over some roots and watches her peel them. She still looks so small! She is only eleven. How can she become a woman next week? This must be some powerful magic.

"Shaymaa. What will they do to you next week?"

He has startled her, and she dumps over the basket of roots.

"You are not supposed to be in here anymore, mother said. Don't bother me, I have to finish this," she whispers as she scoops up the roots and looks around.

"But what will happen to you? What turns you into a woman?"

Shaymaa looks into Khalid's eyes, and he can see much fear there, yet she manages to betray her feelings with a calm voice.

"I will become pleasing to my future husband and bear him many sons," she states from rote.

"Shaymaa, Dumb as a Camel, this I know. HOW is this accomplished, I want to know. Does it hurt? Is it a kind of magic?"

"Khalid, One Who Stays With The Women, how should I know? Mother has not let Duhiya tell me and Mawia is of another family now. Why do you ask the wrong questions? I will live through it, Allah Karim. Haven't you noticed that you cannot see a Woman many days after the Rite? Everyone looks sadly at me, and mother cries, but she says it is because I will soon be of another family. Whatever happens, I am sure it will be bad." She says this last part so forlornly that Khalid's heart beats faster in his chest. He wants to save Shaymaa, his best sister and closest sibling, but it is an outrageous thought. No one can interfere with any of the traditions.

"I miss you Shaymaa. I cannot come to the women's tent anymore, and I have no one to play with." Without thinking he puts his hand on her head, and she puts her hand on top of his and lets a few tears fall. Then there are voices outside the tent, and she snatches her hand away and hisses, "Get out of here!"

Khalid moves back out into the failing light, past his mother, who stands right outside the flap.

"Are you pestering your sister?" she says half sternly, but Khalid walks past her, pretending not to hear her words and hiding his tears, just as a man should. His mother's breast fills with pride.

The moon is bright, floating over the heads of all those gathered, washing the desert white in contrast to the red faces around the fire. Khalid has to look hard to see who belongs to which pair of eyes, but he can tell by their voices. He notices that a few camels have come near to be by the fire, or by their masters. He thinks they must belong to the chieftain and his headmen, because they look like they are listening, bending ever closer to the men's faces as if to ascertain their fates.

"The Raulu are getting closer."

"They will surely invade our territory."

"There is drought to the south… that is why."

"So what will we do? They are fierce fighters… they number five to our one."

"They will be weak from their journey. Besides, if we let them cross our plain, all the Bedouin will know we are yielding. We must fight them!"

A murmur rises up from the group. Khalid's voice, too, shakes like a birthing she-camel, unnngh, unnngh, fight, fight! A new voice speaks up calmly, yet stills the mumbling instantly.

"We have just come back from a raid. Our animals are tired, too. The Raulu won't come this far, Allah willing. Better to let them cross our lands than to have no lands after a war with the Raulu. If they attack, we will fight. Otherwise, we will wait."

"Waiting is for women! We will ride out to meet them, surprise them! Then we will know the joy of victory!"

"Mishal ibn Faris, your heart is like a leopard's, your prowess is known to all. Your words are admired by all. As the wind blows you would do as you say. But we have slaves and women to provide for. We may be facing drought. We will abide by Mataa Fuaz's council: fight if attacked, otherwise wait."

This is the voice of the chieftain, Hassan al-Amud, the recognition of which lies more in the heavy measured beat of his words than in the timber. Wise he is, and certain to help his clan survive. This group of sixty men is the smallest of the Bedouin tribes. All the other small groups were conquered long ago by a larger band, but these men would die to the last in order to maintain their autonomy. "Hassan al-Amud keeps us free," they say. "He is a fox: not big, but alive and free." Khalid has heard as much from his brothers.

As his chest swells with pride for his people, he feels bitter that he has never been on a raid. He is almost eleven. Nuri is allowed to go, and he is only twelve. His father ignores Khalid's pleading until he can't stand the noise and gives Khalid a look from hell. His mother gets big sad eyes when Khalid begs her to intercede and says, "There will be killing enough in your life. Why rush to death? Play, go and play with your friends."

Khalid thinks of his decision to stop spending so much time in the women's tent like a little baby. Maybe now he will be considered for a raid. He thinks with sadness how he must begin his total separation from all girls tomorrow, though he likes the girls, especially his sisters. They talk stories all the time.

Khalid's attention has drifted away from the war council proceedings. His father suddenly notices him lurking just beyond the reach of the fire's light. "Go to the tent," he barks, cutting short the boy's timid argument about his brother Nuri staying up with a sharp glance. Khalid knows the men are going to stay up late, perhaps never to sleep tonight. This is important. As he walks away, he hears his uncle muse, "If we ride, I will have to kill Wudiyeh's foal in her belly, she is too close to ride with that burden."

There is always a problem, always something to be killed. Khalid thinks about how he will ride off himself someday to kill their enemies so no one has to die anymore, no one will have to worry. He thinks if they would only let him go on a raid, he could kill all their enemies.

The wind is whispering about the jinn who fly at night. Maybe it is the jinn themselves, moaning back and forth to one another, "hoo, hoo…" Khalid wants to run to the tent, but then the men will know he is afraid and they will laugh at him. They will say, "He is still a child." But he can't keep his feet from walking faster, and he fears they may run off without him. He wonders when he will be far enough off for the men not to see him. He can discern the outline of his tent and consoles himself with the belief that once you get close enough to see your tent, no spirit can attack you. He slows down and walks in like a man.

Lying under a camel hair blanket, Khalid's mind is racing, and he cannot fall asleep. He thinks:

"When Menwer died from a big slash, when he finally died and spit blood, they slaughtered his camel right over his grave in the sand so the evil spirits would take the camel instead of him. My people are very wise. We can out-smart spirits. There are a lot of them, so this is important. I asked my father if there were as many spirits as our enemies, and he said, 'Ask Farhan, I do not know much about these things.' I asked Farhan, and he said, 'As many as there are men, there are spirits.' I asked, 'And what about the women?' He held his chin, scratching his beard for a louse, and finally said, 'Once women were as men, and men as women, but the women did bad things and lost their souls. There are no spirits for women.' I did not understand what he said at all.

"Tonight, it feels like every man is by the fire but me. I think there must be women spirits howling around our tent right now. They are the evil spirits. They are angry that they lost their souls, they are afraid of Women's Rites, they act like camels. Farhan is the Sufi, he knows everything. I have heard him say as much. I think we should give them honey so they will be nice to us. What if the jinn know what Farhan has said and take revenge? I must make a sacrifice. I will give them something's blood and some honey. That should make them happy. I will ask Duhiya to give me these things. She will get them from Mama for me. She is a smart girl, a good sister. I wonder if she is seeing things over there in the woman's tent. I wish Nuri would let me snuggle with him like Duhiya used to, but he said I am not a baby anymore. So, they will know how big I am when I save the Sufi!

"Will a gecko's blood be enough? I will stone two geckos to make sure."

Shaymaa is bleeding. Khalid gave her his wooden horse, Nijm, so she would show him. His dung horse was replaced by a carved horse a few days ago. Khalid reasoned that he is learning how to ride the big Nijm now, so he doesn't need toys anymore.

Shaymaa showed him a piece of camel wool dark with blood. Khalid knows she wears it between her legs.

"What did they do, Shaymaa!?"

"Mama told me never to tell a male or I would be cursed."

"Well, who did it to you?"

"Mama, Mawia, Alia, wife of Ali, Mother of Mamoud, all the women."

"Did they cut you?"

Shaymaa just nodded her head yes and tears filled her eyes. She gave Khalid a quick squeeze with the horse clutched in her hand and ran off. Khalid remembered Mamoud saying that women have a hole in their bodies, a deep hole right between their legs, a hole for men. Khalid knows they made a hole for Shaymaa, that is why she bleeds. She got a party. Papa is proud of her, everyone thinks well of her now. It is like Menwer: bleeding is a proud thing.

★ ★ ★

A year has passed, and Khalid has replaced his relationships with his sisters for those of his brothers. He is now being considered by his father for a raiding party. He is twelve.

"He handles Nijm well," Nuri speaks up. Khalid thinks how Nuri taught him to ride, taught him how to navigate by the stars, taught him addition and subtraction. Some say Nuri is too smart and should be considered for the position of Sufi. This is not what Khalid thinks. He thinks Nuri, Bahroum, his oldest brother, and he himself will be the terrors of the desert, fighting side by side.

Both boys see from the look on their father's face that his silence is only polite. Khalid will not go this time. Their father wants to say no right away but is going through the motions.

"I hate the Shammar! I could take three camels by myself!" Khalid impetuously shouts at his father. Nuri rolls his eyes as if to say, there, now you don't have a chance. Khalid sees this was the wrong thing to say and listens to his father's reply.

"You are brave, Khalid, that is why I need you safe now. I will need you soon. And the women are frightened without you near."

"But the enemy won't come here! The women don't need me."

"You will not go this time. This I say."

Shaymaa brings in coffee while Khalid's mother carries in food on a flat basket tray. His mother does not look at him, but Khalid can tell she is well-pleased with this decision. Shaymaa looks sadly at him for a moment then swiftly looks away. "If I had camels to trade, if I could win some in a raid, I would get Shaymaa something beautiful," Khalid thinks.

He has had two days to think about this raid, and Khalid has decided to go. He remembers hearing stories about brave boys too young to go on raids who stowed away in camel bags, and he will do just that. He will put both water bags on the same side to offset his weight; no one will know. For once his smaller size will not work against him. Khalid helps carry the provisions and packs them onto the camels. While his two brothers and father are preparing their horses, Khalid saunters over to Katib and moves the water bag from the left side to the right side. He climbs with difficulty into the left saddlebag, letting several small parcels drop to the ground while pulling others back in on top of himself.

He holds his breath. No one comes. He has done it.

He will drink no water and eat no food for several days, this he knows, but rations are very thin on a raid anyway. "Hunger sharpens the claws," as the men say. Khalid thinks only of killing the enemy, of becoming a man among his people.

The men leave within the hour, in the early morning. Khalid is in a fetal position in the saddlebag but for a long time it is not uncomfortable. He gives himself over to imagination. He imagines riding the great war horse Nijm, the red tassels on his reins blown back by his speed as they fly across the desert so fast the dunes blur. He sees his tribe attacking like a sand storm, leaving the enemy's dead too numerous to count. He sees his father weeping, embracing him, saying, 'My son, you are like the fragrant wind, swifter than the creatures. Great are your deeds this day!'

He thinks of the women greeting the victorious band of raiders, singing high notes in the desert and running alongside the creatures of war.

Khalid has never ridden long distances on a camel; he has never known this soreness. After five hours of hard riding, every part of his body has cramped and un-cramped, ached, then fallen asleep many times. Khalid worries that his body will be too broken to be of any use, if indeed this motion ever stops. His pain is growing. He regrets his choice for only a moment, though, and then the thought of the women sitting around the cooking tent makes him glad he stowed away. He tries to flex various muscles to keep them in shape in case he needs to move quickly. Many times he has wanted to call out, but he forces himself to endure, having come so far. Mercifully, he falls asleep.

Khalid awakens when Katib suddenly stops moving. He hears shouts from many voices, all of them steeped in the rattled hysteria caused by adrenaline. Every word teeters on the edge between terror and self-command. Khalid orders his body out of the bag, and when it does not respond, he shouts in the same frenzied voice as the others. He hears the horses being readied for the attack. He feels the camel stomp anxiously, clearly unwilling to obey any command that is not reasonable. This is why his tribe does not fight with camels. They are not brave like horses.

With loud groans, Khalid manages to use his head, neck and thighs to propel his body out of the top of the bag. Luckily it was not tied shut because he still has no use of his arms. With one final thrust, he pushes himself up and over the rough opening and lands on his back in the sand.

Khalid realizes quickly that he is the only man left with the camels and supplies. All the others have ridden out to meet the enemy on horseback. By grabbing Katib's front legs and dragging himself up, he gets to his feet, scanning the desert for his tribe. He can see the riders skirmishing off to the north, and he hears the same shouting, only now it sounds as though it were coming from the bottom of a well.

He must get to them.

With a curious force, his outer extremities begin to tingle, coming alive again. Small jabbing pains arch through his feet and hands making him wince, but he can move and that is all he needs. He unties Katib from the other camels and tries to climb up on his back, but his legs are not responding. He hoists himself up by pulling on the saddlebags and manages to straddle Katib. "I only need to hold on," he thinks; "I only need to ride."

Not a hundred yards from where the camels are tied, Khalid sees a terrible battle taking place. At least a hundred horses swarm over one another like bees, spurred by their riders to run at one another. Khalid cannot tell who is from his tribe and who is from the Shammar, although he knows the Shammar has more men. He begins to pick out individual riders. He sees them goad their horses forward then turn to flee, only to turn and surge forward again. It looks as if a great spirit were rolling beneath the sand, causing the horses to lose their footing. How can anyone tell what is happening?

Suddenly Khalid sees Nijm and he knows Nuri must be on his back. He sees Nuri and Nijm begin to skirmish with another rider. At the same time, he realizes that Katib has slowly been backing away from the fighting and Khalid spurs him forward, in the direction of Nuri. Khalid sees Nuri retreat after a pass at the enemy rider, but before he can turn Nijm to the attack again, a third rider emerges from the ball of horses, spear out, riding hard on Nuri from behind. Khalid is lashing Katib to speed now as he screams his brother's name over and over again, his voice lost in the melee created by the wind and the shouts of panic. Khalid tells his brother to turn around, to watch for the second rider, but as Nuri wheels around the new rider's lance buries itself deep into Nijm's flank.

At that moment, Nuri sees what he thinks is his little brother on a camel hurrying to his rescue. And then Nijm is falling sideways, all four legs working furiously to find some footing among the terror and pain, sinking into the sand like a rock in water, flailing about wide-eyed as if demanding an explanation for her legs not being on solid ground.

Someone rides by and slashes viciously at the man who drove his lance into Nijm; the horse-slayer falls from his saddle. Nuri leaps from Nijm's back right before she hits the sand. She lies there with the spear sticking out of her like a tent pole. Nuri grabs his sword and runs at the fallen man, and a sound like the vortex of a storm comes screaming out from his lungs, the sound of death.

Khalid does not see his brother dispatch the man who took the life of his childhood foal because a new and different pain in his leg makes him turn around. There are men everywhere. Khalid is in the middle of the fighting. He looks down at his leg and sees blood; he cannot tell where it came from. His camel is constantly moving, dancing this way and that in utter confusion and he needs to twist his fingers through her wool just to stay seated between her hump and her neck. Khalid talks to her gently, trying to get her to respond to commands. Katib takes a prancing side step, and they are nearly hit by a rider who plunges right under Katib's nose. A second rider sprints after the first.

The second rider looks like Bahroum!

Khalid can't seem to hear anything. He can't move. His mouth gapes open without a sound as he watches the first rider wheel around, raise his sword and lunge to attack his oldest brother. Bahroum is taken by surprise. He is slower to raise his sword, and when it is nearly raised to the level of his shoulder, the first rider hacks his arm off as he makes his pass.

Bahroum's arm lies in the sand, still holding the sword. An arc of blood sprays out of his shoulder with the force of camel piss. Bahroum totters in the saddle for a brief moment, a look of pure consternation on his face then he falls off backward. The first rider is driving his horse in victory to the fallen body when his hands suddenly fly up and he falls forward. Khalid sees the spear sticking out of the man's back as he slips dead from his horse, feeding more blood to the sand. Behind the fallen enemy he sees his father reign in his horse and jump to the ground. He runs to the fallen body of his eldest son.

Khalid watches Mataa Fuaz, his father, stare in silent horror at Bahroum. Mataa does not bend down, because it is too late. His son cannot be saved. Mataa Fuaz will not bring his son's spirit back into such a twisted body by touching him or even addressing him. Khalid sees his father look up to the heavens and scream, and the sound of his anguish is so powerful that several riders stop in mid-flight.

Khalid has managed to get his camel to trot to where his father stands. He sees that his father's eyes are wild, his father's sword is dancing in his hand. An enemy rider careens past, and Mataa, seemingly without looking, cuts his leg off, slicing right through to the belly of his steed. Another pair of horses comes dangerously close, and Mataa distinguishes the friend from the foe. He grabs the reins of the enemy horse, puts his foot on top of the foot already in the stirrup, and, swinging himself up into the man's face, hits his throat so hard with his sword that the man's head lolls back, barely attached to his neck. Then another horse rides up and Khalid himself spurs Katib into the enemy horse, knocking the man over. He watches triumphantly as his father dismounts and runs his sword through the man's chest.

And then it is over. Khalid sees maybe twenty horses turn and flee on signal. He sees other horses standing as still as his camel, listening to the curious wind now free of war cries, listening for more riders, more attacks, but there are no more. Their enemies are dead or have fled. The Shal'an have won, out-numbered five to one.

All is silence. Khalid is dizzy and parched. His beating heart pumps blood from his leg. It slides down his trousers and drips into the sand. He stares in amazement at his father standing at Bahroum's side.

"Father!" Khalid finally speaks. But Mataa does not respond. He shows no recognition of his youngest son. He bends over Bahroum's form. He stays that way for a long time. Then he looks around and finds the arm. He picks it up and, cradling it, pries the sword free, making strange sounds like the frogs at an oasis.

Khalid does not cry. He feels something hardening inside him. This, his first battle, has engendered in him what will be an enduring sense of power and resolve: he will kill the men who did this to his brother.

The other men are gathering, some with camels in tow, laden with the bodies of the dead. Khalid gets down from Katib and helps his father load Bahroum into the crook between neck and hump where Khalid was just sitting. Nuri is holding onto the mane of some horse, his face sallow from a wound to his shoulder, silently looking on. Neither his father nor his brother considers the fact that Khalid is there; neither question how it came to pass. Where ever Mataa looks, it is as if he is looking far away. His eyes will not focus.

"You have blood on your leg," Mataa dully states.

"I will bind it," Khalid answers.

Mataa looks around and seems to take in the others with their dead.

"How many dead? Khalid, you count them," he whispers from his stupor.

After a few moments, Khalid whispers: "Eleven."

His father nods, the tilt of his head accentuating the irony. Only eleven dead, an amazing rout, but why did one of them have to be his eldest son?

Seeing his father in such a weakened state makes Khalid feel very queer. Never has he seen his father this way before.

They tie Katib and his gruesome burden behind Mataa's horse. Khalid and Nuri follow behind on captured horses. Bahroum's body is hideously shapeless. Khalid turns around in the saddle and counts many horses and camels that were not there before. His father has four new horses and a new camel as well. None of that matters now. Gone are the glory and possessions, the proceeds of war that had once occupied Khalid's thoughts. Now, only his father's sorrow fills his chest. Only hardening anxiety about the next raid and thoughts of how to beat the Shammar captivate his mind.

Katib keeps lagging behind to sniff at Khalid's new horse, and the macabre specter of his brother's armless form on Katib's back is more than Khalid can bear. Slowly, a thought forms in his mind: I will never lose. This he swears softly, inaudibly, to the grotesque heap that was once his oldest brother.

No one ever mentions Khalid stowing away on that raid. His mother's grief and anger over the loss of her eldest son are too intense for her to give much notice to the change in her youngest son.

Unmarked, too, is the fact that Khalid has ridden out on the last two raids. He proved to be a vicious warrior. Nuri, though significantly older, does not have the drive and fury that overcomes his little brother once in the saddle. The other men see immediately that Khalid has special abilities on the battlefield. These things simply come to be, and no one ponders them.

Mataa, for his part, lost his aggressiveness the day he lost his eldest son. He cannot be accused of fear or timidity; he merely lacks interest now. If Khalid had not turned out to be such a great warrior, Mataa would have lost much standing with the tribe.

Many years have passed, and Khalid carries the family name far past the mark where he unwittingly picked it up. That Khalid has sworn a death-oath against the Shammar is clear; their numbers in the Nufud are thinned regularly by the Sha'lan. He sees his tribe grow in stature, due in large part to his leadership. He is asked to accompany the chieftain Hassan al-Amud during many a raid's planning, deep into the night.

Khalid married an older girl named Misha'il roughly one year after Bahroum died. He instructed her carefully in his need to have male children, and her dabbling in the arts practiced by women in order to secure this demand became a well-known secret among the women. Despite two years of marriage, however, only a girl has been produced, several fortnights ago. He has often gone to the women's tent to see the child, doing his best to hide his marveling at her tiny features.

Another raid has been planned, and as he busies himself in preparation, Khalid thinks about his wife. She is fifteen and has produced no son, but she is deft at putting up and taking down their tent when the blood-avengers of the Shammar are on the move. If they do not move fast, a few are always sacrificed. "The Sha'lan are foxes; who can find their burrows?" people say. He thinks how like his mother Misha'il is and how well they work together. His mother likes her. Perhaps he will give her another year or so to have a boy. As his mother says, having a child is not easy. Khalid is growing rich from the camels he captures, traded for goods with the Agheyls, the Camel Traders.

There is time for a son. He will not take another wife.

Khalid thinks to himself, "I am my father's right-hand man. It should be Nuri, but he does not like to raid. 'Do you ever get afraid?' Nuri asked me once in a hush while riding back from a raid. I never answered, for love of my brother, and I understand his fear. Most men have it. But, no. I am never afraid. On the contrary, there is a pleasant quivering in my stomach. I think Khanjar can feel it as I sit bolt upright on him, ready to ride out and kill the enemy. This feeling of anticipation heightens as we approach the camel herd and I mark the lookouts. It becomes a strong, almost musical vibration shooting up through my heart, and like a dream my body fuses with Khanjar's. It is as if a lightning bolt comes down from Allah and strikes the top of my head. It stays that way, emitting a light that blinds my enemies and fills my body with holy wrath. I am invincible when I attack. Allah's strength is with me.

"Nuri is hesitant, that is why he was wounded on our last raid. As he lay ill we even brought in his wife, fearing he would pass without an heir. Indeed, she is with child now, Allah be praised, may it be a son. Nuri will never be a great warrior, so he needs a son. I will train the boy myself, perhaps with my own son, may Allah grant his birth soon. 'Misha'il will be a good breeder,' my mother has said. Let it be true. My mother is never wrong when she gets a feeling for the future, may Allah preserve her."

He is startled to see he has done everything without paying the slightest attention, so many times now has he prepared his horse for war. Every able-bodied man gathers. They ride.

★　★　★

"How is your brother Nuri?" The chieftain Hassan al-Amud addresses Khalid as he stoops to enter the tent.

"He would be here if he was well, but he remains stricken with a mysterious illness," Khalid answers, scarcely hiding the shame his older brother's weakness makes him feel.

"The Wolf would be the one to report to me, in any event. Sit, please, and have some tea with me. Tell me about the raid."

"Ten camel, five horses, no losses. Ten Shammar are dead."

"You take out their scouts before they know it is not the wind, but a Wolf!" the chieftain exclaims with pride. "Khalid, you are brave. You are smart. We will not have to raid again for some time."

"Hassan, I have a concern." The elder nods his head to indicate Khalid should continue. "It is spring again, the rains have been generous, and everything is green here in the Hamad. I don't think we should stay here, we have too many enemies. Our strength is in our fleetness, but I hear many of the elders expressing their desire to stay. They are fatted on the plenty, like lambs. 'Too much killing!' 'For every son born to me, one is lost on a ghazu!' This is what they say. But our losses have always been small compared to those of our enemies. Do foxes eat grass? Are we not to raid?"

"Khalid. We have made peace with the Raulu, may the covenant stand a fortnight at least. The Shammar have gone north, such is the report. What more can you do? Even foxes run for pleasure in the spring. Everywhere enjoys the rain. No one is moving on us now, and they have no reason to. How we have grown! All fear the Desert Foxes now. One of our men is as good as five of any other tribe's, and this is because of your leadership. You shame us all with your fury! It is unnatural!"

"Hassan. Please let me ask: do you tell me we do not move?"

"We will stay and let the young ones grow, animal and child."

"There will be attacks. The guard is thin, some nights only one man. I am ill at ease in my heart."

"I will increase the guard. Now. You are too young to worry even when the battle is won. Zal has asked if you would like to go hunting with him. He has trained a new hawk. Zal! Where is my first born?"

After a few moments Zal enters, slight of build next to Khalid but handsome and good-natured. The two young men exchange a glance of friendship. They decline the chieftain's offer of tea and head out to hunt together. Zal brings his hawk, eyes bound, and they mount their horses.

They talk as they ride.

"Many of the elders believe there has been too much killing, Khalid. My father has told you this, hasn't he? 'For every son born to me, one is lost on some ghazu!' You, too, have heard the talk."

"And now that all fear the Desert Foxes, we hibernate? Do you support your father's views?"

"Yes. We have made peace with the Raulu and the land is rich. 'Locust come regardless of the moon's phase.' Who can tell when hard times will return? When else will you let your women rest?"

Khalid falls silent, and Zal respects his privacy for a while then asks after his new son.

"I have ordered Misha'il to nurse him every hour. She is not to cook or leave the tent but must keep him by her breast, should he grow hungry. A strong infant grows into a strong man. But even a son is nothing certain. The Sufi Farhan says my older brother Nuri may become a Sufi. It is unexpected. He is sick and weak. I laugh to think my father had no idea, observing me as a child, that I would have any use at all. It must be impossible to tell."

"I believe you will become chieftain someday."

"You are his son, it will be you. You are my equal, Zal. I am content to hunt and fight."

"You may be content, but I am not your equal. I will not rule."

The young men are silent again. A fine mist of rain begins to coat their faces and both their hearts soar. The camel grass is up to their horses' thighs, and with their every step, crickets and locusts fly up and scatter. A bustard breaks from its cover. The air smells so fresh and moist it seems to be alive, like the scent of a newborn thing. Khalid's mind turns to his newborn son, and suddenly he sees the narrow grinning eyes of his wife, the woman who is strong and obedient but does not admire him. She has never spoken against him or disobeyed him in any way, but she has a look in her eye. He has come close to hitting her for that look many times, but she would then have reason to speak against him, and as his mother had predicted, she is a good breeder. Two fine girls and now this healthy boy. Perfect, because the older girls can care for the boys to follow. Yet, if his father had known he would be the mightiest warrior, would he have not found him a more beautiful wife? Misha'il has eyes like a goat!

Zal is lost in his own thoughts. They crest a hill in time to see a hunter far below ride hard after a gazelle. Across the sweeping plain coated with rare green grass, they watch as the herd veers off, circling away in the opposite direction of the rider. The hunter pursues a large buck that he has expertly separated from the herd. Khalid tries to think who besides himself and Zal can hunt like that, who carries himself that way in the saddle, but he cannot place the determined slope of the back. The two watch as the hunter swiftly turns the animal again and again until the exact opportunity presents itself and the spear is thrust into the beast directly between the shoulder blades: a perfect kill.

The animal's forelegs crumple like burning straws, but its mighty hindquarters refuse to go down. The hunter leaps from his horse and throws his weight on the spear, forcing the stag down and onto its back. Then, dodging its lethal hooves kicking madly in the air, the hunter pulls out a khanjar knife and slits its throat. Now he is running back to his horse, he has a leather bag...but this is how a woman hunts! He is catching the draining blood in the bag to enrich some recipe. The hooves churn slower now. Would a man bother about blood? It is unclean!

Khalid's horse leaps forward, apparently spurred by his movements, but he does not remember deciding to approach. Zal follows. He sees the hunter has taken note of them, has turned his body ever so slightly to monitor their approach. His hand rests lightly on the dagger at his side; the other holds the leather flask of blood.

As they get closer, Khalid calls out, "Omar?"

"Who rides upon me?"

"Friends."

"Of whom?"

"Of God."

"Then God's countenance be upon you."

It is a woman! Khalid is awestruck. He reigns in, remaining in the saddle, and stares at the woman. Zal rides up and leaps off his horse. The woman's face brightens in recognition.

"Fida, wife of Zal ibn Amud. We watched you take this stag from that crest."

"Oh! Zal, it is you! It is a good day to hunt. I'm sorry if I scared the herd."

Khalid dismounts and hesitantly walks up to them. Zal addresses Fida.

"This is Khalid, son of Mataa Fuaz. You know him, surely."

"All have heard of The Wolf. Khalid. My husband holds you in the highest esteem. Would that I could have watched you hunt instead." With this, she lets the kerchief covering her mouth drop and smiles at Khalid openly.

"Well. Yes. We will be hunting soon," Khalid averts his eyes while answering this mysterious woman who has him completely befuddled. Frustrated, he tries to conjure up some image of her from their tribe, but he cannot place her. Still, he has an uncanny sense that he knows her. The unexpectedness of this meeting and the feeling it engenders in him cause him to respond with fear, which shows itself as anger.

"Who has taught you to hunt?" he demands of Fida.

"My husband, and I have watched Zal, he is a very good hunter. Also, I have been hunting since I was old enough to hold a sling."

"You have skill surpassing mine!" Zal teases good-naturedly.

"I was lucky, this one was easy to divert," she states, motioning to the stag.

"So you hunt with a sling as well?" Khalid asks, unable to hide his incredulousness. She reacts to the heat of his queries by dropping her head and blushing. Khalid then notices several bustards and a hare hanging from her saddle.

"They have tolerated me. I have always loved it. Despite three wives, my father never had a son, so I was taught to help."

She isn't even embarrassed! She is actually proud of her hunting! Khalid scowls. Puzzling these thoughts, he vaguely hears Zal and Fida talk about hawking.

"I don't hunt with a hawk."

"But why not?" It is Zal, using the teasing voice again. Zal likes this woman!

"It is not fair!" She says loudly and with a hint of criticism.

"Not fair to whom?" Zal laughs.

"Not fair to the hawk or the prey. To set a hawk upon a gazelle, just to blind it! It is not natural. It is a hawk's nature to take and eat its prey."

"It is a woman's nature to stay with the tents!" Khalid hears his voice boom, sounding much harsher than intended, but he cannot help it, he cannot think.

He notices she does not seem upset. Perhaps she has defended herself against such criticism before.

"I do not ride with the men, I would not presume to do so. I hunt alone. No one takes much notice. This blood is for my mother's mother. She will die before we move again, though the nutrients in blood have sustained her past the point she wishes to live. Yes, you are right… it is strange for a woman to hunt."

With these words, she takes the anger out of Khalid, but not the fear. His feelings present themselves as something amorphous, incomprehensible. He has not had to deal with any feelings like this before. It suddenly occurs to him that he admires this woman.

Without another word, he turns and walks over to his horse. Zal offers to help the woman get the stag onto her horse and he calls out to Khalid for help.

"Hey, come back. This old man is heavy. Help me get it onto Fida's horse."

Khalid turns and walks back. Zal is looking at him so quizzically that he nearly turns to leave, but Zal quickly motions to the hindquarters, and together they heave the beast onto her horse. Khalid thinks she may need another horse, the load is so heavy, but Fida hops up into the little 'v' left by the stag, covers her face, nods her thanks, and slowly rides off.

Khalid moves toward his horse. He can walk. He can move and think. But something is different now. He swings himself up on his horse, and he and Zal head off in search of small game to try the hawk out. He can feel his horse's muscles moving. He notices the smell of wild lavender and chamomile. Dotting the grasses are flaming red caterpillars. His hand is shaking. He sees Zal prepare the hawk, taking the cloth from around its eyes. A hare breaks cover and they reign in, Zal giving his arm a slight flap to send the bird darting after the hare. He catches it in a matter of seconds and flies back with it.

"Heh! What a good hawk. We will catch twenty hares today! I wonder if he will be consistent after the first few kills. This hawk was a good buy," Zal goes on, never noticing that Khalid is not following his banter.

Khalid watches the hawk soar. Suddenly, the creature jags left and comes flying at Khalid's face. It seems that the hawk is going to take Khalid's head off. In evading the hawk, Khalid falls backward off his horse. Zal laughs spontaneously, but Khalid is sterner than ever.

"Khalid, old man, that was a close one! I've never seen a hawk fly so close to someone's face."

Khalid brushes himself off and leaps back into his saddle. Still he is silent.

Zal becomes concerned that Khalid might be hurt, so uncharacteristic is this bad humor, and they agree to return to camp. Zal points out sights along the way, inwardly remarking how absent-minded Khalid has become, who remains silent for the duration of the ride.

Khalid is unable to rise the next day. He lies in bed. Misha'il tends to him. She is actually more concerned than she lets on. Her eyes have a soft look, like pity. Khalid notices this and feels drained, more tired than he has ever been. He stares at the top of the tent and remembers riding on a dhula, a racing camel, running hard away from a mare, something else...a dream he has had just now.

He begins to piece together memories of the dream. A beautiful sorrel mare pursues him on the racing camel; he glimpses it over his shoulder to gauge its distance. The race seems to last a long time. He suddenly wheels around to face his pursuer. There is no rider on the sorrel mare. She immediately falls to the ground and starts to die, rolling her big soft eyes at him. This is not what he wants. He feels responsible for its pain, but he turns away. Blood begins to run from his right arm. His camel takes a few steps, and he sees a bird lying in the sand. The bird is white, no bigger than his hand, curled up on the sand. He wonders if it is dead.

The tent seems to be breathing. Images from the dream float in and out of his mind. He sees the eyes of the mare. He remembers having dreamed this dream before; he has pondered its images more than once. He cannot tell if he has fallen back to sleep and is dreaming about remembering this dream or if he is awake recalling the dream. He does not have any understanding of what is happening to him, and this disorientation makes him feel he is dreaming even when he is awake. He cannot keep the two clear.

He suddenly remembers his wife and looks about for her. She is there, sitting on a rug looking at him with curiosity and weariness. He seems to feel differently about her, as though he had never disdained her or she him. All he says is, "Thank you." She smiles and leaves, but returns with some broth and helps him drink it.

He has not gotten up for five days, and his father has brought the dervish Zoohair to hear him tell the strange dream, a version of which he has had every night, always with the camel, the mare, and the bird. Zoohair, a dervish from another tribe, does not even pause to think upon the dream but begins immediately.

"The camel is The Wolf. The mare is your heart, which has been dead for many years, slain by the death of another. Something has smitten your heart and made it beat again. This something is the bird in the sand, but it too may be dying before given the chance to live. Thus is life. You must catch the first animal you see when you go out tomorrow," and when Khalid tries to speak he says, "you will go out tomorrow. It will be young. Nurture it until Mushtari (Jupiter) enters the tent of Parwin (the Pleiades) then let it go. Eat no meat for three times thirty days. During this time, pay your mother a visit."

Then the dervish yawns and says he will be going back to his tribe. Khalid's father gives him gifts and he leaves. Khalid has no idea what the dervish's words mean and is resolved not to follow his instructions, but Misha'il sees to it that they are followed to the letter, and for once Khalid allows her to rule.

Miraculously, he has the strength to walk out the next day, and soon a small lizard catches his attention. It is a gecko. He grabs it and keeps it in a bag, feeding it on bugs. His daughters find it quite amusing to catch grasshoppers and, holding them down with a tiny stick, watch the lizard devour them. Khalid takes note of his tiny daughters; they are so beautiful!

His convalescence takes a few more days, and during this time he thinks often of Fida, no longer feeling anger but something closer to a hard longing. He wanders about camp, at times despising the ease and growth of the spring as it fattens into summer. Some nights he falls into a fever again, though never as severely as in the beginning of his illness. During these long nights, dreams and visions of wild monstrous beasts and bare-breasted women who beckon to him in lewd ways plague him. He fights against these images as he fought in battle, always winning, winning back his control, beating back the images or slaying them even as they emerge onto the beleaguered contours of his mind.

At times, too, various odors assail him, causing him to ask his wife, 'Has a lamb been slaughtered just now?' or 'Is it raining?' Her looks to him are gentler than they have ever been. He senses this, but he cannot respond with affection, except on those nights she takes it upon herself to enter his tent and attempt to arouse his manhood. With some effort he couples with her, passively, allowing her to lead. He feels little pleasure at such times, but he takes note that Misha'il seems happy and exhausted. This is something he has never paid attention to before, and there is some contentment in it.

Gradually, Khalid resumes his position of strength and, as before, out does himself. He knows two things only: how to kill and how to lead men in battle. The tribal elders choose him to be chieftain. Hassan al-Amud's strength is waning; Hassan and Zal support this decision.

Khalid accepts it without pride, because he is single-minded and knows he will help his tribe grow in honor.

Khalid has decided that he must eradicate the Shammar and kill their chieftain. Then his people will not suffer their death-raids. This becomes his goal, and he gradually convinces the tribe to undertake a special mission. He prays to Allah to guide him, for he knows in his heart he is attempting to set straight something that happened years ago: Bahroum's death. He blames the Shammar chieftain, Amir ibn Saud, for all the pain in his life put in motion by that death.

Khalid, Zal, and Mishtari, son of Mishal, make up the vanguard. The raiding party numbers forty-seven men. Yesterday scouts brought information that the Shammar are encamped some fifty miles east. Several days of hard riding is to bring them within range of the enemy camp. The plan is to strike at night.

They leave several hours before daybreak. They will camp when the sun reaches its zenith, then travel again under the cover of night. They ride in silence.

On the first night, Khalid is not feeling his usual confidence. Sitting bolt upright in his saddle, his ears are alert and his eyes, well adjusted to the darkness, easily take in the moon-swept outlines of hills and shrubs. His nocturnal vision is exceptional.

He wants to call out to his men to be alert, but there is no cause other than his sense of foreboding. He feels the minutes turn into hours without his anxiety abating. Cresting a short hill, he sees out of the corner of his eye a line of beasts moving.

A line of beasts moving! The Shammar!

Have they dared a full-scale raid on him? What if he had not exhorted the men to ride yesterday? They would have all been slaughtered...

He lightly makes the clucking sound of the pintail grouse to signal danger, and Zal immediately reins in. Like magic, each man in turn reins in, and within seconds, the entire army of men has stopped moving. They stand in complete silence. With gestures alone, Khalid communicates the location of the enemy riders. He commands that the group split into two, one group to flank the enemy, one group to approach from the rear. Without a word, they break formation and move off in opposite directions. Khalid leads the group heading to flank the enemy; Zal, the group heading to the rear.

The Shammar have not yet noticed them. Khalid and his men move quietly through the dim moonlight until he hears a shout. None from his tribe would shout, so it must be that the Shammar have spotted them. He springs into action, spurring his horse into a full gallop. He hears the men behind him do the same. They are a stone's throw away before the Shammar manage to assess the situation and turn to charge their attackers. Dawn is just about to break.

Khalid feels the breeze created by his speed float the hairs of Khanjar's mane. The lightning bolt has struck the top of his head and he is electrified, invincible. His horse streaks through the dark carrying him closer to the enemy until he sees their tribal colors and makes out the broad outlines of their faces.

A scream rips from his lungs, and he hears the cry taken up by the enemy ahead and his men behind. He hacks at the nearest enemy rider and sends him flying from the saddle. He tears through the enemy ranks, slashing with his sword left and right, looking for their chieftain. Didn't he ride out with his men? He begins to shout.

"Amir ibn Saud! Amir ibn Saud!" He looks for signs of recognition on the faces flashing by.

He knows there must be a hundred Shammar here, nearly their entire clan. Not wise. They have come to destroy the Sha'lan once and for all. As he works Khanjar through the throng like a hawk, he feels more powerful than he has ever felt before. He is certain he has already taken out twenty men. That will even the odds. Toppling one man after another, he hears his voice as if it were someone else's, screaming, "Amir ibn Saud! Amir ibn Saud!"

Suddenly a rider bears down on him. He sees a bearded face twisted into a snarl, and he thinks he hears the man howl, "Wolf!"

In seconds they are upon one another, swinging their swords once and passing. Is that pain Khalid feels? This is it. He wheels Khanjar around and sees the other preparing to make another pass. He reins his horse in and sits facing his attacker until the last possible moment. Then he slips from his saddle and does something he has never done before: he slices through the horse's forelegs.

The horse slides off its legs and crashes to the ground. The frantic rider flies over his horse's head and lands in the sand.

With lightning speed, Khalid sprints to the flailing figure and, catching the man's sword beneath his foot, drives his own sword into the man's chest. For an instant their eyes lock and Khalid knows this is the chieftain Amir ibn Saud.

Still looking into his eyes, Khalid pulls the sword out and plunges it back into the man's chest, hissing, "Bahroum!"

Immediately the man's eyes grow hollow, and he moves no more.

Khalid stands over his dead form. He waits for the impact of his deed to hit him, but nothing happens, nothing has changed. This is a just another dead man.

Minutes after it began, the battle is over. The surviving Shammar have ridden away. In silence, Khalid helps the men finish off the fallen, friend and foe alike. The dead lay forty-eight Shammar, nineteen Sha'lan.

Khalid walks back over to the body of the chieftain, dimly noting the blood dripping from his own right arm. He looks down at the face twisted in death, sees the blood oozing from the holes in his chest and finally feels satisfied.

Within the hour, the men have loaded the Sha'lan dead onto horses and have rounded up the enemy horses. They head back to their tribe.

Zal rides next to Khalid.

"How did you know?"

"I did not know."

"First, that we should ride on that very night and second, the flanking maneuvers. We were out-manned five to one!"

"I did not know. Allah guides me. I suddenly know what to do, and I do it."

"That was Amir ibn Saud you fought and killed."

"Yes. The murderer of my brother is now dead. I am satisfied."

The two ride on in silence, Zal feeling awe and admiration for his friend and leader, Khalid beginning to feel nothing at all.

Now the ground is hard and many years have passed. The only scent in the air is that of dried grasses and sand. Khalid has ridden out, ostensibly to hunt, but he finds himself sitting on a hill, gazing out into the bleak desert.

He has three sons and two daughters and is proud of this. He has one wife still, never being able to pay attention to more than one, though his wealth could have supported a second and third.

The wind is picking up and seems to move all the hairs on his body, especially those on his face. He feels relaxed, caressed, and time is of no consequence. His mind drifts back to the huntress, Fida. He has watched her out of the corner of his eye, wary and mistrusting, all his life. It suddenly becomes clear to him that he loves her and has always loved her. He has loved her as much as he loves his brothers, though he has never consciously entertained the thought of loving her for fear of the havoc it would create in his very structured life.

The damage to his tribal relationships, had he acted on his love, pales in comparison to the vulnerability his love for her creates in him. It is unthinkable; he has never even permitted himself to consider it before.

But now he thinks there is no one left he loves besides Fida. He *knows* his wife, his sisters, his mother, and maybe he loves them, but not like Fida. His father has long passed away; his brothers, both, passed away. Three children, one in infancy, passed away.

He sits and feels very poor. He is the richest man in their tribe, the most feared, the most revered, the leader, yet he is impoverished. His life has been an empty vessel. The only thing he has ever loved is Fida. He has always done his duty and that has given him much to care about, but not much to love.

He sees this as one might see their hooked nose for the first time, with horror and surprise. He stares out over the miles of barren sand. The wind dies down.

After awhile, he thinks about getting up, but he does not. He feels a slight pressure growing in his chest, and he begins to sweat. He cannot move. The pain increases slightly, and the part of him that fights is suddenly not there.

There is no fight.

He feels his pulse begin to race, and his heart jumps in his chest. He feels the sensation of it, objectively, as though it were happening to someone else. After several minutes he leans heavily to one side then lets himself down onto the sand, lying on his back facing the sky. The sun is very hot, though it shines near the horizon. It has blinded him: so much light, so suddenly.

His breathe comes fast and shallow. He loses track of time, lying in the sand, listening to the wind pick up then die away again. His breathing is now so shallow even he cannot detect it. He realizes he is dying, that he will die any minute. It is a curiosity, an intriguing prospect, something he has prepared for every day of his life. With contentment bordering on gratitude just for this elusive death, he passes away in the sand.

Khalid after Death

He stays in his body for many hours, staring out of his dead eyes, knowing completely that he is dead: his body will never move again. At first, being dead is startling. He lies inside his dead body, confused and agitated. After awhile, looking up at the sky, he notices it is growing dark. The sun disappeared and he never even noticed. Another sunset missed.

Kami (The Sentient Being Who Was Khalid) feels cheated. After all the battles, all the death, he takes one look at his own emptiness and his heart gives out!

What is a heart for, if not to pump blood?! It is absurd! It is not right!

Now, in the eerie dusk, he thinks about his wife and his children. His sons were bound to bring him honor. He thinks about Fida and Zal, his father and his brothers, his sisters. Going over the memories he has of them makes him feel happy yet regretful, elated yet crestfallen. If he had tears, they would be falling. If he could move, he would be rolling across the sand and down the hill, but he is not really in his body. There are no tears; there is nothing to move.

He thinks about Amir Ibn Saud, and he feels sad that he killed him. He was just a man. He thinks about all the men he killed, and loneliness overtakes him. His life does not make sense. On the one hand, he sees his life with his family and friends, a life he spent little time in, a life he never treasured. On the other hand, he sees his life in battle, where he spent all his energy. If only he could shift the energy from one hand to the other! He would go back, hold his wife, play with his sons and daughters and look in on his mother! He would take Fida in a fit of passion!

And all the killing, to what end? Where are the dead now? Who were they?

Somehow, in the midst of these thoughts, he finds himself hovering in the air over his body. In the barest light of the moon he sees his haggard face, his fallen form. He scoffs, "How fierce you are, Khalid! The bravest man who ever rode the sands of the Nufud! Not fallen in battle, no! Not finally killed, after all you have killed, no! Dead in the sand from your heart giving out! A simple death, an old man's death! How pathetic!"

Suddenly, a pintail grouse calls out for his mate and Kami holds his breath. The warning call, is it from his men? He waits. There is no reply. And then the same call, closer this time. He makes out a small bird hopping among the dry grasses. It is just a grouse. He laughs at his own foolishness.

"It is your call, little grouse. I will never steal it again to trick men, to kill men. Ah, why, why, why!"

His head is spinning with questions, questions he cannot even formulate. He thinks about staying near his body to see if they will find him or if the desert jackals will come. Both options are abhorrent. He thinks about trying to find his tribe, and in his mind's eye he sees them carrying on with their activities. The world has not stopped. New leaders will arise, fortunes will fluctuate, men will fight and die and babies will be born. They do not need him.

Then it suddenly dawns on him. "I am a jinn! I have become that which I feared as a child! If I go back, no one will know me as anything but a spirit. I will scare my own grandchildren! No. I will not go back."

And so, floating above the hillock upon which he died, Kami says goodbye to his tribe.

"But where do jinn go who do not want to scare their loved ones?" he wonders to himself.

Instantly he is in heaven. Heaven is almost like earth, with the same hills, the same sands, the same birds, but there is no threat, no extremes of heat or cold, no hunger or sorrow.

Kami's heart rejoices. He feels a warm sense of bliss as he wanders about in heaven. He meets other sentient beings, none of whom he recognizes, and they often sit by a well or on a hill and talk about deeds from their life just past. Sometimes they cry and grow still; sometimes they laugh and smile. Kami understands everything they are saying to him and he feels perfectly heard. The days and nights pass in a syncopated rhythm.

Kami stays in this blissful state for a long time. After awhile, he cannot remember stories to tell so he listens silently. One day, he cannot remember anything from the past. There is no desert, no friends to talk to, no wind, nothing. He is floating in darkness, yet he feels content. In that instant, he finds himself in a queue with other sentient beings.

There is a being mind-talking with the being standing in front of him. When he disappears, she turns to Kami and smiles.

"Hello, sweetie, here you are again! So, you have chosen. I have a gift for you, a thought-gift. It is this: You have put aside the fear of losing your body. Replace it with love."

With the word 'love' swimming in his head, the Being Who No Longer Remembers Ever Being Khalid is instantly born again.

Transmigrations

Khalid to Keizo

Karlos/Mei Hua/Khalid	becomes	Keizo
Merlo/Bau Yu/Fida	becomes	Tatsuo
Victor/Ying/Misha'il	becomes	Midori
Karlos' father/Shu Chi/Amir ibn Saud	becomes	Aoi
Emilio/Madame Wang/Bahroum	becomes	Aiko
girl who was given the voice/Shaymaa	becomes	Hiro'chan
Nuri	becomes	Hiromi

KEIZO

First life of consciousness

How is there an ant in Tokyo? I know there are ants here, that is obvious, but where do they come from? Ants live in ant holes; I am on the third floor. How many days does it take for this ant to crawl up here? Does it go back and forth every day, does it take an ant-life, do its offspring know instinctively where to go, how to get back to the ground floor, to that measly garden of Kato's, who actually eats the eggplants he grows under the dim sun lording over this city, this very spot?

Koriyama wasn't such a good place, either. I always knew I would leave Koriyama, and here I am, far away from Fukushima province. It was expected of me. Well, for the most part, I am glad to be gone. I can't have ants crawling about my room. Perhaps I should just maim this one as a warning to the others, but she would, most probably, find it somewhere within herself to drag her broken body back downstairs and die near the hole, a fine mist of azuki paste on her back lending an undeniable palpability to her body. So she would be a kind of advertisement, and they would all rush up here after nibbling at her body. Ants will eat anything that was once alive and even things that are in the process of dying. Azuki paste was alive once, beans and sugar cane with bugs running all over them. So many things were once alive, the simple objects around me—boots, soup, sweaters—but we choose to ignore this fact and carry on as if it weren't true. There, now she's gone; I've waited too long to squash her, she's crawled down into the oily straw of the tatami.

This room is disgusting. To think I went through what I did to get this room! "Possibility for advancement." "An honorable position." A government clerk. How will I ever sail around the world on my paltry salary? I need a new tatami; three would be nice, then the whole floor would be covered. Even my father, a simple school teacher, can afford rooms covered in tatami. And a little rug at the shoji, is that asking too much?

And if I don't sail around the world? How can I justify my existence? Well, it is hopeless at home, anyway. Better here than at home, even if I never sail anywhere.

Damn it all! I can't send back any more money. But I will. Why didn't they stop after me, why in the world would they go on after Hiroshi? I would have stopped if my child was retarded. Well, we are all accidents.

At least Aiko's handicap is mild, a clubfoot; she is married and out of the house. What can be done for Hiro'chan? So I send money.

Oh no. It wasn't my leaving that soured my father's face. It was my refusal to be a school teacher. He thinks I scoff at him. Well, he's an old fool, anyway. Is it my fault that I see it? But I try to treat him respectfully... I can't change what is in my heart.

Oh, damn Sundays. I've got to get out. Harajuku? Ginza? I hear, like a little tanuki in my heart, climbing up my throat and into my ear, a call to go! Go! Or come! Come! I don't know which and here I am, rolling onto my side, looking at the picture of a British actress I stole from a magazine in the anteroom at the office.

I wonder what her name is. I know some English names: Veekutoriya, Yaleezabatu... Well, I will call her Veekutoriya, a queen's name for a beauty queen.

What if it were really her name? I have no way of finding out.

Hmmm. Everything is well with my brother, my mother wrote. He is weaving baskets in town. What a dreadful life; and he likes it, too, I'm sure. When Hiro'chan got his new Go Board, he practiced for months then challenged me to a game. I can still see him grinning, looking up at mother and stuttering, "Ma! Big Brother's first game, and he is winning!" Like it was a good joke, how I could beat him my first try at a game he'd been playing for weeks. He has no concept of his own affliction. That neighbor boy, ten years his junior, loves to play with him. Oh Hiroshi, how sad that you were ever born!

I've got to get out of here or else I'll go crazy, CRAZY!

This is my favorite park; all the young lovers come here. Hiromi would come here with me, she always stops to look up at me and smiles whenever I pass, and in the morning she always says, "Ah! Good morning, Mr. Inagaki." She would probably let me make love to her. She's polite and yielding so I treat her nicely like everybody else does, but I hate the pathetic type. I don't care for weak women. Now, just look at that woman! I bet she's not weak, I bet she's meeting someone, maybe in secret. She looks good in Western dress: late twenties, unmarried, no children... That would be my guess. She's leaning up against that tree, a maple, all the leaves have fallen but two... Yes, there are only two, at least from this angle, dried into stubborn brown curls like teeth in an old man's head.

I like it when all the leaves are gone and the dark trees stand naked, nothing more than skeletal silhouettes. The sky will become gray, and it will begin snowing until a thin coat of frost coats their branches. A chill wind will blow her skirt above her knees. Then she will be the most beautiful she's ever been. In a week or two, winter will be officially here.

A young man has come, they hurriedly walk away, heads bowed, talking in whispers though never looking in one another's direction, as if they were spies passing information. But the war is over, for now. Now it's the war between men and women. I'm for women.

Leaves have blown up around my shoes; yes, the wind is growing steadily stronger. I'm sick of scouting out lovers. I need the right woman. I feel like I could go to sleep right here on this bench. I should go home and read some Ibsen, make myself some miso soup. I should break into the theater, girls think I'm cute, I could act, I know I could. I'll polish myself in my free time. The modern theater is just being born in Japan, a fledgling dove, a baby mujina scurrying through the dense forest of western tradition. What's that moving in the bushes?

A dog? No, it's still now, a dog would keep moving. There, again! I don't know, I can't go over and start investigating the bushes, what would people think? I have lost my watch. Alright. There, alright, see, there's nothing in the...what is it? Ah, a grouse or pheasant or something, see, with a broken wing. I'll bring it back and feed it, nurse it back to health. Damn it! All right, if you don't want to come, don't. "Here little baby, come here little, tku tku tku tku tku." Okay, stay there, you're probably safer.

It's almost dark. Winter's sunset, one minute day, the next night. I must have been here for hours; I think I'm losing all sense of time. I must get a watch, that's the first thing I should get. And a new overcoat. Yes, everyone's heading for home, they're going to have lights on in their houses and apartments. Maybe they'll sink their legs down in a traditional kotastu, that's what I miss most, but I must save money. One stinking radiator! Being modern is a cold business! Maybe Kato will be at home. Of course he will. We can play some Go. So home, I'll go home to my room now.

★ ★ ★

A flock of white pigeons careening down from the tip of a gray stone flying buttress. The futon...it smells. The bitter scent of chilled sweat. Some birds against a gray sky, what? A building, an old western building, a woman, birds. Fat white birds. Gray. My feet are cold; it's morning. Yes. Time to get up. What was I dreaming? I've got to have some tea, got to piss. God it's cold! Down the hall to the toilet. I don't want to go down the hall, my feet are already too cold. "Poor circulation." Who said that? And there was something moving, something trying to invade me, cold and frightening. I dreamed it. What did I dream?

I can't remember. Oh, shit. Hito's in the toilet. I can hear him farting. Where are my slippers? Okay, I'll put the water on to boil first, but he better be finished by then, I can't wait. I'll pound on the door! Damn him, always trying to invade me. I want some tea. I've got to go to the office, but I want some tea first. And I'll roll that rice into little balls and sprinkle them with sesame seeds, I should have done that last night, there's no time now! Well, I can do it now, while I wait. My hands are shaking. Don't spill them on the floor or you'll really have something to be upset about.

Yes, there, he's out, that was the door. I'm next. Ah, good, right by the door where I left them. I want a candle, I'm afraid. Don't be ridiculous, you know the way by heart, five years! After five years, you should know. Five years of my youth, gone, gone, nothing to show for it at all! If I would have slept with Hiromi, that would have been one thing. But I am going to know people in the theater, and when I write my play, introduce the Nora of Japan, oh yes, I'm going to write it, I'm just saving up my ideas and experiences.

I have to sleep with someone first. For free. Someone I know. Then my father will be astounded, he'll have nothing to say! Should I stay and try to take a shit? But I don't have to now. This always happens to me. On the train I'll have to. "Can't force nature." Somebody said that to me once, maybe my mother. I was always trying to force nature when I was little. Or maybe the nature of things was trying to force me.

Where are my ties? No, my tie, the black and red one, it would go nicely with my suit, it would go with the day. Ah, in my socks box, I must have dropped it there. What? Wash your face first, your groin, armpits. Oh, I hate doing this, it's so cold. I should move to Okinawa or somewhere nice and warm. I can't take this. Well, Tokyo's warmer than

Fukushima. Tea at last. Now I've waited too long, it's on the cold side. Better a little cool than too hot. I wonder what it's like to bathe in tea. What?

Yes, they forced nature on me when I was young. There are gaps missing from my education, that's it. That's the thought I've been trying to grab, it explains everything. Somewhere along the line, in elementary, one of those years, it seems they just passed me through. "You're so fortunate to be able to go to school." Mother never went to school; she doesn't know what it's like. She can barely read! "Good women stay at home;" that sounds like my father. I'm definitely the smartest one in my family. My cousins are still farmers. They call me The One Who Went to Tokyo as if it were some bizarre action on my part. Even so, there are whole sections of the multiplication tables I can't even remember, the sixes are especially bothersome, and anything over ten, say, four twelve's, well, I can do it by saying two twelve's are twenty four, four and four are eight, two and two, four, so forty eight, but the other guys in the office can just pop out with "forty eight," as if it were nothing. Got to get on the train; when did I walk to the platform?

And that's not all. It's getting crowded in here, and as usual I'm starting to get a headache from the smell, when the bar scrapes over the electrified cable. It's hideous, really. I should get a bicycle. No, but winter, it would be impossible once the snow comes, really any day now, isn't it? Shogatsu comes up on one so quickly. The nights come quicker and quicker and suddenly it's the New Year and you're supposed to change or be changed or something, but I never feel any different, only depressed by these great expectations. Great Expectations, English writer, I should read it. I want to read everything foreign, and my contemporaries, who? No one's really writing in Japan. Well, there are the new Japanese playwrights, Hojo Hideji and Watsuji Tetsuro. They have something to say.

What a monstrous western building, not that it's unattractive, especially the sculptured cornerstones. The thick stone ledges at the top and around each floor are quite stunning; the stone stands out a full inch around the door, and it seems, around each window, I never noticed that before. Not an ugly building, no. Not for a western building. But it is monstrous, gigantic, like America, so big and new and solid. It was built after the earthquake, of course, not that I know this for a fact, but it's certainly obvious. I was a little boy in Fukushima then. I was being teased because of the deformities of my brother and sister. Where are those noisy little brats today? Still farmers. I, on the other hand, am an aspiring writer in the city, I work for the government.

People say they remember where they were the day the quake struck, people my age, but I don't remember a thing. But see, this building looks like a mountain, feels like a cave inside. Not at all like a Japanese building, no matter how big. They look like a gusty wind could sweep them away, they feel hollow, like the trunk of a tree, like they were big hollow trees and we Japanese were trolls, like Grieg's trolls, loping about inside. That is how Westerners look at us, I'm sure of it: like we were little trolls aping their ways.

We certainly build better ships than they do, our textiles are just as fine if not finer, we're recovering from the war better. We must learn their ways to keep up, to compete, I'll give them that: they finally forced us to acculturate. But now we know all about them and they know nothing about us; that is our advantage. We will be stronger, twice as strong, as it were, knowing ourselves and them. Their near sightedness and their lack of peripheral vision will be their downfall.

"Ah, Good Morning, Mr. Inagaki!" Hiromi sings out respectfully.

"Uhhm. Miss Meguro," I nod, heading on up the aisle like a ship looking for a spot to moor, past the parallel rows of desks to the third row, left hand side. But her voice yanks me back like an anchor inadvertently dropped too soon.

"Mr. Inagaki."

"Hehh?"

"Hirata-san would like to see you at nine-fifteen this morning."

"Hirata-san?"

"Yes."

"Did he tell you on what business?"

"No. He only said, 'Tell Mr. Inagaki I want to see him at nine-fifteen.'"

"Oh. Thank you."

She looks at me with a big happy face. I'll bet she knows what he wants and that it's something good. Maybe I'll be promoted at long last. Maybe it's something big.

Stop thinking, you'll pump yourself up and it might be nothing. Hiromi likes you, you know. Hirata could certainly detect any excitement on my part and no doubt find it unbecoming. So don't think, be blank. You've read Bushido! Sit down and do your work; you lack self-control, you're a disgrace. Good, mail on top. Do mail. Don't watch the clock! You have an hour and twenty minutes. Ask Hiromi to call you at nine-ten. Yes. That's how it should be done.

Haven't I been to the boss' office before? Yes, certainly, but how could I not have seen her? It's impossible that I wouldn't have noticed her... Look, I'm still shaking, I might never stop shaking. Who is she? She must be new, that's it. She must have been rotated in from some other department. It's not likely she'd be hired off the street to such an important position, unless she has connections, and she doesn't look like that sort. I must find out right away, tomorrow, there is no time to lose. I may never meet another woman like that and I've already spent twenty-six years searching!

The way she crossed her legs beneath her desk, suddenly tilting her whole body to the right, back kept perfectly straight, aligned with her head, just a dip to the right and back up again. I see her doing it over and over again. What an exquisitely lovely movement!

She must have seen some Western actress do it in a movie, maybe the actress on my wall, and she picked the gesture up, without thinking, she just does it now, it's become a part of her. Yet she has a very classical Japanese beauty, like a Heian woodblock print: almond eyes, straight nose rounding down into the nostrils, petite mouth, rounded chin, oval face... I don't remember her ears. Did I even see them? I don't think so. Her hair must have been covering them, a kind of Western cut, down to her shoulders, longer in the back? I can't remember. Next time I see her, I'll memorize everything.

And how tall is she? I have no idea. Maybe she's a clubfoot. No, impossible! Not everyone is deformed. She wore a lavender dress with a tiny print of yellow flowers buttoned up to the neck, with a tan lace collar, the dress sweeping down to her ankles, or maybe mid-calf. And I'll bet she wore boots, though I didn't see them. Her interests must be similar to mine, otherwise how could she know how to dress? It may just be her individual taste pitted against what's available in the shop windows, but I doubt it. Maybe she has dreams of traveling overseas, too; we could go together. I'll have to see. It would mean rearranging plans I have meticulously laid out. In my mind, I always travel alone and meet tall exotic western women on the boat or in cafes. We'll see. If she wants to go, we'll go.

I'll have to ask Hiromi tomorrow, no more delays. It's been over a week, yes, eight days, since I saw her. If I don't ask tomorrow, I'll have no self-respect left.

I had some heart-burn just now, a little round bubble of moistened, partially digested food. I can't remember what I had for dinner. I can't even remember what I ate an hour ago! I'm losing my mind. I am in love.

I've turned off the light. Here from my tatami I can see building tops and a faint red glow hanging in the middle of the street. The wind blows softly. It's a perfect night. The chill air pours through the window; I snuggle down under my futon. I'm content to lie here forever, looking out the window on this perfect night, fighting back all thoughts but those of her. If someone, a little black Kami or a Holy Ghost offered me the chance of forgoing the rest of my life to lie here, caught in this moment until time fades out, I would accept the offer.

Even now the moment is lasting an incredibly long time, the chill air, the rich blue darkness overlaid with a faint red, the breeze, the snuggling, existing on and on and on. The only thing threatening the peace is a little urge in my head looking for the little voice in my head saying, "Too perfect. Too much. Something will interrupt this flow soon. A bicycle horn, a thought... This can't last." And there, that very thought has come through, others hot on its heels, taking over, irrevocably changing this moment. And I think about the beautiful secretary, money, Hiroshi, the theater, resolving to fall asleep, to take these things down with me into my dreams.

"I'm sorry to bring you to such a shabby place..."

"Oh no, this is fine. Actually, I eat here quite often when I'm in a hurry, it's so close to the office. Ah, how is everything at the office for you?"

"Just fine. Oh, yes. I have been appointed to begin the department's English language study program, and I'm sure you know what that means."

She is looking at me with such a bright, hopeful look on her face. I can't help getting the impression that she is happy for herself somehow, as if my eventual promotion is in her best interest.

Our noodles have come with side dishes of small broiled fish and pickled cabbage, cucumber, radish and seaweed. We were fortunate to get a table against the side wall; others, mostly men, are beginning to line up against the wall in front of the serving counter, arranging their dishes in a space about six inches square on the ledge running down the wall. I hate eating while I'm standing, although I do it more often these days. I always seem to be in a hurry. You make your own little space, everyone eventually gets the same amount and you ignore those encroaching on either side, once you've examined what they're eating and what kind of shoes they wear, which should tell you all you want to know about them. I always pretend I'm eating on the deck of a ship looking out to sea. I don't know; it's the only other situation I can think of where I'd be standing up and eating. The others must be imagining, too. I wonder what? Well, maybe not. But they are making a place in their heads just like they make a place on the ledge.

That's the trick, when you want to get to know somebody. They all have boxes in their minds, each only so deep, so wide. You have to pick the right box, the personal box. I guess you could call it the memory box; that's all we have that's truly personal, after all. You've got to get into that box, then you can enter any of the other boxes you want, though exhausting that one box should take all your energy. I've never gotten there with another person, perhaps not even with myself. At least, I haven't exhausted my memory box, and I don't want to, not now. My immediate past is too stifling.

I must start right off with that box, with her. I must ask, 'What did you say to yourself when you were alone as a child?' Maybe we should eat bread with marmalade, very British. I'll wipe some marmalade on the back of her hand, her left hand, and take it up and lick it off before she can act.

It might work. I must think of more ways, have a barrage of methods to try, one after the other, until she lets me into that box. I will concentrate all my free time to developing the appropriate methodology. And I must be prepared to let her into my box: I will confess my deviousness.

There, Hiromi is slurping down the last of her noodles like a dockworker. She is the first door. How should I begin? Ah yes, the promotion.

"Well, I'm quite excited about learning English. It's been a life-long dream of mine. I've studied some in Second Form, but you know how that is."

"Oh yes, I studied English too, but I'm afraid I can't remember a word. Oh yes, 'ka-tu,' a cat. I'm afraid that's all that comes to mind. Terrible, isn't it?"

"Oh, your pronunciation is quite good and that's most important, isn't it? But you know, when I went to see Hirata, there was a new secretary there, I've never seen her before. She behaved quite oddly. I can't imagine where she came from."

"Ah, that was Miss Saito. Midori. A friend of mine went to school with her, though Midori was three grades ahead. She's older, you know."

I nod knowingly, hoping she'll go on.

"She was born and raised here in Tokyo. They say she lost her parents in the earthquake. Isn't that sad?"

I grunt. "Well, maybe that's why she behaves so oddly."

"Oh, do you think so? But she is very efficient, Hirata asked for her personally."

"Then her whole family's dead?"

"Oh no, she has a brother and sister living. I believe they're quite close, in an odd sort of way."

She has paused again, toying with me. She knows I want to know about her. Midori Saito, she said. I feel like she's eking out every bit of control she can gain over me with her knowledge. I can't seem too curious, or she'll figure out my motives and won't tell me a thing. But there, she's opening her mouth: she wants to keep me interested.

"Well, my mother says her family drew closer after the earthquake. Perhaps just the reminder of how transitory life is, the possibility of more loss, made them acutely aware of one another's presence. Still, I never heard any of them acted oddly."

Oh! She knows quite a bit about Saito, that's obvious from the corners of her mouth, turned up slightly as though she were suppressing a smile.

"No, you're quite right, that's no reason to behave oddly... At least it may not be Miss Saito's reason."

Now she's getting up! I feel like a bunraku puppet, but I have no choice, I must play it Hiromi's way. I get up as well; we stand hesitating by the table. Is it because of the crowd in the doorway or that on the sidewalk, or is Hiromi feeling guilty for thwarting my desires? I try to smile and nod for her to edge past the men in the doorway. As she goes, someone jostles her and I scowl, wanting to hit the man. Do I read too many Western romances or is it because she is my treasure chest, containing the precious knowledge of Miss Saito?

Her name is Midori. I know her name. Somehow, I feel very grateful toward Hiromi. I have a feeling she will lead me to Midori, if I just give her enough attention.

Out on the street, everyone has a purpose, an appointment. I alone seem not to care anymore. I have nowhere definite to go. I have just a face now, with a name, behind one of the doors on one of the floors of one of the buildings in this sprawling manic city. Is she painting her nails on her lunch break like an American actress? This is the vision I have of her, and I wouldn't be at all surprised if I were right.

Luckily, Hiromi seems to be as lost in her thoughts as I am. Before entering the building, she turns and gazes inquisitively at me.

Abruptly I say, "I enjoyed having lunch with you. Next time you are free, we should do it again."

"Oh, I am mostly free. I don't ever bring a lunch, and if I don't feel like battling the crowds, I just go to the park and skip lunch."

"Yes, a walk in the park would be relaxing, though there's no nutritional value in it."

She laughs at my little joke; she releases three little bursts of laughter, actually. Well then, we will control each other, I imagine, until we both get what we want.

Staying in that building the rest of the day was agony, though I'm not particularly happy to be in this box again, either. I actually bit the inside of my cheek with the effort it took to stay at my desk. God, how I wanted to run upstairs and just blurt out 'I love you!' and see what she'd do! But I can't afford to lose my job. In fact, I must climb as high as I can, maybe District Officer, or no, Personnel Manager, I'd be good at that. Then she wouldn't be stand-offish! What objections could she have? I'm rather handsome. My body isn't unattractive, is it? No muscles, really. Does she want a muscular man? It wouldn't hurt. I should get a dumbbell. But I have a good job and I'm a rather good dresser, I think.

Ah Midori! Midori, Midori, the unfathomable ocean! How I love you. It hurts my chest. I can't breathe, rolling off my futon and over the floor, eluded by comfort, hounded like the warrior Kumagai by a vision, a sprite, a fox-spirit whose beauty is like no woman I've ever seen. See, in the fetal position, the most comfortable, though my hip pokes heavily into the linoleum-covered concrete. Still, it's more comfortable than sleeping in a cold empty bed, more comfortable because of its discomfort. How it suits the mood of my soul.

I will always remain curled up in rigor mortise unless she, Midori, comes to smooth out my body, to touch it just once, like the Jesus cured with one touch: I just need her to bend over and touch me once.

I'm shivering. I can almost feel her touch. I can feel my golden rod reaching for the ceiling, calling out for her, for Midori, only Midori. She will be the first and last woman I ever make love to. I must win her or die.

Why do I waste my time on Hiromi? It's like trying to catch fish with my bare hands. She will not lead me to Midori because she has her own designs on me. I should just write Midori a note and tell her how much I love her, ask her to meet me in Ueno Park, her Mystery Man, her admirer. Does she have a soft spot for the Haiku? I will write one. Or does she like free style? I bet she knows English. Maybe a non-traditional Haiku, that's it:

> there is no one to see
> bare tree limbs moistened
> by the moon's milk

No, no, I'd better not include a poem. I'll just send her a note, terse, but vernacular. Has she no curiosity? She'll come. I'll tell her I'll die without her. Yes, women have big hearts.

"Why are you so curious about Miss Saito, anyway?"

"Well, I must admit, secrets, and especially odd people with secrets, have always held a certain fascination for me. I read Strange Tale novels. And she seems to be one of the strangest people I've met," I answer with all the sincerity I can muster.

"Oh, that she is. My friend Kazu says she is abnormally fond of her brother and that she and her sister make no secret of their dislike for one another. And as if that isn't strange enough, she collects cats, all kinds of cats. You know, little ceramic things. I don't think she has a real cat. Kazu and Midori have a friendship of sorts. She doesn't have any real friends. I believe she lives in Shibuya. And she even brags about how good her English is, how she loves Shakusuperu. Well, her boisterousness can easily be attributed to the fact that she has no parents. Kazu says she became strange out of sheer grief, which I guess is understandable. But still, it doesn't begin to explain everything."

"I heard that once, during Shogatzu, when everyone is supposed to be tranquil to usher in the New Year, she purposefully dumped a cup of hot sake in her sister's lap! That's rather strange, don't you think? Being an orphan should have drawn her closer to her sister."

Hiromi is getting quite excited about all this, almost malicious. Yes, she understands everything that's going on and will paint the worst picture she can. Hah! If only she knew how much more I love Midori, hearing of these odd happenings.

"Don't you agree?" Hiromi pouts, as if out of laziness I had forgotten my lines.

"Oh, unquestionably. It is quite curious behavior. But perhaps it is the brother's fault, perhaps he has pitted the one against the other. Families, especially bereaved families, are very strange things, you know."

"Oh, but that is not the case here. It is a constant source of sorrow to the brother, that such enmity lie between his sisters. Really, it seems he loves them both equally. It is Midori's conniving that serves to set them all apart, trying to win all his affection, even that bit dedicated to Aoi. Aoi is the other sister, you know."

"What are their ages? Perhaps, if they were close in age, their contention could be viewed as nothing more than a spat between siblings," I say, affecting a good natured unwillingness to find fault in another, an effort which is physically beginning to tire me.

"How can you say that? You have several siblings yourself. The closer siblings are in age..."

"How do you know I have siblings?" I demand vehemently. But she's not shaken at all; rather, she responds with an air of condescension.

"I am the secretary of our office, aren't I? I must type and preserve everyone's file. That's how I know about you, and that's how Kazu knows about Midori, at least the background information."

"And do you know how close I am to my brother?" I can't help spitting at her. I am very perturbed.

"Of course not. The file just says you have a brother and a sister, 23 and 21 in age, respectively."

Ah, then she still doesn't know about their deformities. It's certainly not something I put down on the Personnel Information sheet. Good. Suddenly I feel quite light, gleeful. She knows nothing of me, knows next to nothing about Midori. I don't want anyone to know her secrets but me. Really, Hiromi is a sneak and a gossip, fueling her petty daydreams with the imagined truths of other's lives. I should never have come to lunch with her again. It is too much of a commitment. Heavens, my coworkers may think I'm interested in her! I should have just sent the letter as I had promised myself. Oh, what a worm I am. Perhaps I don't deserve a woman like Midori.

"Mr. Inagaki, is the eel all right?" Hiromi asks.

"The eel? Yes, no, the eel is fine, don't you like it?" I answer confusedly, my thoughts interrupted. And there, she's giggling a little. What's so funny?

"Miss Meguro, what is it?" Again I can't hide my angst.

"Ah, nothing, nothing! The eel is delicious." She's obviously trying to keep from hysterics. What's so damn funny? Well, forget about her, let her get all the amusement she can from my wretchedness. What is that? Ah, a cockroach has jumped off the table onto the floor. I shoot out my foot and smash it, rubbing the sole of my shoe back and forth against the warped boards. I look up with satisfaction. I see Hiromi has stopped smiling. Good. Her face seems to say, 'Really, I can't understand you!' No, she can't. No one can.

"I have learned from a coworker that you are originally from Fukushima Prefecture, and as that is my home prefecture, too, I am very curious to find out whether I know any of your relations. There are not many Tokyoites from Fukushima-ken, eh? Perhaps we could share a cup of tea after office hours one day and see if there are some hidden friends we have in common. You may find it odd that a stranger has taken the liberty to write you a letter. Our secretary mentioned that you, too, are from Fukushima. Really, it is not odd at all for countrymen to meet and discuss their home province. Tu Fu would always converse with anyone from his home province.

"If you are curious to see what I look like—if you can't remember me from among the other workers trooping in and out of Mr. Hirata's office—I believe there is a photograph in my Personnel File.

"If you have any interest in a brief meeting, please take the liberty to determine the time and place. Of course, we could meet outside the building, if you like. Well, let it be according to your convenience. I hope you do not mind responding through the office mail. This fifth day of the eleventh month. Inagaki Keizo."

It sounds horrid, but it will have to do. I've worked it and reworked it. Look, I have splashed ink on my futon, but I leave it there. I hope it sinks in and stains, in memory of my first letter. Such a commitment will certainly vouchsafe more letter-writing nights like this. I wish I could be more frank; I long to unwrap my heart. But soon, soon! I can tell. I know she will love me as I love her.

No, it's not her that makes me feel so sad tonight, not the prospect of her refusal. Everyone is bored and therefore curious, at least. No, it's something else. I feel oppressed by this room, by my background, by my status. I am a minnow in the ocean. I have done nothing. What could I do, burdened with such a family? Even if I work very hard from this point on, I won't get very far. People must be saying, "He is a chrysanthemum," blooming years after the rest. If only they knew the load I've had to carry! Literally, I just barely escaped carrying loads as a laborer or a farmer. But will they say, "What a great thing you have done, how far you have come from the rice paddies of Fukushima?" No, they will say, "He is the oldest, he should go the farthest."

I should have joined an acting troupe as soon as I reached Tokyo, then I'd be on stage right now, playing Hamlet or Doctor Faustus. My calling is to be an actor, but no, fate would conspire against my native talent. How can I become an actor when my parents expect money each week? Greatness takes time and suffering, and I could have bore it well if I were on my own. But no, how can I go on this way? It is all past now. There is still a chance, I say, to achieve everything, but I don't believe it. Ha-mu-re-tu! Just like Hamlet. I am what I do. If I do nothing...but this letter! It will be my first step on the road of a thousand miles!

I can't seem to feel anything, dangling here from this strap. Everything seems the same—the smell of electricity still nauseates me—all the faces are blank or frowning, as usual. But I am not anxious or happy or depressed—I can't think or feel. It's been like this all day. I somehow expected to be dancing, or at least glowing inside. Well, the shock just hasn't worn off. I can barely remember the note. How short it was! Something like, "Mr. Inagaki: I think meeting is a good idea. Hibiya Park, Sunday, 2:00pm? If this time and place is acceptable, then I shall expect to see you there, at the western entrance. Otherwise, you can contact me again in the same manner. This seventh day of the eleventh month, Saito Midori."

I've got it here in my pocket. Yes, that's exactly what it says. I've memorized each syllable. Well, it was good she waited a day to respond. If she had sent word to me on Thursday, I would have gone crazy trying to keep myself from running upstairs to peek at her; now I have only a day and a half to wait. I'll go into the office early on Saturday then read Western plays for the rest of the day. On Sunday I'll have a good breakfast out and spend the rest of the morning getting ready. Perhaps I should buy a new shirt to go with my gray flannel slacks. I'll wear the tweed jacket and the "spy" overcoat. Maybe I should scout the area tomorrow to find a cozy kissaten coffee shop. We'll be so thoroughly chilled from our walk, we'll stop for a coffee and some cake; it'll be romantic, dimly lit. I'll have to find one that plays western music. As we listen to Hoagy

Carmichael I'll ask her all about her life. Maybe, clutching her hand over the table, I'll tell her how much I love her.

Oh god, it will be so good, everything, I'll make sure it's perfect. I cannot wait that long. I'll ask her to meet me...what? Did she just say Shibuya next stop? Damn. That must be Shinjuku Gyoen to the left. I've missed my stop. Damn! I could stay on the Yamanote Line and circle around to Hibiya, or get off and hail a cab. Why not? I'll stay on and loop around. When everything's arranged I'll rest easier.

Is she late on purpose? Well, maybe she's not late yet, I don't have a watch. I've got to get a watch, a Swiss watch. Will she be taking a cab or walking? The sun is almost hot compared to the last few days. I could take my overcoat off. It won't be a long walk for her from the station, it's so close.

There she is! She looks so...so odd, yet beautiful and stylish. She's not smiling, though she's spotted me. I begin to walk over to her. Yes, now I see her features more clearly, she's curious, expectant, with two fine creases across her brow.

"Miss Saito. I'm very glad to meet you. I'm Inagaki."

"Mr. Inagaki. Yes, I thought so. I'm very glad to meet you," she says perfunctorily. She's terrifically preoccupied, like a cat following flies, darting looks from side to side. I doubt whether she's really took in what I look like. A swell of frustration is making itself felt in my solar plexus, as if I've failed once again to make contact with her, though her body is right here in front of me.

I, too, look around, for lack of any appropriate words to say, and now I can feel her looking at the side of my face. I turn slowly. Her gaze is sweeping my form from head to toe, as a ship's radar monitors the water. I can feel my cheeks reddening. I seem so incredibly vulnerable before this self-possessed woman. I can't stand anymore.

"Ah, well, would you like to stroll through the park for awhile? It seems there are a few trees with color on them yet," I stammer. What is she thinking?

"Oh, let's do that," she agrees, making me feel as though it were her suggestion. She gives her scarf a definitive toss over her shoulder.

It feels good to walk; my muscles are slackening with the rhythm. I've consciously fallen in step with her. Those boots she's wearing, they're rather old fashioned, the kind that button up. But on her legs and calves they are made very fashionable, classic. There, that lady passing by in a kimono, she's noticed them, too. But Miss Saito walks so nicely! It's difficult to remain in step with her as she is neither striding nor mincing. She seems to be placing her toes down on the pathway first, as if testing its solidity then allowing the heel to settle for a moment. This is incredibly strange, like a dream in which trees begin to move, startling the little birds from their nests. They fly around your head pulling tufts of hair out with their beaks.

I cannot believe it is Miss Saito walking next to me. I think we should stop and talk, I need to talk to make it more real, to stop these queer thoughts. Thank heavens, there's a bench under that maple.

"Let's sit down for a minute, do you want to?" My steps are already heading for the bench. In answer, she makes a humming noise through her nose. I hope she's not thinking strange things about me. I pull out my handkerchief, sit down, and spread it out beside me. She suddenly smiles at this gesture, looking warmly into my eyes. She is stunningly beautiful, yet it seems I have a chance.

"You know, I feel as though I've seen you before, though I am from Iwaki. Weren't your people originally from Koriyama? It's just a guess. It gives me the most peculiar feeling."

"Well, you looked at my file, didn't you? You got it from Hiromi? My picture is in the file."

"No, no, I mean before that. Besides, that picture doesn't look like you at all. Really, you look much handsomer in person, and more humane."

She is looking at me intensely and I realize now, behind the quiet self-possession, is a beggar eyeing a bowl of millet, unsavory as it may seem to one well-fed. If it weren't so absurd, I would swear that she has just made up her mind to be my lover.

But I'm imagining it, perhaps; wishful thinking. Yet surely I'm not bad looking. An interesting man, one looking to be personal, is undoubtedly hard to find. Or perhaps she's done this before. Perhaps she takes a lover at each new season. No, don't think that way! She's not that kind. I don't know who she is, but she's not like that.

"It's cold."

"Isn't it?"

She is lost in thought. I, too, seem unable to shake myself from the constant chatter in my brain. A double pane of glass our brains, mine and hers, separating us from each other. How odd that I can sink further into myself with her simply sitting next to me. But I feel sad. Sinking into myself is not at all what I wanted. I can feel us, the two of us, sitting like this, together but eternally separated. It feels very real, like a dream too real to be true.

I don't want to feel this way. A love, an unmatched love and titillating passion, that is what I want, to possess every bit of her, nothing held back! She has sat with others in this comfortable isolation, but not with me! I am different, truly different; she has never met a man like me before. And when I break this glass barrier and another threatens to ease up from our feet as in a weird world of paper leaves and steel trunks, wire stems and clay blossoms, I will smash it down again. Because I love her. I love her now more than ever.

I see her staring ahead, catatonic, maybe envisioning us together, maybe thinking of her past, drifting far out into midstream like a toy boat one grabs at as it drifts just beyond reach, bobbing imperceptibly further away with each renewed stretch of one's arm. What can I do or say? I must grab her mind somehow.

"Are you thinking of your brother?" I say evenly, almost coldly, understanding with the last syllable that I have hurt her, have gone too far.

"Who told you about my brother?" she hisses, stunned, as if I had, out of the blue, struck her full force in the face. She seems to want to stand up and flee or hit me back with something tangible.

"Midori. Forgive me. I have no right to ask you about your brother. It's just that you were so far away. I wanted to startle you."

"No, but who told you about my brother? You obviously know quite a lot. Hiromi? What did she say? She likes you, you know. She would lie, would say anything. What did she say? You must tell me, word for word. How the hell did she hear about my brother? It must be that Kazu. She is two-faced. All women are two-faced! And most men, too. What right have you…"

"My brother is retarded and my sister is a club-foot!" I blurt out, horrified and expectant.

Her face is going through the strangest contortions! The anger is replaced by shock, the shock by pity, then confusion and consternation. I can't say more; it's already more than I've told anybody. She leans a little closer and says, "I'm sorry to hear that, I am. Have you told me this because of what you said about my brother? But there's nothing strange about my brother, he's perfectly normal, and so is my love for him. He loves me too. Is that odd? Did Hiromi say we were odd? Please tell me."

"Don't be sorry. They're quite happy, actually, happier than I am, it's just that I've never told anyone. But Hiromi? No, she said something like, 'She's too close to her brother. She's strange. Her family is strange.' That's all. I thought it was wonderful, intriguing. And I know Hiromi. Believe me. I don't accept half of what comes out of her mouth. Listen, don't be upset. You're trying not to cry, aren't you? I'm sorry, please, don't be upset. I'm sure your brother is a wonderful man. I'd like to meet him. Are you crying because of him?"

"No, no, it's not that. I just feel so peculiar, emotional, I don't know why. I don't care what people say, really. I'm just so emotional right now; I don't know why I'm crying."

"Listen. We'll go get some tea. I know a nice place near here. Do you mind walking? Look. We've missed the sunset. Would you take my arm?"

"Yes, I would like some tea. It's too cold out here, and so dark. I'm fine now, I'm sorry I lost control."

"Don't ever be. Your honesty means more to me than I could ever explain."

"I'm usually quite reserved."

The wind whips her skirt around her lace-up boots. Although she seems quite tired, she is still placing her foot down toes first. In the chill air, the smell of burning pine seems to travel undiminished, as though a ring of fire were surrounding us. I am suddenly jerked by a strong shiver running up my spine; it is the impact of a tiny voice saying, "My, what a strange dream this is!"

I'm going to Midori's house today. She and her brother and sister all share a house, rebuilt on the original site after the fire, south of Yoyogi Park, in Shibuya-ku.

I am going to see my beloved again. I can see her lips in my mind's eye, unsmiling yet not severe. Whenever I try to conjure up the rest of her I can't, but sometimes she appears unsolicited, looking as she did that first night, walking toward me at the entrance of the park. It is maddening not to be able to see her face in my mind. I always thought that when you really loved someone, you had the vision of them before your eyes constantly. Am I not in love? No, I am sure this must be real love, not some romantic notion.

Something special will happen today, I can just feel it. Perhaps she has arranged for us to have the house to ourselves. It is surely time. If she does not allow me to touch her body soon, mine will explode. She must be feeling the same way.

It's nothing she said, specifically, about today being special. We've been dating for four months, I think; let me count it up. After we had tea that first night, we've had lunch many times, and I've taken her out for dinner, formally, at least a dozen times. Last week we lunched in the park near the office, nibbling delicacies from stacking lacquered boxes she prepared. She invited me then. It was so cold! How strange when the sun is so bright it hurts your eyes, yet the air is so cold it chills your bones. On the park bench she said, "I have arranged something for this Sunday, at my house. Can you come?" Yes, she said "arranged." That's what has led me to believe it will be today.

Oh, god, how I want to touch her! The curve between my thumb and forefinger would fit so nicely around the back of her neck. I will trace her instep with my thumbnail, and when I have touched everything I will fill her and she will scream my name. I can hear her now, gasping, demanding, "Keizo!"

I will clean my nails.

"Midori-chan!" I yell hopefully over the wooden fence in front of her house. All these old houses are hidden by tall wooden fences to create the sense of an isolated garden in the front. Only the green tiles of the inverted triangle-shaped roofs are visible from the street. All down the length of the lane the houses are lined with the same wood, perhaps from the same forest, six feet high and a mellow worn brown like the curved wooden comb belonging to my grandmother.

"Keizo-chan?" she calls back softly. She is so close! She's been waiting. The wooden gate opens, and there she stands in a kimono, her hair swept up and her face painted white! A tanuki could run at me and bite my calf and I could not be more surprised. Her expression is patient, but I can feel her excitement. The colors of her kimono are so odd - muted lavender with a print of tiny purple mountain flowers, colors for an old woman. And yet the obi! A sunset pattern done in orange and yellow with a grass green cord. It is perfect for her, perfect! Not a blending, but a stark division of old and new, a schism. Her eyes are laughing at me.

"Have you never seen a kimono or is this one just terribly distasteful?"

"No. Yes! It's great! Too beautiful, really."

"Well, Come in!"

She turns and minces across the garden's stone pathway leading to the raised wooden porch where the shoe rack and slippers wait. I feel like I am observing every little thing, causing time to slow down, drifting into the seconds it takes to lift a foot and place it twelve inches ahead. With incredible contentment I climb the steps, turning softly to the right to see the slippers and shoes lined up neatly on the rack as it was at my house when I was a boy. You could tell who was in the house by the shoes on the rack. I feel giddy. The slippers are like fruit in the market: which pair shall I choose? Black is for men and would match my suit, but I find myself reaching for the blue pair with small white cherry blossoms. I feel free.

She slides the door open and we enter a narrow hallway of wood.

"Please, to the right. We will sit in the family room. The kotatsu is warm." She slides the shoji open.

Something is very wrong. I suddenly feel trapped, though I'm still moving. The atmosphere has jelled. There is a man, handsome, and a woman. Both are sitting around the kotatsu stove.

I will not be making love to her. I can't move.

"Please enter, sit down," Midori's voice wafts to me from behind. I step inside and she turns ceremoniously and slides the shoji shut. Now she moves around me, eying the man intensely. Becoming even more formal, she announces me.

"This is Inagaki Keizo, we are coworkers."

"Ah, Inagaki-san. Please. It is good to meet you. I am Tatsuo," the man says warmly as he sweeps his arm out to the left, indicating that I should sit next to him.

"Ah, Inagaki-san, pleased to meet you, I am Aoi," the woman says, bowing her head.

I move to the kotastu and look back at Midori as I sit. Her head is down, her bangs casting a shadow over her face. She waits for me to sit first. I slip my legs down into the hole in the floor cradling the tiny wood-burning stove. I suddenly feel as if we are all moths clamoring for our deaths. I want to laugh. Midori sits next to Aoi, her right foot coming to rest on top of mine. Eerily the warmth from the kotatsu moves up my calves and my torso shivers; she's not going to move her foot!

"Would you like some tea?" Aoi asks pleasantly.

"Ah," I nod. She begins to pour for us all.

Each cup is different, undoubtedly the cup each is habituated to using. Mine is a light sea-green color, cracked glaze style, man-size. Her father's perhaps?

"You admire the cup? It was my father's. Not his everyday one; he only used it when guests came," Tastuo says.

"Exquisite" is all I can manage to say. Tatsuo's tone is...well, not hostile. No. Testing. He's examining me. I feel as though I have been dropped from an air balloon into a maze that only these three know how to run.

"This one he used every day," he says, slowly rotating his own cup with his fingertips. It has an uneven brown glaze, like the seaside dirt in Fukushima. Of course Tatsuo would use it. He is an intriguing man, a difficult man. He looks more like Aoi, their foreheads slope a bit. Is it the mother's or the father's influence?

"Please, help yourself," Aoi prompts, breaking the lull like a tree limb crashing into a pond. She is hard. Tea-drinking snacks are in the center of the table: deep-fried peas, barbecued eel, pickled radishes, cakes of azuki bean jelly, sugar cookies from Denmark. What an odd assortment. They are waiting on me. I take a few peas and crunch on them miserably. Midori stifles a giggle.

"Hehh. Are you laughing at my snacks?" Aoi is agitated.

"Midori, are you mocking the snacks of our family?" Tatsuo asks and starts laughing. Midori laughs harder. Aoi sits quietly, her face now completely composed. Tatsuo and Midori are really having a good laugh. I am chuckling.

"Have you two been drinking already?" I tease them, looking from one to the other.

"Yes, we have been drinking a lot. Drinking since we were three. Usually drinking together. But Aoi never becomes inebriated," Tatsuo says half laughing.

"I do drink," Aoi insists, looking me straight in the eye.

"Oh, yes, but you only drink whiskey!" Midori squeals, sending her and Tatsuo off on another laughing jag. I cannot understand this humor and I feel left out, jealous of Tatsuo. Aoi and I exchange glances, mine quizzical, hers disgusted. Tatsuo and Midori are now making little grunting and sighing sounds, slowing down. Aoi very slowly and elegantly reaches for the teapot, deftly moves upward until she is standing and leaves the room. Tatsuo and Midori settle down. Midori looks over at me and smiles prettily, as if she had just realized I was still there. Sensing my puzzlement, she says, "We laugh so we don't cry."

"No. We laugh in order to cry," Tatsuo says almost solemnly. I think they are thinking about their family's tragedy. There is something disturbing about their intimacy.

Aoi returns with the teapot. Her movements are too precise to be graceful. It's incredibly still. I don't know what anyone is thinking. Aoi pours tea all around. It seems Tatsuo's words are going round and round in the upper reaches of the room like a butterfly looking for a way out: we laugh in order to cry, to cry, to cry... I shudder.

"Are you chilly?" Aoi bends forward and asks, glancing swiftly at Midori as if to chastise her for failing to see to the comfort of her guest.

"Ah, no, thank you..." I answer, but I feel everyone waiting for me to explain my shudder. Was it that noticeable? "I thought I saw a butterfly. Just imagining things," I venture.

"No, there are many butterflies around here, inside the house as well," Tatsuo says, the gleam in his eye lighting up again.

"Yes, they wound themselves trying to find a way out. It takes them a long time to die. I find them and put them outside so they can at least die where they want to be," Midori says sadly.

"A blessing is the death that brings fulfillment of desire," Tatsuo says softly.

"It's disgusting. I would never touch a butterfly," Aoi says with startling vehemence.

"You never do, not even when they land on your nose!" Tatsuo teases. "Aoi doesn't deal with messy things that are hard to corner," he laughs.

Aoi dismisses him with a short gesture and continues. "It has gotten so one can't walk in the garden. They approach from behind and leave a legacy of powder staining one's clothes. And if one has the misfortune of brushing one with the back of the hand, the stain won't even wash off with soap."

"I think it would be lovely to have a kimono colored with butterfly powder stains. But it would be awfully cruel to the butterflies. I have never understood people who enjoy hanging dead butterflies on their walls," Midori states unequivocally.

"I'm personally quite fond of butterflies." I find myself speaking for no reason. "Once, in my landlord's garden last spring I saw two simple yellow butterflies joined back to back on a leaf. They stayed that way for the longest time. I couldn't stand it, so I approached, thinking to separate them, but they wouldn't move. So I shook the stem and they flew up, still connected, and floated over the wall. I looked over and saw they had landed by the side of the road, still connected. Then a young man rode by on a bicycle and crushed them. It seemed one of them might still be moving, but it could have been the breeze."

Everyone is looking at me. I look at Tatsuo and our eyes lock. It's as if he is seeing me for the first time. I have solidified before his eyes. In his gaze are remnants of sorrow and hope, like an offer of friendship. Finally, Aoi breaks the silence.

"Would you care to see the house? It is modest but done in the old style. It looks very much like the house we were children in."

"Yes, please," I answer, looking at Midori to see if she would show me around.

"You'll forgive me if I don't show you the garden?" Aoi says politely, nodding her head to the right with a stiff jerk.

"Of course," I nod to her. She gets to her knees then stands without looking around, walks straight to the shoji, slides it open and walks out.

I follow her. I feel that we are to leave Midori and Tatsuo together for a while more than tour the house.

Tatsuo is in there, talking to Midori. I wonder where Aoi went? I was hoping Midori would come out to the garden, knowing that Aoi would not show me around. How long am I to stay here waiting like a stray rooster? I feel like I have been here for days. My mind wanders, and I see myself on stage. I'm playing some Western role, stomping and pleading, making wild gestures with my arms. Midori is in the audience admiring me, for once awestruck. I leave the stage when the curtain drops, trembling, groping my way to my dressing room. There is Midori outside the door, waiting. She falls into my arms; I am aflame.

I've got to stop thinking like this. Why am I still sitting here? Does she have any intention at all of being my lover? But then what am I doing here? Why would she toy with me? They're probably all huddled together, deciding whether they'll let their dear Midori sleep with an outsider. Really. I am getting angry. I don't have to put up with this! I will be a great actor someday. I don't have to put up with this! I'll just go now, turn on my heels and leave. Oh, but I must say good-bye. What would Tatsuo think? Oh damn it. I'll go inside. I'll be strong with Midori. Her family has opened up to me. I don't need to be so polite.

"Kei-zo! Oh Keiyyy-zo!"

I whirl around and there she is, playfully calling my name. My breath catches, I am so glad to see her! She is beautiful.

"Hi," is all I can say. She traipses up to me like a child, her eyes sparkling as if waiting for a surprise.

"So she's left you out here on your own, eh? She really is adamant about her dislike of insects, it's not just rudeness. What do you think of our garden?"

"It's beautiful. Who tends it?"

"Tatsuo and I do on the weekends. Sometimes we have a gardener in, but Tatsuo won't let anyone else touch his cherry trees. He's raised them from saplings. The bonsai are his as well, though he doesn't have the time to spend on them."

"What is Tatsuo's occupation?"

"He is a stage designer for the Kabuki Theater. He does very well. Actually, he's an artist and a scholar. He just does the stage design for money because it is fairly undemanding. Someday you must see his work."

"Well, it must be hard to find someone who lives up to his expectations," I throw out, immediately feeling bad. What is wrong with me?

"My brother's expectations are not my major concern," she says coolly. "I am concerned with what is meaningful to me."

"You haven't found anything yet?" I ask softly.

She turns her head and stares at the garden wall as though it were a vast unbroken horizon. Midori. What does she want? Yes, and she was so happy just a moment ago. What was she so thrilled about?

I have to get out of here. I reach out and take her arm, a little too forcefully. It feels good.

"Shall we go have dinner somewhere?"

"Where can we go? Should I change out of the kimono?"

"It's been hours. You must be uncomfortable. Well yes, go and change. I can sit with your brother and sister. They won't mind, will they?"

"Aoi is resting, and Tatsuo... No, let's just go. I will get my purse."

"Shouldn't I say good-bye?" I'm somewhat overawed at this change in events.

"I'll be right back," she whispers and turning away, glides silently up to the door and disappears.

Suddenly I feel chilled and alone. The sun has just dipped behind the roof's ridgepole.

I think this is her favorite kissaten, right off of Shibuya station. She sits with her tea and biscuits, watching the people come and go, lost in thought. I can look at her all I want because I know she can't feel my eyes when she is so absorbed. I think her eyes are beautiful. Everything about her is beautiful. I can see her neck sweeping out of the back of her kimono. Such a graceful line. My mind follows the flesh down her back, along her spine: such creamy flesh! I need to pull her to me and put my mouth on her body.

At the same time, it occurs to me that I haven't the faintest idea who she is. This thought, the contrariness of it, the wrongness of it, makes my mouth ache more. I know what I need to know. This is not some kind of joke. There is no other woman on earth, as far as I'm concerned. I need Midori. I need to know what will bring her to me.

"Midori," I say, pulling her gaze from the people milling about the café front to my face. "Are you hungry?"

"No, I'm fine." She looks at me curiously. I think she must know what a hungry fox I am for her flesh. She begins to smile. I take her hand; it is too much for me. I am aroused more than if I were touched down there. I see her shiver.

"What can I do for you?" I whisper. She doesn't answer, but keeps staring at me, as though she is trying to decide something. Oh, it is to determine if I can wait. Oh yes, I can wait. What else is there? Of course she cannot give herself to me; not now, not like this.

"I should go home," she says with fatigue in her voice. Hearing this statement is like someone turning off the lights, although I expected it, it must be this way.

"I will take you back. Should we ride the train or take a taxi?"

"The train is fine. I like the train."

"The smell nauseates me most mornings when I'm riding to work."

"Oh, is it so? It smells like everything new in the world."

On the train, I ask her if I can see her every night. She laughs and says of course, every moment. 'We will live together, so we won't miss each other!' she says. She's just kidding around. She doesn't know she has put into words my heart's desire.

Tatsuo is awake when we get to the house. Midori knows because the lights in the dining room are on. Midori asks me in for a little sake and I agree. Tatsuo nods in acknowledgment of our arrival, managing the barest of smiles. We sit and slide our legs down into the kotatsu. The temperature is perfect. It reminds me of my home in Fukushima. There are little broiled fish, pickles, and a flask of warm sake. I could cry.

Tatsuo seems to know what I am thinking because he asks me about my family. Without pausing, I tell him about Aiko, her clubfoot, her lucky marriage to a farmer from a good family. I talk about Hiro'chan, how he is not smart but has a good occupation that brings in a little money. Father, high school teacher. Mother, selfless housewife.

Through all this, Tatsuo only breaks eye contact with me once to glance at Midori, who raises her eyebrows as if to say, 'I don't know why he is telling you all this. He is a frank person.'

Tatsuo begins to talk when I have finished. He speaks slowly, methodically. He describes being alone with his two sisters and how his father worked in the theater. He elaborates on the beauty of Kabuki, the joy he feels being able to work in the theater himself, what a blessing his life has been, overall. He missed having a child, a wife, but it must have been in the stars. Given the chance, he would have been good at both, he feels.

He speaks from a vast knowledge and a mild view of life. His voice is strong and slow, filled with the patient curiosity of a powerful cat. He is content. He has desires he has achieved and those he looks forward to.

I feel respect and love for him. I want to know him better.

As he talks, it quietly dawns on me that I am no match for his sister. I have an urge to push myself up to my feet, explain that I am in the wrong place, thank him for his hospitality, and leave. Really, I am close to it, but my baser desires hold sway.

We sit in silence a little longer, and then I say I must be going. He does not offer more sake, and Midori gets to her feet. Tatsuo's eyes find mine and we look at each other. Then I smile and stand, leaving him sitting with his legs still tucked in the kotatsu.

"Tatsuo-san. Thank you for opening your home to me. I have great regard for your family," I say. I bow to him.

"Heh. Please come again," he says and then looks away. I follow Midori out.

It is many months since that night with Tatsuo. I have only seen him briefly since then. I asked Midori to marry me. She refused. "For now," she said, "I cannot." "Is it Tatsuo?" I had asked. She looked askance and said I questioned her too much. I said I wouldn't push. I asked her to pillow with me, some weeks later. We met at the park. We kissed for quite awhile and as usual, I was beside myself. Then she said yes. I am going to meet her at Shibuya station. I have a reservation at a hotel near the heart of the city, a nice hotel with a reputation for helping out young lovers in need of discretion.

I am on the train going to meet her and I feel sick. I can't parcel out all these conflicting emotions. I'm thinking she's done this before. I could not be the first. Is that why she won't marry me? I got a promotion at work, not much, but enough to fix my little place up, which she has still never seen. It's as if she doesn't want to get to know me too intimately. I think I'm in line for another promotion. They really like me in my office. I've been working hard ever since I met Midori. My superiors have noticed my potential. Appreciation at work is a necessity that does not feed my soul.

I am going to have sex with Midori. I think about resting my face on her breasts when we are exhausted. I think about her buttocks. Is it my clothes that are not right? I have a hair growing out of my cheek from a strange place. Once again I have forgotten to pay attention to eliminating it. Oh, how nauseating.

Walking to the station tonight, there were snails all over the sidewalk, all crushed to death. Has it been raining? How could I not have noticed? I couldn't step on the snails, couldn't abide the feel of them under my heels or the sight of their soft little bodies staining the sidewalk. I know how weak this is. I can only hope no one saw me dance around their dead bodies. They just make me sick.

Tonight I will have more ecstasy than I have ever known in my life, but something is wrong. You will have more ecstasy than you have ever known! You have lived for this moment. What is wrong with you! Take a breath, you idiot. Suddenly, all I can see is that idiot brother of mine grinning and saying, "Ma! Ma!"

Oh, an excellent plan. Think of your brother, destroy everything. Think of Midori! Is she going through the same thing? This is not romantic.

Panic seizes me. I'm going to get off the train. I'm going to vomit. I must get some air, walk around. And if I am late? She might not sleep with me. She'll be angry. What? Was that a bird outside the window? Train's going too fast. Birds can't fly that fast. Fly at night. Too late for insects. Who cares what it was?

I went to the hotel last night to make sure it was alright. Such a strange place! The place seemed modern. Some kind of red material draped over everything, lots of angles and black wood. I love places like that, but it doesn't feel right now, thinking back on it. Garish. What if Midori thinks it's tasteless? I should have picked a traditional place.

No. That would be worse. Well, red it is. So Chinese, though. What? Who cares where we are?

I remember a dream I had, was it last night? I was coming out of work, it was crowded, people everywhere, but I noticed a girl from another land, maybe from China; she had smiling eyes, and I felt compelled to go over to her. I was chasing her in the crowd and she was gone from sight, but I felt her, just ahead, just out of reach, when two big mean looking guys pulled me aside, leering into my face as though they were going to bash my head in. I struggled ferociously, but I was losing...

It's Shibuya station. I can't stop trembling. Oh how noxious I am, this is absurd! I will have to leave if I can't calm down. The train is stopping. I search the platform.

She's there, walking along the platform instead of waiting at the coffee house. She must be late, too. So, a different rendezvous point, I'll run after her, no problem. Okay. What a face. What a beautiful woman. She's mine. I'm going to take her in about 60 minutes. Again and again. I have certainly practiced enough. I'll see how many times I can manage. I will let no thought intrude. She hasn't seen me.

I jump off the train and run after her. Is she going to the kissaten or running away? I never know where I stand.

I was going to surprise her, but she turns and sees me coming. Is it her sixth sense? Our eyes meet and suddenly we both have the same secret. She is smiling. I feel myself grinning, thinking, "You should smile. I am going to make you a very happy woman tonight." I lean over and press my hands softly against her upturned face. I glance around quickly. No one is watching. I let my hands travel down to her breasts. I squeeze them lightly and wrap her in my arms for a moment, then let her go. She rebounds to a distance further than need be, but I can see from the flush in her cheeks that she liked it.

I play along, keeping my distance as I guide her the two blocks to the hotel. We are so clandestine. Before we go in, I see a scarf tucked into her coat collar. I pull it up and arrange it around her face so she can't be seen clearly. She blushes. I push the doors open and we enter.

Is this the same place? It does seem garish, painfully so. I'm glad I rearranged the check-in process. I go to the front desk and ask for room number 22. I get the key and we head up the stairs, Midori leading the way. I can see her haunches alternate with each lithe step. I'm going to touch her there, I'm going to see the flesh I have watched moving beneath her clothing, for how many months? This is it.

"Keizo-chan?" Midori says, turning to look back at me. I am quite shocked by the sound of her voice. I almost feel like saying 'no talking!' I don't answer. We walk down the hall to number 22.

"It's right here," I say, as if this is the answer to my name, and open the door quickly. She steps inside to see a four poster bed, raised high off the ground, with red covers and odd paintings on the walls. I look to the right and see the bathroom door; I arranged for a room with a private bath. A chandelier hangs from the ceiling. A straight-backed chair with a brocade cushion stands in the corner.

This place is great. I feel like someone else, which is just what I wanted. I am someone else. I can do anything.

"Keizo," Midori says again. She does not seem to need an answer, as though she is saying my name to reassure herself. I walk up behind her, put my arms around her waist and just breathe in her smell. I am so far away from everything. I begin to squeeze her.

"I'm going to," she doesn't finish her sentence, she is anxious. I'm glad she is afraid.

"Go, go!" I laugh and sit down on the bed. I watch her disappear into the bathroom. I take a bottle of American whiskey from my coat pocket. It is very expensive. Maybe I'll always drink this. I feel so alive right now. I take a quick drink and wince from the alcohol burn in my throat. I bend over, untie my shoes and slip them off. I take off my coat. I undo my shirt. Maybe I should get all the way undressed, but she comes out of the bathroom, riveting my attention.

She is only wearing a slip. She does not seem the same. She does not seem apprehensive. The whiskey is making me brave. I walk over to her and push her breasts up with my hands. She stands there. I step behind her and squeeze them again, playing with her nipples with my middle fingers while I gently bite the back of her neck. My golden rod is rearing up, its thick head scenting the hunt like a great beast. I push it into her buttocks so she can feel what she has done to me. She shivers and sighs.

I don't even want to take my pants off. I'm going to make this last forever. Fifty thousand years of waiting. I release her, step to the front again, lead her over to the bed and take the whiskey out. I offer her a drink and she tips the bottle back; a little whiskey runs out of the corner of her mouth. I act as though I am going to lick it off her face, but she pulls her fist up and wipes it away herself, then laughs. I laugh too. I have no idea who I am, no idea who this woman is, but I already know her body.

Let me see what I know.

I take off my shirt and pants, leaving my shorts on. I tip her back on the bed and begin with her feet. They are so tiny and cold! I rub them between my hands and feel my rod flare again. I reach over and switch on a little table lamp by the bed. I run my hands up her calves and half way up her thighs then I stop. I straighten up and look into her eyes. She is hungry too. Good, I am doing it right. She suddenly reaches out and grabs for my rod, bumping it with her hand. Then she takes hold of it and squeezes it. She hurriedly pulls it from my shorts and runs her hand up and down, up and down. I look down and see the head red and swollen. I pull away within seconds of having an orgasm. I stand still. I stand over her and take a deep breath.

"Hor-ra, Midori-chan! Take it easy, cute baby," I growl at her. She grins and lies back again. I take my shorts off and begin moving up her thighs, as if I never stopped. When I reach her lotus, I push her legs up and apart, like a frog's, so I can see the entryway. Her bud is running wet with the dew of love. The pink is outstanding. I have never seen this before. I think my throbbing rod is going to explode just looking at her.

I hear her breathing in short bursts. I leave her thighs and pull the slip up over her head. I carefully caress her belly and run my hands over her breasts again. I caress her throat. I take her face in my hands and just look at her pretty mouth and eyes. Then I kiss her while I play with her nipples. This is too much for me. I straddle her body and begin rubbing the moistened top of my golden rod against her tiny gate, murmuring, "Ooh you are cute, so cute." I can feel her ready to go and rub so softly and slowly she starts to get really noisy, making sounds of exertion. Her body is convulsing. I guide my rod over the edge and through the gate and start pounding on it, I'm saying something, I don't know what, and she is calling out and making a sound like the lowing of a new calf. All my muscles are taut. I teeter there, hanging in midair, shaking, holding on for another minute then I just burst inside of her. My head is in the stars. I collapse at her side.

We lay listening to each other calming down for a long time, not moving or talking. Our breathing matches. I'm going to keep this woman. I will do anything. I have never been alive before this moment. Yet I'm afraid to look at her, so I don't. I am content to lie still. But no, I can't just lie here, so I turn my head to see the side of her face. There are tears running down her face. I look down at my wilted warrior and see no blood. Do I remind her of the one who did this first? I don't care. Did I make her happy? That is all I care about.

"Hey, Hey, Mi-chan, what are you doing?"

"It's nothing. Keizo. Keizo."

"What are you crying about? Are you happy or sad?"

"Happy."

She offers no more, I ask no more.

Still I look at her face. Very gradually, I begin to feel alone. I don't know what Midori is thinking. I turn my face away and look at the ceiling. Now I'm struggling to keep the peaceful feeling. I reach my hand over and place it on her thigh. She rolls over onto my chest and buries her head there. I feel her body slowly relaxing, her breathing evening out. She may be asleep. She may be thinking. I call her name softly. No reply. I comfort myself with scenes from our lovemaking. At last I feel sleep overcome me.

It is fall again, the most melancholy time of year. I have grown to love the rocking of the train beneath me, holding onto the strap, winding my way back home. It is the end of the week. I will have some time to work on my orchids tomorrow.

What is this burden I feel? My melancholy comes and goes. Has it always? Was I a sullen child? I think I was. It doesn't matter. Or rather, something matters only I don't know what it is.

Hiromi is used to it. I don't think she ever tried to understand, didn't care as long as she had me. She never asked, not once. I told her she was an empty head, during one of my then frequent tirades against her. I told her she was cold and inconsiderate, not to care what went on inside me. She acted like she was not even curious like a simple animal might be. In her usual nonchalant way, she meekly countered that anything I told her would not make her happy, so it was better not to know. "I allow you your thoughts," she had said.

I don't believe for a minute she is so calm inside, but she would no sooner give me her most private thoughts than inquire into mine. She's right. It is better this way, things not being what either of us wanted.

Every now and then I think of Midori. I never share this with a soul. My thoughts are like an old tree standing in a garden, never changing in any significant way. Why did Midori leave? Why wouldn't she marry me? Why didn't I follow her?

After that first night, the only night, Midori grew strange. In fact, we only saw one another again six or seven times. I talked. I poured out my heart. I tried to get her to make love with me again, somewhere, anywhere. I tried to get her to talk to me, to tell me what she was feeling, but it made her sadder, more distant. I bought new clothes. I gave her presents. The more I advanced, the more she receded. Finally, she broke it off completely, said she didn't want to meet anymore. Soon after that, she moved south for a while, I don't know where. She never said a word. No letters, no phone calls, nothing, just like that.

How could the most beautiful experience of my life cause her pain? I cried when she broke it off. It remains the darkest day of my life.

I have posed many possible theories over the years. I got too close, I got into her box with my passion and it scared her. She couldn't leave her brother. Her love for me was too painful. She could not conceive and so felt she could never marry. Perhaps she made a pact with her brother and sister never to marry. I did something wrong. My personality was wrong. She was too mature, too developed for me. It stopped mattering after I married Hiromi, yet I still ask myself the same questions.

I did not see her again for three years. I married Hiromi right before she came back. Maybe she came back because she heard I married Hiromi. I like that explanation.

I still love her. I cannot understand why her rejection of me doesn't seem to alter that fact. I wish it would.

I never loved Hiromi, as Midori never loved me. Maybe Midori couldn't marry me because she is not cheap like me, she would not marry just for comfort. I didn't follow her because I knew this, knew that I shouldn't try to make her go against her heart. Somehow, I knew this from the beginning.

It is just too sad for words. How could I love so completely and not be loved back? The truth is I know that I am not loved at all, not by Midori and not by my wife.

She lives here in Tokyo. She moved back in with her brother and sister, neither of whom ever married. After she returned, after I married Hiromi, ran my department, got a nice apartment, buried my father and my brother, I contacted her. I contacted her in the hopes that she would consent to being my mistress. I was sure she was having sex with someone, why not me? Of course, being the opposite of Hiromi, she knew this without my having to say it. She never responded. Such an arrangement would naturally be untenable for either of us. I sent her ten letters then I gave up.

Ah, yes, this is the little stream of thought I follow to its end every few days, or maybe it is months now, I don't know, I don't keep track. My Whiskey Track. Whiskey will make it go away when I get home. I would feel sorry for Hiromi if she suffered even a moment from my mental unfaithfulness, but I know she doesn't, so my loathing for her gets a little fuller every year, like an old man's middle.

Tatsuo will be home. Yes. I think Hiromi got a little riled when I insisted on calling our son, our only child, Tatsuo. She never once mentioned Midori's brother, she merely said the name sounded noxious. "It's a noisy name," she stated calmly, an adjective nearly indistinguishable from all the other nonsense descriptors she uses. Nothing she ever says has any meaning. She lives in a great intellectual void like a dumb farm animal.

Oh, she is a good mother, clearly, maybe the best. Probably because she is so devoid of feeling, she is even-keeled. Good wife. Good cook, good worker. My mother is very happy with her. She lives with Aiko on their farm. I still send her money. Men I know envy me for having such a dutiful and docile wife. I want to scream, "She's not even aware enough to reproach me!"

I used to berate her and she seemed to take some perverse pleasure in allowing me to do so, never speaking a word in her own defense. In the end, nothing stopped me but myself. One day I stopped yelling at her, stopped expecting something different. Now I live in the silence of my own thoughts. It is not as though putting them into words created any understanding in her. The fact is I do not like my wife. I never did. My son is even something of a pain, being lethargic like his mother, but he gets good grades. I do not understand the dull, how they can excel in one area and be entirely bereft in another.

Once, many years ago, I had a very strong desire to get out of this situation by killing myself. I thought constantly about it for a week; the thought became a comfort to me. I don't know why I didn't. That week, when I was closest to it, I had a feeling it was just too selfish. I do not know to whom. I would not be missed that much. Something held me back. Shortly after that, I developed stomach pain. I suffer now every day. Hiromi has noticed, has asked after me, but I tell her nothing. I suffer alone.

It will be nice to work on my orchids. I love them very much. They are so delicate, mysterious. They come from the jungles of Borneo and are extremely fragile. I have been trying to grow a black orchid, but each one eventually withers before it blooms.

Well, Tatsuo is in college. I'm glad I can afford it. My mother is living with Akio, so the money I regularly set aside for her now goes to him. There is no break in the rhythm. The pain has gradually increased, but it, too, has a rhythm about it and never changes in nature.

A strange thing has gradually taken shape, though. The stronger my pain grows, the weaker my loathing for Hiromi becomes. She brews me fine broths and medicinal teas every day. She brings me my medication. I don't know what I would do without her.

It is cancer. The doctor has said it will kill me soon. He gives me painkillers; I sleep a good deal of the time. I go to work still, but only in the morning. I do very little there, really. It is not strenuous, at any rate. They let me stay on out of pity.

I cannot read anymore. I don't go out anymore. I listen to the radio.

The hospital has been a cold tomb. Hiromi has taken a job at a green grocer near the hospital to supplement my pension. She comes to see me every day.

Yesterday I told her that I didn't want her coming every day. I know there is some kind of war now, things are getting worse. It must be hard for her. I am in constant pain. I am skin and bone. She answered that fruit prices are going through the roof. It was a perfect answer. I predicted it, actually, in my mind, before she said it. I laughed and she laughed, too, like a child. I took her hand then and told her she was a good woman, too good for me. I could not finish. She looked into my eyes and nothing I said seemed to register. She asked softly if I would like to listen to the radio, as though all along I was trying to ask her if she would turn it on, but just lost my way into other words. "Oh. Sure," I answered. She turned it on, leaned back, and began to hum.

My breathing is thin now, thinner than it has ever been. I think constantly about death. I am really quite afraid, yet undaunted, all at the same time. I am curious. I think death is a dark silence and this seems acceptable to me, but for how long?

I can't breathe. The pain in my bowels moves out through my entire body. The pain is almost exquisite, it is that excruciating. I can't call out for more medication, though I try. My voice isn't working. I feel tears sliding down my face, but there is no sound, no movement.

Odd. Nothing is working but my tears. Suddenly, the pain stops.

Keizo after Death

The pain stopped and I am in this tunnel. It is dark and I am scared. It goes on and on; I can't see the end. I think I see some light, a pinpoint, in the direction I am heading. I think I turned around once and there was no pinpoint, but I can't be sure because even now I'm not sure that I am seeing light up ahead. It may be something else. My eyes may be playing tricks on me.

I think I've been walking very fast through this tunnel for three hours or so. It may be days. All I know is I'm tired, but there is nothing behind me, so I keep going forward.

This is ridiculous. Where am I going? I can't remember. The pain stopped and I was here. This can't be right. When I get to the end, perhaps it will make sense.

But this is ridiculous! I'm not going to just keep walking! I've tried running, I didn't get anywhere. What is this place? I can't stop, there's nowhere to lie down, the floor of this tunnel must be filthy. I look down to check and good God! There are layers of people right under my feet! Where the hell did they come from? I can't touch them, but I can see them vaguely, it's so dark in here... Hehh?! There are people next to me, moving in the same direction, at the same pace. Some of them are looking from side to side like I am; others march with their eyes straight ahead, as I have been doing. Have I just now looked around? I must have been in here for half a day! Did the others just appear?

I run to catch up with one of the people near me, but she looks right through me. She can't seem to see me. I try shouting, but there is no noise, not even the sound of our feet, nothing. Perfect silence. I want to throw up but my stomach's not upset. I stop. People of all ages and colors keep moving past me. I watch them go. Whoa! There's a funny one, so short and black. And there's a really tall, very white girl. Look at all of them!

I can't sit or lay down, there's no space without people. I get tired of watching them; my neck hurts from turning my head from side to side. I look up, and Whoa! There are people walking up there, upside down, the tops of their heads must only be a few feet away, but I can't quite tell because it is so dark in here. I turn around full circle. There are people everywhere, all of them moving, some looking about like me, some staring straight ahead. I'm still moving. I thought I stopped. Even when I stop, I'm moving.

Okay. They're all over the place. I start to run and everyone runs. I slow down and everyone slows down. I look up. God! It's the very tall very white girl rushing past. She's up there now. Now she's gone.

I think this is some kind of slowly spinning tunnel that loops back on itself. I don't think there is an end at all! I think I'm trapped here forever!

"Hey! Hey you, look at me! Look at me!"

What the hell! No reaction. Nothing. Did I yell? I didn't really hear myself. I think I've been running. I'm so tired! I'm going to die from exhaustion. Die.

Die.

Die, die, die, die, die, die, die, die. That's it. I'm dead. The pain stopped and I died and now I'm in hell. That's what I get for my life. I knew I wasn't doing it right! I knew I would go to hell! God in heaven! Now it's happening!

No way. I wasn't that bad! What did I ever do? I wasn't a murderer. I didn't even have a mistress. What did I ever do?

I'm not staying here. I stop. Nothing else stops. I just stay right here. I sit down right over someone's head, but they don't mind, they're moving, and I could still be moving, I don't know, but I'm sitting down.

This is crazy!

"No way out, idiot!" I shout to a funny man, but of course, there is really no one there. That's what I think. And if they are there, then they're doing what I used to do; they're running for what they think is a little speck of light.

"It's not light you fools!" I cry. I wish I could cry, but no, not even tears. No voice, no tears, movement that gets you nowhere, stillness that always moves...

"Nice hell! Nice hell, cruel creators! But not really! You left out quite a few things..."

Leaving things out; leaving things out. I have always left things out. That's why I'm here! I left out my brother, Hiro'chan! When you died, I didn't know you, hadn't seen you in so long! Aiko, who is Aiko? And you cared for our mother, you're still caring for her, aren't you, my sister, whoever you are! Pa! Pa! Are you here in this hell somewhere? I left you out and you left me out. Pa! Why'd you do that?

Hey Keizo, ask yourself!

Midori, Hiromi, Tatsuo my son. I left you out. I left my life out! Why? What the hell was I doing? I was thinking, mostly.

You were thinking about yourself, all day every day, whenever you were with anyone, and now you are all alone with all these people.

Why, why, why! I didn't mean it that way! I wish I could do it all over again!

Whoa!

Whoa-oa-oa!

Hey, there is a light! Beneficent Heaven! There, oh God, it's getting bigger! It's getting bigger! Am I running toward it? I can't tell. I don't know anything anymore, just please, please, I beg you, let me leave this place. I won't do it again! I won't do it again!

I'm running out into the light! Has anything ever been so wonderful? So beautiful, so light, so sweet, so soft, this must be heaven! I escaped from hell!

I can't see anything, it's so bright. Hey, somebody's up there, they're walking toward me, it's a boy, I think. Hey, that looks like Hiro'chan!

"Hiro'chan? Hiro!!!!"

I'm running toward him. It is him! He's smiling and I grab him up and hold him in my arms. I will die again before I ever let him go. Oh, Hiro! I love you so much! Hiro! Hiro! Can you ever forgive me?

Thank you, God. Thank you for this boy, my little brother, the most precious human being on the face of the earth! Hiro! It's me, Big Brother! I'm sorry I didn't come back to visit you!

Oh, it's okay! Hey Big Brother, you made it to heaven! I saw you die, and I had to wait a long time before you came here. That tunnel's pretty spooky, isn't it! Hey Big Brother! You can beat me at Go, but I went through that tunnel a lot faster than you!

I bet you did, Little Brother! I thought I was in hell! Wasn't that hell? Oh, Hiro!

I bury my face on his shoulder and just cry and cry, and as I cry, I hear him laugh and laugh. He's thinking, "Oh, Big Brother. Boy, are you a baby! I never got so scared as you in that tunnel! What are you crying for? Jeez. You're getting me kind of wet now. Hey, it's okay! The tunnel's gone, see? Keizo'chan? Okay, how's about we play some Go, 'cause I think I could maybe beat you now! Jeez. What a baby! You're noisy, too! Paying me back, huh? You always said, 'Hiro'chan. Shut up, will you? So noisy!' Hey, Keizo'chan, shut up, will you!!! So Noisy!!!"

I do quiet down, but I don't let go of him. He is still retarded, even in heaven! Hiro! Why didn't I protect you?

From what? You never make much sense. Hey! I waited for you a long time! Are you done crying? Can we play now?

How do you know what I'm thinking?

Oh, 'cause this is heaven, no need to use words. I never talked so good anyway. This is much easier. Mind-talk.

Everything I think?

I don't know! Now can we play finally?!

He walks off in exasperation, motioning me to follow. I follow him over clouds, through fields of berries, past a swing, past a brook with a little damn built over it—"That's mine!"—I hear him think—"I'll show you everything later!" There is a Go game set up on a little table under a blooming cherry tree with a pot of tea and a tray of cookies right next to it. Hiroshi turns around and just beams at me. He thinks, "Are you ready?!"

We sit and play Go. Tears stream down my face. It's starting to bug him. I can see him twist in his seat a little and cast me a look that says, "Big Baby!" Every once in awhile I manage to get them under control, but then he does some cute little thing and I'm crying again. Finally, he shouts, "Okay, cut it out! I love you too! Sheee, what a little baby you are!" I stop crying, just like that, and the pleasure I feel is exquisite.

The smell of the berries in the field is the most stunningly gorgeous smell I have ever experienced. The wind is blowing ever so slightly, and the temperature is perfect. I can hear the cool clear sound of the brook, and the ground is made of clouds.

I am happy. I want this game to go on forever.

I notice that he is actually beating me. I haven't been trying to lose, but he's beating me. I think, "I should let him win." And he thinks, "You can't let me win, I'm winning on my own! Huh, Big Brother! It's true! I'm winning on my own! Winning on my own!"

He gets up and dances around, and where ever his feet touch, a big flower pops up until he is surrounded by flowers, singing at the top of his lungs, "I'm beating Big Brother! I'm winning, I'm winning!"

I get up and dance around with him, twirling and jumping. I have never danced in my life! I'm shouting, "Hiro'chan is beating me and I'm trying my hardest! The little scoundrel's been practicing up in heaven and now he's beating me! Hiro'chan is beating me, he's beating me, he's beating me!!!" And he's laughing at me so hard tears roll down his face and I howl, "BABY!" at him and he's shouting, "I'm beating you I'm beating you I'm beating you!" We fall down into the flowers, we roll around laughing and my heart is soaring through an eternity of peace and joy, with the most profound sense of beauty and unfathomable richness: a gift from my little retarded brother, my Hiro!

After awhile, we both calm down. "Hey, finish the game! You have to finish losing. I always had to finish losing!" "I will, with great pleasure, and I am trying my very best, and maybe I won't lose!" He grins madly and pulls me to my feet and plops me down in front of the Go board.

We drink tea. We take our time. We eat cookies from across the ocean. I think I make a couple of brilliant moves, but Little Brother just laughs and laughs.

Eventually, I lose.

"Ha! First game after you die and I win! I win I win I win! That was fun. Now I'll show you how to do everything because Pa showed me, otherwise I never would have got it. And you showed me how to play Go, remember?"

"Hiroshi. What did you say about Pa?"

"Pa taught me. Pa was waiting for me, and I said, Pa, I'm going to wait for Big Brother. I said that after Pa and me played Go and did a lot of other things here. We did a lot of things, and then Pa had to go, like I have to go. Because it feels like the time to go, then you go."

He sees the look of confusion on my face and makes an impatient gesture with his hands and says, "Okay. See? If you want something, just think about it. If you want to see someone who's alive down on the earth, just think about it and you can see them. But don't try to see dead people, because mostly they've left again, unless they are waiting for you like I was. I wanted to go for a long time, but I wanted to see you, too. So now I'm ready."

"Go? You can't go! Don't go, Hiro, I'm telling you, I'm different now, I want to be with you!"

"I know, I said that to Pa and I couldn't believe it when he disappeared, but then I learned about when it's time to leave. So it's okay, you'll see. Don't be a Big Baby!" he says with an angelic smile on his face and a teasing gleam in his eye. I'm shouting to him, "No, don't go, I'll go with you!" but he fades away, just like that.

He just disappears.

This is crazy. I don't believe it. Was he ever here? Where is here? This must be Hiro's world. I like it very much. I sit back down and cry. When I'm done crying, I eat another cookie, but I think about some soba noodles and then there is a bowl of noodles just the way I like them on the little table. I taste them. So perfect! Better than anything I ever tasted on earth, the best! I eat them all and sip the soup out of the bowl then I lay down in the clouds.

'Just think about what you want.'

I want to see Midori.

I can see her. She's squatting over the toilet, her skirts hitched up around her hips. She's so old! She's biting at her nail. This doesn't seem right, but I can't stop watching. Midori? This is my Midori? There are lines around her eyes and mouth. I don't want to watch anymore.

Where is my mother? I see her sitting at the kotatsu, alone. She's sitting and thinking, I guess, because she doesn't move for a long while. Finally, she gets up and moves off into the kitchen. I follow her there. She starts cleaning the dishes. She seems too absent minded, but there she is, my mother. Watching her doesn't feel right, either.

And Hiromi, and Tatsuo? I see them. They are sitting down to eat. Ah. Hiromi has made soba, like the bowl I just ate. They talk about mundane things.

Whatever happened to my body?

It doesn't matter.

I watch them all night long. Hiromi helps Tatsuo with his homework. They listen to the radio. She puts him to bed. She reads for a while, humming to herself. She gets up and sways a little back and forth to the music in her head. What is she thinking? I have no idea.

How long have I been gone?

I see my son sleeping in his bed. How frightened he would be to wake up and see me! Can they tell I'm watching? I want to sleep now, that's what I want, right on this cloud. Instantly, I am back in Hiroshi's made-up world. I fall to sleep.

When I wake up, I think about climbing in the mountains. Then the mountains are here and it is so beautiful. I climb for hours.

I think about acting on a British stage, and I am suddenly on stage, but it does not feel right. I don't know the lines, I can't act. Who are those people watching? It's all in my mind...

As time passes, I spend a lot of time thinking about the things I have always wanted and then experiencing them, but nothing feels right, it's always superficial. It is because there are no humans here, no one to play with, just illusions. Finally, I think about the world Hiroshi made and I am there again. I sit and think for a long time.

The fact is I never loved anyone when I was alive. I needed them, I wanted them, but I never loved them. I say I never loved them because I didn't know what they were thinking. I didn't know what they wanted. When I see them now, I know they are the people from my old life, but that is all. Why is that?

I wonder about this. The sun rises and sets in a regular pattern. Am I doing that?

At last, I realize I treated everyone pretty much the way I treated myself. Who was I, what did I feel? There were times I knew my heart and at those times others may have felt my love, but mostly, I never knew. I never got past the constant chatter in my head. I never worked out why I wanted the things I wanted. I stayed with the desire. I saw the tree, not the roots underneath.

I am convinced that I must get to know myself, but how?

I immediately find myself in a queue and a person comes up to me. The being thinks, "I feel like I know you."

"I feel like I know you, too. Did you just die?"

"I don't know. Some time ago, maybe. I can't tell. I got all confused in that tunnel."

"The tunnel was horrible. I have been here for a long time. I'm going back down now, I think. I want to go. I'll do things differently this time."

"You won't remember. I don't think we remember. Did you remember the last time you were there?"

"The last time? You mean I may have been born before? God, there was a time before?"

"Well, yeah, I think so. If there is this time and we're going back now, then there must have been a time before..."

"No, I can't remember anything. I don't think there was a time before. This is my first time."

"Maybe. Maybe this is my first time, too. I don't know. Maybe we'll remember everything when we go back."

"I hope so. Good luck to you."

"And to you."

The being who was talking to me turns back around in the queue and a third being talks to him for a while then he disappears. This same being turns to me and thinks, "You have learned a lot. You have chosen again..."

"Did I choose before? Is this a choice?"

"Good question. The answer is yes and no. No, you don't really choose what you learn, but you choose when and how you learn. Learning is inevitable, like walking down a road. You decide when you stop your journey and when you begin again. You can wander away from the road, look for it, get back on it, or travel along in the wilds for just as long as you want. But sooner or later everyone walks down the same road. We are all the same."

"Will I be hurt? Will I have to die again?"

"If you are alive, you will be hurt, you will die, but those are only a few of the marvels that you will experience. You may say, this time, that it has all been worthwhile. 'Don't be such a Big Baby!'"

"Everyone keeps saying that to me! Someone I used to know, I can't remember now..."

And I feel myself being moved in darkness and unknowing.

Transmigrations

Keizo to Marta

Karlos/Mei Hua/Khalid/Keizo	becomes	Marta
Merlo/Bau Yu/Fida/Tatsuo	becomes	Jon, husband
Victor/Ying/Misha'il/Midori	becomes	Jon, son
Emilio/Madame Wang/Bahroum/Aiko	becomes	Little Marta

[girl given voice/Shaymaa/Hiro'chan --- does not enter this life]
[Nuri/Hiromi --- does not enter this life]

MARTA

Harmony achieved

I feel the day slipping away. It will be dark and I won't be finished. My weariness is already strong even though the sun still hangs low in the sky.

I have a spot of time, it seems, otherwise I would be hoisting that dang laundry basket and loading it through the back door, but I am not bending down, so there must be time to take a moment. The sun is fast approaching the horizon. The autumn smell is musky. I love the maple changing her color. I wish I were as beautiful, I wish I had her colors. I am such a plain woman. Still and all, I stand here and am grateful; Jon must have seen something lovely in me. The birds come to life at dusk; they are starting to raise a commotion. There are too many calls to pick out just one, which reminds me of my brood.

Where are they all, how can it be so quiet? Little Marta may be at that bread already, bless her heart. She's not so little anymore, and capable as any ten year old.

The boys would be out with their father still, tying up the last of the straw into sheaves. Little Jon, he's a good one. He'll help his father get the fields ready for spring planting next year. For once, there is enough laid by. Sweet Lord, we haven't had such a good harvest in many years.

What am I doing still standing here? I don't have supper nearly done and they'll be scrambling home any minute.

Yet I stay. There is the slightest wind picking up, bringing the smell of hay and early night. I feel so odd this evening! All is beauty, stunning beauty, and I am so happy to be alive. My eyes are filling with tears, and it is not just because of the little one I carry inside of me, or barely carry, it's wanting to get out so badly! A big baby, must be the biggest I ever carried. Number six.

Get on now! Get to work, supper's waiting to be cooked!

Inside the door I almost trip over Uta, our youngest, only two, sitting just inside the door. My voice sounds peculiar to me as I tell her to find a better place to play. "Better yet, come set the table. Can you hold the plates?" Helping her set the table is more work than doing it myself, but I'll take the time tonight. Lord, what a pleasure that little girl is, and now there's this one coming. I hope it's another girl, three and three; then I'll see if Jon will let me rest for awhile, because much as I love 'em, I grow so weary these days. It's gettin' harder. I am happy, but all used up like a rag.

"That was very good, Marta. No woman can do a spot of rabbit like you. Tastiest stew I've ever had. Are you putting more of that cabbage away then? Like you did after last year's harvest? Because if you are, I liked the way you put that spice in 'em, what's it now, something hot? Peppers were it, Marta?"

"Yes, Jon, among other things. I'll do 'em the same, if you like, or experiment a bit again. That's how I came upon that batch last year."

"Oh, yeah, have a new go at it, I'll never be disappointed, not with you cookin'. Come, sit here for a spell. You don't look so good."

"Nevertheless I'll do what's needin' to be done, ugly or no. The Baby's off to bed already, but there're the other four, you know."

"Old enough to make do for themselves. Now, Marta, come by me here, my pretty one."

"I will, I will, straight away, as soon as I check on 'em."

"Have Little Jon and Little Marta put the other two in bed, that's what you need to be doing. They have to learn. You'll be dropping that one there any day now, then where will you be?"

"He's right, Ma. I've seen to Steven and Marc, they're tucked away in their beds and all," Little Marta's voice rings from the stairs. But I'm up to see them good night anyway, as I have done since they were born and will continue to do until they leave me, little precious ones.

I didn't have such a mother, no. Didn't have much of a mother at all. I don't think she liked me much. I don't remember a good night kiss. I don't remember a kiss at all, and then she died.

I move off toward the stairs.

"You can't be climbing those stairs, neither, Marta, it's a danger to you now," I hear Jon call out after me, but I move ahead. Five stairs, six, twelve, up to the top. Perhaps I should stop climbing them. Tomorrow.

Jon, Steven, and Marc share a room, and Marta keeps little Uta in her room now, as of a fortnight ago, in preparation for the new baby. Little Jon has gone back outside to tend the animals. He so loves the outdoors. He is a strong boy, soon to be a man. I go into the boys' room. There they are, the dears, I see their little eyes shining in the dim light of the candle.

"Good night, Steven, good night, Marc. Sleep well you angels, and let's say a prayer." I see them smiling, waiting for me to kneel, but I can no longer. A sudden pain shoots up through my belly and along my spine and truly, it is all I can do not to cry out. I close my eyes and manage a nod, at which they begin to murmur their wee prayer of safety for their family and love for God. Their words are like rain on parched land, and as they finish up, my pain subsides. I wave to them and make my way to the girl's little room under the eaves.

"Ma. Pa said for you not to be climbing those stairs," Little Marta says, chastising me.

"Don't you worry your little head. I'm strong as ol' Wheat the Horse, I am. And you, taking on so much and only ten, Marta! You are sure a blessing to your mother!"

Uta has gotten up out of her bed where she sleeps with Little Marta and is pulling on my dress to get picked up, but I can't bend over. Little Marta gets to her feet and picks the Baby up, holding her as close to my face as she can.

"Alright, alright then, good night littlest angel. Sweet dreams and pray to the good Lord with your sister now. And tomorrow we may bake some bread."

"Bed! Bed!" Uta squeals and runs back to bed. Little Marta's face is full of worry; she won't let me erase it with my smile. 'I love you,' I whisper to her. 'I love you, too,' she mouths back, snuggling down under the comforter with the Baby.

Oh, a house full of blessings, that's what I have. I make my way back down the treacherous steps.

Downstairs again, I promise myself I will not sew, I will not think or worry or fret, but only sit by the cold fireplace and relax. Jon is working at his whittling. I lean back and close my eyes.

I must have drifted off because I come to with a terrible fright. I feel my body heaving for a moment, wanting to leave the chair, but then it gives up. My heart is racing. I look around. Jon hasn't moved; he didn't notice. I fall back exhausted and remember the horrible dream I had.

I am in a garden with my children. They are all young, all about the same age too, when suddenly a bird flies up to my face. At first, I think it is going to take my eyes out, but then it hovers in the air before me, growing larger. It is huge now, and black. It flies lightly up to my shoulders and takes them hard in its talons, and in an unimaginably gentle fashion, it lifts me up and carries me off, away from my family.

I feel a sudden anger at Jon: why wasn't he there, why didn't he stop the bird? It's just a dream, I tell myself, but we all know dreams are portents, and this one must have its meaning. Something bad may be coming. A quiet fear takes hold of me and I begin methodically reviewing all my blessings. I give thanks to the Lord for all we have and I pray the Kingdom Come, so He knows that I will abide in Him and accept His will. Gradually, the eerie feeling of loss dissipates.

"Jon."

"Yes, my wife?"

"Is Little Jon in then, is he safe abed?"

"Yes, Marta, and that's where you need to be."

I don't tell him about the dream, can't stand the horror of it spreading beyond me. He helps me to bed in the downstairs sitting room we have converted into our bedroom on account of the stairs being too much for me in my state.

I lay awake next to my snoring Jon in the deep feather bed that was my dowry. Jon always teases that he would have had any woman who came to him with such a bed. How happy have our times been in this fine bed. It is too fine for us, really, and many were the hard winters when selling it may have brought a much needed spot of beef, but Jon would hear none of it. The bed is a sign of his fortunate marriage to a woman slightly above his station, credited in his mind to some dashing air he possesses. He is not a homely man, but a prince he is neither. Still and all, he's quite good looking, better looking than me. That doesn't matter to him, and it doesn't matter to me.

Ah, I cannot sleep tonight. The whippoorwill and the mockingbird vie for attention in the darkness of the glen. The air moves about mysteriously and I have a great desire to go walk into the dark unknown, to feel the cool, radiating silence of this fine autumn night.

But I go nowhere for to get up would surely rouse my husband, and how could I explain? It may be cold outside or there may be an animal about. Long I lie abed wanting to go out into the night, conquering each yearning as it arises, but the more I order myself to sleep, the sharper come the night sounds, just outside these walls. At last, the "outside" part of me must have won, because I'm edging out of bed, feet heavy on the cold floor, baby and all. I find my slippers, never mind the hat and coat. I'll just slip out for a minute and be right back.

This must be the prettiest night the good Lord ever made. Even the crickets sound magical. Their slow cree-creeing laces the air thick with the smell of falling leaves and the sweetness of fallen fruit. I spy a nighthawk darting for insects. My legs don't want to hold me up, my reason tells me to get on back to bed, but the rest of me is staying put. I sit down in the yard, in the cool dirt. The ache in my legs is immediately relieved.

I find myself thinking back to when I was a girl, my mind jumping over these years of joy to my emotionally barren childhood. I recall a stream where my brother taught me to fish. He hung a swing from a tree limb and I swung on it for hours. Our mother and father never knew about that place. There was honey sometimes slathered on bread when we could steal it, and afternoons of freedom. "I am happier now," I find myself whisper into the spacious night, "I have much more now."

My brother, dead and gone, was the only sweet thing in my childhood. He made the coldness of my parents bearable. He held me in secret when I was beat. I wish my brother were here, but I know he is in heaven. I see him there. I know he is better off, too, and bless him now and forever, Dear Lord.

Now the blood has pooled in my legs. With each baby, my legs grow stouter. It is a price I gladly pay. I have made a wonderful life for my young ones and never raise a hand to them. I give them honey on their bread and read to them. I feel so proud of myself and so happy to be out here tonight! I feel as though I am the right hand of this night, a part of it. I belong in this place. I am happy, in the way that a bird flies and is happy.

I struggle to my feet and go back inside because I know I am not well. I manage not to wake my husband as I roll back into bed. Sleep is swift and sweet.

It is not the fine morning, with its dew and bird song, that has become so difficult but the need to move once the morning has come. I feel as though I could lie here forever, even to the point of death, just to avoid moving. I cannot get my limbs to respond. The day's work clamors at our tiny bedroom door. I hear the sound of the children milling about the kitchen. Jon has gone out to the fields by now. I desperately want to lie abed. Stay in bed. Sleep in bed or stare at the wall, it's all the same to me, but never to leave it, never to move. I am so sore and tired.

Somehow, I force myself to my feet. There is a metallic taste in my mouth and my stomach is churning. With unending effort, I force myself to don clothes and start my morning routine.

Oh, the wee tiny faces and happy smiles that greet me in the kitchen! And one concerned frown from Little Marta.

"Ma, are you all right? Sit down, Ma, I'll get breakfast today. Ma, how high should I put the fire on the stove? Ma, I can't get this match lit!"

Always more trouble than doing it myself, but such a little dear, I show her again. And Marc and Steven tussling, is it over a stick? "Stop that!" I say to them and they stop. I am tired. I am so tired. This baby in my belly is huge and I can't help but resent the poor little thing, what with how difficult it's making my life right now.

"This little one's slowing me down, it is!" I try to sound happy, explaining my condition to the children.

"Ma, is you got one or two in there?" little Marc calls out.

"Ma's having a litter like ol' Woodsy, she's got four baby pups in there!" Marta teases.

"Ma, can you really have some pups for us?" Steven quips.

"Pup! Pup, pup, pup!" Uta sings out.

"Now, you know a human has a baby, a dog has pups! Sillies! This one here is your littlest brother or sister, and I do believe there's just one, though it's weighing on me something fierce," I tell them.

"Ma! If you can't have a pup, can we get us a pup?" Steven asks with some insistence.

"Yeah, a pup, Ma!" Marc echoes.

"Ma, how about a pup, then, for the little ones? I'll take care of it." Marta says, swept up by the boys' excitement.

"I know you could, Marta, you're such a one, so strong and smart, but there's no pup to be had now. Let's see in the spring, shall we? Maybe the Martens' Woodsy will have a litter in the spring. They've got a good bitch there; she's had many a fine pup. We'll see about it in the spring. I must have this wee little baby first!" Their protests silenced, disappointment telling in the slope of their shoulders, they set about eating the cold bread and milk Little Marta has laid out.

I look carefully at each one, except Little Jon who is out with his father. They are needing a good bath. I decide they must have a bath this very day. I'll bake the bread for the week and try to prepare as much food as I can, for this one will come tonight, if I'm not mistaken.

★ ★ ★

I'm at the window finishing up the bread when my waters break, the warm liquid streaming down between my legs. I am alone. The water puddles around my feet. There's an occasional drip audibly joining the mess on the floor, but I just stand here, waiting and thinking.

The first thing I think is how happy I am that Jon put this window in the kitchen for me because I can see the fields and birds and trees while I'm working. There aren't many windows in the house besides this one; windows are a luxury. I had hinted around and Jon just put it in, was that after Steven? Now I think I better send Little Marta out to the fields to get her Papa because the time has come to fetch the midwife, and that might take several hours.

I don't have much time.

"Marta, love?" I call.

"Yes, Ma?" She runs in from the sitting room where she's been playing with the baby. She sees the puddle and her face goes white. "It's the baby. Ma! I'll run and fetch Pa!" and she turns around and runs off that quick.

I watch from my window as she races across the fields. Such a strong, healthy girl! My little girl. And this one here, probably a girl. That's what I'm thinking.

I manage to get myself to the couch in the living room, throwing the dish towel down before I sit. The pain is getting too big and I should be moving to my bed, but I'm thinking on having her right here. But no, it would be bad for the children. Steven and Marc are out back and Uta has fallen asleep on a cushion. I'm quite content to watch her. Sooner or later, I have to get over to my bed. The pain has started in earnest now.

There's Jon shaking me, I must have passed out, he's saying something.

"Now, it doesn't look good, I have to go for the doctor. Now, you just hold on Marta, I'm telling you now, do you hear me?"

"Yes, Jon, stop fussing at me." My voice comes out as a whisper. I can hardly talk. Then a pain takes me, and when I open my eyes he's gone. I lay there for a long time until the baby cries and Marta comes in from the kitchen and picks her up.

"Ma, I put out bread and some stew from last night and we're all eating, and we've had baths, Ma, just like you wanted."

She's beaming, holding little Uta, the very image of her big sister eight years ago.

"Oh good heavens, what time is it? Did I fall asleep?"

"Supper time. Pa will be back soon."

"Lamb, I must move, and I'd like you to walk with me," I tell her softly.

She runs to the kitchen with the baby and I hear her telling Little Jon to hold Uta. I forgot he would be back from the fields. He goes everywhere with his father. I always just think if Big Jon is gone, then Little Jon is gone, too. I call her back and tell her we need Little Jon's help, they'll have to put the baby in her crib. In a twinkling I see Little Marta and Little Jon standing over me.

"Ma! You weren't so sick with Uta, were you? Are you going to be all right? Ohhh, I wish Papa was here!" Little Marta is suddenly beside herself and begins to cry.

"Hush now, just hush up, will ya? Ma. Can you swing your legs over the edge of the couch there?"

It occurs to me that Little Jon has such a strange manner. Not like me, that's for sure. But good. He is such a good boy. I am so proud of him.

"Right over the edge, there..." I can't finish, my voice is still nothing more than a whisper. The children stare at me as I fight back a new wave of pain. It subsides.

"I'm fine now. Walk along at my side," I say as I struggle to sit up. Blood rushes to my head and my whole body feels faint, though the worst is yet to come. I know that much. I may be too old for having this baby. I may be too weak. I hate scaring my children like this.

Jon and Marta walk along beside me, their little arms holding me up. I make it to the side of the bed, but then I think about the mess to come.

"Lamb, could you run get the towels and lay them here, and strip away that corner of good sheet, for I'll be ruining it tonight if I lay on it."

Marta runs off and I stand supported by Little Jon, my legs throbbing. I'm hit by another pain and Little Jon's brow furrows; he's practically scowling at me. Did it hurt this much before? It seems to be worse. I do not remember this kind of pain.

Little Marta hops to my side in a wink and sets about fixing the bed as I directed. No, you don't need to tell that child twice, smart as she is. When she is done, I manage to lie down and it is a great relief. I couldn't stand another second. My back aches, my veins are pounding, and my body seizes up in anticipation of the next contraction, each worse than the last. A wave of pain hits me. I squeeze my eyes shut and bite my lip so as not to cry out and scare them even more.

After the last wave of pain, I open my eyes and see Little Marta and Little Jon looking down at me with fear in their eyes. I tell them to go play at something, now that all are fed and I'm safely in bed. "What will you play at, then?" I ask, huffing and chuffing. They have seen me in labor before, the last time was two years ago with Uta, but it was never this bad. They know this.

"I'll play with my doll, Ma, the one you made for me," Little Marta says. Well do I remember making it! How I thought on Little Marta's joy as I sewed that evening by the fire. Cold into December it was, a Christmas present I managed to hide. Go on, little ones, play. Play and play and play forever and remember the sweet love of your mother, who would lay down her very life and soul for you, so deep runs her love for all the little loves who are her children. But there, I only manage to nod.

Little Jon hasn't moved. I nod at him, but he doesn't move. "Little Jon, go on now," I manage to whisper. He looks angry.

"I don't want to play. I'm staying here to watch over you." Oh, now tears are slipping down my face and he's leaning forward and I can't tell him how adorable he is, but I do manage to smile and say, "Go on now, Little Jon. Come back in a little while." He backs slowly out the door, keeping his eye on me as though I might run off unless he kept his eye on me and if I wasn't so weak I would laugh and laugh.

The pain comes hard as he closes the door behind him. Ah, this last one will be here soon and if not, she'll be the death of me. 'Think on her, Marta, or you'll be cursing her for sure and there's no baby wanting that feeling against her, especially not as she struggles out of the womb.' So I start thinking about her. Her hair will be darker, like Jon's. She'll look the most like him, his youngest, and steal his affections for the way they look the same. How could she be but gentle and sweet like her sisters? I hope she grows up just like Marta. I hope she grows strong and feels the sun on her face even as I have. I hope her life blooms as my life has blossomed and grown, bringing me the sweetest fruits of these days. I hope my offspring bask in the sun and take their places in love and joy, in pain and sorrow. It is a beautiful thing.

Am I lying abed crying to myself then? Is it the pain or the thinking on my love that moves me so? The pain is great and I need not the midwife to tell me something is wrong. Why wrong, what have I done? There's no sense to it. I feel moisture all over my body, the sweat pouring off me from clenching at the force of the pain cooling in the autumn air. Really, I am so proud. I haven't cried out once!

Will Jon never get back with that midwife?

"Ma." A long pause.

"Ma. Are you all right then, Ma?" It's Little Jon's voice, and thick with fear it is.

"Little Jon now, just you go back and help with the little ones. Your ma's alright." I don't know how I manage all that, for my breath is leaving me.

"Ma."

It's Little Jon again. He won't leave me be.

"Little Jon, I'm having your little brother or sister don't you know, and you must leave and go settle the little ones and go about your business whittling or whatnot by the fire. Have you made a nice..." I have not managed it this time, have not been able to finish my sentence.

"Ma. Steven and Marc are upstairs, and Uta too, though none asleep, and I'm looking in on you, making sure you're alright. Do you want anything, Ma?"

And without knowing what I'm doing, I say: "Bring each to me, for I need to see my little ones and kiss them goodnight."

"Aye, Ma, straight away."

He is gone.

Between the ravages of pain all I hear is the crickets; all I know is the crickets. Some folk find them detestable but for my part they are nature's musicians and their fiddling is high and fine. They are the sound of calmest night and I do love them so. There is a wave of pain that no man could bear and then a quiet lull with my sensitive musicians, the crickets. I realize that with every wave of pain, as I lose myself in a sea of agony, I can hold onto the hope that the crickets' song will greet me once again. And again, it does. With each new round of contractions I await the sound, the life-saving cree of the crickets.

Then the door is pushed open and tiny ones pad in. There is my son Steven, with his beautiful little face hovering over my bed, crying.

"Steven, you little dear, stop that crying now and what are you doing it for?"

"Ma. I don't want you to be so hurt."

"Oh sweet Steven, it doesn't really hurt. It is your little sister struggling to get out is all and I'll be fine, though I look a sight, don't I? Now Steven, help The Big Ones and be a good boy for your Ma, will ya now?"

"I will Ma and I have been very good."

"And where is my Marc? Oh there you are. Come kiss my cheek..."

Another wave of pain must have hit and silenced me sure because when I come to, they are all hovering about.

"Where was I then? Marc, it's you, and I'm saying goodnight, and you are a brave strong boy and I love you as I love your brothers and sisters. Be a good boy and go to sleep, Marc."

"I will Ma."

"Mama. Mama!"

It's little Uta, with that face of an angel, sure, and smart too, so smart, though she's still just a baby. And fat, with thick little hands reaching out for me from Marta's arms.

"Marta. Bring that wee angel closer!" I manage to wheeze and there is Uta in my arms. I hold her and close my eyes. A million stars erupt and I am wracked with so many needles that fissures of pain open all along my body. But then as suddenly as it comes, it passes.

I hear my voice rising up in my throat, though it tumbles out in a sound not unlike the crickets'. "Oh little angel, light my way, Oh be my guide through all my days." I am singing and Uta is laughing her baby laugh and Little Marta's face is suddenly pressed against mine and I whisper to her, "Off with you now, and please, dear, take the little ones and go to bed. I will kiss you tomorrow again." And doesn't she lean over my head and kiss my forehead and rub my cheek just a little. And isn't she the sweetest child ever born to this earth.

Another wave of agony comes and goes and I am alone with Little Jon.

I see him staring at me in the gloom of this unlit room and I smell something foul and sense his fear.

"Jon. Listen to your mother. You are a fine strong lad and the best who ever graced a mother with his presence. You will grow strong and big, won't you Jon?"

"Aye mother, as you like, so I will do." He is so serious his voice is shaking.

"Child, fear not. Your father will be home soon and all will be well. Now I want you to leave me be, for this is women's work. See to it that all is put straight then to bed you go, Jon."

"I will, mother, and I'll kiss you before I go."

And leans he over and kisses my brow, and there may be sweeter things on earth, but I know not one of them.

The gentle close of the door behind him scares me. I feel a panic rising up through my being and it would rule me, too, if the pain hadn't gotten here first. But as it is, I cannot focus for long, because the pain steps in every time I think I've got something straight. It's the crickets, the only thing that pulls me back on track and tells me where I am: alone in the dark with the crickets.

After some time there is Big Jon hovering about me, and I think he has taken my arms in his hands, but the sensation is so remote. That's his voice, too, and he's saying things to me, and probably nice things, too, but I cannot hear him. I think he says "Darling," and other fine things that make the pain ease just a little. Yes, tell me Jon, tell me what a darling I am and make this pain go away and I will slave over you until the day I die.

Then Jon is gone and there is a long sea to swim and I am not fit to do it. I cannot take another stroke but I do, because there is a shore to reach, right out there, beyond the darkness, a shore to reach for my little baby. I swim with her on my back. I carry her like an animal. I head for the shore even when there is not an ounce of strength left in me. It's a miracle from God. I keep stroking for the shore and I pray that Jesus, Mary, and Joseph will get me there safe. At last, when it is too dark to see, I feel the solid land beneath my feet and hear the tiny baby wail of a newborn gasping for breath and it is the Little One come…I have brought her here. I hear Jon whispering in my ear, "It is little Gretchen, as you predicted, right again and she is just as right as anything gracing God's earth! You should see her, Marta, see her tiny perfection! If you could just open your eyes, Marta, just a little, and see this baby I'm holding before you. Marta! Now open your eyes! Marta!"

I hear my husband commanding me. I have gotten my lovely baby to the shore, but I myself am sinking beneath the waves. I feel my hands letting go, though I want so much to hold on. Oh, I feel so bad, Jon, to leave you! It is not of my doing, for I have tried, tried to climb ashore, but I cannot. Believe this Jon, I have tried everything I know to come ashore with my baby, but I cannot. The pain is gone, and to hold little Gretchen I would bear it all again and more, but the waves are too strong! They're pulling me down. To hold my baby, this will never be, never be. Jon. You know I am trying, I am willing, but my body won't respond. Jon. It is not I who quit but my body, it won't go along anymore. But to see her just once!

Then I see his eyes swimming with loving tears. I see the baby in Jon's arms, the midwife right behind him who has come too slow, too slow! Oh, the baby is fine! I feel my mouth trying to make words but I hear no sound. If you could hear me, Jon, you would hear me asking you to please find a good woman to help you, to see after the children, and lucky she will be, even raising another's brood, to have such a fine husband as you, and such bright lovely little ones to help her. But he cannot hear me because I have not spoken.

"Jon!" Do I manage to whisper? His mouth is moving but I can hear nothing. I look once more at my newborn daughter and I smile. Now the water is freezing cold and the current is strong. It is growing dark again. It is so strange to die.

Marta after Death

I feel myself floating, I can't tell where. All is light. I feel relaxed and peaceful. I hover without thought. I'm buzzing a little. It's like a little tingle of joy, but quiet, like waking up on Christmas.

The glow begins to clear and I see a glen like the one at home, and there are people there waiting for me. I approach them. They smile and I smile back. They are beautiful. We all sit in the glen on the softest grass. I hear crickets creeing and bees buzzing and the sound of a stream nearby.

I think, "What a beautiful place God has made."

"The God in you," one of the beings thinks. "You have used His Earth as your model and have created this lovely place with your mind."

"Is this heaven?" I ask. It suddenly seems like such a funny question! I begin to laugh and they laugh with me. We laugh and laugh. A deer leaps past. A bird darts up to her nest in a tree. These things make me laugh even more, a kind of joy-laughter, an easy mirth.

"Oh," I say when my laughter subsides, "Don't tell me. This is heaven! And you are angels come to welcome me, and heaven is that which my mind finds pleasing."

"That which your mind finds, at any rate. Heaven or hell, Marta, it is all the same."

And before I can think it, another being thinks, "And now you want to see God!"

The other beings laugh again and I'm not sure what's funny, but their laughter is contagious and I laugh, too, enjoying the beauty all around me. Before I can think again, I hear:

"You'll understand if you think about it some."

I think about God. I thought I would see Him, and Mary and Joseph, and angels with wings. But never mind what I thought. I feel *like God is all around me and inside me and that Mary and Joseph are just beings like us, and these angels around me are like me, only they've already thought these things through.*

"Something like that," one of them thinks. And then there is only one.

"But there is a difference between you and me, you are so advanced. And I sense there is a difference between what God really is and this feeling of God I have. What is it?"

"It is time, only a matter of time. You perceive that which you are ready to perceive. Time brings understanding because it brings experience. Your experience of God at this point in time becomes your reality of Him. You will

have a different experience of Her at another point in time. It is like your lives. First you sacrificed others then you sacrificed yourself. You found out that they are the same. Whatsoever you do to anyone, you do unto yourself. That is the ultimate experience of God."

"The Lord said that."

"Many Lords said that."

"I don't understand about time. What is it, why is it so powerful? Why does understanding take time? If I stay here long enough, will I understand?"

"If you stay there long enough, you will understand. This is where you sleep, where you dream, processing what you have just learned on earth."

I am beginning to remember something, know something. Oh my God. It's kind of frightening. The being said, 'Your lives.' What does that mean?

I look into the face of the being: it has no age, no sex. I cannot tell anything about it, except that it is full of love. Love comes from its eyes and radiates from its entire being and suddenly I am not afraid to remember that I have been to earth before. 'If you stay there long enough...'

I am not only Marta. I am many other people as well; people who never knew of my existence because they came before me. They are me and I am the most advanced version of Us. And there will be more people - I will become them.

"I'll be going back." I think.

"I'll be going back, too. If you are here, you'll be going back."

"Is there a place other than here and there?" Again, this is quite funny and we both laugh. Because of course, besides here, there is no other place but there. I would need a new word for a third place that is neither here nor there but beyond time and space.

She hears all my thoughts. When did the being become a woman?

"To tell you the truth, I don't know about the third place you are thinking about, but I know it exists. Your Mary and Joseph have gone there, and countless others, as many as the stars. I will know when I get there."

The being continues: "I think of time as a string holding together the beads of our experiences. But when you pull the string of time from the beads, there is just one bead. Time is the element that creates the many. When there are no divisions, no time, you exist in the third place we have been imagining. That's how I think about it."

Jeez, this being is so smart!

She teases me: "You are so smart to understand my brilliance!"

"But perhaps, if I weren't so stupid, you wouldn't be making so much sense!"

"How about a game of Go!!!"

My heart nearly stops. A game of Go. A game of Go.

I remember!

Love pours from my face and I want to grab her up in my arms. I feel like crying but it is more like joying, and I don't have to hold her because she is not Hiro'chan. She was Hiro'chan once and thereby will always be Hiro'chan, in a sense, but much expanded. She is Hiro'chan evolved.

"I'm glad you didn't cry! Last time you got me all wet! Boy, was I stupid then!"

I squeal with laughter. He was smarter than me! He has always been smarter.

"Comparisons, still? Isn't it funny how strong our past learning is? Like the moon and the tides, always pulling us back; in some ways, anchoring us. We would be adrift without the confines of the past, at least for now. But the time will come..."

"Or go!"

"When even these memories..."

"Will be forgotten..."

"Yes, because their usefulness..."

"Has passed..."

"Were you a woman your last life?"

"Were you?"

"But we both still are!"

"You just think of me that way, so that's how I appear. Jeez!"

"But I was a woman! I was swimming to save my baby and oh, I was such a good mother. I loved all my children so much. I loved almost everyone! My life was so happy then zip, just like that, it was gone. Gone, gone."

"Oh, just like that, gone, gone!" She's mocking me. She's gotten up and is running around in a circle holding her head, and she's right, because I don't actually feel sad; I only think I should be sad. The truth is I feel happy.

"I suppose you're trying to tell me not to concentrate on the past."

"Yes. Know the past but do not hold on to it. You experienced what you needed to learn. You learned the joy of being selfless. The pain you experienced is not here now, only the understanding. You want to ask me about them..."

Things go so fast up here! I was wondering about what happened to my family. I was going to ask the Being Who Had Been Hiro'chan about my children. They are not mine anymore. They never were. They are beings like myself; they have lived and died many times, they have been to this very place. My love is pure, it is simply expanding.

I remember my last wish, for Jon to remarry, and I feel satisfied. It is up to him now. It is his life.

"I'm not saying pain should be trivialized, or that love is transient. Just the opposite. Pain is the most constant of life's helpful guides, the greatest of teachers. And love is the other. And I am still afraid of them both..."

"Or you wouldn't be here..."

"Heading back there..."

"I feel sad and elated and scared and excited and trembling with joy and fear and love all at the same time."

"Yeah."

We sit under a tree. The place is shifting from Hiro's old dream place to my glen from this death, to others that just come unbidden, visions from the four corners of the world. I think about the last time I saw Hiro, here in heaven. Was it yesterday we played Go? It is seductive, the thought to stay here and fool around...

"And postpone experiencing God, postpone sharing that experience with others who need you so badly..."

"But if time is an illusion..."

"Not to them. Listen, I need to go. Again. I've waited for you twice! I think I'm going to be a singer..."

"Really! You can tell what you're going to be?"

"No, I can't tell, I just think about what I want and, karma permitting, it might happen. It happens up here, why not down there? I can't remember once I'm down there anyway, so I can't be disappointed. Or maybe I will remember this time. But think about it. We get the life we need, we remember what we need to remember, we learn what we need to learn. Time is dynamic. All of us are interacting with each other on so many levels, from so many planes of prior existence, making choices about what to do with what is being handed to us..."

"We succumb to the illusion of predetermination."

"Exactly. Just because things happen in order, according to certain laws of existence, doesn't mean it's happened before or must happen. Each person is choosing constantly, in unison, so how could anyone predict the outcome?"

"Will I remember all my lives?"

"I don't remember all of mine. I remembered you enough to wait for you so I could forgive you, forgiveness being my favorite sentient-being experience. I don't even know why I waited for you again, but I'm glad I did."

"You have been so helpful. You have shown me that all I need will come to me. Maybe I'll see you again..."

"Sooner than you think!"

And she is gone.

I spend no time dwelling on Hiro or our past lives. There is something I feel I need to do. I'm not sure how, but I think I've been waiting for someone, too. I remember a man who killed me, whom I then killed, and he's coming here. I don't know how I know these things, I can't remember everything, I just know. I saw him in my mind's eye not too long ago, maybe a second ago. I saw him die and he did such a nice job! He gave up his seat in a lifeboat and even if he was an Imperialist, he deserves a break for that! He saved another man so the man could be with his wife in the lifeboat. He must be learning something. He sure is spending a lot of time as a male down there. I want to help him wipe the slate clean.

He's probably caught in that tunnel. I wonder if I could go through that again. Oh, I have gone through the tunnel more than once, only I will never experience it as frightening again. It was so light and nice this time! I wonder what he's seeing.

Ah, there he is! Boy, what a mess! Poor guy... He's running to me, he's putting his arms around me...

We just hold each other, and as I hold him I remember that he was my father a long time ago and he nearly killed me, he raped me, he made my life a living hell and I became an angry spirit. Yes! Then he actually did kill me! But by doing so, he saved me because I repaid my dearest friend, to whom I owed so much, and later she became my husband, Jon. The being I am holding brought me to the happiest moments I have ever known on earth.

I killed you, too, didn't I? You were busy learning important things about life but I killed you. I felt bad about it. That was what it was. I learned a lot that life, it brought me to consciousness. So I have you to thank, doubly, and here you are, all shaken and weepy. Yes, I'm an angel. You can't hear everything I'm saying, just the parts you like. Oh, soak up the love, that's the best part. You'll know next time around. Here, I'll make things simple for you.

"The tunnel is gone. It's okay now. You did spend a long time in there."

"I ran through the tunnel. It wasn't really a tunnel. You have to keep running or they catch you..." He's hugging me again. Glad to be of some assistance. Oh, I like this one so much!

"Come here, now, I'll bring you to a nice place... "

I take his hand and lead him. I'm a female to him, and I can see why! He has been a man fighting men for so many lives. The place I bring him to is partially Hiro's place and partially mine. It has the trees and berry fields from Hiro's place, with the glowing azure sky I saw after I died this time. The being that just emerged from the tunnel falls down into the grass, into the ecstasy of heaven. He's weeping, looking at me so gratefully, shuddering from time to time with memories.

We spend a lot of time together, as much as he needs. I listen to his thoughts and answer all the questions I feel will be helpful. I teach him about looking back into your life... There is a woman he can't forget. She wants a child... Yes. It's okay now. Look if you want to. Make up whatever you want to, see? And when you are ready, go back down.

He's looking at me with great foreboding. "I'm not going back down."

"Well, maybe not. Maybe you'll stay here. I love you very much, but I need to go."

"I know you from somewhere... "

"We will meet again."

"Stay here with me!"

"I'll tell you what. I'll do a lovely little dance for you, but then I have to go."

I begin bobbing and twirling in all earnest, while I whistle a little song from his place and time; I don't know how, it just pops into my head. And this is suddenly very funny to him and he begins to laugh. He falls to the ground and begins to roll around, and I fall on top of him and we roll around together, laughing. Once in awhile, when he seems to calm down, I whistle that song again, looking ever more serious, and he bursts into howls of laughter, and that's it. I made him laugh, he'll be okay now. I give him a hug, and I disappear.

I'm standing alongside the line for rebirth. Jeez. Everyone looks so apprehensive and all their thoughts are so loud!

There is a line with three beings in it. The first being turns to me. It is thinking it will die right away, as soon as it is born, because it is scared of life. The being can't remember that this has already happened its last three times on earth. I mind-talk.

"How many times can a baby die? Is there anything sadder? When you die right away, as a baby, you have nothing left to fear, but you miss all the good stuff about life, too. What will you learn? What would happen if you kept on living? I think you should go for it."

His face gets softer and he disappears.

The next one moves forward. She isn't thinking or feeling anything. She has forgotten everything. She killed someone in her last life. I mind-talk what pops into my head.

"The first shall be last and the last shall be first. You will be forgiven if you can forgive the world."

Its face softens and it disappears.

The last one in line starts talking to me first.

"I want to go back and do it over again, I just want to get it right, I want to do this one damn thing right! Do ya see! Can ya send me back?"

"You can never go back, you can only go forward. Concentrate on what is right and it will happen."

His face softens and he disappears.

Now I'm going down and there's no one to give me the talk. I begin to laugh and laugh as every great thing said by every great being that ever walked the face of the earth goes running through my head.

"Love is all there is."

"I'm having a hard enough time with this life, don't ask me about the next."

"Return to the un-carved block."

"Pain is an illusion."

"A stitch in time saves nine."

"When the tree falls over, the monkeys split."

"What is the sound of one hand clapping?"

"The lord will provide."

And I'm off.

Transmigrations

Marta to Molly

Karlos/Mei Hua/Khalid/Keizo/Marta	becomes	Molly
Merlo/Bau Yu/Fida/Tatsuo/Jon, husband	becomes	baby in traffic
Victor/Ying/Misha'il/Midori/Jon, son	becomes	Henry
(girl given voice/Shaymaa/Hiro'chan)	becomes	Mr. Prizzani

MOLLY

The scope of existence widens

If God knows everything, then he knows I'm making up sins for confession.

Well? I can't remember everything I did wrong the whole week! I bet Jane remembers—she remembers everything *I* do wrong. I hope those ants aren't the kind that bite. I like to sit out here a lot. After I cleaned the bathrooms, Mom said sure, go pick some strawberries.

This is my strawberry patch. Because I called dibs on it, and Jane and Sammy don't care about it. One little strawberry for the basket, one for me. So sweet! Not even sour at all, not like the fat empty ones from the store.

I wonder what they're doing. Everyone's cleaning house, that's what. I'm glad I don't have to dust the whole house! I already did the toilets - that's bad enough. But I don't mind one bit. I don't know what the big deal is with thinking toilets are gross. It's the easiest job.

Two for the basket, one for me. I'm going to make a pie this time, if I have enough. Or I'll make a really little pie, if Mom shows me how. That's what I want to do.

In church they say that God is Love. If God is Love, then why does he want to hear the bad things? I don't get to tell the good things. Plus, if God can already see and hear everything, why do I need to tell the priest what God already knows? He saw me push Sammy, which was his fault for taking my seat, and He must have forgiven me right then and there, because He saw what Sammy did first. God is fair. He knows the rules. Two for me, one for the basket. Two at once are good.

I don't like confession. I think the priest tells on you. He probably tells the Sisters and that's why they are so mean. They're probably mad at me for stuff I didn't even do, because I made it up. That's how nuns are. They are crabby, for sure. And, okay, lying is a sin. But to even go to confession and confess my sins, I have to lie and make some up because I can't remember. So going to confession is one more sin on top of all the other sins I can't remember.

I always think God will strike me down dead for lying. I wait in the back of the dark smelly church, not at all like it is on Sundays, all dusty, no music, being quiet in line. I always get nervous and try to make things up quickly and wish I would have thought up some sins before getting into line. But God never strikes me down, not in line and not in that little box, which it's only job is to hold sinners talking about their sins, which is a waste because they could be good hiding places or little forts and certainly tree forts, if you could get one up in a tree. And then the priest should know I'm lying because I can't talk right, and I say pretty much the same thing every time, but no, he says the same thing every time right back to me.

And I've got to say, anyone who goes home and prays all the prayers that the priest tells you to pray to make up for being a sinner like holy homework has got to be a nut because who would know if you did or you didn't? But Jane says her sinner prayers and she's perfect, but I don't because God knows I don't mean the bad things and he sees everything and stuff. And of course, I never remember, so at bedtime I just say things like Hi God, sorry I forgot what I was supposed to do for the fake sins I made up because I can't remember everything I do wrong. I'll be good, though, tomorrow, and will I get a new bike for Christmas? If the answer is yes, make the light come on. Okay. If the answer is no, make the light come on. So I'm probably getting the bike. Thank you!

I really think God is too busy to pay attention to all that. First of all, he's got a lot of starving Chinese people to try to help. And he's got all the bad people he's got to mind and one hundred angels over there and everything in the whole world he's got to make happen like the sun and rainbows and taking all the sick puppies and people away to heaven and stuff, so I'm lucky that way because he's busy and all. Otherwise, I would be in big trouble all the time.

I can't find any more strawberries. There's none even hiding under the leaves. Is that it? Did I eat them all yesterday? This isn't going to make a pie, there's just a little bit. I might as well eat them all. Or I could bring them in to Mom. Or I could just eat these few because there aren't that many. But if I never ate any, there would be enough. So I won't eat any more and these go to Mom, and I'll put 'em in back of me so I won't eat them.

When I get a little too hot, then the wind blows just right. I don't know where it comes from. It just comes over me and goes away. That's pretty amazing. You can't even see this spot all winter long because of the snow, but now, when the strawberries come out, I really like this place. I'm going to sit here for awhile.

Yep. They never even talk about the worst sins. Neither do I. I don't think any of the other kids tell the truth, either. I think the worst sin is picking your nose and eating it. You have to be very careful no one sees you because if they do they say, "You have cooties! Sick! Mom! Molly ate her buggers!" And Mom looks so de-scusted, she makes me wash my mouth and my hands and I'm still de-scusting, I think she's going to put me in the shower. It's some kind of disease you might get, but I still do it all the time because I can't help it. And touching your poop should be some kind of sin and playing with your mom's bra or your dad's underwear when you're folding the laundry or even thinking about your mom and dad's privates. Now that's de-scusting and that right there is a sin of thinking about bad things, and I really would confess thinking bad things, but I won't remember this and so that's my whole problem.

I'm going to check on the strawberries. Those aren't the kind of ants that bite, but they eat strawberries, I think, because they're crawling all over them. I should blow on all the strawberries so I don't bring ants in the house.

Other real sins are eating things off the floor, especially ice cream, which I can do pretty good, you just have to slurp real fast. And looking at naked people or trying to see the people you know when they're naked, like accidentally walking into the bathroom with the broken knob when you know they're in there, but Jane just shouts, "Mom!" Jeez. What a big mouth. But the worst thing is pulling the butts off of lightening bugs or the legs off of Daddy Long Legs. Well, it's the worst to me, but maybe seeing people naked is actually the worst.

All the church sins, I don't even know what they mean. Once I said one of those, I said "Bearing Falls Witness," because that doesn't sound too bad. Bearing Falls Witness gets you the same punishment as hitting your brother, which is surprising. But I never confessed any of the other bible sins, like "Coveting." Sick! I wouldn't try that one. I think it's sick. Anyway, it sounds sick. But all the actual sins I do, I never tell, really, except lying and pushing. But I never say, "Bless me Father for I have sinned, my last confession was a week ago, and since then I've picked my nose and ate it lots of time because that's my bad habit. I also eat my scabs and try to see people naked. I'm sorry." Hah! No one says that, ever! I would just like to see someone say that to Father Burke! Then they probably *would* get hit by lightening in the church, but I'm not going to try it because the sins I make up are good enough.

Well. I blew on all the strawberries. Maybe Martha Macken is home. I could go play with her. She lives closer than Jennifer Langston, who's kind of crabby and wants to be a nun when she grows up and that makes sense to me. Martha wants to be a movie star. I'm the only one I know who doesn't want to be anything yet.

I used to think I could be a nice nun, like the Flying Nun, but then I think just be a bird if you want to fly, because that's all I really want to do, not be a nun. But the Flying Nun can eat ice cream and watch TV but birds get attacked by people like Eddy who thinks it's wonderful to shoot a bird, which is not a sin I have and is worse than pulling the legs off a Daddy Long Legs so he's in more trouble than me. But see, it would be better to be myself and be able to fly, which is impossible unless you went to Ali Baba and got a magic lamp, that would be my first wish, but it's not going to happen, I've tried a million times.

So I'm going to give Mom these strawberries and hopefully Dad won't have anything stupid for us to do now, because half the day is gone with church anyway, and I can go over to Martha's. I go in through the garage door and mom can hear me with her eagle ears.

"Is that you, Molly?"

"Yeah, Mom, I brought you a surprise!"

"Did you take your shoes off? Molly! You're old enough to remember without being reminded every time you come into this house! Go back and take them off *right now!*"

"But I'm eight, Mom, which is not a good remembering age I don't think, and I've already walked over here, so the floor..."

Mom gives me that look, that "I'm not going to hit you because I'm going to walk away now and hope that when I turn around you won't be standing there bugging me or I will hit you, that's for sure" look, so I go back over to the rug and tug my shoes off and then I remember I should untie them, which is hard to do when your foot's not in them, so I don't get hit or yelled at or get the look and I think my strawberries are stupid now.

Around the corner and there's Mom, hunting for dust balls so she doesn't have to clean the whole floor again, but I wouldn't clean it even with the dust balls because they really aren't dirt, and she jumps when I get near even though she knows I came in. She does the fake Mom voice meaning "I'm not really upset, but I have every right to be."

"Yes, sweetie?"

"Can I go over to Martha's?"

"Hmm. Okay, for an hour or so. Be back by five, okay sweetie?"

"Okay Mom. Hey, there is a surprise for you on the counter..."

"Uh Huh? Okay, honey, I'll see it in a minute."

She's just spotted a dust ball and she's down the hall, grabbing it with a wet washcloth. She uses washcloths for everything, like healing the sick she just puts Vicks on it and wraps it around your throat and pulling stuff out of the oven and swatting flies and scrubbing my scraped knee which I hate, I'll just do it myself or better yet leave it alone, hide it from her, because she was a nurse and she says you've got to scrub it until it bleeds so all the dirt will wash out with the blood but what about me crying? I don't like her washcloths and I don't ever use them myself, except for the old rag ones, which I clean the toilets with.

I go put my shoes back on, which is so dumb, but that's how it is. I wonder where Sammy and Jane are, but it's no good asking questions, someone might ask you to do something, like dad might come around the corner and say, "Hey, help your brother wash the car." It's best to leave when you can. I go out the way I came in.

It's a nice sunny day. I can hop on one foot, though not all the way to Martha's house. I don't know why it's so much more tiring to hop but it is. You go over the same ground, the same distance, but it makes you more tired. There. I'm getting too tired.

A caterpillar! A fuzzy orange and black one. I love these guys, except they, yep, it just pooed in my hand and I hope it's poo because otherwise it might be guts and you've got another sin, but I didn't squeeze it very much when I picked it up and God knows that. It's all curled up in a ball. You can stretch it out, though. If you rub it's back. Like that.

I should put it down before I get to the door, there, in that bush, that's a nice home. But it will never see its own home again because it could never find its way back. It would probably take a caterpillar five years to get back, even if it knew which direction to go. I should put it back down the road where I got it. Maybe it was going home. Maybe it was going to its friend's house. I wouldn't like it if a giant picked me up. I've thought about that a lot. That would be about the worst thing in the world. Every time I pick something up, I think a giant will pick me up and carry me far away where I could never find my way back, but I forget and pick up little guys anyway.

Where did it go?

"Hey, dumbbell, whatcha doing on the porch?"

I turn around and there's Eddie. He's so stupid. And he's mean. He's a fifth grader, so he's probably naturally like that.

"Is Martha home?"

"Is Martha home?" He's teasing me, using a girl voice. I ignore him and ring the bell.

"Hey! Don't ring the bell, my Mom's sleeping! Yes, she's home. Just go in, you idiot."

I don't even turn around. Eddie's trying to get me in trouble, of course. I wait by the door. Mrs. Macken opens it.

"Well, hello Molly! Are you looking for Martha? Well, come on in. Eddie, did you take the trash out? Bring it out tonight, angel, or you'll forget."

I turn around and give him a look like, "Yeah, ANGEL!" and he sneers at me and lumbers off. Eddie is mean.

Mrs. Macken has already turned around and walked into the house, saying, "She's in the backyard, I think, go ahead out honey," and Mrs. Macken glides behind the counter in the kitchen, going at something in a bowl. I go to the sliding glass doors and let myself out.

Martha is lying in a lounge chair with her sunglasses on. There's an orange plastic cup balancing precariously in the grass next to her chair. She looks kind of funny, trying to be like Doris Day or something, but she's a lot chubbier than Doris Day, who I think looks dumb but Martha thinks she is great.

"Hey, Martha."

"Oh, hello, darling."

"Whatcha drinking?"

"Wine!"

"That is not wine! It's probably water."

"It's a martini, I made it myself. Do you want some? You can be the make-up girl and we can drink martinis."

"I don't want to be the make-up girl. How about if I'm a movie star, too?"

"Oh, okay, but in a different movie. I'm Doris Day. You can be... Who do you want to be?"

"I want to be Little Joe's girlfriend. Did you watch The Ponderosa last night? Remember Little Joe had that one girlfriend? I could be her."

"Okay. So anyway, darling, what movie are you making now?"

"Martha, is that water? Because I'm kind of thirsty."

"Oh Jeez. You're not very good at pretending."

"But this is stupid. Why don't we pretend we're kittens who get lost in the woods, and this bear comes along and we have to hide but then a dog comes, who's really nice, and he leads us out of the woods..."

"You want me to get you a drink of water?"

"Yeah, sure, thanks."

"Come on in."

She gets me the water and we go up to her room. We get out her Barbies, which she has a lot of and she plays movie star while I play house. We would play with Skididdle Kiddles and Trolls if we were at my house because they do a lot more and that's all I've got. Jane has Barbies she keeps neat and tidy in their cases at the bottom of her sparkling clean closet and won't let me touch. I ask for Barbies, too, but mom forgets so I forgive her because I forget a lot, too, and that's one of the nice things about me, I can forgive you really quick.

Martha won't play with anything but Barbies, so we always have to play at her house. I'm getting really bored and my bottom hurts and my legs from sitting down so long. I go over to her bed and hang upside down and listen to her talk on and on.

"Oh no. I don't want to go out for lunch again. Let's stay here and go swimming. Okay. Where is that Ken? He was supposed to be home an hour ago. I have to polish my nails. I don't like this dress any more. I'm going to change again..."

I think I'll go home. It's probably close to dinner time. My head is starting to pound from the blood. When you hang upside down all the blood goes into your head and plumps it up fat and then you sit up and it drains back down to your toes. It's kind of weird to have blood all over inside your body. I can smell something. Martha's mom is cooking something. I sit up slowly and feel the blood gushing around. Weird!

I see Martha's reflection in the window. I hate Barbies. The shoes fall right off their feet and the clothes don't fit and after you dress them up, there's nowhere to go, except maybe to the woods. I could take Barbie to the woods and have some fun. This is boring. I don't like Barbies. Martha sees me staring out the window and says, "You want to play doctor?"

I feel my eyes scrunching up because I'm pretty sure I know what that means, doing something nasty, but I'm not sure, either. I don't think I want to do something nasty. Abby Goodman made Angie Steterson do something nasty and she said it was really weird and she'll never do it again. I don't want to do it ever.

"Let's not, Martha."

"No, let's, it'll be fun. Come on. Oh! You never want to do anything fun. Come to my tree fort with the doctor kit, it'll be the hospital!"

I forgot all about her tree fort! I love to go up there. We could go up there for a while, especially if Eddie isn't around, because if he sees us, I'm not going up there. He'll figure out some way to do something mean.

"Okay, let's go to the tree fort, but I don't want to play doctor."

"No, I mean *real* doctors. And if you don't want to play then go home."

Well, I think about this. I could see if Sammy is doing anything. Is it time for me to go home? I never know. But the tree fort is fun. I don't like it when other people get these ideas and get me in trouble.

"Okay. I'll play, but only once, really quick."

She grabs the doctor kit, one of those white plastic jobs with the scalpel things and fake pills and everything. I had one of those once, or it was Sammy's, it was pretty cool. I follow her out the sliding backdoor and down to the giant sycamore tree. This is such a cool fort!

She climbs up right away, holding that bag in her hand. It takes me longer to get up because I haven't climbed it as much as her. I have to hunt around for the next board because I don't want to fall. I don't know how she climbed up with that bag in her hand. I get to the top and swing my butt around and sit down right there because you could fall real easy and die for sure. I want to think about standing up. I might just crawl on my hands and knees so I can't fall. I look out across the yard and just sit still. The fort has three walls and a roof but this part is open with a railing. It feels good up here, although it's a little scary. But that's the fun part. I pull my legs up and scoot back and I'm safe. I scoot to the wall and hug my knees.

We talk about Robinson Caruso and what if we lived in a tree house without our parents, how great that would be. I ask her if we could move up here and just go visit our parents or get them to bring food and stuff to us. I'm having such a good time. Then Martha says, "Oh, you poor, sick child! Let me see what's wrong with you!" and she pushes me onto my back and goes fishing around in that bag and then she holds up the knife.

"Your nipples need to come out! Lift up your shirt. I need to do an operation!"

It's kind of fun, so I lift up my shirt and she pretends to cut out my nipple. I feel all funny and the knife is cold and I worry for a minute that she might actually try to cut it out for real, not that I need it or anything. I guess you need them when you're older, but I don't think I'll be using mine. But my mom would get really angry if my nipples were actually gone. I can just hear her: "Young lady, where are your nipples! How many times do I have to tell you not to let Martha Macken cut them out!" I start to laugh from the cold knife and my mom saying stuff in my head and Martha is laughing, too, and her eyes are all happy like that. She's talking away as usual.

"Oh my gosh, this nipple is sticky. I'll put it over here so you can take it home and put it under your pillow..."

"How much do you get for a nipple?!"

And we're squealing with laughter and Martha cuts out my other nipple and falls over laughing. I pull my shirt back down real quick and she sits up as fast as she fell over and shouts, "Okay, my turn! Cut my nipples out!"

"Okay, lay down and pull up your shirt," I tell her. I talk doctor stuff that makes her laugh really hard.

"Sutures! Nurse! Snoggle that indecision! Oh my gosh, she's losing a lot of blood! Put a washcloth in there! Nurse, you idiot! Did you lose her nipples? She has to put them under her pillow to get some Nipple Fairy money! They're probably worth fifty cents! Yeah, I wonder if the Nipple Fairy knows the Tooth Fairy? They're probably sisters or something!"

She laughed the most when I called the nurse an idiot, so I say it some more.

"Nurse! You idiot! You are an idiot, nurse!"

She's saying it too and I've already cut both her nipples out, but she just lays there laughing with her shirt up and she looks really weird with her nipples sticking out of her chest like that and I'm not laughing anymore and she sees me looking at her and our eyes meet and I feel pretty funny but in a good way until I hear Eddie's voice.

"Um-ma-ma-ma-ma! What are you nasty girls doing?"

Just his head peeks over the edge of the tree fort. He's standing on the boards, spying on us. Martha pulls down her shirt and scrambles over to the edge but Eddy is already climbing back down. She tries to spit on him, but it kind of just runs down her chin, so she shouts, "Eddie, if you don't get out of here RIGHT NOW, I'm going to tell!"

"'I'm going to tell! Mom, mom, Eddie saw me playing doctors with Molly!'" Eddie says in a squealy girl voice, teasing her.

But Martha doesn't even wait a moment, she starts screaming right there and then and Eddie gets so rattled his foot slips on the board and he falls, and his mother comes out and she's listening to his explanation and not believing much of it. She says something to him, then tells us girls to come on down, it's almost supper time, and I know I'm probably late so we skinny down and I tell Martha thanks for having me over and she smiles at me and I start running home.

It feels sad to be suddenly alone and all the bad things come rushing in and the air is losing the light. I think I'm in trouble. I think maybe I shouldn't go home, but then I would get in more trouble, so I should go home faster and my legs feel funny and suddenly I'm looking at the gravel up close and my knee burns and I want to cry. I'm picking myself up and brushing the rocks from my hands, which are stinging, and it's getting cooler and I'm hungry and I can smell the smell of food everywhere and I look down and see a dribble of blood going down the front of my leg, coming from my knee and I start to cry. But just a little.

I start limping home and when I get in the door my mom shouts, "Molly? You're late. Go wash up now and hurry."

And I feel like I'm in so much trouble because my mom's voice is weird and something is wrong. How does she know about the nipples? Did Eddie call her? Did Eddie tell Mrs. Macken and Mrs. Macken called her? Oh God, that would be really bad. Oh why, why did I ever do what Martha said? See? It never turns out good. I always get in trouble for having fun.

I wash up and try to touch my knee with a wet wad of toilet paper and I get most of the blood off but every time I look at it I start to cry a little. I go to the kitchen table and everyone's there and they're looking so strange and angry. Does everyone know about the nipples? How could this be happening? I sit down across from Jane and she gives me one of those looks like, "Just shut up and be really good," so that's what I do.

There are rolls and canned corn and mashed potatoes on the table and mom gets the fried chicken out of the oven and finally sits down. Dad says grace in a weird way like shoes that are too tight and everyone starts eating. Sammy of course gets the chicken first and takes the drum stick and I want to say something, but I can't because of Jane's warning look so I be quiet, feeling worse and worse until the chicken gets to me and there is a drum stick left and that's good.

No one says anything, we just eat. Fine by me, I'm hungry.

Jane looks sad and I wonder what's going on. But she does look sad or angry a lot. She's the oldest. All the oldest are angry a lot. I'm glad I'm the youngest. Sammy's pretty fun, though, because he's even younger than me.

"Hey Sammy, wanna play a game after dinner?"

Everyone looks at me and I figure out that no one has been saying anything so I shouldn't either and Sammy's eyes say, "Yeah, sure," but he doesn't say anything but mom says, "After you help with the dishes."

Okay so hurry up and finish eating. My mom takes the longest. I just sit there and then my dad gets up before mom is finished so dinner's over, and I start clearing the table and stacking up the dishes. Jane washes and I dry and when it's all done I run to find Sammy. He's playing records real low in his room, which he's the boy so he doesn't have to do dishes and he gets his own room, but if I said that to him he would say, "Okay, so you take the trash out! I have to do all the big jobs not just splash a rag around in the toilet goofing off like you do." So never mind the fight, he has some games I like and I would rather play than fight, unless it is wrestling which is so much fun but we better not.

"Hey Sammy! Want to play Trouble?"

So we play Trouble in his room and he plays those little records soft like Rubber Soul, which doesn't mean anything but the music is good. I love the Pop-o-matic. I would always play even if I always lost, just to push the Pop-o-matic. Some genius thought of that. When I grow up,

I'm going to think of stuff like the Pop-o-matic and play games until I die. I'm getting some lucky rolls. I feel so happy.

Jane sticks her head in and says, "Man from Uncle is on," which we always watch together on Sunday. The game was over a long time ago and I'm just fooling with the Pop-o-matic and Sammy's switching around different records so we go to the den and I get to lay down on the floor and Dad is on the couch but where is mom? But the show is starting and then it's the commercial and that's when I go out to the kitchen and mom is sitting there with a cup of tea staring into space and I say:

"Mom, come watch Man from Uncle with us. It's really good," And she like wakes up and smiles a little and says, "Okay, dear," and keeps on sitting there. She does that all the time. It's pretty weird.

Then the show is over and mom says go to bed and I wonder if she was watching the show or if she just came into the living room right now? She never has any fun and I won't be like her, ever, because it is so sad and boring. I go do everything I'm supposed to do and Sammy's getting in my way in the bathroom, which he loves to do. I get into my PJ's and I'm in bed but Jane's not, I don't know where she's been all night and mom comes in and says prayers with me and says Jane will be here in a little while and mom looks at me just a moment with her love eyes like she's not going to be around in the morning and has to say goodbye with her sad eyes. Then she does that wake up thing like she was sleeping while she was staring at me and she gives me a big hug and sweeps out the door clicking the light off and pulling the door closed as she goes.

I don't like the dark, but I'm not afraid of it anymore. Actually, you can see cool things in the dark. I try to make those chickies and duckies on the wall, but I can only do a dog, if it even looks like a dog. Then I hear Jane come in and she gets into bed all quiet and I say some stuff and she says to just go to sleep. Okay fine, Crabby. I lay in bed trying to remember to keep my eyes closed, but every time I think about it they're open looking at the ceiling, which we have a really interesting ceiling with swirly faces and mountains and stuff on it, though it's supposed to be just a white ceiling with bumps on it.

I'm starting to feel bad and my heart starts racing and I hear mad voices and suddenly I remember that everyone probably knows about the nipples and I was supposed to feel bad all night and I sure do now. I try hard to hear the voices, but I can only hear my dad's. I can't hear what he's saying. Maybe he's saying, "We have to do something about Molly and this nipple problem." Like hit me or yell at me in front of everyone and I start crying and Jane says, "What's the matter?" and I say, "Jane, am I in trouble?" and she says, "No, everything's alright, just go to bed. You're not in trouble." And I say, "Then why is everyone mad?" and Jane says, "Don't worry about it. It's not about you." And I say, "What's it about?" and she says with that tight shoe thing Dad does, "It's not about you, so please just go to sleep."

So I be quiet but I feel bad. I know Jane wants to get a room of her own and now she probably really wants one. I wonder how she'll get her own room? There aren't any left. I don't want to be alone. I like Jane even if she is crabby because she's nice, too. Sometimes, like now. Even though I cut out people's nipples, she says it's not my fault. So I shouldn't worry.

Now my body's starting to feel warm and that's real nice. There are dragons that are small enough to hold in my arms and they follow me, but I don't tease them because they can grow real big and turn left, turn right, don't hit the mailbox, I can fly right out of the window like a bird and miss all the trees and get cotton candy the man says get in the car but I don't want to get in the car run away run run run but not fast enough but run run run as it gets dark, turn left, turn right on a bike I found and it's not mine but I need it now so it's okay and it's working, the man's not there, but keep going, just to be sure, down an alley, in a city where I've never been before but somehow I know the way.

Nobody seems to understand that I'm not a baby anymore. I still can't stay up as late as my friends and I have the dumb chores still and it's just the way everyone treats me. I can't explain it. I know I cry more than anyone in our family but that is because I feel more, not because I'm a baby. But whatever. I don't even care anymore.

Everything's easy in the ninth grade now, compared to all the other grades, when I did poorly. Of course, no one in my family has noticed that. Sometimes I think I'm invisible.

I watch Annette Segal and Amy Siden and all the popular girls and I can't figure it out. I don't know why they are so popular. They are stupid. They talk about stupid things. And I never say they are stupid, I'm always nice to them, but they still don't let me "in." Okay, I'm going to Amy's Bat Mitzvah, but so is half the class.

I'm tired of being alone. There is not one other person who thinks like me. Terry is my best friend and she's a good friend, too, but she doesn't think like me. She doesn't think up cool stuff to do. She has no guts. I always have to make her do everything. After we ran around on the golf course in broad daylight, running through the sand traps and water holes with this guy shouting, "You kids get out of here! Nick? That's it! Call the clubhouse!" I got us out safely, but after that, she said she's not doing any more of my ideas. But she floated down the creek with me and we got leaches stuck to our butts oh my god that was so funny, and Terry was saying, "Just leave them, just leave them alone, Molly, don't *do* anything!" I looked at her butt because she said it felt funny. That right there is too funny: "Oh, could you please look at my butt? It feels funny!" I scraped them off with a stick and Terry had scabs on her ass for a week, not that she could complain about it to anyone but sit a little funny in math like she's always got to pee, and by the time I pulled my pants down apparently the leaches had drank their fill and fell off or something and Terry was so miffed. "Miffed." That's the only emotion, besides tears, I ever get out of Terry.

You'd think the boys would think of some cool stuff to do, but the boys are even worse. They only want to be with the sexy girls who are stupid. Except for ugly boys, like Jimmy and Cameron, they want to be with me but I'm not that desperate. Well, I'm not that desperate for a boyfriend; I *am* desperate, in general. And what a creep I am to think such thoughts. I try hard to rise above the mundane, the physical, but it gets so confusing. I'd rather not have feelings for anyone. That right there is the truth. I don't have feelings for anyone.

Maybe Jimmy is like me. Kind of. Except he's nicer. But he's really not like me, either. I just like his smile. He thinks I'm funny and I think he's funny, that's about it. He doesn't get it, when I'm talking. And besides, I would get teased so bad if I went out with him, he is sooo ugly. No one would talk to me again, except Terry, and she's getting a little tiresome. I don't think I could kiss him, either. He'd be all trying to put his tongue in my mouth and I'd be choking back vomit, probably.

But the thing is, intellectually, I'm alone. No one gets me. For example: I want to be a black man. Can I say that to anyone? Of course not. But here's the deal: They are totally groovy, they sing and dance much better than white people and they talk about what really matters in the world, like what the meaning of life is and how to live. They say what they have to say whether people want to hear it or not, the world be damned. I wish so bad I could be like that, not care what anyone else thinks. At least I stand up for my music, which is probably why I'm not popular because I apparently have potential, thanks to decent looks and a nice house in a nice neighborhood.

Stevie Wonder is my favorite. Everything he says is absolutely true and important. That is rare. And Sly, he totally knows what's going on. And Jimi Hendrix. If I could be as cool as those three guys, that would be it for me. That right there.

No one at my school even buys records. Okay, they buy them, but only if the songs have been on the radio and then they only listen to the radio songs. I have everything Stevie or Sly or Jimi ever did. The best songs are not on the radio. I listen to Joni Mitchell and Cat Stevens, too. Some people look, *and* see. Some people just look. It's about change, doing things differently, is that so hard? Is it so hard to make this generation different from the last one? Everyone at school doesn't even think about the words. They do what their parents did, in the same tired way. I can't hardly stand them. Even Terry says, "Why do you listen to that music? I mean, you're so crazy about it." Yeah, like listen to the radio, be sane, eh Terry? And she means black music, which is all I really listen to, besides Joni Mitchell and Cat Stevens.

Anyway. Terry really loves me, so I try not to be too mean to her, but I am kind of mean. I heard people think I'm a snob. Do I have a thousand dollar Bat Mitzvah at the mall? No, I don't care about your money and I don't grovel, so you say I'm a snob. Lackey or snob, take your pick.

They are so blind. Never think about where they came from, not their people, not their birth. Never think about all the other people on the planet. Never think about death. They think about their life, but not with their own thoughts. I swear they are programmed like robots, so predictable. I know no humans, only these thoughtless robot kids. Even Terry is a mama's girl. She'd never cross her mother. She would never take a step outside the invisible circle around her. She doesn't even see the circle. "Look at me, I'm the first and only person on the planet and my sniveling little life is all there is!"

Oh to hell with it. I'll always be alone. I have a weird fate, I guess.

I honestly believe that without my music I would die. Without it I would have Amy and Annette and John Sample and Frankie Hardaway's deep thoughts like, "Hey. Why don't we make them serve pizza in the cafeteria?" They want me to join their protest. I go door to door to get McGovern elected and they want to change their lunch fare. That's the big deal with them.

Stevie says, "I don't even have to do nothing to you, you'll cause your own country to fall," and that's the truth. I see the bigotry and hypocrisy and I just can't take it sometimes. And I'm not even black! I don't know what I'd do if I had to deal with prejudice and idiots and people like my grandma saying, "Why, I like blacks, I do! I like Sammy Davis Junior!" You know what the worst thing is? I'm so invisible to my grandma she couldn't even see how much I hated her for being an ignorant racist! Ignorant racists everywhere, and they'll all be gathering at the Bat Mitzvah.

I have to get ready for the Bat Mitzvah. I don't even know what they're for, except to say, "Hey, I'm a rich Jew!" What do the poor Jews do? I guess they're not really Jewish. You don't see the rich Irish Catholics trotting around throwing their cash down the drain. No. They sleep on their cash. Got it sewed up in the mattress. Wear rags and eat weenies, in case there's another famine. Who'll be laughing then? My dad says the Irish are my People. Just as crazy as Jews. So what does it matter?

I think all religions are nuts. It's like, they set up a religion and make some rules, and the first thing everybody who signs up does, is break them. Jesus said to love everybody, so Christians have been starting wars and killing people and saying everyone else is going to hell ever since. And the Jews were slaves for eons, poor and downcast, and their God said don't be making golden calves and worshiping the things of this earth. So what do they do? Make sure they are the richest folks around and look down their noses at everyone else. I think I'll start a religion where everyone has to live just for themselves and if my little theory is right then they'll be nice to one another. But probably not. Maybe people are just born low and selfish and there's no way out.

I look fat in every dress I own, which is two, and two skirts. My mom says, "Wear those pants, those are fine. Those are *fancy*. After all, it's not a ball!" She should have married Mr. Rogers. He thinks a lot of stuff is fancy, too. She doesn't get it.

I don't know why I'm going, anyway. Terry wasn't invited. I'm more popular than her, god only knows why, because I know everyone thinks I'm weird. I don't think I'll go. I could stay home and watch a movie or M.A.S.H. or something. Someone's walking down the hall. It's mom, and she'll just walk right in without knocking I got to pull this dress on first jeeze I hate that.

"Molly, are you dressed? Oh Hi, Honey. That's nice. Isn't that your Easter dress?"

"Mom! Could you please knock?!"

"Oh, didn't I knock? You're so silly anyway, what does it matter if I see you?"

"It clearly doesn't matter to you but it matters to me, Mom! That should be enough. And this isn't my 'Easter dress.' Do you think all clothing is named after some Holy and Apostolic Church holiday? Yeah, these are my Christmas tights and my Lenten shoes, Mom."

"You're sure in a mood today."

I'm in a 'mood' today. I wonder what it would be to be sans mood? 'Yesterday I was moodless.' Mood is such a weird word. Mood. Mood. Who thinks up these things? I want to be on the panel of word-makers. Dill. Salamander. That guy should be proud. Let's see. Crankation. Now I'm proud! Oh, there she goes, Mom's picking up my room without asking, with a gentle smile on her face, totally oblivious. She doesn't even care that I was just mean to her, which is kind of a good thing because I don't mean to be, she's just such an idiot sometimes. I don't know how I could be so different from her, but thank God I am.

God, I know so many people who are just like their moms. They are invariably dull, but often quite nice, like Terry. I should've gotten Amy to invite her. I feel bad going without her. Sometimes I think being popular is more important to me than my friends, or at least for awhile in the seventh grade it was. I'm not like that now. It was the thing to do; everyone was trying to be popular. I tried a little and got close to the top, but I saw right away there was no point. What do you get? Sick to your stomach and mostly at yourself, if you have a brain in your head, which seems to be my biggest problem. Not that I test high or anything, but Jesus, I can mentally tap dance around almost everyone I know.

"What are you thinking about, Honey?"

"I just don't know if I want to go. I look fat in this."

"You look fine. You have a nice body. You're developing so nicely and..."

"Mom! Please don't talk about my body! You sound like Mr. Rogers! My pants are fancy, and my body's fancy..."

"Jeez! You are in such a mood! Anyway, do you want something to eat before you go? They're not going to have dinner there, are they?"

"No, I think just snacks and stuff. I don't feel like eating."

"I have that stew on the stove. It should be ready by now. Sammy's over at band practice and Jane is... I don't know what Jane is. Where Jane is. Isn't she going out with Ted tonight? Anyway. Come on down and eat some stew. Maybe you want to put on some of my make-up tonight. Do you want to wear my perfume?"

"Mom, I don't wear make-up and I really don't care if people think I'm pretty or not. Why just hide what you are with a bunch of goop on your face that's probably going to make you look horrid when you're old? I don't care what I look like. The Lord giveth and the Lord taketh away. Who am I to say, 'Ah, sorry Your Holiness, I like this feature you gave me, but this one here, well, I'm going to have to do something about that. What on earth were you thinking?' Maybe God knows what's beautiful better than we do."

"Whatever, dear. When are you supposed to be there?"

"Oh my gosh, in like thirty minutes. I won't have time to eat."

"You can eat."

"Mom, can you please just drive me there?"

"Okay. But take something in the car."

"Mom!"

But she's already walked out of the room and no doubt I'll be chewing on some dried-out gristle just to make her happy while we're driving in the car. So I'll have beef-breathe when I meet the boy of my dreams.

That's *really* why I hate these things. I start dreaming about meeting someone, having some boyfriend who thinks like me and I get all stupid. I don't care if I never meet a boy. I wish it were frontier times and I could just marry someone who saw me in the newspaper and drive out and live on the prairie with them because what difference does it make who you choose, or if you choose? You live. You die. Why am I going to this thing?

"Here, Honey, take this bowl."

"Mom, I don't..."

"Oh, just eat something! I don't want you filling up on junk."

She wins. She used that voice that says, "I only seem weak. I could take you out with a thought." Times like these I think about how strong my mom really is, parading around as a weakling. I wouldn't mess with her. I take the bowl and get into the car. It's an Electra, which I think is pretty neat. At least I won't be showing up in a stupid car. It's amazing they spent the money. This is pretty good. No napkin. I pick around the carrots. Got to put carrots in everything. My grandma, the good one who died, she used to put carrots in everything, too. We're almost at the mall.

Suddenly I feel guilty. What is my mom going to do tonight? Hang out with Dad? Oh, that's always a good time. Mom never goes out. She never gets to do anything. God, I hope I don't end up like her. I feel so bad for her!

"Thanks, Mom. The stew was really good. What are you going to do tonight? Why don't you go out with Dad?"

"Go out with Dad? We don't want to go anywhere, Honey. I have some ironing to do."

Ironing? On a Saturday night?

"Don't do the ironing, Mom. Why don't you take a bath or go see a movie or something?"

"Oh, I like to iron. I appreciate having the time to do it. I'll watch something on TV. When should I pick you up?"

"Annette Segal is going to give me a ride home. They live near us."

"Oh. Okay. But call me if you need a ride. Do you have any money?"

"You gave me five bucks yesterday when I went to the mall with Terry and I didn't spend it. I'll call if I have any problems. Don't worry, Mom. I'll be fine."

"Okay, Honey. Have a good time."

"I will, Mom. Thanks. Thanks for the ride and everything."

"Have fun, dear."

"Bye, Mom."

I kiss her soft cheek and get out of the car but I can't walk away. I turn around and wave at her. She can tell I'm hesitating on her account and she waves me on, begins to pull away from the curb. I feel sad. I turn and head into the mall.

I feel sad that my mom isn't doing anything and Terry isn't doing anything. She's probably having Harriett over to watch some TV. God, Harriett is an idiot. Her name alone tells you what kind of night Terry's going to have. They'll probably make brownies, the little do-gooders. I wish Terry didn't hang out with the geeks. I could get her in to these things. But she doesn't want to go. Well, I'm going to see a few things before I die. I want to go everywhere.

Is this the right place? The mall is so empty. Second floor. There's Mike and Cameron. Was Jimmy invited? They see me.

"Hey, Molly."

"Hey, Cameron. How's it going?"

"Are you going to the Bat Mitzvah?"

"No, I'm window shopping. I like shopping at night."

Mike looks at me like I'm a snob but Cameron smiles. He knows me, kind of.

We walk up the stairs to the second story together. I'm thinking of something to say. They're probably thinking of something to say. Now we're trapped in that thinking-of-something-to-say-so-it-better-be-good thing. I've got something.

"Oysters."

Mike, deepening puzzled brow, Cameron smirking, he got it, but there's Samantha on the balcony, leaning over, there's Angela, who calls out, "Hey, guys. How's it going?"

"Hey, good, Angela," Mike pipes up, obviously grateful that he doesn't have to deal with me anymore, but someone more sane, like stupid, stupid Angela. Oh my God, she's got on this gorgeous dress! It *is* like a ball! I should've known. And she's wearing make-up! And Samantha's all dressed up, too. Probably their mothers dressed them. Oh, to hell with them. If people don't like me for my mind, then I don't really care. I'm not going to sell my soul for Mike Jacoby's attention, that's for sure, or anyone else's.

Oh my God. This is like a huge ballroom! It must have cost a thousand dollars to get this place! The hall is as big as a football field and everything looks like it's made out of velvet and gold. Amy is Queen for a day. "Yo daddy's rich, and yo ma is good looookin." Nobody's mom is as good looking as mine, actually. I wish I didn't come. I look stupid in this dress. No, I like this dress. I look good. At least I look groovy, which is more than I can say for most of the other girls here. It's like they're wearing their mother's clothes! They look so stupid! Anyway. Whatever.

There's Amy. She's got all these girls around her. I walk up and move in closer. I listen for a minute. They're talking about Annie Lacey, class slut. Oh, she went to third base with John Sample. Big news. Everyone laughs and looks around like they were touching themselves in public or something. But I laugh, too, because Sheila Goldstein keeps nudging me. I hate myself for it. I'm such a hypocrite.

Finally, we go over to the buffet table and get some punch. Some of the girls have drifted off. Me and Amy and Dawn Clausen are standing around looking at all the other kids and I ask Amy, "So. You're having your Bat Mitzvah. What is it, exactly?"

"It's when you turn thirteen, well, between thirteen and fourteen. You have to memorize all this stuff, not that I did. In fact, I couldn't remember much at the synagogue this morning, not that you can just flunk or something. I don't know. It's just like, you're Jewish, and you get this cool party!"

She sees the look of consternation on my face and adds, "Well, it's about saying to God and your family that you believe in being Jewish and you'll continue the traditions."

"That's pretty cool. So are you already done, being Bat Mitzvahed or whatever?"

"Yeah. We did it this morning. This is just the party part. Yeah. It's pretty cool. Oh! There's Angela! Oh my God! Is she going to dance? She's going to dance with Frankie! Oh how cool! I'm going over there!"

And she's gone, and Dawn runs over there with her, so I'm standing here alone. Oh, shit! I *knew* I shouldn't have come! If I was another girl I would have run after them, for no reason, like be a follower, which I'm not. Why do I go to these parties with people I don't even like and why do they invite me? Maybe I could get someone to dance with me. Cameron would dance, but then I'd get teased. Everyone would think we were going out, which we aren't. Screw it. I really like the mirrored rotating ball hanging from the ceiling throwing rectangles of light around the room. And I like the smell in here, like a new troll case when I was a kid, mixed with the smell of warm chocolate. Should I eat more dessert? Where's Cameron? Oh, he's over in the corner talking to some guys. I'm going over there. Don't go over there! I'm going over there.

I can feel myself walking across the floor. I feel beautiful. I think some guys are looking at me, but I'm so cool, I don't even glance around. I am, at least, very cool. Not like most of the girls here. Not like any of them. I'll go where I want to go. Cameron sees me and smiles.

"Hey, Molly."

"Hey."

"So, what're you drinking?"

"Whiskey."

"Where did you get the whiskey?" this guy asks and it's like I see him for the first time. I mean, I've seen him before, I think, in the hall. He's not in any of my classes. Have I ever seen him before? Oh my God, he's gorgeous. Shut up. Why did you say that about whiskey? Say something, you idiot, they're looking at you, Cameron and this guy and John Sample...

"I'm just kidding. It's not whiskey. I'm not allowed to drink whiskey at Bat Mitzvahs..."

"Oh yeah, but you drink it at roller skating rinks, right?" Cameron is my friend.

"Yeah. Only when I'm skating. It's an Irish thing."

"Are you Irish? You've got black hair." Oh, the dreamy guy's talking to me, smiling at me, who the hell is he, what's his name?!

"Uh, Black Irish, yep. That's what my folks tell me. I'm taking their word on this one."

"I say she's not Irish," John teases.

"She's got green eyes, though," Cameron says. Shit! They're all looking at me, three guys! They all like me! Play it cool.

"You see, the Moors came up from the Devil Land and impregnated Irish wenches, and so some of us have black hair and green eyes. The lucky ones, I guess. It's a sign of evolution."

"Hey, that means my people impregnated your people," the dreamy guy says. He's staring at me, he's smiling too much, but he's so cool, too. I'm looking right at him. I should look at John or Cameron, but I can't.

"So you're a Moor?"

"Yep. From the Devil Land, as you say."

I look quizzically over to Cameron as if to say, this guys putting me on, right? But Cameron shakes his head 'no' and says, "He's a devil, alright. He's from some United Arab country down there. Exchange student. He's staying at Jimmy's house. Didn't you know?"

"Jimmy's house? Hey, where is Jimmy? Did he come?"

"He's getting some Vodka. Don't ask. He's going to get some Vodka, out of his cousin's car, I think, and he's going to sneak it in here!"

"No! Jimmy would do it, too. He's so crazy. Look, I'm not drinking any Vodka. I was just kidding. I don't drink."

"In my country, we are not supposed to drink, either. But I don't really fit in there. My mother is from America, actually, that's why she sent me here. I'll drink. Where's Jimmy?"

And like, on cue, Jimmy comes sauntering in. Five foot eleven, towering over everyone, grinning like a maniac at me, all the way, all the way across the floor, grinning at me until he steps up a little too close, bends over, whispers, "Hey, Molly."

"Hey, Jimmy. What the hell are you doing? Do you have..." but I can't think of the right word to say because I can't say 'Vodka,' everyone will hear and we'll get in big trouble, but what's a slang word to use? 'Hooch?' 'The stuff?' Before I can think of something, Cameron says, "Chicken pocks?" and we all roar because Jimmy's face is all marked up with zits, which is what makes him ugly, that and his huge nose, and Jimmy lets a little anger float gently over his face then he's laughing with us.

"Have fun, Johnson. No, actually, I don't have anything. Well, I *might* have something for a friend, like Molly, or Shudree here. Let's see. Anything for Cameron? Let me look. Nope. Nothing for Cameron."

"Come on, Jimmy, I'm just playing. Did you get the stuff? No shit! From your cousin? You are sooo lucky, man. I'll be good. You can hit me, if you like, if that'll make you feel better. It was a joke. I couldn't pass it up. Come on, man, where is it?"

"Oh yeah, let me just pull it out and flash it around. Show and Tell. Do you see why you're not in charge of an operation like this? We've got to have some punch to pour it in. Ho ho! Molly, would that be punch you are consuming?"

"Fine, take it. I'll go get you some more. A couple of things. One, don't pour it out here. Go to the Men's Room. Two, I'm not drinking any. Because I don't want to, so don't ask. Now then. Do you want a couple more glasses of punch or don't you?" I'm getting a little riled, because this is soooo much fun, but I don't like being pressured into anything, and Cameron is looking at me all goo-goo eyed again, and Jimmy is proud like I'm his kid or something, and this new guy, Mr. Dreamy, is slouching, hanging, he's cool, trying to ignore me, so I know he's into me.

"So lovely, yet so daring. Yes, doll, I would like a couple of glasses of punch. And I will heed your sage advice."

'Sage advice.' That is why Jimmy is so cool. Well, one of the reasons.

"So off I go, on the mission of my King," I say and head over to the other side of the giant hall. Some kids are dancing, oooh yuck, there's Angela 'getting down' to a Sly tune. She is so fake. She can't move for beans. I only glance over for a minute, then I continue heading for the buffet when that guy appears at my side.

"Thought you could use some help, Molly." He says my name funny, but nice.

"Yeah, thanks. You mean to carry them. Yeah. Thank you, Shu...how do you say your name?"

"Shudree. Like Shoe-tree. It means something in my country."

"What does it mean?"

"I don't know." But it's like, he knows, but he's not saying, or like meaning in names is ridiculous or something. Then he asks, in a very serious voice, yet with devils dancing in his eyes, "What's your name mean?"

"It's a kind of tree, actually. A beautiful flowering tree."

He screws up his brow in mock consternation. He scratches his head for a moment. Then he states in a loud, authoritative voice: "Bullshit!"

I look at him for a minute and then we just crack up. Oh my God, that is the funniest thing I have ever heard. I can't breathe. I'm probably blowing stuff out my nose. I probably look retarded. Right when I'm about to gain control, I hear him whisper, "Bullshit!"

And we start laughing again. He's says it really funny. He's taken my arm and pulled me closer and we're both doubled over and I can smell his breath, it's nice, and he's breathing hard and he's saying everything in a whisper. "Now, Miss Molly or whatever your name is, you can bullshit me no longer. I am on to you, as they say. Enough of your crap!"

He whispers 'crap' so it sounds something like 'cap' and I'm laughing again, leaning on him now, whispering back, "Okay, okay, I'll stop, just let me take a breath here!"

And I think for a moment that it's like the movies, because I really want to kiss him and stay with him forever and I can tell, for some insane reason, he feels the same way and we look at each other and we stop laughing and it's one moment two moments three moments I think he's going to kiss me! But no. He says 'bullshit' again and we laugh it off and turn to the buffet. We get four cups of punch and carry them back to the guys. Tina Sweetwater is there now. Too bad. I was enjoying the attention. But she's cool, as far as girls in my class go. She's a little more funky, like me.

"Hey, Molly."

"Hey, Tina. How's it going?"

"It's cool. Got some punch, did ya? Thirsty?"

"Nope. The gentlemen here are thirsty. Here you go, Sir Jimmy, Cameron," and I hand them the punch. They stand around holding them for a minute and I'm about to say something, but Brick House comes on and I love that song. I start moving a little and look from face to face. I can't stand it. This is how all my favorite songs go, I never get to dance. I finally say, "Anyone want to dance?" and then I look right at Shudree, but he grins and shakes his head, says, "I can't dance."

All the boys chime in with 'I can't dance,' and I'm riled again but Tina says, "Come on, let's dance," and I run out to the dance floor with her and just close my eyes because I don't care. I don't care about anything anymore. And I figure Mr. Dreamy is watching me, and well, if he doesn't like my dancing, then he doesn't like me and I may as well find out sooner than later. I rock my hips and move up and down on my knees like I've seen blacks do. Of course, there's not a black in the room. But Shudree's pretty dark. Tina is bouncing around like an idiot, enjoying herself and what can I say? I couldn't look worse than her and who cares anyway?

The song is over and Tina and I run back over to the guys. They seem more enamored of us than before. I've got a grin on my face and I'm flushed.

"What're you smiling at?" I demand of Cameron in mock indignation.

"Nothing. Nice dancing. You girls dance good."

"We could teach you, for a price," Tina says, and Shudree says, "How much do you cost?" and Tina says, "More than you have!" and she's flirting with him! The whole thing makes me sick. He can't decide who he wants. See? That is why I hate guys. One minute we're having the Hollywood moment and the next he's hitting on someone else. I know immediately who I want and he, he's going to play the field a little, see if there's something a little better out there. Guys!

Cameron touches my arm and says, "Later, doll. Got to go to the Men's Room," and he and Jimmy saunter off, and John Sample and Shudree, who's been talking to Tina, they turn and leave, too. Shudree shoots me a glance as he saunters off. I don't even care. This party sucks again suddenly and I'm almost angry at Tina but she's smiling at me, says, "Hey, you wanna go dance some more? Hey, there's Amy and shit in the middle, let's go stand on the dance floor and block everybody," and so we head over.

The guys come back but they kind of hang in the corner and talk, point to people, laugh. I'm not going over there again. They should come over here. Am I desperate?

Brad Walker asks me to dance and I do, trying to catch Shudree's eye. He's looking at me but I can't tell what he's thinking. He shouldn't have flirted with Tina. Brad Walker is the captain of some obscure sport, which is better than being on the football team, and he's nice looking, but not much else. Not enough. I cross the room with him when the song is over, hang out with Amy and Annette and a bunch of people. I hang out and try to be cool, but it's getting old and I decide to go walk around the mall by myself.

No one notices when I leave. I go down the steps to the lower level and just head out, looking at the clothes in the windows, wanting them and wanting not to want them because I'm not going to get them and materialism is so rank. Then I hear steps behind me, fast and strong, and whirl around to see Shudree heading toward me, and I can't help but give him a big smile and he smiles back. I can tell my smile is like a whisper and a prayer, like a rainbow over a battlefield. I hope he feels the same way because I already want him so much. But I can't tell what he wants.

We walk along together and just talk. We get off the subject of clothes and materialism and move on to music and books. He likes a lot of the same stuff I do, he's read Salinger, he likes funk, but he knows some authors and music I've never heard of, like Leonard Cohen and Russell Koban, and he promises to turn me on to them and it's late and we're back at the stairs and there is Annette Segal and she's mad that I disappeared and her mom's been waiting and I look at Shudree with eyes that say, 'Can I be with you forever?' And he looks back with eyes that say, 'You are so amazing. I don't want you to go. Can't you stay here, can't this last a little longer?' And we don't really say anything except, 'Hey. See you later,' or something and I go.

When I get home, my dad's in the living room reading. He looks up at me with his usual look of consternation and suddenly I feel guilty. I was thinking about Shudree all the way home. I was silent as a mouse in the car, which was no great loss since Annette and her mother babbled the entire way home, yadda yadda the decorations like a movie star yadda yadda the food like a millionaire. I haven't thought about anything but Shudree. Am I late or something? I feel like I've betrayed my father somehow, because I don't love him anything like I love the boy I've just met and I don't want to hang out with Dad but he says something and I say what? And he repeats.

"You're out late, aren't you?"

"Mom said I could... It was a Bat Mitzvah at the mall..."

"Don't you have school in the morning?" Jeez, it's like he's trying to get me in trouble. Am I not the perfect daughter? Do I not get good grades, obey my parents, spend little to no money and *never* stay out late? What time is it? This is probably the latest I've ever stayed out my entire life.

"No, Dad, it's Saturday, tomorrow's Sunday..."

"I know what day it is. I said don't you have homework to do? Did this thing cost money?"

"No and no. I had a really good time, Dad. I'm tired. I'm going to go to bed."

"Goodnight," he says with that harrumphing thing of agitation. My dad's always agitated, so it's hard to tell if he's extra agitated. I'm just glad he didn't go off on me. I go up the stairs to my room and think about leaving some day. I'll marry Shudree and leave and he'll never tell me what to think or do again.

I lie in bed and think about Shudree and how gorgeous he is and smart and cool. Is he going to be my boyfriend? I can't believe it. I have to make sure he never meets my parents or that will be the end of it.

I start to breathe deeply. I'm thinking about traveling around the world with Shudree. I bet his country is so cool. I don't even know where it is! I'll look it up tomorrow.

But wait! Don't! No, wait! What was that? Wait a minute. Wait now. There it is. A bald-headed man...and what? Jane left me alone, left me standing on the highway in the dark, took the shirt off my back, asked for it, I gave it to her. So creepy. Yes. I went back into the dark building, a man was there, big, the bald-headed man, a vicious killer, he pissed me off so bad just by looking at me, threatening me with his eyes, I took his head in my hands and smashed it through a window pane. I had to reach up on my tippy toes to grab him by the back of the neck, smashed his head right through the window pane, then another, and another, an entire wall of window panes and I smashed his head through them all. Rape me, will ya? Have you had enough? Have you had enough yet, you bastard? Think you scare me? Huh? Who's scared now, huh?!

A dream. There was another part, what was it? Can't remember. Got to go to school. Oh yeah. School. Shudree. What happened last night? It wasn't last night, it was the night before. He loves me, that's what happened. All I want to think about is him. And all I want to be is beautiful. I lay in bed, mentally going through my wardrobe. What should I wear? Oh God, it has to be special, so special. I'm going to get that boy.

Shudree and I have been together a year, over a year, actually. I'm in the eleventh grade now and I met him toward the end of the ninth, so yeah, about a year and a half. I'm turning seventeen in a few days and the day after, I'm going to get my driver's license.

We go everywhere together. Terry says she never gets to see me. Get a boyfriend, Terry, we'll double-date. Shudree is just so... it's like he knows me and I know him, and whenever I see him, my heart races and I'm almost not cool anymore, that's how much I love him.

When he gave me flowers my sister teased me and my mother looked worried. Dad, of course, just looked angry. I can tell he thinks he raised me too liberally and now he has this to deal with. He thinks he made me. He doesn't even know me. But everybody knows Shudree now and they're not so worried. I just want to spend all my time with him. He said he loves me.

We kiss. I feel so good. I'm not nervous anymore. I used to be afraid that I wasn't doing it right. He is so perfect at everything. I don't feel worthy of him. He plays tennis, which my father loves. He is smart, rich, polite, and very intellectual. He knows everything about books and music.

Sometimes he says I should do this or that and I try. Like when he wanted to play tennis with me. I just can't and I don't care enough to learn. He says I'm insecure and I know I am. It makes me sad that he's better than me, but should I walk away because of that? I can't. I would die without him, my feelings are so strong.

He loves me, too, I'm sure he does. He went away all last summer and it was unbearable. I thought I was going to get sick. I felt sick. My heart ached but he said he would come back. We talked on the phone every Friday, took turns calling and wrote each other almost every day. When he came back I was so happy. He had to convince his family that going to school in America was the best thing for him. He had to be sure his host-family would keep him, which really wasn't any problem. I talked to Mrs. Hillside almost as much as I talked to him. When he stepped off the plane we fell into each other's arms and both of us cried. We didn't care what anyone thought. We didn't care then and we don't care now. I know he loves me as much as I love him. I don't know why, except for my mind, and I'm pretty, actually, I look pretty good. But other than that I don't know why he loves me.

He has touched my breasts. They're too small, I want to die. I want to tell him they'll grow. I don't say anything. I feel weak. He has too much power over me, how I feel. I would rather he didn't touch my breasts, but I let him. I let him put my hand down his pants—was that after he came back? That's all we do, if we can get a second alone and the coast is clear. It upsets me, but I would do almost anything for him. Maybe anything. I don't know.

He has to go again in a month, home for the holidays, which Islam doesn't even celebrate. They celebrate some other holiday, I can't remember what. He says he's not a Muslim, really, only by birth, which matches me perfectly, because I'm not a Catholic, either, except by birth. But I go to church. I would love to say to my father, "Hey, I don't believe in all this hypocrisy, Mr. Money-worshipper whose place in heaven will be behind the camel going through the eye of a needle," but I wouldn't dare. I'm lucky he doesn't forbid me to see Shudree. I'm not about to rock the boat.

Shudree says it won't be any problem coming back. I worry, though. When I'm seventeen, I think I could go with him, but he hasn't asked me. I would go live with him in a minute. The United Arab Emirates. I would go live there. I would become a Muslim. I would do anything to be with him.

Yesterday I cried and cried, thinking about his leaving. He just held me, rocking me, stroking my hair. I think he cried, too. It's going to be the longest three weeks of my life.

I can't believe it. Shudree says that he can't come back, not right now. He said his father isn't doing well and he has to stay. I begged him to let me find a way to go live with him in his country. He said it wasn't possible. His family knows about me and they don't approve of our biracial relationship. Biracial? We're not that different. If they could only meet me! How long will it be? He can't say.

I've been crying. I told my mother why. My dad's not interested. He would be more than happy if I never saw Shudree again. He doesn't believe in relationships, not without marriage. But we will get married! We've talked about it! We just have to wait a few more years. What is time to us? Our bond is strong enough to survive anything. I am so lucky, lucky to be loved by the man I love. I am so miserable and happy at the same time!

I'm lying in bed, staring at the ceiling. I can't remember to close my eyes. Sleep would be good. Go to sleep. You can't feel anything when you are asleep and that's one more day gone; one more day closer to being with Shudree.

I feel my body twitch. I smell the cold. My feet are cold, but I'm too comfortable to move. Get another blanket. Not getting up. It's cold out there. Need more heat, always keep it so low. What? Man in a hat, monkey following along behind, turn the corner, now on a bicycle, a big floating egg coming down from the sky, he looks up slowly, the egg falls in slow motion, it seems huge and heavy, is it going to land on the man? On his head and break his neck? Before the egg gets close, it cracks open. Out comes a rainbow bird, a bird of prey, with multi-colored plumage over huge, soft wings. Effortlessly he rises up, up, up, floats five feet up for every downward stroke; downward stroke, five feet up, floating through the air. It's gone. A woman stands looking at me. A plain woman. She looks disgusted. The sun is so bright. She's wearing a summer dress, but she's wagging her finger at me, shame shame shame, shame on you. What did I do?

I can remember someone, a couple of men maybe, chasing me, secret agents hiding everywhere, out to get me. And what else? Something else. Before the secret agents. Oh yeah, the dream with the egg. I remember the whole thing. I go over it in my mind. The alarm's going off again, how many times? I'll be late for school. No. There's no school today. I smell something really good, and I want to laugh and cry.

Shudree wrote me. He's been away for six months. He doesn't write but once a month anymore, but he always assures me of his love. Now this. I got the letter three days ago, and I've been numb. I think I should rend my clothes, scream and cry, but I don't really feel that way. It feels quite natural, what is happening, so my response has been relatively even. Of course. Of course he has dumped me. Love me forever. No other girl for him. And just like that, I'll never see him again.

He slept with somebody, someone from his homeland, something something about meeting her, and has to go to school in France. But it's not because of the other girl. He doesn't care about that. It meant nothing. We're getting older something something. Hey stay in touch.

I just feel empty. No. That's not all. I'm starting to feel stupid. Really stupid. Who was I kidding? Have you had enough now? Have you learned anything, you idiot Molly? Do you have any questions, anything you haven't figured out yet? The new girl slept with him. He kept bugging me about that. I would never do it. I guess I *am* Catholic. She slept with him. He never did love me; he only needed me while he was in America.

The truth is...the truth is my life is over. I am broken. Who could throw such love away? I would have done anything for him, anything. Well, almost anything. But why would he ask for something that made me feel so bad? Because he never loved me, he just liked being loved by me. But I would never hang out with someone who loved me just to be loved, if I didn't love them. Never. I would not be an emotional hooker that way. I did love him. I do love him. I will never love anyone else.

But that's over. The truth is so clear now. He doesn't love me now, and he only kind of loved me before. He just doesn't know how to love as deeply as I do.

But why did he weep when we were reunited? Where did that go? I know he loved me, I *felt* it. Was it just too hard? Did something else happen, beyond his control?

But see, you loved him more, obviously, because nothing could ever get in the way of your being with him. That's not how it is for him. That's how it is for you. "For you, there may be a brighter star, but in my eyes, the light of you is all I see." I will walk the face of the earth alone and unloved. I will love and not be loved back. I have been abandoned by my soul mate, may God forgive him for being so weak. Forgive him for not being able to love at my level. I know he will suffer for it all the days of his life. But he probably won't know he's suffering.

I should make him feel it somehow.

But no. You loved him, that won't change. Let him go, if he needs to go. Go and have a good life. Except I curse you. I hope your children are born green, all green and... No. Have a good life. I don't curse you. You are free. You have always been free. And now I am free, too.

What do I have? There are guys who want to date me. I'll date them. I have my drawings. Mr. Talbert says they're really good. I know they are good, Mr. Talbert. I don't need your approval. But it feels good because not many people think they are good except my mom. I could puke on a piece of notebook paper and my mom would call it art. I love my mom.

Now I'm crying. My eyes are swelling shut. I have my mom. My mom always loves me. And Jane, she's been so cool. She'll take me out. She'll take care of me. And Sam, too, he's been a doll. He's so good. I remember all the games we played when we were little and how he looked after me at school and when we shared that bedroom together and wrestled every night with Mom sneaking in on us to catch us playing and hiss, "You kids get to bed!" and we'd leap across the room into our beds and fake-sleep just to appease her. He's so fun. I love Sammy so much. And Terry loves me, although we've drifted apart. Thanks to that shit Shudree. Why did I abandon Terry? But she still loves me, I know. We will always love each other. And my dad is always there. But I don't think he loves me. That's the truth. My dad loves me because I am his child, but he doesn't *love* me. Not as a human being.

Oh why, why did this happen to me? I wish I were never born.

No I don't. Tears subside, get off the floor. Forget him. He never thought much of my drawings. He never said much. That's why I thought they weren't very good. Mr. Talbert says they're good. See, that right there should have told me the depths of his love. But I loved him. I loved him. I loved you, Shudree! Can you feel that? Can you feel my pain reeling across the miles, searching for you? I loved you. I loved you.

That's enough of that, now. Get it together. There's always tomorrow. Who knows? Maybe he'll be back. Maybe in a year or two. Or when you are famous, he'll be back, apologizing, whatever. This is like the Grand Canyon now. I don't wish you any harm, Shudree, but don't come back here. Never again. It's broken now. It's broken. So stop thinking about him, stop it!

What do you want to do? See where Jane's going. Call Cameron. Call Terry. Get your oils out. You haven't even used them yet. I'm afraid of oils. Big league. What have you got to lose?

Okay. I'll get on with it. I'll wish him the best. I'll love the ones I'm with. But I'm just faking it. I will never be the same. I won't be alright. I'm not alright. I will always be broken. Always.

I would have done anything for you. Get on with it. A hole in my heart like the Grand Canyon, I can feel the wind blow right through me. That's the truth. Fine, that's the truth. Go out tonight. Go crazy.

At first I was so psyched to go to college, now it's quite the grind. But North Western's a good school. I miss Jane. She married Chuck like I knew she would. Oh, it was romantic, blah blah blah, he's not half the person she is. We have that in common. Always hooking up with men who aren't half of what we are. Why is that? She's lost the baby, too. Was that two years ago? She's studying Egyptology. She is so smart. I want Jane.

And I want Sammy. He's in New York, of course. Going to school. Fucking off. Good ol' Sammy. That's the way it should be. No one holds him down. Well, that's not entirely true. He can't seem to get his love life going. Who can? Is it just us, my family? No, of course not. There are merely the honest and the dishonest. I would rather be around people who lie to me than people who lie to themselves. That came out wrong. The thing is, I think people who lie to me are also constantly lying to themselves, that's it. I would rather be around people who tell the truth. Not that I always know when I'm lying to myself. Discovering my own lies has been one of the most painful experiences of my life.

I'm taking a course in psychology. There are actually people in class who think we humans can know ourselves. The Prof believes that, too, or at least he makes out like he does. What shit. That's like monkeys trying to figure themselves out. Really, when you read the text... it's like classification equals understanding. Do I need to explain how lame that is? I have a word for you, so I know you? In the beginning, there was the word, a word for God, so zip, just like that, hey, we know God!

How long must I wait for everyone's cortex to evolve? Am I advanced? If I am, that is a sad commentary on the species.

The problem is I think too much. When I direct my mind *at* something, I stop *knowing* that thing. Like Alice in Wonderland, I can't see it if I look straight at it. To tell the truth, I understand how this works and I even do it successfully from time to time, looking sideways to see something clearer, but I don't really know why it works. Maybe it's because I get myself out of the way.

I wish I was in Marrakech. That was such a good trip. Dad gave me his frequent flyer miles and I just took off, by myself. I went to New Delhi and Agra. The Taj Mahal was absolutely amazing but I shuddered to think how many people died building it. Most peoples' lives seemed to be worthless in India. Besides, what does Holy mean when everything's Holy? I went to Bali: too beautiful for words. Everywhere I went I met some good people and I met some bad people. I wish I had more money. I wish I had a ton of money, then I would just paint and travel around the world. Would that spoil some vast eternal plan? Am I asking too much here? Well, yeah. Like, I get to eat every day, so what am I bitching about?

I went out last night, Saturday night, lots of expectations, all dashed, as usual. I was sitting with Luke in that Cafe Boucher or something. Café Bigass. We had just seen a dumb movie, one of those movies that make you wish you were someone else, with a plot that reconfirms the deep discontent you've always felt by retelling the crazy fairy story of being happy, loved and fulfilled. Why is this screen-person so happy, loved and fulfilled? Because the screen-person is so very, very different from everyone else. Oh yes, she stands out in a crowd. Oh yes, he goes to Oxford but is a sweet loving man. It could happen to *someone*, just not to you, because you're not *special* and see, these movie folks are very, very special. Oh, the fine super-humans. How I love them. How I love the cinematographic stories of their lives!

I looked around the theater. Looked like ordinary slobs to me. I *know* they suck like me. They're leaving the theater saying, "Why isn't my life like that?" It's as if people are paintings: some are good, some are bad, some are worth millions, and others are worthless, hidden in closets or burned.

I was telling Luke about these ideas of worth and relativity. I told him I would rather date one of the extras than the star of the movie. I, like Chuang Tzu, would rather be a live turtle dragging my tail through the mud than a dead turtle hanging on the ancestral palace wall.

Luke said, "You're just afraid."

"I am. I know that. Everyone is afraid. Only these movie people aren't afraid, that's what I'm saying! It's such a bizarre lie that we all constantly want to hear, that we'll pay good money for! Mommy, tell me another story, please? The fact is, what you are is what I am, like all the suckers in the theater, like the people who make the movies, like our diarrhea from too much coffee and our pettiness from discovering one thing we do better than others. Like our fantasies, richer and stronger than anything in real life, no ability to distinguish between the two. We are all the same.

We insist that the movie people are different because we don't like reality. We make them what we wish we were. It's sad, really."

"Come on, Molly. You are so much better—smarter, prettier, stronger—than most people. That's the truth. That's just a fact."

"But you are wrong. That's what *you* see. Is that what I am? And even if others see me that way, does that make it true? I don't think so. I don't think attaining what the majority of people deem desirable has anything to do with happiness. Or Goodness. That's the Great White Lie."

He looked at me a little angrily. He didn't get it.

"See? Everything is relative. For every action there is an equal and opposite reaction. One life is no better than any other. We are not actually doing the things we do, we have been set up to do them, genetically and socially. The only freedom is free will, and how can that exist without consciousness? You're living out some play you didn't even write. It really doesn't matter if the star pulls off a wonderful performance or if he stutters and fails. He's the same person. Maybe because he doesn't have as much feeding his ego, I figure the extra has a better chance of knowing what love is. Love is the only measure of a person; it is the only measure of any value on the face of the earth. All the rest is acting."

"You're just smoke-screening. I'm saying you're afraid of success, that's why you don't show your work."

"I'm not successful? I'm sorry, what do I need to do in order to be a successful human? I always seem to miss that. See? That's the thing. You would love me more if I were famous, even a little famous. You would, because that would make me better. But the painting is the same, where ever it hangs; I painted it, where ever it hangs. Don't you see that? So maybe I don't want my world to change, or maybe you would like to fuel some fantasy about being with someone great. Or maybe you date an unknown because you are afraid of the same thing, of being successful."

"You're doing it again. If it's true, what you say, then it wouldn't matter if you were a successful painter or not, you would just be painting. And why paint? So only you can look at it? Then why not paint over your canvases..."

"I do..."

"And it pisses me off! I'll buy you canvases! One paints to show. You paint over because you're afraid."

"One does not paint to show. One paints. That is all. You don't get it."

"Maybe you don't get it."

Sometime shortly after that we left the café and I never got on track again and Luke dropped me off with a small kiss, though he was feeling more. He felt bad for throwing me off, and I felt bad because I couldn't just turn around again and be this little lover thing he had envisioned even before he picked me up for the date. And I think, you make love, you don't make love, what does it matter?

Do I have to be in a war for something to matter? What the hell is wrong with me? Nothing's wrong with me. It's the world. "People tell me, it's a sin, to know and feel too much within..."

But today, now, I'm thinking about all that. If I'm thinking about it, it must have cut deep.

I do like this coffee. I think I would like to go back to bed, maybe masturbate, maybe eat a lot of chocolate. I could run out and get some. No, going out would be bad. And why not drink some wine? And why not snort some coke? And why not just mainline heroine for the rest of your life?

What are you looking for?

Get busy then. What am I afraid of? Oh, so much. I need to list my fears. List my fears. This coffee is so good. I'm hungry. Bread. There's half a loaf of bread in the fridge. Ahg. It's stale. Toast it. Toast is great. I want to listen to some music, nothing too heavy, don't set the mood, match the mood. What then. What then. John McLaughlin. Jack DeJohnette. Something like that.

I can't paint. How do I paint all these fears? I wish I could spit back at Luke, "I am not afraid!" If I take my fear out and look at it again and again, will it get smaller? That's what happens. That's what happened when I was young. What a different list I would have written ten years ago when I was thirteen. I had no power then. Shudree proved that. He ripped me open and I saw my fawning weakness, so that was a good thing. Now I can make myself strong and brave, I can conjure up an Angel of the Lord who will hold me in love and acceptance.... Or maybe I can just lie to myself better now.

See? It's still there. It's always there. The voice of reason turned upon itself, like a snake swallowing its tail.

Death is the ultimate fear. But, really, it's not. Even in death, one can remain oneself. That's what I think. What is worse is to not be oneself, not know oneself. I fear that success would show me someone I don't know and that, in and of itself, would show me there is no bottom, I have no substance. Worse. I fear that success would automatically change me, which would mean I am not now nor ever have been the captain of my own ship. That is my deepest fear: That there is no ship, no captain, only illusion. And I think, well, that would be nirvana, then, and you would be actualized, but then I think actualization would suck, because it would be the death of *me*.

Nonexistence. Money and infamy erase you, if you have no substance and no one has any substance, not even me. If it erases you, it erases me. So it is a kind of death. And what for?

Let's say I become erased, which is to say I become lost in the tidal wave of humans, isn't that what I always say I want, to see the oneness of this body of humans? Like mitochondria?

I don't know about want, but it is what I fear.

Oh. Nice head. I've painted a head. It doesn't look like a head of fear. What is it? I need some ocher the way a junkie needs smack. I need berry, black berry. I need vermilion and cornflower. I will die without them. Mix, mix, mix. Mix faster. It'll go away. The images and ideas will fade away. The colors will abandon you, you've been untrue. Where do they go? Where does a flame go when you blow it out? It is latent. It is still there. All the elements of fire are there, rediscovery is all that is needed.

What time is it?

Who cares? Is it time to paint? Time not to paint? Besides being here and doing this, is there something else, someone else, an item perhaps or a paper bill or a person who is me waiting for me in a place owned by me and ran by me? When I am tired, will I see me loitering outside waiting for me while I close up, hoping that I will just go away and not cause a scene? What is it time for?

More toast. That is the only time I know. I know bed time and meal time. I know two times. No other times count here. When you don't limit your times, (and two, maybe four, is all you should honor), you end up becoming a slave to structure. You have a million times for performing various activities and that's it. That's all she wrote. I am afraid of nonexistence and I am afraid of demands on my time. They may be the same thing.

Two fears.

Ah. A nice head and a baby with foliage. This is looking better.

Don't think too much. Don't tell yourself what to do.

This is coming along. And what should I say about it? "Do you see the image first?" What's a good answer to that? "No, I just make it up?" Great painters see images first. Do they? Maybe great painters lie. Maybe they think, what should I say? And they figure, great painters see images first. So that's what they say. You know you are not great when people are asking you those kinds of questions. Once you are famous, no one asks them or you can say any shit that comes to mind, or not answer at all. You don't give an interview.

What the fuck does it matter what I say? But when you're a nobody, you want to talk them into showing your painting because just looking at it isn't enough, they need someone to tell them what to think and feel about your painting, and if you're a little man, that someone is you. Will you be seen and felt and cherished for once, if you talk right, if you convince someone to hang your art in a public place?

That's bullshit. I see a lot of people playing that. It's the Emperor's Clothing and I really hate it. That's why I don't show, I fear I may succumb. I'm too easily duped and swayed. Duped and swayed, duped and swayed.

I like people from afar. They're like mountains. They look good, maybe even beautiful, interesting. But you get up close, and there are thorns and rocks and danger, and when you're done there's exhaustion and if you're lucky you force yourself up to the top and you see something you've never seen before. I want somebody to force their way to the top of me.

Landscape (With Head). This is great. I got more than one head here, though. That's okay. Perfect. What good are S's anyway? The Chinese don't have S. They just figure it out. I'm liking this. It's looking good.

I like Chinese. Chinese everything. Can't stand the Spaniards. No idea why. Mr. Wang says, "You rearning Chinese whole rot betta dan any student, you rike Chinese, huh, Ma-li?" He's so wonderful. So simple. About the opposite of me. Yeah, Mr. Wang, I like Chinese.

Spanish anything makes me shiver. Don't like the colonialists. Don't like South America. Don't like Mesoamerica. The most barbaric forms of animism I have ever encountered. The Japanese were vicious, too, and their animism was twisted, fecal matter and demigods. But for some reason I like the Japanese. Their goofy creation stories in the Kojiki don't bother me. I kind of like them.

Luke says I'm prejudiced. Maybe.

Liking this. Where's that brown blood color? Fuck, is it gone? How could I have used it all? Gone? Mix up more? Skip it.

Can't skip it.

Record's over.

Record's been over. Use that dark green, cut that with some...

Can't. Not right. Make some more.

What time is it?

Oh, time again? Do you need something? Are you ready to quit? Is that it? Shot your wad?

Maybe. I want some chocolate.

Put the brush down. You've lost it. You're just going to fuck it up.

Are you coming back to this? When? Another unfinished painting? Why don't you stick with it?

Because I don't like this part. This agonizing part. This dragging myself through to the finish part.

Do something.

Okay. Get a grip. Open the curtains, light some incense, find another record. Paint all night long. This is your only chance. You have to go to work tomorrow. Go to class. Off you'll go, to your real life, where everyone knows you. You're such a nice person when you're not painting. Why do you bother? You're nothing, O'Connell. You're no different than anybody else.

Stop it. You said it doesn't matter, what's finished, what's not, where the damn things hang. You like them. You like painting. Is this your bliss or not?

It is and it isn't. I need to stop for now. Maybe I'll work on it again. I'm going out. I'll just walk the streets. Call Luke. I am so alone. Look at that! I've been painting for six hours. Feels like six minutes.

★ ★ ★

My classes are weak. That's my fault, I guess, because I don't know what I want to do. It's amazing to me that people decide 'who to be,' or 'what to be.' I can't seem to do that. I paint. That's true. But I am not a painter. It's something I like. It's a hobby, according to most people who see my work. It's not that bad. I know it's not bad, just no one can see it right; no one knows what it is. That's my fault. That's why I'm not a painter. A painter would be able to communicate better. Fine. But would you want to 'be a painter?' Aren't you a little bigger than that? Moot point anyway since I'm not 'a painter,' and don't apparently have that choice right now. Will I ever? Oh, how badly I would love to show, to sell something!

Well. You're a 23 year old college student who paints, just like a thousand others. But really. Stop at the store, you have nothing in the house. But it's rush hour, I hate rush hour! Are you going to go home, wait an hour and then go back out again? Go now. Now. Turn left. Take Jefferson. Stop at Smith's. Do it now.

I take the corner, keeping up with the traffic. Everyone's moving fast like they're going to die or something if they don't get ahead. No one's going to get ahead of me. Hey, fuck you too, buddy. Asshole. People can be such creeps.

What? A little girl, a toddler, standing on the curb, two blocks down, where's her mother? I can't see! God damn it! God damn it! She's going to step into the traffic! Three lanes this way, three lanes that, why the hell is she alone? There's no one there! She's alone and she's about to step into the traffic. She's going to die, Molly! SHE'S GOING TO DIE!

Is anyone stopping? Someone will stop. YOU stop! YOU are the someone! Stop now! Pull into that street, now, now! For the love of Christ!

I'm slowing, someone's honking behind me. I can see her little face clearly now, she's so scared! Oh little baby you're so scared! Shut up, you bastard! You'd just plow right into her, wouldn't you, you ignorant moron!

She's so scared! Sweet Jesus, you're too late, you're spooking her, she's stepping down off the curb, stepping into traffic, roll down your window! Be soft, be fun…

"Hey, sweetie, stop! Don't step down! Don't move, baby. Don't move! I'm coming, doll, it's okay, it's okay honey."

She can't hear me anymore, but she stopped when I said stop, thank the Lord, thank you God, Blessed Jesus! I've thrown the car into park and race over to her and just swoop her up. Just that easy. Snatch her from the jaws of death. Precious baby. She's crying now and I want to cry too, but I don't. I hear my voice light and happy and I amaze myself.

"Hey, sweetie! You are such a good girl! You did really good! Thank you for listening. How old are you?"

She stops crying as soon as I start talking. She's just looking at me, blinking her eyes like she can't believe what's happening. Now she's giving me a slight smile, she likes me! She's grateful! Oh, you can like me, baby, because I love you. Maybe she's too young to talk, or maybe she's too afraid. When do babies start talking? But I know what she wants.

"You need your mommy, huh sweetie?"

Her face immediately screws up into a ball and she nods her head and lets out a big wail.

"It's okay, baby. I will find your mommy. See? I will find your mommy. Oh yes. Let's find mommy, okay? We'll find mommy! We're going to find mommy and everything is just fine, okay!" I'm a blithering fool, chattering away in a high happy cartoon voice and she's paying attention as though she is deciphering my tone of voice and facial movements into her own language, in her head. She has accurately interpreted me: she smiles, she knows. She knows I will take good care of her. She feels it.

She's looks at me with her big beautiful eyes and grabs hold of my upper arm in a little death grip, like she knows she's found her savior and she's not letting go until I save her all the way.

This is the best feeling I have ever had in my life. She's smiling at me.

"That's right, baby. You're safe. Everything's alright." We are smiling at each other! What a beautiful baby!

Who would do this to a baby?

Who would ever let their baby get into this situation?

I look out onto Jefferson. Cars whizzing past like nothing is happening. No one sees us or pays any attention. I scan the cars for a minute. Hell, I'm not going to find her mother this way. I turn and look down the street. No one.

Holding her—and she's holding onto me for dear life and I wouldn't let go of her for anything—I walk down the block. Circle the block. Back down on Jefferson and she doesn't like that, doesn't like the sound of the traffic, she's freezing up, getting all tense in my arms, she's going to cry! I can't let that happen.

"Okay, sweetie pie, no problem, not going to walk anymore. See? We're almost back at my car. Can you come to my house? Can you come in the car? Just sit in the car, drive a little, and go to my house! Then we'll call the big people who find mommies, okay? The Mommy Finders. They'll help us find mommy, okay?"

And she's smiling again. I guess I'll take her in my car. God, I feel like I'm kidnapping her or something. And I wish I could. I could live and die with this baby and never ask for another goddamn thing. What a precious little angel. There, she won't let go of me to get into the car. I smile okay, whatever you want, sweetie, and we both get in together, on my side, the driver side. Then she's willing to move over into the passenger seat. She didn't want to lose me! Little Angel! I won't let you lose me, or let anyone hurt you.

It feels like three minutes and we're at my apartment. I go so slow and light with her, easy breezy, no worries, sweetie. Everything's fine. I put her down in the kitchen and she won't stay on her legs, it's not where she is most comfortable, she sits immediately, begins looking around. She's curious, yet so settled in herself. I get her some milk. She looks at it and almost laughs, like she's saying, "I always wanted one of these! I never got this kind of glass before! Only Big People get these!" She moves the glass up to her lips, keeping her eyes on mine, and spills a little down her front and onto the floor. Her eyes widen apprehensively but I just smile. She transfers the glass to her left hand and runs the fingertips of her right hand through the milk on the floor. I get her some toast and put it by her then get the phone. 911. I never called 911 before.

"Is this an emergency?" Yes? No?

"No."

"Please hold." But I don't want to hold! I should have said it was an emergency.

Then a voice, a female, comes on the line and says, "What is your emergency?"

"I found a baby that was about to step into rush hour traffic on Jefferson!"

"What is your name?"

"Molly O'Connell."

"How old are you?"

"Twenty three."

"Where is the baby now?"

"At my house!"

"Where do you live?"

"344 East Congress Street, Apartment 15. Over the old theater. The one..."

"Your telephone number?"

"577-6203."

"What is the name of the child?"

"I don't know the name of the child, she doesn't speak!"

"How old is the child?"

"She's maybe one year. No, maybe eighteen months. I'm not sure."

"What is the sex of the child?"

Is this woman mentally challenged?

"She's a girl."

"Please hold."

I look down at Angel. She's playing with that milk. She's trying to dribble a little bit at a time onto the linoleum, but she ends up making a big splash, which thrills her to death until she thinks it might be wrong. Then she looks up at me and I nod as if to say, 'No, you're right, baby. Go ahead, doll, that's good. That's what one does with milk!' and she grins and splashes a little more out of the glass.

"Ms. O'Connell?"

"Yes?"

"Is the child sick?"

"No, she's perfectly fine. She's beautiful. She's fine. She's drinking milk."

"An officer will be over as soon as possible." Click.

Weirdoes. Do you have to pass some totally cold weirdo test before they let you answer the phone at the police department? I look down at Angel.

How soon is that?

I don't want them to come get her. God, I just feel so close to her. Okay, O'Connell, get a grip. This is not your baby. Her mother must be worried sick. You just need to keep her happy until the cops come.

Hey, I've got a rubber duckie in my bathtub. I should get that for her to play with. I start to leave the room and I hear the strangest sound, like a whimper. I look around and there's Angel's face all knotted up in that ball, ready to break.

"I'm not going anywhere, sweetie! I was just going to get a toy. But never mind! We have toys here, huh! We have happy, happy milk and all kinds of good stuff, huh!"

And just as quickly, her face breaks out into a grin and she's playing with the milk, drawing on the floor with it, moving it around with her fingers. I get another glass of milk out of the fridge and we both pour a little onto the floor and trace it around with our fingers. Angel really laughs when I do it. She's so smart! She knows we're not supposed to be doing this and she knows that I'm doing it because I'm desperate to make her happy and, Sweet Jesus, she's looking at me with that grateful look in her eyes.

"I'm grateful to *you*, sweetie. I never met anyone I liked so much!"

Mushy part over: time to get back to playing. She crawls over to the cabinet and pulls it open, taking out pots and lids, always looking back at me just like a little grown-up, "Is this okay? How about this? Am I allowed to play with this?" I let her do whatever she wants. And she's a good girl, too, she never does anything bad.

After awhile she eats some toast. I can't believe how long it's taking the cops to get here! I've been studying Angel. She is kind of dirty. Her clothes are certainly not expensive. What if she's being abused? What if her mother sucks? What if they can't find her mother? I'll keep her, then. I will. No one's going to hurt her. She can stay here. She won't be any bother. I could figure something out.

Then there's a knock on the door. I rush over and open it and a big cop steps in.

"You need to ask folks to identify themselves before you let them in."

"Sorry, officer."

"Well," and that's all he says. He looks at the baby playing in the milk on the kitchen floor. Now I feel a little embarrassed. He walks over to her, like he's going to pick her up, but I stop him by saying, "Excuse me. What is your name? Did you find the baby's mother?"

"Officer Sheehan. Yes, her mother's been worried sick about her, called her in an hour ago. I'll bring the baby over to her."

"What's her name?"

"Who, the mother's? Can't tell you that. I better be going," moving toward Angel, who stiffens up a little. I've had her over an hour? Why was she on that street! I'm getting angry. This isn't how this happens.

I tell the cop, "I need to know she'll be okay," and then whispering so Angel can't hear me, "What the hell was she doing about to step out onto Jefferson?!"

In the same whisper, Officer Sheehan tells me the baby was dropped off at the neighbor's to play, she wandered off, the neighbor called the mother, who called the cops, happens all the time.

"I've got to return her to her mother now."

"Can't I go with you? She'll be scared."

"No, ma'am, you've done all you can do. Thanks for your help."

Happens all the time. Bullshit! She could have been killed! Why the fuck did that mom leave her at the fucking neighbor's who clearly doesn't give a fuck and couldn't keep track of a zit on her ass.

He's lifting her up and her eyes fill with tears. Okay, this is going to happen. You're going to lose her now just like you found her. Make it okay for her. Make it okay for her.

I put on a smile, the happy-happy voice I've been using, no different.

"Hey, Angel! This man finds mommies and he's found your mommy! Hooray! You are going to your mommy's now! Isn't that great? Thanks for playing, Angel. You sure are a good girl!"

The officer throws me a look like I'm a little whack in the head, hoists her up on his hip, and turns to go out the front door. I hold the door and watch my little Angel go, and her eyes are tearing up and my eyes are tearing up but I wave to her and try to say with my eyes, "Yippee! Going to mommy's! Yeah! Good for you, baby." And she is gone.

I turn to clean up the milk but end up standing in the kitchen on the old linoleum floor of this fleabag apartment. They rent exclusively to students. No aesthetics. It's a dumpster for Americana counter-aesthetics.

I saved her. She is my baby. If you can't take good care of your baby, then you shouldn't be allowed to keep her.

She was my baby. I know she loves me. Dear God in heaven, please make sure Angel's mother loves her a hundred times more than I do, then she will get the love she deserves because she is the most beautiful baby in the world. Dear God, please make sure Angel will be alright.

I'm crying, the tears are salty in my mouth, I'm making a whimpering sound like I always do, like little Angel did, a "whooo whooo" mournful sound. I slump down to the kitchen floor and just let go. I sob and sob. My chest heaves. I have no one, ever, I never have anyone, I'm always alone. I will be alone all my life, and some pig will get Angel.

I'm starting to calm down.

I feel something wet under my butt.

It's the milk.

I start laughing through my tears. Everything's okay. Angel's better off with her mother. I begin to dream about my baby. I think about Shudree, how I thought he was the one. That's the thing about babies. They have fathers. I don't know about Luke. I don't know. I was wrong about Shudree.

I see Angel's face before mine. Such a small apartment I have. This would never do for a baby.

This is the most intense thing I've ever experienced. I'm going to call my mom.

I've been talking about babies a lot lately. It's not just because of Angel, though. It's like she was a catalyst or something, but I think about it a lot. How long has it been since I found her? Four or five months.

Luke's starting to look a lot better.

He can tell I'm thinking like this. I made him dinner tonight then we watched The King of Hearts. We're listening to music now, and I'm suddenly getting nervous that he's going to make some move and I don't feel like it. I want him, but I don't. I just want a baby. That's no reason to get hooked up. And do I want Luke's baby? I can't stop thinking.

He can tell I don't love him like he loves me. I've told him before that I'm broken. He reaches out to touch me, so I say it again.

"I done got broke, baby." He narrows his eyes at me.

"You may think you're using me, but you're not. This is it. This is the thing you've always looked for. Idiot."

I just raise my eyebrows. He continues.

"Do you want me to let you off? Is that fair? We can't talk about this?"

"I don't know what's going on. I don't know what I feel. I don't know what I want."

"Can you possibly just entertain the thought, for a moment or two, no matter how foreign it seems to your brain? Good love between man and woman exists. Not perfect love, good love. That's what we have."

"Look, I don't want to talk about it. Can't we just hang out?"

"No, goddamn it! You say you want a baby. I say, let's have one. You screw up your nose. Are you stringing me along, Molly? Because it sure feels that way sometimes. One minute you're warm, the next minute you seize up on me like a fuckin' epileptic. One minute you love me, the next minute you don't."

I start to cry. It's true. I should just let him go. I'm using him. I love him, but not like, well, not like I want to. What do you want? Moonlight and candles? I'm a fuckin' mess. He tries to put his arm around me. I say, "Look. I do love you. I'm just a fuckin' mess. Can I see you tomorrow? Can you go now, Luke?"

He's going to say something to make it alright for him to stay, but I feel my eyes get cold. I want him gone right now. He sees that cold in my eyes and so he covers up the hurt with a nice piece of anger and storms out.

Shit. Shit, shit, shit. But he's not the dream I've always had. He's not the One.

I stop crying. I play Leonard Cohen, the most depressing music I know. I start to paint. I cry and paint and drink beer.

Why can't I love?

You do love. You loved Angel. You've loved a lot of people. And you love Luke. You do. You just want too much.

Maybe that's it.

At least I know how to finish paintings now. This is the third one I've finished. I think I'm going to show. At the university. It's a start.

Time passes, but I'm not aware of it. I made something here about killing men in order to make room for children who cannot exist without men. My skin crawls and my heart races. I hear a saxophone whisper. It tells me to blank out, there is no coming to a rational conclusion: these are the things you *feel* to understand.

I'm tired. I sit in my armchair and suddenly the night is all around me. It talks to me, it is full of people, thousands of people who know me, that I know, everyone in all the boxes next to mine, I know them, we sing our separate songs with the same notes.

I smell... I smell dust or something mixing with myself, it's a nice smell. The earth smells like dust and the sky smells like water. There is some food somewhere, I'm hungry. What time is it? I open up the window and get knocked back. It's fuckin' cold out there. I hear the background sounds. Cars and animals and nondescript sounds. It's a nice night. I'm hungry. I feel really good. I should marry Luke. I'm going to go out for some food. Denny's would be open. But it's five blocks away, maybe more. I could ride my bike. Don't go out in a college town at night. Anywhere.

Hmmm. You know, but if I can't go out, what's the use of being on the planet? If I have to fear all the other humans, humans just like me, forget it. I'm no weakling. Take the bike.

Wonder what time it is?

Good God its cold out here! How I wish I would have worn a hat! You're too vain for hats, aren't you, Molly? Never know when you'll meet Prince Charming, always got to look your best for Prince Charming. I wish I were a lesbian.

I'm pretty hard on myself. I know where I get that, too: my dad. "The opposite sex parent becomes the root of all neuroses." I wish my mom had been a more profound influence in my life. Nothing can be done about that. It's nature. The Nature of Things. At least the same laws govern everyone.

I'm studying C. G. Jung. What a great man. Everyone gets his ideas confused with Freud's. I tried to explain it to Luke: "See, Freud is like the Republican. More traditional, less metaphysical, not going half as deep, intellectually, theoretically, or in terms of interpreting the data. Jung is like the Democrat. No, like a write-in candidate. Anyway, Jung is brilliant. Even I don't understand some of his work." Luke looked at me like he was going to vomit.

What is it about me and this huge ego? Someday I hope that what is true and what is my ego will gracefully delineate.

It is so fuckin' cold, Christ! My ears are going to fall off. It's giving me a headache. I can hardly grip the handle bars. I've got to get my car fixed. This is the park coming up then the bridge, then the shopping center and Denny's. I'm going to eat everything on the menu.

There's a man there and I must have hit a bump in the road or something because I'm down on the frozen ground, this guy's pulling my bike off me, helping me.

Fuck.

Fuck! He's! Look at his face! What's he saying?!

"Little girls shouldn't be out late at night, unless they're lookin' for a little action. You lookin' for a little action?" And he just springs on me and I'm trying to get my knee up and he's pushing it down, has a hand on my throat, ow, my arm, he's broken my arm.

I can't move! Utter hysteria, I can't move, paralyzed, he's got me pinned. Is that his knee?

He's going to rape me.

He's going to rape me! I'm struggling against his weight, my head hurts, it's on an ice patch or a cold rock, I'm shaking...

What's he saying?

"...better fuckin' hold still if you don't want to die, little Bitch!"

What!

He's got a knife, a long shiny thing, he's cut me, where's that pain from what this can't be happening hold still you idiot. HOLD STILL! I CAN'T! DON'T BREATHE! BE DEAD. BE AS THOUGH YOU ARE DEAD. HOLD STILL, HOLD STILL has he pulled my pants off? Am I cut? My pants are off! There's no way this is going to happen, no way, I can take this fucker! REMEMBER WHAT YOU LEARNED IN RAPE SURVIVAL CLASS! I'LL KILL YOU MYSELF IF YOU DO ANYTHING STUPID! LIVE TO FIGHT ANOTHER DAY! IS THAT A CAR? IS THAT THE MOON? WHERE IS YOUR LUKE? WHERE IS YOUR MOTHER NOW? YOU'RE GOING TO DIE!

 don't move, don't breathe don't move don't breathe don't move don't breathe don't move don't oouu. COLD. CAN'T FEEL ANYTHING, CAN'T BE ANYWHERE.

WHOA! WHAT THE! SWEET JESUS! OLD MAN HERE, OLD MAN HERE, THE GUY FELL OFF DID THE OLD MAN HIT HIM? OLD MAN SMILING HERE Hey, you okay? Get up, let me help you up, you'll freeze to death. Come on, dear, my car is warm, we'll go call the cops. HE PICKS ME UP. WHERE ARE MY PANTS? WHAT'S GOING ON? Never mind, dear, get in the car, it's safe. I think he's down for the count, but we should go. I Hit Him With My Cane! Whacked him on the head! COLD COLD COLD CAR SEAT SAFE DRIVE DRIVE DRIVE!

OLD MAN WITH MOVING LIPS TALKING TALKING SMILING OLD MAN BLESSED OLD MAN SWEETEST OLD MAN WALKING THE FACE OF THE EARTH I HURT EVERYWHERE ALL PAIN ALL FEAR ALL PAIN ALL FEAR. HOT TEARS, OLD MAN TALKING.

"I saved you! Just happened along, really, right at the right moment, I think. Never saved anyone before! Not bad for an old man! Here we are, dear, at the Denny's, you just stay right here, I'll keep the engine running, be right back."

I'M COLD, SO COLD. CAN'T STOP SHIVERING TEETH ARE GOING TO CRACK, WHOLE BODY SHAKING, GOING TO DIE, NOT GOOD. DON'T DIE. WHOOA.

BIG LASHES CRYING LADY POKING HEAD IN AT ME you poor little lamb, are you okay? Are you okay, honey? Nothing to be ashamed of, now. Nothing to worry about. Happened to me once. You'll be okay. This nice man saved you, you're very lucky! BIG HEAD LADY GETTING INTO CAR NEXT TO ME, TOUCHING ME PLEASE DON'T, DON'T COME NEAR GET BACK WHERE'S OLD MAN, THERE HE IS HI OLD MAN! HI OLD MAN!

"She's in shock. I told you she needed this blanket. Someone needs to stay right here and say nice things to her until the cops come, I saw it on TV. Hell, I lived it!"

"Well, *I'll* stay with her, I saved her! Let me see her! Are you okay, dear? That was a nasty shock, wasn't it? I hit him with my cane, had the presence of mind, quick thinking, I was in The Big One, you know..."

"You the folks who called about the rape?" WHAT'S THAT VOICE?

"Where's the ambulance?!" OLD MAN.

"It's coming. I was just around the corner. Where'd you leave the perpetrator?" SAME VOICE. A COP. I KNOW A COP.

"What's that?" OLD MAN.

"The rapist, where is he?" COP

"With the cane over there, I hit him, had to, nothing else for it, what do I care? Is there an ambulance or not? This girl needs a doctor! I think she's bleeding," OLD MAN.

BIG OL' COP HEAD POKING IN ON ME, AROUND BIG LASH LADY, "She's shaking pretty bad," "rocking," "signs of shock," "keep that blanket on her." "They'll be here soon."

"Well how soon is soon, goddamn it! I pay taxes, so does Nancy here, never needed a cop before in my life, now I need one, where the hell are you people when you need one?"

OLD MAN GONE. I WANT OLD MAN. SIRENS. HE'S COMING BACK. I DIED. BIG LASHES GONE, TOO. I DIDN'T DIE. WARM NOW, THOUGH. WARM NOW. WARM IS GOOD. SCARY NOW TOO SCARED. TOO SCARED. NO GOOD. GOING TO DIE. You're not going to die, Molly. The Old Man saved you. You're lucky.

Where's that pain coming from? Moving me into an ambulance. There's Old Man.

"Thank you! Thank you!" I try to shout. Did I say anything? Crying now. Old Man waving to me, says everything's gonna be alright. Oh yeah. Everything's gonna be alright. Everything's gonna be alright, Bob said so, I believe him and I believe Old Man. Easy. Alive. Warm.

In the back, close the doors, we're moving. Another lady, not that old, really. What a brave woman! Good brave woman working as an EMT. She wouldn't have gotten raped. Never rape her, no. Hot tears. Lots of tears. She's talking into a thing.

"I gave her ten c.c.'s of Demerol. No. No. 82 over 60. Yep. Yep. Uh-huh. Yep."

Driving in darkness. Is it just before dawn? That's when the darkest hour is, yep. With one hand on a hexagram, a bird in hand is worth two in the bush. Siren's aren't going. I'm fine. But I was raped. Was I raped? I don't know. Cry, cry, cry. Sob and weep. She gives me another needle. Warm now, I'm going to fall asleep, don't want to sleep.

★ ★ ★

I picked up and moved forward. Maybe it's because there was no penetration. That does make a difference. I think it does. He cut my arm with that switchblade, whatever it was, but I'm fine now. Ten stitches, all healed. It doesn't matter. I'm going to be more careful, that's all. He plead out, no trial, that was a good thing. I never had to see him again, don't know who he is, don't care, could be anyone who had a bad life. I see the whole episode as a random, strange gift because I have changed, and for the better.

Mom and Dad came out. Dad was actually very cool. We spent some time together. Well, we went to the store once and we watched a couple of movies. I didn't want to hurt him much, or tell him to leave often, which is an improvement. But I swear, if I talk to that man, it's just a fight. He doesn't like me; that's the sad truth.

I know I'm no kind of person to him. First of all, I'm a female. Second of all, I'm a loser because I was dumped by Shudree and I'm in a field where I'll never make any money. Those are his rules. That means we don't have much to say to one another. Sometimes I have to be careful not to fuck things up in my life on purpose, trying not to be his ideal woman. Is there the slightest chance that could happen? What is it he wants? I should be intelligent yet passive, pretty but celibate, working some high-power job while I raise fabulous children. I cry sometimes because I don't measure up. I am too weak. I am too strong. Did my singing please you? No, the words you sang were wrong.

We used to argue about art. We argued about school. It's better to argue; I don't know what to do with this nice dad. The first few days, perhaps because my mom held sway, he was eerily nice. He bought me a book of Impressionists. I like some of the Impressionists, Monet, some of Sisley's work. I look at a lot of art, though some of it just irritates me. Now I get to be raped loser kid.

Don't be an ass, Molly. Your dad loves you. He did some nice things. What's your problem?

My problem is he's a hypocrite and we can't talk. I feel like there is an invisible barrier between the truth and myself and somehow he keeps it there, it's there because of him.

I think too much. *I* am the hypocrite.

Luke has been the greatest. My parents met him and liked him, but I guess that's okay. Everything's been so strange.

I can touch Luke. In fact, I touch him more now than I did before. Because that creep didn't ever touch me. Not in any way that counts. Not in my heart. He just scared me. I wonder what would have happened if that old man, Mr. Prizzani, hadn't come along. God, I love that old guy! We had this big party for him. Actually, my dad threw the party. He wanted to give Mr. Prizzani money, reward money or something, but Mr. Prizzani absolutely refused to take it, so we drank wine and ate pasta and listened to Astor Piazzola. Mr. Prizzani is Italian. He said he was going to steal my mother away which actually pissed my dad off. This thrilled me and mom. It was a great night.

Mr. Prizzani had some of his war buddies come along, and Nancy from Denny's was there with a couple of friends, and we all went to this Italian restaurant where he knows everyone including the owner and all night he's saying, "Hey, Rickie, this is the little gal I told you about!"

"Hey, you're a hero, eh? A regular Hero, Al."

"Whattaya sayin'? I only did what you would have done!"

"What a hero, eh? Eh, Miss?"

"What hero? You're making me embarrassed, forget about it. I'll go down to Rodolfo's next time!"

"A regular hero, Al! Say what you want, there's a lotta fellas wouldn't have stopped, wouldn't have done nothing, so you want to yell 'cause I'm telling the truth, go ahead. That ain't stopped me yet!"

"Come on, Molly. What does Frank know? I was only doing what anyone would have done. Frank would have done it. I watched him with my own eyes run in front of machine guns to pull this guy to safety. It was Henry, remember Frank? Killed himself ten years later. What a waste. Frank here, he's the hero. Got the medals to prove it."

"And you ain't got no medals? Miss, he's got a wall full of 'em. A born hero."

On and on with my father praising him and my mother crying and old man Prizzani having the time of his life. Really. Bigger than the war, I think he feels. He is so happy and proud. It's funny, how my misfortune gave this old man something to live for. His son is gone. The other one's a "bum in L.A." Who knows what that means? A falling out. Wife died eight years ago.

It's in all the papers. Seventy-year-old hero. Good for you Mr. Prizzani. "Call me Al. I'm your Godfather now!"

You saved my life. I believe in everything now because of you.

I had Jackson ten months ago and now I know what life is. I had no idea before him. I have never known anything, although I still think I do, only now I *do* know something. A little bit of something.

Something is Jackson.

Name just came to me. That's all I can say. Everyone has to ask. My parents are unhappy about his name. Whatever. Not married to Luke, but Jackson is so clearly his. Besides, we both know we don't sleep around. I just didn't want to get married, not because of the baby. It would have felt forced.

I think I'll marry him soon. I know my heart doesn't swell like I thought it would, but Luke is here. He's the one who's next to me. He's too weak, but only because I am too strong. He's so happy with the baby. He's so good to me. Just finished his degree, has a job clerking in a law office, going to grad school, MBA. Weird. But he wants to start a business, wants to market skis. I thought he was going to be a bum with me. Now that Jackson is here, I'm really glad he's practical.

I'm nursing Jackson. Oh my god, he's such a love. He looks at me with those big eyes that say, "You are my mommy. I live for you. I feel your love. You give me life. We are one."

We *are* one. We are inseparable. Even when I'm not with him, I feel him. I can live the rest of my life making sure he is happy.

Luke is great. We get along. That's the thing. I am not high, he's not low; we get along. I really can't talk with anyone else. I see shapes move in the shadows, the shapes of smells, colors that move, sounds that stick to my canvas and adhere to my face. There are feelings that sing to me, and at those times its better not to go out in public. Eyes strip me bare.

I can share these feelings with Luke. He's heard it before and he loves me, better than I love him, still. He is more capable of love, I recognize that now, I envy it. And I love him for it. No soul-mate this lifetime, but that must be another goofy idea I was taught and haven't thrown out yet.

I've been going through all the thoughts I accept without question. Every single one. This is the source of my art.

I have to go back to work next week.

I paint whenever the baby is asleep. Oh to make a living painting! But really, the more I paint, the less anyone has to say about my paintings. I must admit, some of them are pretty bad. I wear a scarf and sunglasses, I tote the things under my arm to the gallery or Mr. Johnson comes here. He seems to be interested. He must be as mad as I am. He is 35 but he looks 21. He's a strange child.

I work at a flower store. I may have to go back to school. I don't want to go back to work or back to school, I want to paint.

I've had two shows. I paint all the time. Luke and I got married before Julia was born. She's six and Jackson is eight. You should see Julia. She is...she is perfect. Delicate and rough and petite and strong. My dream daughter. Am I projecting onto her? I want her to be free, especially psychologically. I monitor what I think and say, I teach her to be her own person.

Raising these two children is all I need to do. It's like God said: "Molly, go to earth and prepare your womb. You will have two sweethearts. That's your big assignment." And I say, "Thank you, God. I accept this assignment. I will raise these sweet babies for you and that's it, okay? Don't be asking for more, because that's all I can do." Of course He knows that. You know, I still can't think of God as a chick. I can think of Him as being amorphous, ambidextrous, and amphibious but not female. Maybe in Julia's time conceptualizing the Godhead as female will not be a major strain.

My children, my husband, are all I need, besides, besides, besides this art that gnaws at me. How I wish I could be free of it. It gives me pleasure but it gives me pain. I like the double-takes when someone looks at me and then at my paintings. I am not what they expect. I am glad I don't match their ideas about how I should look. I stand firm against the projections. I hold on with my teeth.

I quit my job at the flower store years ago, though I was really good at it. One of the few jobs where you can be wacky and no one knows. It's a one-man job, mostly. There were people, other workers, mostly women. They came and went. I liked some of them and they mostly liked me, perhaps because I wore my street face at work. Had to. The world will not accept me as I am.

Now I stay at home and paint. Luke has a ski distribution business. Not a big business, but big enough. I don't ski and he doesn't paint, so it works out well. We are different, that's why we get along so well.

I made $20,000 last year. I sold twelve paintings. Not much, huh? I made more in the flower shop. Luke makes enough. I don't know if I'm any good or not. I love my work. My work does not pay.

I think about what else I could have been, could have done. Does my focus on my art detract from my mothering? I don't think so. I wish my mother had been fulfilled. Isn't that good modeling? The world of visions, my waking dreams and my sleeping dreams, truly take up more than half of me. But the other half is vibrant and alive, when she is mothering. It's alright. I know I'm a good mother. I seem to have been born with that ability.

The truth is I have no choice but to paint, except to be very unhappy.

I'm not sure I've ever been happy. I'm not sure anyone is happy. Everything is relative, of course. I am relatively happy compared to some, and especially so when compared to my past.

At least I can paint in this century, a woman can do that. I'm not dismissed out of hand and I have no man running interference for me. In fact, I don't know many other artists and I certainly don't hang out with any. But I knew one. I almost slept with him. His name is Henry. I met him in New York. I met him in Chicago. I almost slept with him in L.A. Our friendship is ruined. He said he was in love with me. There were places in my heart he touched, but I know not to act on everything I feel. I know how that goes and I understand it's not on me. He'll have to work through his feelings just like I did with Shudree, and in some ways with him. If I had been alone, or maybe if I had been younger, I would have gone over to him. But I am neither.

That was the last time I spoke to him, at his request. Was it just last year? He is a good artist. Not as good as me, not that you could tell him that. Real artists are men, you know. They have muses. Yet, I thought I was falling in love with him. I battled it for a long time. That night in L.A., I went up to his room but I stopped before it went anywhere. I couldn't do that to Luke. I couldn't do that to myself.

Luke does not know about Henry, will never know, because I love him more. I let my shadow side take me some place. Here is the truth I found: Ever since I was a little girl, I thought a special man would come and undo the harm my father did. But of course no such man exists, not outside of me, anyway. He is right here in my head.

I paint me. I cannot get me right. I don't know what's there, underneath my persona. I cry in the night, alone in the dark, I don't know why. I have pain from some other time and place, I was born with it. That's the only explanation I can find. I don't believe in life after death. This plagues me. I don't know where I came from. I don't know where I am going.

There are a few things I do believe. I believe we are all fundamentally the same, and there's some research to back that up, though no one wants to hear it. What evil our species is capable of! I believe that the universe is evolving and that I make no difference whatsoever, but somehow I make every difference in the world. I believe that doing good things for others brings happiness and that doing good things for oneself brings happiness. I struggle to accept what I find on this earth, the good and the bad. Sometimes I feel like the world is here to give me what I need. I do get everything I need. I find that amazing. I realize how incredibly lucky I am. I hope my art has given something back. I believe that benefitting others has always benefitted me, even if I never make the connection.

I have made choices that benefit others. I stopped the car for Angel. I could have followed Henry, could have taken the children's father away from them; I could have lived the bohemian life of an artist. But I stayed. I watched over my children, and put them first, and they became the source of all the growth and joy in my life. Where would I be if my children had not brought me to this place? To Luke, to this home beyond sexual desire, beyond like and dislike. We stand next to each other like two trees, as though we have always stood here together in this silent forest. And gone is the dream of Romeo, that archetypal demon, thanks to Henry. For that I am most grateful.

Has Luke had an affair? I am not only certain he has not, I am certain he suspects me in no way. Therein lies his happiness. He is a happy man, happier at base than I am.

This toast is cold. But soon I will be rich, rich, rich! Rich beyond my wildest dreams! I throw the cold toast into the trash. I will make new toast, warm toast! I will take off my shirt and let my thirty-something breasts sling around in my bra as I paint. Music. Music. Stravinsky. No.

Grieg. No. Iranian guy. Yes. That's good. The blessed unholy, he is, the alpha and omega of life's lust.

Work until the kids get home. Go to the park. Order out. Ha! Take a long bath when Luke gets home. Is that the smell of fall descending over me? Is that the scent of dried leaves and sad souls and skipping angels falling unnoticed from heaven? Who could say life is not good on such a day?

I am inside out. I feel all the fires burning around the globe. Energy moves up from my feet and vibrates through my legs. I want to know.

I want to know everything! Then I'll be quiet.

I told Luke, that's it. I'm only going to paint what I want to. He looked at me quizzically as if to say, "When did you paint for others?" I'm making money now, lots. All my paintings sell. I don't get it. Well, I kind of get it. I always knew I have this thing, but I didn't think it would ever be recognized. My worst paintings go for the highest prices. My best paintings are not for sale, and no one wants them anyway. Three coins in the fountain bleu. Three gypsies traipsing through the tall grass in front of my house at the end of a dirt road in the middle of nowhere.

I had a dream. It was dark, and I was flying over the compound of the evil humor man. I wanted to go see him, but I was afraid. I wanted to get away at the same time. I started to fly away.

A large bird came to lead me back to that which I most fear.

I followed the bird, down, down in the darkness, through the layer beneath the lowest layer. In the hidden chamber I found candlelight and a queen. She held out a mirror. She admonished me not to squander my riches, not to cast my pearls before swine. She was very hesitant but she gave me the gilded mirror. My breast swelled.

Let me be worthy. Let me be worthy.

I awoke. The kids were rustling around in their rooms. I made pancakes. I kissed them and they shrugged me off like ones who are sure they are loved, ones who are ready to take the world for themselves. They don't need me at all. That is good. I watched them from the window, saw them walk over to the old VW Beetle, Jackson throwing his books in the back and sliding into the driver's seat. They never seem to know how I watch them; I look at them all the time. Julia will be driving soon.

They pulled away.

I drank coffee. I drank every drop, waiting. Then the call came saying I had the opening in New York.

Now it will get too complicated. I will go to more openings. I will sign things. I will meet people. People already write and ask me to come stay at their mansions. People want to use my work in their books, their flyers, I don't know what all.

No. I did the paintings. I did my work. I put it down as it came, imperfectly. Enough. That's it. I can't go down that road. I have a profound dislike for power and fame. Somehow I feel like I've been down there before. It's not better than here. It's definitely worse. Open your eyes and pay attention!

I need to stay focused. I need to stay focused on being unfocused. I have to be myself. Don't let go, don't let go. Don't lift a finger. Don't go where they say. The land of milk and honey. I have milk. I have honey. What do you need, Molly? Do you need more?

I don't need more. Luke says we're fine. Let's go skiing. Let's take the kids snorkeling. Never mind the rest.

Never mind the rest. The world of people is a squid: it spits black ink at you when you get too close. The world of finance is an underwater cave. You can get lost in there. What for?

Am I still chicken? No. I don't think so. I need to maintain myself in the quiet, loving life I have found. I'm not going to enter the art world. It sickens me. Just look at my paintings, put them places, leave me be.

The kids are in high school. Some of their classmates know of my work. Their parents want to meet me. Oh yes, I am a snob. Feels like high school all over again. I know the emptiness and rejection, the soul-rejection, waiting there for me. I do not respond. Life is too short. Let's just watch the basketball game, shall we go?

Julia plays basketball. She's really good, for being so short. She looks like her father. Jackson looks like me. He doesn't do sports: he thinks. He'll be going off to college next year. So scary. Out go my babies.

That's the thing, see? I need more babies. God said I did such a good job I get to watch over more babies. Soon, when the kids are gone, when they fly away into the world, I will help the motherless children. Luke says it's fine.

Someday I will fly away into the unknown. I will be alone, like I was before I was born. Let me know, sweet God, what all this pain and joy was about. I am drinking it up, like you said to. I am living this life as I was born to do.

Did I fuck that up? Look at that color! All wrong! I can't get it right. I don't know why anybody buys my paintings. What am I doing?

My babies are grown, with jobs and families…just starting out. I am fifty five; it's a good age to be. I am growing round and wily.

I think Julia is going to get pregnant any day now. Jackson has a little boy. I go stay with them. Luke is futzing around with his business and helping me with my second job, my "free" job, as we call it. I turned one of the rooms into a nursery. I take in babies who need a place to stay, toddlers, sometimes, on an emergency basis. Child Protective Services asks me to take in more, always more. I can't. Don't ask, I tell them, or I won't do it at all. I'll tell you when I can. I give the little dears the touch of my hands and they give me joy. Then they are taken away. Sometimes they stay a week, sometimes a month.

My painting is structured now because I sit with it. The images take hold of me and I sketch for days and dream back the colors. I am as careful with it as I am with these young souls. I sit and hold them without moving or speaking for hours. Some are so filled with pain I cannot take another for months. They burn my arms, they scald me. I had one skinny little guy, twelve pounds at three months and writhing every moment he wasn't sleeping, born with crystal meth in his veins. I almost quit after that, but I realized no one can see the future, who knows which souls will rise from the ashes and which will fall?

Most people my age have written off the earth just as their parents had when they got old. They spiral into gloom, they say it's over, global warming, war and deceit, but I believe the earth will heal, anyone can heal, anything. All things will become new again. I believe in that little boy. I painted him. He looked like a city.

I went to hear a Siddha Yoga woman speak last weekend. I was just curious. That's it for me. There is no truth but that in my heart, and if I want to know it, I have to work for it.

I was angry after I heard her speak. Well, maybe such people do some good, but in my book anyone who tells others what reality is when they are well-fed and worshipped doesn't know. She was like a meek version of the Queen of England, untouchable. Is not the contradiction obvious in any religious tradition? They should give all their money and power away and speak through a proxy then I will listen.

I'm filled with anger today. I could retch, eat clay, and hide in a cave for twenty years. There are wars going on and she said we choose our reality. Only someone who has never known war could think that people choose it. It is so simplistic! The things that make men pick up guns, the things that make old women say we must kill, are very complex. We are forced into warring situations, we are driven to them. It is how we humans are. I have never heard of a time or place without atrocity, though we long to find a people who have learned to live in peace. It is always a hoax. We will isolate a gene for it one day, no doubt, the Killing Gene, to balance out Higgs Boson, the God Particle.

I don't care if I deserve to be happy because I have good karma from my past lives. The bottom line is that my sisters and brothers are suffering while I live in peace and comfort. How can that be right? I am furious with sorrow in the most selfish way: it could just as easily be me or those I love. What if they create another war and draft my grandsons? It is all so needless. When will we learn?

New Age thought doesn't go far enough, it's a stone's throw from tradition, mere Calvinism wrapped up in a sari, blaming people for their circumstances. Don't they know it's going to be them, next time around?

What the hell kind of color is that? There's no word for it. But it'll work. Big'ol ugly painting. Won't make any money on this. Probably take me fifty years to finish.

There's a river of sludge and it is not mine, but I inherited it. The fish cannot be eaten. Their unnatural ears prick the thick gloomy surface. They are beyond pain and pleasure now in a most human way. They are crystal fish, beautiful and good for nothing. The bears that come to drink and eat can do neither. A thin girl rides one of the bears to the edge of the river that cannot be tasted. The bears should know better. They will have to travel many miles before they find something of value.

The feeling is deadness but the creatures are so alive. That is the hope. We always find ourselves at this pass.

The holy woman said life can be bliss, constant bliss, but my experience has been a mixed blessing. Maybe I *do* bring this suffering onto myself because I screw up. It is true that I am often not fully in the present moment. I do not pay close attention for days. I fail to move my body in the ways I like, fail to love who I love, forget I could be dead tomorrow. That is when I cause myself pain.

Nothing wakes you up like pain. Why diminish this great experience? Jesus suffered, Gautama Buddha, Confucius, maybe not Lao Tzu, but a lot of swell guys. And females, girl saints, they suffered, too, Mahadevi, Noor Inayat Khan, St. Teresa of Avila. The only ones who were paid any mind were the ones who wouldn't have sex, but I'm not going there. Patriarchal virgins! Don't get me started.

I have been told this darkness, this very painting, is inside of me. And I do believe it, but the darkness feels external. I am a light in external darkness, waiting for the world to catch up.

The woman said we know everything we need to know, we have only forgotten. I disagree. Some things I have forgotten, but other things I am learning. These are things I have never known before, not in another life, not in this. Even animals and plants learn. Evolution is a mixture of inter-generational learning and chance. What learning comes without suffering? What suffering caused our thumbs to move that inch, becoming opposable, giving birth to the neo-cortex? Utterly amazing.

To imagine the end of suffering…only the concept of the Bodhisattva makes sense to me, someone who could cross over into Enlightenment but refuses to go until all beings can cross over with her. The Buddha, who just goes straightaway, makes no sense.

Are we wrong in this wrong moment, choosing to suffer? If I didn't suffer, how would I learn to walk without falling so many times, boinking my little skull, squeezing out my thimble of tears? How many times did I do that before I learned about gravity and my body's relationship to it? Do you know what happens to children who are physically incapable of feeling pain? They have no empathy.

It is dark, I need a light but I can't bear to move from the canvas. I will paint in the dark. When I need red, I will slit my tongue.

After I learned to walk, I walked to my pain, and ran, and bicycled, and drove, and flew to my pain, unendingly. Just like gravity and that nameless state without gravity, that which would exist without Higgs Boson, couldn't there be pain-free learning, or growth, or existence? I don't accept the setup, with pain being the evolutionary motivator. I think about it. There exists X number of elements creating matter within time. I'm sure I could figure out some pain-free way to put it all together.

It is so cold I can't hold the brush. Talking fingers, ssssaying they disagree with me. I feel the wretched, the sorrowful. Over five billion sentient beings can't be all wrong. So we're fuck-ups, so what? I like my pain, in my own way, and revel in it; it is no longer perverse to me. On the other hand, I never avoid joy; it feels like I don't get enough. I choose joy, I get pain. I accept that pain is here for a reason. I learn from it, without choice.

Mostly, I identify with the child's pain because it is undeniably blameless. And if we are all one as you say, then I am certainly as right as you.

Not even wind can cut this dark water. It is not water. What is water's opposite?

We develop certain ideas precisely to separate ourselves from the reality of the people suffering all around us because we fear that suffering. We know it could be us, but we don't want to do much about it because at this very moment, it's not us. 10%, we'll give that much, no more, like a superstitious hedge against bad times. Maybe we remember suffering, unconsciously, from a past life and it horrifies us so we shun those who suffer. We need witchcraft, a religious spell, to keep it at bay. Doesn't work for shit. We are primitive and fear-based, like monkeys tearing apart the albino who is different. We hate the idea that all these suffering people's reality could be ours someday, no matter what we believe. It heightens our cruelty. We've seen it time and time again.

I want to master my fear of all possible existences. Are they that far from my own? What will be next for me? Are there experiences I haven't had? Will I fight and die in a war my next life?

Magenta. Dried blood. The ripped womb. Ringing the lips of the fish.

If I don't want to fight and die in a war, if I don't want to be a baby killed in a war or a woman raped in a war or a man maimed in a war, I must stop all wars for everyone.

My god, why is that so hard for us to see? Helping others *is* self-serving.

Sometimes I think I might become a blistering bum on a bench, drunk and wheezing, hoping for death, killing myself slowly, so slowly that a shift of the hip on a hard bench brings tremendous relief. Is that relief any less than your bliss during meditation?

This painting bears witness to the God-ness in a glass of water for a thirsty woman who didn't plan ahead when she entered the desert. I like her. I am one with her stupidity. I cherish her contentment in drinking that cup, without flavor, without a holy book or Knowing Way, without a friend. I like the way she doesn't say thanks and gets herself in the same fucked situation again tomorrow or the day after because she didn't think ahead. God is held within the moments of her experience.

She smiles at me, the Black Madonna, her touch from the core of the earth. "Be here with me."

Five billion of us are with you. We are called the Undeserving. We are described as lazy, petulant, mad-on-purpose. We are told we choose this suffering, by those I can only describe as the ultimate control freaks. They come by it naturally, of course, things being what they are, so I forgive them and hope they may one day see that all of life is held in these dull hopeless painful moments. It is through our collective experience that we feel the heart of humanity. It is *our* heart, and it is as divine as it is vile.

Look at all those sad eyes. We condemn others with our eyes even as they fill with tears for ourselves. Shame on you for being thin and haggard, and why doesn't he love me? Barely clinging to life we are turned away once again. Only then do we see the Madonna rising in the forest behind us. These trees know how to turn everything around, they are starting the process: turn around little girl, turn around.

You take the high road and I'll take the low road and I'll get to heaven afore ye. With all the dumb useless lost ones, an army of forsaken idiots, even as Christ said he was forsaken, crawling desperately toward the pearly gates and falling right before we get there because we have mental illness and didn't plan ahead.

And our God, the God of the five billion suffering, un-planning, always fucking up numbskulls will usher us in with the grasshoppers and the toads and we will reign in the frantic beat of a heart, waiting for you few who have so much, waiting for your fall. Only in your utter failing will you excel. The last will be first.

I am coming to know the God in all of us, how this very moment is most perfect for being imperfect; it is perfectly fucked for most of the world. Do you know how most people on the planet live? Struggling to get water, the very basics of life? Is this moment perfect simply because it is?

Existence equals perfection.

And we do get a glass of water from time to time right when we are about to die of thirst, and we escape boulders crashing down the hill, and manage to make whoopee as often as we can. We feel things, lots of wondrous things.

If you grasped reality you would understand the concept of free will for a man falsely accused in prison. You would know all about choices for a two year old who watches her drug addicted mother beat the baby to death. And you would say, "This little bliss theory of mine is good except for genes, neurobiology, and circumstance."

And then maybe you'll begin to supply the glass of water if you have it and stop talking out your ass. And if you don't have the water or you do but keep it for yourself with some lame philosophical excuse maybe at least then you will have some respect and shut the hell up.

Masters do not take money for teaching and Saints suffer.

I let the spiders go where they will. I keep the doors open. Let the fissures gape. Let the cord tangle; it will anyway. You cannot stop it. Your white dress will turn to gray and you will be on the bottom. That will be the best day of your life, eyes wide open, sucking air. Everything will be so goddamn real you'll forget all about your breathing.

I wish I had more love. I wish I travelled more, held more babies, helped more people. I wish I could make my belly undulate like Martha Macken. My life is full of awful and wonderful experiences, and perhaps enough love, broken and crippled and short of the mark as it is, to say, "This love of mine is like a tree, it feeds the planet something necessary though unseen."

I have a few friends and at least eight people I am fully convinced I would gladly give my life for. Maybe more.

When did I leave my painting? I got upset and went outside. Wind bends the stalks of corn in the field over there, somebody's corn. I have sat in it. I have run through it, silk tassels overhead, surprising crickets that scatter up into the air, zooming, foaming crickets. Their song makes my foot tap and I move in the wind, I call it dancing, take me, take me up, take me up…

Night is falling. Perpetual dusk and grace. I sit here on the back porch and I think. The future. The past. Looking back today I feel there is nothing I can't remember. I have been very careful all my life to practice remembering. While others were snapping pictures and making scrapbooks to jog their memories, I have been watching carefully with nothing between me and reality. I don't have facts or dates but I have images with smells and feelings, with temperatures and sounds, all swirling about me with every second of memory. I remember Jackson and Julia in the tub squealing, the white light of contented angels in the belly of time, the sense of freedom that comes when you have full knowledge of evil. Luke holding himself just one more minute, a drop of sweat on his nose, sweet salt and skin taut and shivering, the final squirt of semen, the intense release, forcing open his eyes to look down at me, the fading of drums, talking drums, what were they saying?

The faint strain of fine heavenly music, all light. All light.

Most precious memories.

My memory is selective and vast. There is enough here to keep me busy for a long time. I will add white to make the fish come alive. Go back in. You know what the painting needs. Give it.

I have only completed two paintings this year. My mind is growing blank. My thoughts are so strange there are no longer words or images to capture them. It is the Golden Age of my existence.

The world is finally ready for my thoughts right when I am done with the world. As it should be. The day I have waited for all my life: I am through with this world! Most days I feel as though I float high above it, pulled gently along by a sweet red and white paddle boat plowing through the clouds.

The kids tease me. I taught them that. I tell them I am the Paddle Boat Queen. The grandkids wrinkle up their noses and look to their parents for some kind of explanation. Sorry, no explanation. Get used to it, wee ones.

To control urination is the first order of the day. To overcome control is the second. To piss oneself blissfully happens naturally.

Oh, the simplicity of life!

I have never been happier. I piss myself from time to time. I drink tea. I laugh at Luke. Gosh, he's an ugly old man! He has hair sprouting out everywhere. He has wrinkles that catch the dust. That man has to wipe himself down every hour or so if he wants to be clean, what for the dust settling on him and the slobber. Okay, he doesn't really slobber. But we are old!

So nicely old.

We have a little place here in Colorado, out in God's country. We play the banjo. Well, I do, and dance around naked, pulling my knees up to the sky. See? I can jig. I never could when I was young, but now I jig like a maniac. The sun feeds my soul when I dance. It fills me with another day, just one more, which is all anyone needs, really. It is all I need. Just this one more day.

We have a little place in North Carolina where the kids live. They both live there, wanted to raise their children so they'd know each other. Good thinking. We spend half the year there.

Incontinent. Not a continent. I am not Africa. I am not North America. I am an old woman who pisses herself.

Oh, Lord above. You should see what a fuss they make over my paintings. I guess you could say I'm famous. Anyway they call me on the phone and tell me they are going to call me on the phone so I sit right there. I pick it up when it rings. Then they say blah blah about your paintings and what were you thinking? And I say a paddleboat or crickets and I laugh too much. They tell me afterward, phoning me up again, that it was an excellent interview.

Well, wonderful. Things couldn't be easier.

Julia is a mother. Jackson is a father. They used to bring the wee ones to me often. Actually, the grandkids are getting quite big. Are they teenagers now? They are adults. Jackson has a son, Julia has two girls. Who knows what they do. They are choosing things to be or things are choosing them. At any rate, they are lucky not to die in a war, not to starve, not to be beaten in prison. They are lucky to live their privileged lives in this country. I think I have transmitted that much to Julia and Jackson. I think they know they have to disperse their privilege, or flat out reject it, in the name of justice.

Well, you can't teach your children shit. You have to watch them make the same mistakes you did, and they don't go out of their way to share their mistakes with you. But it seems my children have done interesting things. Julia is a violinist. I would have liked to do that. Jackson is a high school teacher. I would have liked to do that, too. I also like what I did with my life.

We're going to Alaska next month then we're going to Africa. Nice juxtaposition. We will go see the Yukiguni, the Snow Country, the birthplace of the neo-cortex, and then the Sun Country, the birthplace of DNA. Isn't it rich? The mother of all creation, of all men, is a Black Woman. God, I love that. Maybe I will be a black woman in my next life. Maybe I will be a scientist. Maybe God will ask me to die for something. I was spared that, this life. Or maybe I will find it a blessing.

I know less now than I ever have. Everything just gets more and more confusing. What a complicated world! We make it too difficult. As I did, in my time.

But I know a thing or two. I know that toast is the finest food, with real butter and berry preserves. I know that babies are the finest things, better than cars or skyscrapers, far and away the most valuable things on the planet. I know that black is not a color and white is not a color. I don't care what they say. I know every color in between like the palm of my hand.

Oh, check that. I've pissed myself again. My kids wonder how I can go trotting around the world. I could have an operation for this, but I choose not to. I have yet to fall beneath the knife. No car accidents. No surgeries. Once a knife cut me, was that five lifetimes ago?

The kids have already sworn to me that I can die as I like.

There's old Luke. Old Man Luke. What a fool. His ski business paid the bills, never "took off" as they say. People look at Luke as the failure, me as the success. Stupid, stupid people!

Look at him out there! I'm going to bring him some lemonade. I made it myself. I make pies, too. I make bread. I paint pies and bread only folks don't know that's what they are. They see the name on the painting, they buy it. I am quite valuable. Tee hee! Jokes on you!

Look at that old man out there. He's using a scythe. A very old scythe. I bought it for him to display as an antique, not to cut the fucking lawn with! The grass is so high. He says there'll be snakes, so he's got to cut the grass. I think going by way of snake bite would be just too perfect. And any fool can see he's putting himself in more danger than the snakes, swinging that damn thing around out there. But it gives him pleasure, and me to watch him.

The children's children will soon have children. Here at last. Come in, come in, Little Ones. Take this world now, and see what you can do with it. Hah! You move as one in six billion, you have no idea about your connection to all the others! But from afar, from the heavens, you are ants moving without much thought. You are in a choreographed ballet, a part whose machinations you have unwittingly committed to heart. The unconscious. Well, fine.

The babies will see how difficult it is to make a new world by yourself, or buy yourself, seems more like it to me these days. Oh, help for you, you Bacchian hordes, blind to your own doom! Woe unto him that seeks fulfillment outside of herself. Extro-punitive little snots.

Ah, jeez. Luke's doubled over. Oh. He's just hacking up phlegm. Good. Back to hacking up the plants.

When I think about dying my heart races. I am quite afraid. But I am not an obsequious sycophant currying favor from Death. Hoo no, not me. I'll take it. I know I'll do okay. Did I scream when the kids were born? Well, maybe I'll scream some, but I'll get it done. I swear it's not the pain; I'm not worried about that. Dear God, grant me a quick passing so that I be not a burden on this earth, to those who still have so much life to live.

The airplane ride was as good as any. Alaska. I can smell it. I am imbued with the cold wilds and the stark bite of survival. I think I'll go back to Alaska.

We have arrived at the Seychelles, the Islands, where the hell are they? Off the east coast of Africa, in the Indian Ocean. It is very beautiful here and I am grateful to be able to afford this travel. What an unusual spot, what a strange piece of land, yet a place like any other under the sun, a stretch of ground.

I am happy here.

I let my old shriveled skin soak up the sun, white sand at my feet and monstrous trees at my back. What do I have to fear? Luke is next to me, reading or sleeping. I can't tell which. Sleeping would be good. I think I'll take a little nap...

Molly after Death

The sun is so very warm and comforting! Not too hot, not too cold. Where is the breeze that was blowing? Gone now. The beach is gone, the ocean is gone. The mountains, my husband, the children, all gone. Only light, warm light, confusing my awareness. I can't see anything. I feel like I am floating, slowly drifting upward, floating with the slow fandango of heaven's clouds.

I have passed on again. Yes, again. I know this feeling. Luke will go on without me. Who knows? Maybe he will scale a mountain still. The wee ones will go on without me, making their way in the world, being where they come to be, coming here again someday.

I am free, free as a bird, free as the clouds I float amongst. Free, free, free, and so happy in that freedom.

Julia will laugh that I passed away on a beach. How will they move my body? I am sorry for that; sorry Luke has to deal with my body. But never mind. He will be happy for me. It was such an easy death! Just like that! He knows that's what I wanted. I am very lucky...

I am happy to stay here. This is a good place, this is a good feeling. All joy and holiness, all grace and happiness, all blessedness, to just be.

I can feel the universe breathing, like a newborn, like myself.

There is no time, only light.

There is another here. Another thought? Another feeling? I know I have been here before. I have a longing in this heart that was so peaceful just a moment ago. I feel sad, I feel heavy. I am growing angry. What is it?

It is my father! Where is he? When did he die? He died many years ago. I remember the funeral. He died slowly and I wasn't there for him because he wasn't there for me. All these long years, I have been sad about my father. I have pretended to be happy around this sadness, like a rock in my heart, like a pebble under my tongue, like a grain of sand inside a pearl.

It is hazy now, the light is gone. There is a mist swirling about unnaturally, the colors of the lower spectrum, the colors left of center, deep hues, low sounds. I wander in the violet low notes until I see him standing in front of me. It is a man. Is it my father? He is waiting for me. I think he must be sorry. Is it you, then? Are you sorry for what you've done?

It is my father!

Dad!

He is smiling. He is not sorry, he does not look downcast; his face is light, beaming. He smiles at me and holds out his arms, saying nothing.

I want to run and fall into his arms, but I don't. Why isn't he sorry? He was never there for me; he doesn't even know who I am!

There he is, smiling. My hesitation has caused him no pain. He will stand there with his arms open, with that look of love on his face, forever.

I want to go to him.

But still I linger. I hold tight to the idea that it was he, he who caused all the heartache in my life. It was his love I sought in others, looking for his acceptance all my life and he withholding. Well, now I am the one withholding! No love for you, Dad. No attention when you most want it!

I look at him. We are quite close now. His face is shining, his arms are open. He knows my thoughts yet his face is shining because he loves me.

And then I hear his voice—kinder, deeper, freer than it has ever been before. He intones a single word:

"Molly."

It is as though he takes a step forward, but he hasn't moved. It is as though the timber of his voice is of the higher hues, a midrange tone, it is green and it brings the light sweeping back in all around me. The knot in my heart is sliced through, it breaks open with tears and I go to him. We hug each other. I am growing in his arms. I am his equal.

He is just a person, a person like me. This is a feeling I have never known; it is very, very good.

And suddenly, resting my head on his shoulder as he rests his head on mine, I can feel all those I have ignored. Caught up in my striving. Pursuing my dreams, seeking my 'self'. It is not because I didn't love them. It was because I didn't love myself, couldn't love myself.

But now I can.

I step back and we face one another. Beyond his smile, superimposed on his face, I see the faces of my children, my grandchildren, my Luke and my siblings, so many faces, flashing one after the other. They do not hold me responsible. I did the best I could. I see the forgiveness reflecting back from the multitude of faces floating over his face and I know: these faces are my own reflection: they are my mercy on myself.

The Sentient Being Who Was My Father is having the same experience, looking at me. I can sense this.

Warmth radiates through us.

"I never meant to cause myself the pain of ignoring you," he thinks to me.

"I, too, have caused myself unnecessary pain, pain that affected others. Thank you for helping me forgive myself."

"It is you who helped me. Thank you for waiting."

"But you waited for me."

"No. I didn't know you were coming. I was somewhere else."

"So was I. It is the same for me."

We are floating a few feet from each other. Suddenly he changes form again, this time with his entire being: changing sex, changing race. He is transforming into other beings from my past, and my past before then, and my past before then. I was a child, she hit me. I was a lover, I scorned her. I was a brother, we played.

Back further and further. I killed you. But then, you killed me first. But no, I must have killed you first. How many times did we kill each other?

I was lonely and you laughed at me, you used me. You are lonely and I am laughing at you. Your name is Hiromi. I remember now.

I wanted you so badly, but you didn't want me. Then you wanted me, but I didn't want you. Your name used to be Ying. Now it is Misha'il. Now I want you again, Midori, but I can't have you.

Now we love each other because you are my son, Little Jon. How amazing. Then we almost had a sexual union and we did love, but it did not last. You are Henry.

And I loved you Bau Yu, more than was possible, and my love for you threw me ahead in my cycle of rebirth. I chased you through the centuries and you brought me to the experiences I needed, until you were my husband and we were happy. We were lucky. And then I paid you back for all you gave me. I saved your life because I took it once, though with the right intentions. You were the little girl in the traffic, weren't you? I didn't know...

I can remember everything. I see my past, a myriad of lives, mine and others', swirling into and through one another, overlapping and piercing one another. I am a sentient being busy with the activity of rebirth. And that is what you are. We are exactly the same.

For a long time we stand, watching each other's past lives reflected in one another's faces, revealed through the other. Have you seen your lives too, Father? But this is not my father. She is someone else's mother. He is someone else's child. He is a being moving through time, like me.

Slowly, the transfigurations fade. We are quiet. We fall asleep. It is a kind of sleep where you do not close your eyes, you do not move, you do not even have a body to move. We are masses of energy displaying ourselves as light; we hover.

After awhile, I sense other beings, many other beings, all around me. They are discrete masses of light. They are hovering like me. Any one of them could be the father I had my last life. I do not know. It does not matter. I wish for my Father, one of the myriad lights here, all the good things that can come from existence.

The masses of light seem less and less discrete. I could be my father from my last life. There is no distinguishing now. I am filled with a singular thought, like a sound and a color, like a midrange note of emerald green: I hold this green wish that we all live in happiness.

I am at the place for rebirth and I help many sentient beings be reborn. I know who they were and what their fears are. I give them special encouragement. Suddenly, there are no more in line and I find myself alone, in a sensory void. I review every nuance of every past life I ever lived. Memories come so easily; lifetimes come in seconds until there are no memories left.

I float in light.

I feel myself preparing for rebirth. There is a little boy with a twisted foot, he is blind. He approaches me, and I pick him up. He grows. He is my equal. His eyes shine as he looks into mine. Suddenly, I can feel that he is my great-grandson, born blind, died when he was one year old in a car accident.

Have I been gone that long?

He mind-talks to me.

"Do not confuse yourself with me because you are me. We were a killer. We will be a saint in our next life. We will help us all move forward." As he speaks, I feel myself become him. I remember every detail of the car crash: I am the only one who dies. What great sorrow for my parents! Then I am not him anymore. We smile into each other's eyes.

I give him a little squeeze and he shrinks back into the form of the twisted little boy. I put him down. He disappears. Immediately I am reborn again.

Transmigrations

Molly to Krishna

Karlos/Mei Hua/Khalid/ Keizo/Marta/Molly	becomes	Krishna
rapist	becomes	Tom
(Merlo/Bau Yu/Fida/Tatsuo/ Jon, husband)	becomes	Morani Botsu

KRISHNA

All is new again

Sooner or later the light overcomes the darkness. Sooner or later the darkness overcomes the light.

She was a beautiful lady who came to me in my sleep. She moved with music, an alternating pulse, all music a pulsing, her eyes round and smiling, her dress simple. In her hand was a book. She gave it to me and the music came with it, high and fine, lilting, a Goddess' voice, an Angel's. Soaring with the high notes, dropping back to the low tones of earth, pulling itself up again... it was the voice of love.

I could not see her after a few moments because my eyes were shut in ecstasy. I saw *within* her.

She said, "All this. Giving away all things, you are given all things. Do not chase. Do not flee. Be where you are, little one."

I fell at her feet, my leg was twisted, and she raised me up. My leg straightened and I grew. I was equal to her. I was a man. I was in her arms, with the heavenly sound of love enveloping us.

Light as a cloud, arms like reeds filled with glowing light, head floating upward, expanding over the mountains.

I am bursting with pleasure. I recall everything. I sing praises in my heart. I will become the man she envisioned.

The dream is a gift, knowledge I received from my inner feminine. I add it to my Night Journal. I say "Krishna, Night Journal, record" and speak my dream out to the media-surround, a function of our central computing system. It will time-stamp and catalogue the dream for me. When I am done I say, "all senses," turning off the stimuli-eater, then close my eyes again.

Bird song, the muffled sound of distant human activity, and the scent of baking roti swirl around me. Light plays in my mind and shines against my eyelids. I am like a feather in the breeze. I distinguish the separate bird songs drifting in through the open window: that's a wood snipe, that's a swift of some kind, a thrush, a rosefinch... they are returning from their morning feast, talking to one another.

If I could trill like that, I would.

I give it a try. Ptree, ptree.

Not bad.

I roll over on my bedding, laid out on the floor. The morning light streams in like butter melting. I love the warm summer. I will pick the ripe papaya in the far garden, near the bael and tamarind trees. They are a special hybrid for this climate. Our village only has those two papaya trees so we share them. I will pick some after breakfast for our restaurant.

What was that dream now? Oh yes, the smiling Lady, she gave me a red book. I recorded it.

My chest rises and falls. My breathing is like the sun, warm and fluid. I feel my body and it is happy. Happy feet, happy arms. I open and close my eyes. Fireworks burst against my lids when they are closed, and the window reveals the Nepalese Pine and Betel trees when they are open. I should have a tree with me where ever I go, I love them so much. There is no kind of tree I don't love.

Really. I have studied almost every kind of tree. They are helping us get to the bottom of the soil rejuvenation project. Their precious roots are teaching us. All roots are magical. All mouths and digestive systems are magical. They are the key to our planet's sanity and health, same as us.

And there is Devaki, not five feet from me. I have not disturbed him; he can't hear me because he is still cushioned in his stimuli-eater.

He looks so tiny! He is six. His skin is light, like an American peanut. I am twelve and I am brown like an almond. That is because of genes. Many of my genes are the old equatorial genes. His genes are the newer north-country genes. They have come together in my family because all of us have been mixing for thousands of years.

I know my genetic make-up, of course. We are all assessed in utero. When they discovered my problem, they tried to fix it in the womb but it didn't work. Mama brought me into the world anyway. She told me she knew I was perfect in my imperfection.

That is how I feel. Everything is perfectly imperfect.

We could be living anywhere, but I am glad we are here outside of Katmandu because I love the Himalayas. Papa brings us climbing high in the mountains. I can see the peaks from my window. I pull up on my elbows and there they are. Deepa is the best climber of the children because she is the oldest. Deepa likes the places on TV more than here. She says she's going away to school soon.

I like the mountains. I like the trees everywhere. Katmandu is quite temperate and has deciduous trees, while just ten miles to the north, into the foothills of the tallest mountains on earth, the trees are coniferous.

I get to enjoy many different kinds of trees because of the Himalayas. They make me cry when I stand in their shadow looking up.

Mama keeps up with Papa when we hike. She is smart and strong. "Drink electrolyte water, even when it is cold," she reminds us. We have nice gear, light and useful. We have protein-sewn brown rice paste for body fuel. That makes it easy. I feel like an astronaut when I suck on the tube. I could be in space. No trees in outer space, though, so I don't want to be an astronaut. We humans go to outer space every day. Some people want to go. I don't.

When I was Devaki's age, life was found in our galaxy using spectral analysis. All the old theories have fallen away. The answer was right in front of us for many years, but it took someone like Morani Botsu to see it. Such is the nature of truth.

I don't think that's his real name. Could be a woman, too. The movement for anonymity is very strong. No one lays claim to the glory of discovery and invention anymore because the effort is always collective. Plus nothing messes up your self-concept more than fame.

We sent probes and are awaiting verification. Unless we think of another way, verification won't be obtained until after my death, but we will probably think of another way. 'Carbon-based only,' that's what researchers used to say. Now we know different. We have identified many planets where carbon-based organisms exist, but there are alternative possibilities for life's basic structure.

What do we know? We only know what we are capable of perceiving. We rarely mistake that for reality anymore. We, as an international community, know the futility of thinking we know everything. We are therefore in a position to learn so much more.

Devaki is moving around. Hah! He rolls over, opens his big eyes and a smile comes over his face. I feel my skin contracting with goose bumps from joy for my little brother. I see his mouth moving, saying, "All senses," to turn off his stimuli-eater.

"Hi!"

"Hi, little brother. Did you have a nice sleep?"

"I dreamed something. I was big. I had an elephant."

"Did you get a book from anyone?"

"No, did you?"

"Yes, from a beautiful lady."

"Yeah, but did you get an elephant?"

"Nope!"

He rolls off his tatami mat and begins rolling across the bamboo floor to me, trying to roll right over me. I push him away and he rolls back and I roll him back and forth across the floor. He likes that. He is giggling. I play with him all the time, for all the times I wanted a big brother and did not have one. It is almost the same thing, being a big brother to him.

The curtains flutter against the mango-plastered walls and light plays on the computer generated art hanging here and there. Besides some silk-covered cushions there is nothing but our bedding on top of our tatami mats on the floor. We like it simple. We like to be on the floor. Our clothes and other belongings are put away in bamboo storage cabinets recessed in the walls.

"Krishna!"

That's Deepa. She must be downstairs. They might need help. Or maybe it's just breakfast.

"Hoy. I'm awake! I'm coming!"

"Bring Devaki, Mama says let's eat!"

She is a good big sister. She wants to show her beauty on TV. Okay, that's fine. Could be fun.

"Always keep track of the lucky things in your life," my mother says.

It is easy. I do it every day.

But gosh, Devaki is so skinny, he's a little monkey. His hands are so small. He waits to see what I will do. I will get ready to go downstairs and join our family. You can do it like me, Devaki. I won't steer you wrong.

We skip into the bathroom and wash our faces with warm water, then skip out and get dressed. We wear baggy pants and T-shirts and dailies. They used to be called tennis shoes. Why did they call them tennis shoes? No one played tennis much, only the rich. That was when the world was more divided than today and everyone followed the people who amassed wealth and power. They knew it was through deviousness, but power is very seductive.

Actually, I have no idea why they followed. They weren't all starving.

Or maybe they were.

What were they starving for? They needed someone else's attention to feel alive. It is so archaic, that drive for communal attention, although it still happens.

We fly down the stairs taking two at a time and burst into the main dining room. Our restaurant is full, maybe thirty people. These are our friends, the same people who always come: Narada, Yun, Tom. They eat the morning and evening meal with us. They are like family. The big room on the main floor of our house is also beautiful: stone, wood and bamboo, warm colors with lots of light. We nod and greet all the people sitting and drinking. Maitreyi and Ushasta are co-owners, they do equal work in the restaurant. I see them in the kitchen. They must have opened with Mama and Papa a while ago. They smile and wave.

We have many machines to help make the food and I know how to run them all. No one has to work hard. Not at making food. We work hard at other things.

It's a special treat when the papayas ripen. We don't use a machine for those. I skin them myself and slice their slippery flesh with a handheld knife, placing them carefully on recycled circles of purple paper, dusting them with powdered sugar. I like to gather the specialty foods we prepare. Tonight our guests will have a surprise, I hope. If the papayas are at last ripe.

Devaki, Deepa, and I sit and eat while Mama and Papa serve our guests. I like warm buttered roti bread and chocolate soybean milk and bananas. I like every kind of food, except for meat. We don't have any meat here and no one ever asks for any. There is a store on our lane that has meat in cans. I guess the Westerners eat it sometimes. I don't know. They'll probably throw those cans out. It's not good for you. It tastes nasty and it hurts the environment.

I can feel the soybean milk going down my throat. I can smell the roti cooking. My brother smiles at me. People are talking to each other. I feel like I am soaring. I hum a little song I made up. Devaki hums it, too.

He learns so quickly!

"Hey, monkey boy, wanna go pick papayas with me? We'll give our guests a treat tomorrow!"

"Mama, can I go get papayas with Krishna?"

"Yeah, sure, go ahead you two. Be back in a few hours. Papa and I want you to watch the news with us, and you have school on the computer."

"Sure, Mama. We'll be back soon, I promise."

We skip toward the door and there's old Tom the Westerner at his usual corner table. His accent is funny. He makes me feel strange. He is the only one I feel that way about, I don't know why. I try to understand but it is just beyond my reach. He says something as we pass.

"Hey, Krishna! You little scamp! Going out to play?"

"Yes! We are going to hunt papayas, but don't tell anyone. It's a surprise!"

I stand and look at him because I know he loves me. He sees the feeling in my eyes and he is grateful just to look into them for a little while. He is smiling. He knows I am pausing for him so he says, "Go on now. I'll see you again soon. Why, I'm going to have a little surprise for you tonight, too!"

"Now I'll be wondering what it could be," I say, grateful to be released. I run off, that funny feeling floating around like something's not quite right.

★ ★ ★

How I love the feel of the ground beneath my feet. My leg works so well now after all those operations. Mama tells me stories, how I cried from the pain, and I think I remember. It's okay, though. I run pretty good now. Maybe that is why I am a scientist: because science allowed me to run. How lucky I am, huh Mama!

Pad, pad, pad. I love the soft sound of my dailies in the dirt. Devaki is trying to stay up with me. I slow down so he can. We are outside of the village now, on the dirt pathway to the orchards. We run under the trees, our arms held stiff at our sides, looping like hang gliders. I've been in one before. Wow, that was a special day. Mama turned forty so Papa took us all hang gliding. Mama likes things like that, she likes to soar.

I like to soar through the trees with my little brother. The earth flies beneath my feet, we are fast as the wind. Bird songs in my head, singing in my brain, air filling my lungs. The sun is so mild, like a kind father wanting only to give enough light for life.

We reach the section of the orchards harboring the papaya trees. They look ripe! I hunt around for the knocking stick we leave in the corner of the garden.

"Krishna, I bet you I could shimmy up there. Why don't we climb?"

"It's too dangerous. Also, when you hit them with a stick, only the ripe ones fall. We just want the ripe ones. Look, Devaki, here's the knocking stick. You can go first."

He stands there waving the stick around, little beads of sweat shimmering on his upper lip and forehead. He misses the tree altogether, his first swing. Closer, closer, now he's hitting the tree, up high, and down comes a papaya. I manage to catch it!

"Chango! Nice aim, Devaki! Try to get another one!"

"Do you want a turn?"

"No, that's okay, you go ahead. I'll try when you are tired."

He knocks down two more that I don't manage to catch. I set them with the other one in the dirt. Then I take my turn with the stick, knocking down one more. That's four. That's about all we can carry, and I don't think any more are ripe on this tree. Four isn't enough to feed everyone, though. We could try the other tree.

I get a couple more while Devaki watches. That's six, that's enough.

We walk back down our lane carrying all the papayas. The kitchen has been cleaned up and Papa has pulled the shutters down until dinner time. We don't serve food for lunch. We fill everyone's bento boxes with lunch-time snacks, fruits and nuts and grains and beans, simple fresh food.

I prepare the papayas for tonight and put them in the refrigeration unit. It's huge. We are really careful because Devaki is still young enough to get trapped in there. Then we go up to our rooms.

We have four rooms upstairs over the restaurant. The bedroom is very big because all five of us sleep there. We use the stimuli-eaters if we don't go to bed at the same time. But mostly we do. Some families sleep alone in little boxes, but I would be too lonely. It is much more fun this way. I know about copulation, my parents told me about it and I have studied the human body extensively in school. Sometimes Mama and Papa use the total black out function on their stimuli-eater and I know what that means. I look forward to copulation when I am old enough and find the right person. On the other hand, Papa says Love is something one waits for. I haven't decided if I will wait for love or do copulation for fun. Mama says not to worry, because I'm not old enough to decide. She says it's like deciding how to die, takes all the fun out of it.

We have a big bathroom, too, with two separate compartments. And then there are the two libraries, one with the research computers and one for the other computers. They are all networked differently.

We go into the main library and watch the news. There is no financial gain from news reporting now and I shudder to think back to the time when it was otherwise. Who could ever believe a thing on the news?

After an hour we have got the primary report: Rangoon is being evacuated again because of flooding and Ache is mobilizing due to questionable seismic readings in the Indian Ocean. The west coast of the United Americas has been notified, because they are usually hit next. There are talks over the re-enforcement of old treaties across the globe. Papa said it is important to follow the Peace Works and never take them for granted. His people are from Burma and he knows what happens when we do not feed the people who are alive, when we let them be born without food or the means to enhance their lives. I pay attention. Papa is right. Everyone must be actively engaged in order to maintain the balance so many have died for. Even an earthquake could throw us back into war, because war is not about good and evil, it is about fear and scarcity of resources. We have the 48 Hour Relief System to redistribute resources if something bad happens.

After our family news time, Mama goes into the research room where I will join her after my classes. The three of us kids network into individualized educational systems, connecting to other kids all around the globe. I can see and hear all the people in my classes and they can see and hear me, but I can't hear Deepa or Devaki because of the stimuli-eater. It saves a lot of space.

In my first class we're studying the New Exact Freelance History of the World. We are on the section about studying the history of history. People have not always had the luxury of honesty as we do now. People wrote histories to gain influence or to curry favor, or simply because their written history would not get published unless they wrote it in a certain way. Most everything was written to control the way people perceived the world. Sometimes, the writers didn't know any better, they were projecting the prejudices and ignorance they were raised with.

Other times, they did it on purpose to control others but it never worked for very long.

Of course, only a few people had access to literature and publishing back then, and consciousness was not a component of education, as it is now. People had to memorize what the few had to say, in huge schools. What a stupid way to learn. Fear was far more powerful in the world then.

It makes me sad. Sometimes, especially during history, I cry. Other kids cry, too. We are sad for our great-grandparents because of all the wars, the ignorance and the spiritual deprivation they had to suffer. And we are grateful to them because we have gained so much through their suffering. We learned from their mistakes.

During class we are encouraged to talk about our feelings and perceptions. Some talk more than others, but no one talks too much. Everyone knows, "The fuller a stalk of rice becomes, the lower it bends." We may struggle within ourselves with powerful feelings and projections, but we must identify the originating thoughts to become open to a deeper understanding of ourselves and the world.

Next I study mathematics. Then I break out into the advanced course of nano and glyco-biology. Everyone is much older than me, but they are kind. They call me the Mad Scientist. I have a good time but I am focused, because Mama and I are working on a global desert reclamation project. Information from water-bearing minerals including sulphates and phyllosilicates were studied on Mars. We learned to combine them with cross-linked polyacrylamides that are 400 times slower to degrade in UV light. It is working, but not fast enough. There must be a better way.

I don't know why, but my mind is fast with chemistry. I know the language of amalgamation like my mother tongue, so I see the patterns in compounds easily. And I love trees and plants, so I am quick in this field. Sometimes my classmates—there are only eight of them, all living in the Middle World——say, "Krishna, you are a whiz, man!" and I don't know what to say. Inside, I say a little prayer that I will always be true to myself, that I will not say it is my skill but the collective skill of the world carried in me, the culmination of eons of work done by others, because it is an awful thing to lose yourself to vanity, and besides, it is always a lie. They know this and let it go with a word or two.

About three hours later we are all done with our schooling. Papa comes upstairs and we telecommunicate with Grandma for a few minutes. We look in on Uncle Bhriga and Raya, too. Then Papa plays Pi'pa for us. It is amazing, his musical ability. He can play many instruments but he loves the Pi'pa most and so do I. Sometimes he gives concerts for the village that are streamed live on the Web, and sometimes they fly him far away to play for halls crowded with his fans.

I tried to learn how to play but I don't have the talent Papa has and I know it. Is that why music seems to be my very soul? Honestly, I might stop living without it, but I don't have to worry. The air would have to disappear before music died.

We all go down to prepare dinner with the sweet harmonizing chords still reverberating in our chests. Deepa has two friends over and so does Mama, and they are going to take care of dinner. We will cook tomorrow. Devaki and I run over to the neighborhood center to get in a game of Highball or Backgammon. Papa goes as far as the Music Hall with us then heads over to the Musician's Corner to jam.

I love both Highball and Backgammon, but there's a game of Highball just starting so that's what I choose. I leave Devaki and head out to the field. We break into teams, and whoa, what a game! My skill is great for throwing, but I am not half as fast as Indra or Junichiro. But together, we are pretty good. It is a fun game because as soon as one side starts losing, we guess-switch players to even it out again. It changes very fast. Everyone has a good time.

After the game, I go find Devaki. He is swinging and talking with some friends. I give him a ride on my back and we head home for dinner. The sun is setting. All our regulars have already gathered on the viewing deck. We drink tea and watch the sun go down before heading in to eat.

This is always a quiet time. I feel the quietness of time here tonight. I feel the world turning. It is spinning inside the book the Lady gave me.

Now that the sun is down, Tom says he has a surprise for us and sings a song he wrote for Desaki and me. It is plaintive and beautiful. Formulas start crowding my head as he sings, which rarely happens to me. And these are quite different from the ones that naturally run through my brain.

I politely wait until he is done, then run to the study to get all the formulas down. I tell Mama not to wait for me, I need to work now, and she nods her understanding, because that's how knowledge comes, unbidden, in bursts. After several hours, I am done. I plug the formulas into the Work, but I am too tired and hungry to wait for the results. Mama made a plate for me, with a side dish of sliced papayas. I go to the upstairs viewing porch and enjoy the food, looking out over the dark forest.

★ ★ ★

"The world has come full circle. What the seers predicted, the scientists have proven. We were in misery, captivated by war, living as economic slaves, and the Holy Ones taught us that money does not make us happy. Following the urges of the flesh does not make us happy. Material possessions do not make us happy. Power does not make us happy. Only love, in all its forms. Love as conviction. Love as dedication. Love as discipline. Love as devotion. Precious love. Paradoxical love.

"Who were the Holy Ones? Ordinary people like you and me who focused on their hearts. They were figuring out the heart while the cortex developers were figuring out the world through science. These are like tributaries flowing into the same sea. Be grateful for the cortex developers, too. How many sacrificed their lives to further medicine, to further science, with no more reward than a house and two cars? How young they died! How alone and unfulfilled! Eaten up. Lopsided. Killed by the diseases they studied, the diseases of misery.

"It was faith alone that propped up the masses prior to our current level of cortexual development. The irony is that the adversity we humans created for ourselves accelerated this intellectual/spiritual development, and it brought the world one step closer to Betterment. They were heroes, suffering to heighten our awareness.

"With the accelerated development of Cortex Fini in certain high-stress areas, a strain of super-empathic humans evolved and began mixing with the general populace. Suddenly, scientific breakthroughs began cascading, laying the groundwork for our current knowing about how the mind leads the body. Science began to prove all the things that the holy ones had said: that wealth can be just as harmful as poverty, in terms of personal death and suffering; and that we are all very much the same, varying only by minor genetic predispositions toggled on or off by environmental factors. These can appear as quickly as one generation now, we are evolving so rapidly.

"Even so, genes are not destiny, and genetic reversals follow the individual's will. Remember the great genetic trials of the 2020's? Thought alone undid many of the splicing, especially those that were involuntarily performed. In this we know, 'Where I stop, you start,' as the great writer Wilma W. has said.

"What does a human seek, then? Health, life, happiness. What gives health, life, happiness? Relationship. In the 2030's we started focusing on relationship and developed the relational principles of chaos, interdependency, intuition, and love.

"Globally and locally, we are only as strong as the weakest link; one person's vulnerability makes everyone vulnerable. There is no way to save yourself if you abandon others because the weak link will attack like a cancer, weakening the entire body. You cannot cut a cancer out anymore than you can eradicate a people: they will both grow back with a vengeance. You must understand its cause and solve the problem. This is what we do in our world, household by household. Through the love and connectedness of each small community, we enhance the global community. This is the next step for our species, building these small centers of love and mutual support across the planet.

"Giving is the key to relationship. Any doubt or mistrust you feel are actually expressions of self-betrayal, because no one can take what you have inside. Only you can deny yourself love.

"The Ones in the East, who first developed intuition and feeling, were finally heard by the Ones in the West, who first developed scientifically. If you are not connected to the body of humanity, you are dying. If you think you are better than *anyone*, you are dying. If you think you are worse, it is the same. Your accomplishments are my accomplishments. We are now proud of ourselves, not as a race, or a religion, but as a global people, a community of sentient beings."

"Krishna, are you coming?" It is Mama.

"Yes. I just had to finish this paper for Sociology. How's the Work going?"

"It's confounding. Come look at this. I think that dream you had must have made a difference, or maybe it was Tom's song, because the soil sample evinces an adiabatic pressure dependence of 2.7. What did you do last night? I mean, I can see the calculations, the adjusted calibrations, but how does it work?!"

"Is it the Gobi sample? For real?!"

"Yes, sweetie, look at this!"

I study with Mama into the evening. We have to get this out as soon as possible. 2.7 microns! Why, that's almost the same as here! We can rehydrate the deserts. I knew it was only a matter of time, but in my time? We will need to run experiments, run the numbers, many times. But it is a compound I know. A simple one, really. Its parts are simple.

After we run multiple tests with the Work, we send everything to The Clan in the Gobi and, of course, to the World Council, who will disseminate it from there. I am very grateful for the people working at the World Council, because that kind of monotonous work would bore me. Well, each to their own tastes and talents. It's funny how the ancient Communists got that part so right, yet everything else so wrong. Of course, the sacrifice must be self-chosen. "Water only flows uphill if you beat it with a stick!" I have a T-shirt with that on it.

It is time to watch the sun go down. This dusk is special. We stand with our arms around each other on the viewing porch, each holding in their hearts the knowledge that soil erosion will be reversed. What this means for all living creatures on the planet! Caged animals, all the endangered species bred in captivity, have waited for this day. We can repopulate the earth with the animals we took from it. We can end starvation. We bow our heads and weep, squeezing each other around the waist.

We maintain silence.

No one treats Mama and me differently because they do not want to tempt our egos. I appreciate it. They are merely grateful to me and I to them. We rock back and forth. When the sun finally disappears, Tom spontaneously starts to hum the surprise song he wrote for Devaki and me. He has a great way with notes. We all join in like insects, like crickets humming goodnight to the sun.

Papa said to give it a rest, so he and Mama went on a date. They are going to the ancient temple with a palm heater and a bottle of Bolivian wine. Deepa is checking out the wide world on TV, and Devaki has gone to play with Junichiro. I'm practicing being happy on the back porch.

The light moves through me and it is like a vibration of color and sound that I can feel, rolling up my spine from my feet and exiting from the top of my head. Then suddenly it fades because something else comes into my mind. Our minds are like the ancient Chinese hero Monkey, jumping from tree to tree with our prehensile minds, unable to sit still. Learning to control my mind is like learning to walk a balance beam: it does not feel natural at first. But I like the feeling when all is silent without and within, so I practice a little every day.

When you get good at happiness, there is no next step.

The stars are coming out. Night animals rustle in the trees, and below on the ground. I think:

May we all reach peace.

There is One Being: We.

And while We slowly awaken to Ourself, I get to play in my head. I get to swing high into the air. I get to suck the juice from mangoes and watch myself grow in the body of everyone I love.

I get to lay in the dark and watch the stars move. I get to stand in the storm and wonder about death.

Maybe I will find a special mate someday, and have a baby.

Maybe I will die in a Transportation.

Maybe I will stay on this porch and just watch the heavens.

Who knows?

Printed in the United States
221918BV00001B/12/P